All
Our
Broken
Idols

Paul
Cooper

BLOOMSBURY PUBLISHING

LONDON · OXFORD · NEW YORK · NEW DELHI · SYDNEY

BLOOMSBURY PUBLISHING
Bloomsbury Publishing Plc
50 Bedford Square, London, WC1B 3DP, UK
29 Earlsfort Terrace, Dublin 2, Ireland

BLOOMSBURY, BLOOMSBURY PUBLISHING and the Diana logo are trademarks of
Bloomsbury Publishing Plc

First published in Great Britain 2020
This edition published 2020

A catalogue record for this book is available from the British Library

ISBN: PB: 978-1-4088-7935-1; eBook: 978-1-4088-7942-9

2 4 6 8 10 9 7 5 3 1

Typeset by Integra Software Services Pvt. Ltd.
Printed and bound in Great Britain by CPI Group (UK) Ltd, Croydon CR0 4YY

MIX
Paper from
responsible sources
FSC® C020471

To find out more about our authors and books visit www.bloomsbury.com
and sign up for our newsletters

To my parents Margaret and David,
for reading to me.

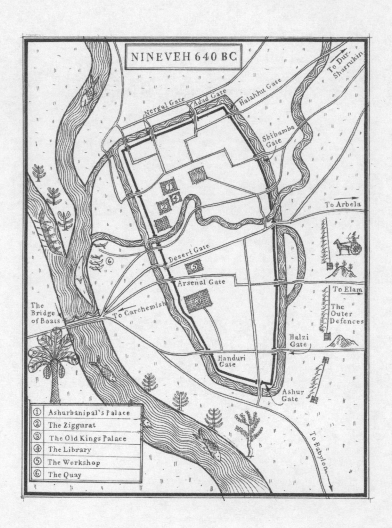

NINEVEH 640 BC

To Dur-Sharrukin

Nergal Gate Adad Gate Halahhu Gate

Shibamba Gate

To Arbela

Desert Gate

The Workshop

To Elam

The Outer Defences

Arsenal Gate

The Bridge of Boats

To Carchemish

Halzi Gate

Handuri Gate

Ashur Gate

To Babylon

① Ashurbanipal's Palace
② The Ziggurat
③ The Old King's Palace
④ The Library
⑤ The Workshop
⑥ The Quay

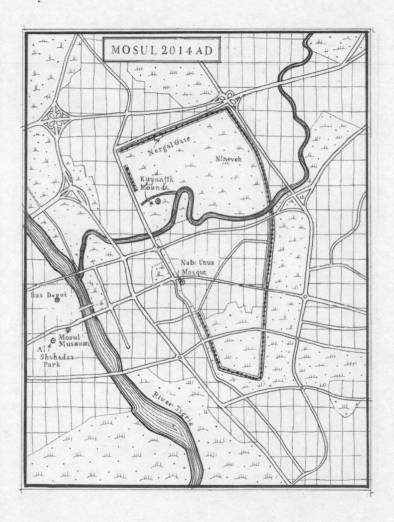

MOSUL 2014 AD

Nergal Gate

Nineveh

Kuyunjik
Mound

Nabi Unus
Mosque

Bus Depot

Mosul
Museum
Al
Shuhadaa
Park

River Tigris

History is sarcastic with its victims
and its heroes

Mahmoud Darwish

BOOK I

The Lion

Aurya

Aurya hated going out into the reed bank. It was a clear morning, but the reeds grew taller than her, and she could never see far. She had dreams some nights that she was lost out there, running and breathless, while something huge stalked her through the rushes.

'Sharo!' she called out, sending a flock of crows bursting into the air. 'Sharo, where are you? I mean it!'

She'd spent half the morning looking for her brother around the village: up on the crossroads where the desert people sold caged birds and rabbits, at the quarry edge where foxes gathered among the hawthorn and wild oak. Usually if you followed the animals, you could find Sharo. But now there was only one place he could be. The ruins of the old village. As she wandered deeper through the sunken thicket of tamarisk, Aurya tried to keep the stories people had told her out of her mind.

On the ground beneath a clump of boxthorn, she found what she was looking for: her brother's drawings, scratched into the riverbank mud. They were sketches of animals, as usual. Carp and pigs, snakes and turtle shells. Aurya followed the images as they became rabbits, deer and doves. Then she spotted the deep footprints Sharo always left in the mud, leading off towards the old village.

'I knew it. Not again, Sharo.'

The undergrowth was denser here, wreathed with thorns that clutched at her woollen sleeves. She tried to follow the paths cut

3

by wild pigs where she could, but the going was hard. The deeper she went into the thicket, the more those stories came back to her: the sounds in the dark that one of the charrer's boys had run from, and the prints the old leather-worker had found at the river a few mornings back, bigger than a man's hand. As she got closer, the shells of the old houses appeared, half-hidden in the thicket. The stench of the abandoned well filled the air, and Aurya saw that her brother's footprints led off towards it. The well had been tainted by flood waters once, and when the villagers moved, it became a rubbish pit, full of the waste of two dozen families.

'Sharo?' she called out, and edged closer. 'Sharo, are you down there?'

A groan of pain answered from the bottom.

'Sharo!' Aurya ran closer, but something stopped her. A sound: a slosh nearby that sent her ducking down into the grass. A crow fluttered from the skeleton of one old house, and then the tamarisk on the clearing edge swayed. Something was out there. Aurya hushed her breath, her heart thumping. It was probably a pig. A large pig. There was the crack of a rotten log, and then something heavy moving in the reeds. Not a pig. It could be a deer, lost in the brush. Aurya thought suddenly of the goat that had disappeared from the village pen in the night, its stake uprooted from the ground.

'Sharo!' Aurya hissed as loudly as she dared, but there was no reply from the pit. 'Sharo, if you're down there ...'

The trees hushed each other. Aurya gave out hurried prayers:

To the god of old things
To the gods of the riverbank
To the god of hunters

The sounds came nearer, the crunch of reeds, the water dropping from branches. And then the rushes parted and her brother stepped out, back first, heaving an old roof beam behind him.

'Smash your head!' Aurya shouted. Sharo started and turned to her, going pale with guilt. The beam he was carrying thudded to the ground.

4

'Aurya,' he said. His eyes were swollen with crying. 'Aurya, please don't tell Father.'

She ran to him and brushed him down, his wool shirt wet and caked in mud. He was a whole head taller than her, with curling black hair and a flat face full of feeling.

'Sharo, I've been looking for you all morning. Didn't I tell you never to come out here? Look at you. You're filthy.'

'Aurya …' He held out his muddy hands. 'I just wanted to help it.'

'You could have hurt yourself.' She took him by the shoulders. 'Clambering around in these old houses, disturbing the ghosts. And what if you fell into the pit? You think Father would help get you out? You think the village would fetch the ropes for us?'

'I'm sorry, Aurya. It needed my help.'

She heard him this time. Sharo was looking over her shoulder, down into the pit. Then that groan came again from below, like a wooden board when a heavy person steps on it. A huff of breath. The noise sent something skittering inside her.

'Sharo, what is it? What's down there?'

'It's hurt, Aurya. Please don't tell Father.'

Aurya turned and crouched, crept towards the pit and peered over the edge. There at the bottom, among the rotten reeds and the shards of a cooking pot she'd broken back before the rains – and been beaten for – and fish heads with eye sockets seething with white worms, and the grinning bones of a lamb from a recent wedding, and old curd spotted with blue mould, and wax seals from beer jars, and the leathered body of a dog that had jumped down there half-starved and never been able to get out, and the pools of muddy water and weeds and wildflowers growing among all the festering mess, Aurya saw the thing she dreaded most in the world.

It was a lion: a young male with a thin black mane, blood caked around a wound on one hind foot. A cloud of flies circled, but its ribs still moved to a slow breath. That groan came again from between its jaws. Aurya shuddered. Beams, like the one she'd caught Sharo dragging, had been dropped over the pit edge, slanting so they formed a ramp almost to the top. Aurya looked back at her brother, who stood guiltily behind her.

'You were going to help it climb out,' she said.

'It was crying, Aurya. Can't you hear it?' Sharo said.

'We can't – it's not …' She struggled to find the words. 'Sharo, how could you?'

'It's hurt.'

Aurya stared down at the creature's matted black mane, the slender arc of its spine.

'Sharo, one of those monsters killed our mother. What were you thinking?'

She saw the hurt look in her brother's eyes, and knew she had to soften her tone.

'Sharo, listen to me – if the lion – if that animal gets out of the pit, it will come for us. It will come stalking through the reeds and into our house at night.'

Sharo's eyes wandered from her down into the pit, so she took him by the chin and forced him to look at her. Then she reached into the pouch inside her shirt and pulled out her knife. It wasn't a knife so much as a shard from an iron blade that she'd once found in the river shallows, thrown from a passing barge. But she kept it sharp.

'Do you know what the beast will do then?' she said. His eyes followed the sliver as it flashed. 'First, it'll find Father lying drunk on the floor. And it will slice open his belly with its claws and eat his guts, just like hot soup.' She made a slurping sound. Watched his eyes waver. 'Do you know what it will do then, Sharo? It will come into the room where we sleep. It will creep through the dark and come over to my mat, and then it will slice open my belly, and eat my guts. Like what?'

'Like hot soup,' he murmured, going pale.

'And do you know what it will do then? It will creep over to your bed –'

'No! Stop!'

He was shaking. Aurya felt weak. This talk of soup reminded her that she hadn't eaten since yesterday. She kept checking the undergrowth surrounding the clearing, at the shaded wall corners

6

and collapsed roofs. She knew those beasts sometimes moved in pairs. She squeezed Sharo's shoulder.

'Try remembering something,' she said.

'I don't want to.'

'Sharo, do it for me. What about the day Father came back from the war? Where were the stars that night?'

'You always ask that one,' he said, his breaths coming in little gasps. 'It's too easy.'

'Well ... what about the clouds? What did they look like just before sunrise?'

Sharo's eyes wandered, and Aurya counted three heartbeats.

'A big one, over the hills. It looks like a jumping hare. The birds are coming home for the season.'

'And what about ... two days later? What did we eat in the morning?'

Sharo took a sharp breath through his nose, smelling the meal he'd eaten years ago as if cooked right in front of him.

'Barley soup, and locusts cooked on coals. They've ruined the crops. People are crying. For the crops, and the men who didn't come home.'

Aurya looked at her brother, at his wide, smooth cheekbones, the swollen pink skin around his eyes. By some intervention of the gods, Sharo had never forgotten a thing in his life. He remembered the position of stars and clouds on far-off dates, the exact words someone had used ten years ago, the patterns of bark and stone he'd seen only once. There was only one thing Sharo didn't remember: the day their mother was dragged away by the lion.

'You have to promise me not to come back here,' Aurya said, and saw him look away. That was the upside of Sharo's curse: he found it impossible to tell lies. 'Sharo? You can't come back out here. That lion – it has to stay down there. If you promise, you can tell me one of Mother's stories.'

'A story?'

'Yes, I want to hear one.'

'Not like the last one you made me tell?'

'No, you can choose this time.'

'Can it be one with lions?'

'You're the one who knows them,' Aurya said, and led her brother away, with just one look back at the pit. 'But you have to promise, Sharo.'

'I promise.'

She pinched him, made a roaring noise. 'Look out,' she said. 'I'm a lion.'

He laughed.

'No, you're not.'

'Yes, I am.' She pinched him again so he yelled, and she chased him through the reeds, shouting, 'I'm a lion and you're a deer!'

When they reached the house, Aurya found a large piece of stone lying on a sledge beside the east wall. Deep furrows in the earth led back up to the road, and the earth was torn with buffalo prints. It had been years since her father had last bought a piece of stone, and Aurya stopped chasing Sharo and stood for a few moments.

'Did you know about this, Sharo?' He shook his head.

'How did he pay for it?'

Sharo curled a lock of hair over his ear as he followed her to the stone. It was beautiful: a flat slab, eggshell-white, laced with veins the colour of sunset. Aurya smoothed her hands over the surface: the hush it made against her palms, the odour of the thick ropes used to bind it. It was strangely warm. She put her cheek against it, and the sensation made her think of putting her cheek against her mother's stomach. She knew it wasn't a real memory: the lion dragged her mother away before she could remember. Aurya stroked the stone and thought of the animal in the pit, and the sound it had made when she called out to it, as if it knew her.

———————

Aurya took her brother back to the cooking area behind the house, the clay oven full of cold ash. She sat him down on the millstone with the weeds growing up through its centre, and washed his face with rainwater from the trough. Their father's snores came from inside.

8

'Are we going to eat ash again, Aurya?' Sharo said.

'Well, did you catch any fish today?'

'No.'

'And did you catch any pigs?'

'No.'

'Then we're going to eat ash. Unless you'd rather be hungry.'

'I think I'd rather be hungry,' he said.

'Me too.'

Her stomach lashed out though. Once they would have begged for food from their neighbours, but now their father owed them all, and they'd stopped leaving out scraps for the mason's children. They would have to go to the quarry camp and steal again.

'Can I see her necklace?' Sharo said. Aurya nodded, and let him play with it, the little cylinder of greenish stone she wore around her neck. Sharo ran his thumb over the lines carved into its surface, and Aurya poured a last spoon of water over his unoiled hair.

'Mother was from Nineveh.'

'Yes, she was.'

That's all she had: a necklace, the name of a city, Sharo's stories.

Sharo took the necklace and pressed it down into the earth, rolled it so the image carved on its surface printed into the ground. A lion, arching its back, surrounded by trees, and a river winding below it.

'Hey, you're getting it dirty,' Aurya said, and took the necklace away from him. 'Come on, before Father wakes up.'

Their father was where he always was, asleep on his sheepskin. In the summer, when he laid it out in the sun, the white lice would crawl out of it, showing blood through their transparent skins. Their father's face looked like it had been carved with a chisel. He kept his hair cut close to his scalp, like a slave. He'd been a soldier once, and if his stories were to be believed, he'd fought the Medes and the Elamites, savage hill creatures with sharp teeth and hair on their bodies like dogs. He'd never been a good father, but the war had made him worse. An Elamite arrow had landed in his thigh, a wound that still troubled him, and when he came home, he was given their house as a reward.

9

The moment Aurya and Sharo stepped into the room, a sharp wind from downriver banged a shutter, and their father jolted awake, coughing.

'What's the wind doing today?' he moaned. 'Where's it always hurrying to?' He rubbed his scalp, the short fuzz of hair broken in places by scars.

'Go back to sleep, Father,' Aurya said.

'Aurya. Look at you. You're getting taller every day; we'll have to weigh you down to earth somehow. Will you go down to the crossroads please ...'

'No.'

'Will you go down there please, and get me some beer? Or some date wine. Tell them to put it on my credit.'

'You don't need any more,' Aurya said.

Her father's face darkened, and he waved her away. His palms were mason's hands, smooth and completely without fingerprints after years of working with stone.

'You'd have me eat clay for bread too,' he muttered. 'You'd have me drink water like the beasts.' Then his eyes fell. 'This demon, Aurya. You know how it's always scratching behind my eyes.'

'You haven't worked for months,' Aurya said. 'Me and Sharo had to go and sell your last chisels. We'll be eating the leather in the door hinges soon, and you want me to buy you beer? With what money?'

Her father's eyes untethered. He leant over and picked up a jar by its neck, the reed straw still in it. He made a movement as if to throw it at her. It was heavy; the momentum rolled him on to his side, and a little beer spilled on to his sheepskin. Aurya flinched.

'I made a big sale.' Her father laughed, and clumped the jar down on the floor. 'Big piece of stone.'

'I saw it. How much did you borrow?'

'Beautiful piece, fresh from the quarry and still full of sap. Guess who bought it.'

'I don't want to guess.'

'Guess!' He pointed a wavering finger at her. 'I bet you think it's Nasirpal on the other bank.'

'I don't care if it's Nasirpal or not.'

'So like your mother.' He hiccupped, and thumped his chest. 'Well, it's not Nasirpal. It's the King.'

Aurya watched him, filled with waves of hatred and pity, and love turned rancid like old curd. She could hear her brother murmuring to himself on the terrace, scratching more drawings into the earth. She took the first step over to the door.

'Our lord, our sun, his mighty mightiness, King Ashurbanipal,' her father sang. 'Last week I heard that agents from the palace were buying up all the gypsum slabs from the quarry. So I borrowed from Nilmaher and bought the largest, flattest piece I could find. The poor old quarry goat who sold it didn't know what he was giving away. When he finds out – when he hears about the palace, and what they're paying …'

He hiccupped again. Puffed out his cheeks to hold in a belch. Aurya took another step.

'Why would the King want your stone?'

'King Ashy-ashy-banipal,' her father said. 'Doesn't just – just saying that name make you think of date syrup, and all the beer you can drink, with flower petals floating in it?'

'I haven't eaten since yesterday morning,' Aurya said, but her father didn't hear.

'The King's men are bringing a barge all the way from Nineveh. They'll be here to take it away: first light on the fifteenth, four days from now. We're part of great things now, Daughter. Great, great things. Ashurbanny-banny-pal. When you go to the cross-roads, make sure you fetch some firewood, Aurya. Fetch some firewood and wash the pots too, with ash. Make yourself useful until you're married.'

Outside, Aurya found Sharo crouching on the ground, still drawing in the soft mud with a reed. She turned her head to see what he was drawing. It was a lion, crouched and mournful, its paws over its head.

'Come on,' she said, 'you've done enough drawing today.'

Aurya didn't go to the crossroads. Instead, she and Sharo went up to the quarry camp and crept behind the workers' tents, listening for voices inside. They had learned to survive this way while their father was away fighting; these days it had come back into use. The earth around the camp was scattered with lumps of gypsum, old pieces of rope and dead rats. Aurya found a sandal there with a broken strap she thought she might be able to repair and sell. They found one unoccupied tent too, and managed to steal an onion that someone had forgotten. They ran back to the riverbank before anyone could catch them and sat on the abandoned kiln at the bottom of their dry field.

While they sat there and shared the onion between them, the north wind came in and battered the village. The women wrapped up the grains and small fish they were drying on their porches, tied down the cloths that covered their doors. Shutters banged.

Aurya did her weaving. The potter's wife sometimes gave her grain biscuits in exchange for repairing palm leaf matting. It was fiddly, but it let her mind wander. While her fingers worked, she and Sharo watched the boats sailing past on the wide river: the barges drawn along the towpaths, the reed-matted rafts, the sleek oared ships heading downriver to the great cities. Aurya imagined what magic it would be to step aboard one of those ships, to let the river's course draw them downstream.

'Nineveh,' she said, just to hear its sound. 'What do you think it's like there, Sharo? In the great city?'

'I don't know, Aurya.'

'I think it must be the most beautiful place in the world.'

Even from out there, they could still hear their father back in the house. He was crashing from room to room and singing. It was an old song about a city that had forgotten its gods and fallen into ruin, but he laughed as he sang it as though it was the funniest thing in the world.

Katya

Katya lurched awake when the plane touched down. She blinked and looked out of the window on to the flat beige landscape rushing past, at the rain, the forests of weeds bursting through cracks in the runway, the shapes of tower blocks lost and far-off in the haze. So this was Baghdad.

The line for passport control took for ever, and Katya listened to the hubbub of other languages as she waited. Soldiers with dogs and guns watched her from the corners and she realised her mistake: she rummaged through her bag and got out the black abaya she was supposed to wear from the plane, pulled it over her hair. It felt like stocking fabric, and she adjusted it constantly as she waited in line.

'Welcome to Iraq,' a sign above the walkway said. She tried to calm herself. Salim would be there. He'd have a board with her name on it. When she reached the desk, the guard tapped his finger on her Iraqi visa – six months, expiring in 2014 – and asked her name.

'Katya Macaulay.'

'Where did you fly from?'

'London, via Istanbul.'

He nodded and motioned for her to take a seat on some plastic chairs nearby. Minutes passed. The man went several times into a nearby office, returned with different papers and stamps. Katya felt her stomach churn as the other passengers went through without incident, and the queues thinned. Something seemed wrong. While she waited, she looked up and saw that a family of small birds had got inside the airport building, in defiance of security. Rain pattered on the roof, and her fear rose gradually: fear that her visa had a mistake on it and she would be sent home, fear that her baggage would be stolen while she waited, fear that Salim had forgotten to meet her. Soon the queues emptied completely and she was the only one left.

Finally, looking a little irritated, the man waved her over. He gave a bang-bang-bang of his stamp, handed Katya's passport back and waved her through. The handlers had already taken her luggage off the carousel. In the arrivals lounge, she held her breath, and scanned the signs people held out, in English and Arabic. Then she saw it: 'Katya'. The man holding the sign wore a crisp white shirt and had a few days' stubble. Closer up, she noted his curly hair and striking grey-green eyes.

'Hi. Salim?'

'Hi,' he said with the hint of an American accent, and shook her hand. 'Welcome to Iraq, Miss Katya.'

'Thanks. Nice to – great to meet you.'

Salim was better-looking than his photo. Katya felt conscious of her heavy outdoor boots, her cargo trousers and old hoodie. She wasn't sure they had the effect she'd hoped for: tough, unfussed, prepared for anything. Outside, the rain was still sizzling on the ground, so they ran across the car park with coats pulled over their heads, and dived into a battered white Volkswagen faintly smelling of tobacco.

'I hope you don't mind the clutter,' Salim said. Junk filled the back seat and foot wells, and Katya noted the familiar accoutrements of a field archaeologist: the weather-proof clipboards and trowel, the folding rulers, rubber-palmed gloves and old boots, all of it at odds with Salim's crisp shirt and polished shoes.

'No, I don't mind at all.'

When he took a pair of sunglasses from his toiletry bag, Katya saw the knurled grip of a pistol hiding between his toothbrush and safety razor. She tried to pretend she hadn't seen it, but he caught her look.

'For protection,' he said, almost embarrassed. 'It's Baghdad, you know. But we're only here for one night.'

Katya nodded, and caught herself tucking her hands into the sleeves of her hoodie.

'Oh, and you don't need to wear that with me,' Salim said, as he started the engine. He kept his eyes focused ahead, and it took Katya a moment to realise that he meant the abaya.

'Oh, thanks,' she said, and pulled it back. 'It itches a bit.'

'Yeah. But put it on when we go out, and at the checkpoints. These are difficult times.'

Salim drove carefully. They pulled out of the airport, past black armoured vehicles topped with guns and along an endless concrete wall made of prefab pieces.

'Is it what you expected?' he said.

'I didn't know what to expect. I didn't think it would be so wet.'

'It's the season. The Iraqi winter. It always takes foreigners by surprise.'

Katya felt stung, even though she knew that's exactly what she was.

'I'm not completely foreign,' she said. 'My dad was from Iraq.'

'Oh, yes? You don't have an Iraqi name though.'

'No. My mum's English. They couldn't decide what to do with their surnames, so they promised if they had any girls, they would get my mum's name, and all the boys would get my dad's. And then they just had me.'

Salim laughed.

'Sounds like the typical luck of an Iraqi man. So you must know some things already. Where was he from?'

'From here, from Baghdad. But he didn't talk about it much. And he died when I was young.'

'Oh, I'm sorry.'

'No, it's fine.'

'Well,' Salim said, shifting in his seat, 'welcome home.'

Welcome home. Katya looked out the window at a family pushing a stalled car through the flood waters, forests of razor wire collecting colourful scraps of plastic bags, and the Tigris's golden expanse bounded by concrete banks. Everything was new; everything she saw tingled with electricity. Every time she became accustomed to where she was, they passed through a checkpoint, each one a small fortress. Soldiers peered in through the windows, opened the boot and rooted around, so the smell of mud and still water filled the car, and looked underneath with mirrors. Katya pulled on her abaya each time and handed over her passport without meeting any eyes. She realised with a shiver that all of this was what her dad must have seen growing up here as a boy, then a student, finally as a journalist – and it was what he must have seen too in the days and weeks before he disappeared.

'There were some bombs yesterday,' Salim said, as they pulled away from the checkpoint, speaking with the same sad embarrassment as when she'd seen the gun.

'Bombs?' Katya said. He nodded.

'In a market and a mosque. Terrible things. After an illness you don't recover just like that, you know. You come back in stages. And Iraq has been ill for a long time. You must promise me: don't ever go outside alone. You're safe if you're with me. And always keep your passport on you.'

Katya nodded, determined not to seem afraid. She brushed her palms on her jeans. Then Salim softened his voice.

'It's been hard to get good people out here. I was glad you accepted. Your paper on the archaeology of plant life in Italy was impressive.'

Katya had spent that summer in Tivoli getting sunburnt, piecing together the planting patterns of Roman fields, mapping the irrigation systems of ancient gardens, sketching the imprints of vine leaves left on clay basins. She didn't tell him about the other jobs she'd been offered this time round: the digs in Greece and Peru.

'Thanks,' she said. 'You can tell a lot from plants, if you learn to speak their language.'

'Well, I'm excited to see what you can bring to our site. My speciality has always been anthropological. Bones and stones. We've probably missed a lot you would've caught.'

They stopped at a roadside restaurant with red plastic chairs and ate a quick meal of rice and chicken, with baba ganoush and pickles in a dish, tastes that reminded Katya of her childhood. They arrived at their hotel as the sun started to go down. It was an inexpensive one, with high steel gates set well back from the street, a bright red carpet in the lobby and fluorescent lighting. Salim shook hands with the owner like an old friend, their hands staying together as they talked over the reception desk.

'We've got a long drive back up to Mosul tomorrow,' Salim said to Katya. 'Once we check in, we should call it a night and start early.'

Checking in, like everything else here, took a long time. Katya went and sat on a faded sofa in the lobby beside a family watching news reports on an old television, their son playing with a toy fire truck on the floor. The boy came and sat beside her, used her arm as a road. The British newsreader was saying, 'Explosions occurred at around the same time on busy streets in the districts of Sha'ab, Tobchi, Karrada ...', and Katya looked at the boy to see if he understood. He just looked back at her.

'We used to watch the English channels when I was a kid too,' Salim said, handing her her passport. 'I used to think they called it "breaking news" because there was always something getting broken.'

In her room, Katya lay awake and listened to car horns hooting softly in the distance, wondering if she would be able to hear a bomb if it went off in the city. She thought about what it would be like to dig the earth in this country. She thought about trowel shapes and mapping techniques, the beauty of a perfect soil profile with all its multicoloured layers, the feel of a sharpened pencil on paper. She thought about the sensations of clay on dry skin, and the sounds roots make when they popped beneath the trowel. She watched a yellow gecko dart across the wall, the wings of a moth jackknifed in its happy jaws.

———

The roads were still flooded in the morning, so they set off later than they'd planned after a breakfast of boiled eggs and diamond-shaped bread. Salim wore fake Ray-Ban sunglasses and another starched shirt, knife-pressed trousers and polished wingtip shoes. He looked like he was going to an office. She tried to gauge his mood, but the sunglasses made him inscrutable and he seemed distracted as they drove through the city. She began to wonder how much she really knew about this man, alone in his car in a strange country. She stared out of the car window at the mosques and radio masts, the bundles of wire hanging like creepers from corners, and thought about the other Katyas, the ones who chose one of the other jobs. Just now, one of the other Katyas would be flying off to the snow-capped mountains of Peru to uncover Inca tombs.

'Do you like books?' Salim asked, out of nowhere. She hesitated.

'Do I like them?'

He nodded, stopped the car and made a motion for her to pull on her abaya. She got out, unsure, and noticed he took the bag with the gun inside. He led her to a narrow street near the river, and she followed, feeling her heartbeat rise a little. When they turned the corner, she saw crowds of people among piles of books lying out on tarpaulins, on tables and shelves and in rotating magazine racks.

'My favourite place,' Salim said. 'I like to give people a good experience of Baghdad before they head north. So you can tell people when you go back home that Iraq isn't all rubble and ruins.'

They walked along the street, and Katya saw books in many languages: textbooks, novels, poetry, encyclopaedias, Qurans with silver embossing.

'At night they leave the books out here on the street,' Salim said. 'That's what I've heard. Because readers don't steal, and thieves don't read.'

'Is that true?'

'I don't know. Do you want a souvenir?'

Katya shook her head.

'No, I ...'

He called out to one stallholder and picked up a book, handed over some notes.

'Here. A welcome present.'

Its cover was an image she knew: ancient Assyrian carvings from seven centuries before Christ, of a king hunting lions in his chariot. *Gilgamesh*, it said.

'Oh. Thanks. I read this in university. Not this edition, but ...'

'The world's first story,' Salim said, a serious note to his voice as he led her into a busy café at the head of the street. 'Written on tablets of clay four thousand years ago, right here in Iraq. This is where all our stories began: the garden, the flood. All our battles with monsters.'

Katya noticed that Salim always spoke in fragments, bursts of information that seemed to crumble away the moment he said them. They sat down on the worn wooden benches and he ordered a couple of cardamom-flavoured coffees, but they didn't linger.

'Let's go,' he said after necking the rocket-fuel tar at the bottom of the cup. 'It's already noon, and it's about five hours on the road. But Mosul awaits.'

Once outside Baghdad, the flood waters dissipated and Salim drove faster, one arm slung over the rolled-down window. Pebble marks on the windscreen glinted like stars when the sun hit them.

'So your family weren't worried,' he said, 'when you said you were coming to Iraq?'

'Yeah. They were worried. My mum didn't want me to go.'

'But you came anyway.'

'I wanted to see where my dad was from. I thought I'd learn something about him. About myself.'

'Archaeologists are all the same,' Salim said. 'They always think the answer is in the past.'

As they headed north, the land became dryer and looser on either side: a spinal landscape, sensitive as exposed bone. As the hours passed, Salim told her about the dig she was joining: a joint Iraqi and international initiative designed to protect the ruins of the ancient city of Nineveh from organised looting.

'The ruins are right in the middle of Mosul. You'll see them soon enough. But that makes them hard to protect. We've seen looting gangs going out at night, digging into the earth, probably stealing things to order. So wherever they dig, that's where we go. Every day they get bolder and more organised. And Mosul is only a two-hour drive from Syria. With the war over there, it's like the Wild West. Lawless. Whole cities under the control of militias.'

'So the looters have more funding than we do.'

'Aha, yes. That's right.'

As they drove and talked, Katya noticed that Salim preferred to speak only about the future: the development of Iraq, solutions for the corruption in the government, grand schemes for hydroelectric power on the Tigris and rebuilding the old railway from Istanbul to Baghdad. He deflected questions about his family, or the recent history of his country. It made Katya think of when she was a kid, how her dad had always changed the channel if the news came on.

The road ahead pooled like mercury. At each checkpoint, lorry drivers lounged on carpets laid out in the shade of their queuing vehicles, smoking and playing dominoes. Katya looked out over the dry, undulating land and thought about a paper she'd once read on the physics of sand dunes, their height and position an emergent property of the amplitude of the wind's wavelength and the size of the grains of sand. When she looked back, she saw that her dad was driving the car. She couldn't see his face properly, but she knew it was him. He was dressed like the ancient kings of Assyria, the way they always looked in their carvings: a tall crown and beard in seashell curls. But he had her dad's scars, the constellation of purple rings and crescents running up his right arm.

'Dad, why are you dressed like that?' She tried not to laugh; he looked ridiculous. He turned to her and opened his mouth.

'You're not going to find me, you know.'

She was going to ask what he meant, but she couldn't summon the words. He raised his finger to point straight ahead. In the distance, black smoke rose over the mirror glaze of the horizon, flashing orange with the light of unseen fires.

Katya woke with a start, her head banging softly against the window.

'Ouch,' she said, massaging the cramp in her neck. Salim chuckled, eyes crinkling a little.

'Tired? We're nearly there now.'

Katya blinked. It was almost evening, a city, a fog of dust in the air. Salim was driving slower, already more relaxed than in Baghdad.

'This is Mosul,' he said. 'The city of prophets, the hunchback, the mother of two springs ... it has many names; depends who you ask.'

Butterflies fizzed in Katya's stomach. Had her dad driven down this same road too, ten years before? Had he looked out at the same slender white asparagus of minarets, the blue eggshell domes and satellite dishes?

'It's big,' she said. Salim nodded.

'We've had some trouble getting you proper accommodation at the site. I tried, but I'm afraid we'll have to put you up in the museum for now. We've got an office set up, with a mattress. Pretty basic.'

'The museum ...' Katya said. 'That's okay, I love museums. So long as the exhibits don't come alive at night.'

Salim didn't laugh.

'Everything comes alive at one time or another.'

The museum was a sleek, modern building on an intersection of roads near a park, a bridge over the river and a heaving bus station. It had high ceilings, arched doorways, floors marked by scuffs and two guards with hennaed moustaches standing outside. It was closed to the public after the years of unrest that had followed the war, so the statues lining the walls were all wrapped in blue plastic sheeting, ringed with sandbags. Katya followed Salim into the echoing entrance hall, flanked by two large stone lamassu, the winged bulls with human heads that guarded the palaces of Assyrian kings. Scaffolding was up in places, the dust of recent building work.

'Your room's up here,' Salim said, leading her up the stairs. She followed him past the concealed statues and exhibits to a disused office that smelled like varnish, a mattress on the floor beside a desk and an old filing cabinet. A bare bulb hung from the ceiling, with a single fly in orbit.

'The Mosul Hilton,' Salim said, checking his phone. He showed her the small staff kitchen lined with humming refrigerators, the toilets and showers. Then he took her back to her room and handed her a sheaf of papers joined with a staple. 'Here, just some forms to fill out for tomorrow. Risk assessment, medical. I'll come and pick you up in the morning.'

'You're leaving?' The words came out in a higher pitch than she would have liked.

'Yes, sorry. I wanted to show you around properly, but there's been more looting at the Nineveh site. Have to check in with the others. I'll be back here tomorrow and we can do a proper tour. You can meet the museum's curator in the morning too, Dr Malik.'

'Of course. He's famous.'

Salim shrugged.

'As famous as an Assyriologist can get, I suppose. He's a little strange, by the way. I apologise in advance.'

'Strange how?'

'You'll see.'

Katya stuck out her jaw and nodded.

'Sure. See you tomorrow.'

'Just one more thing.' He led her back to the main door and showed her the locking mechanism. 'Don't ever open this at night.' He handed her a bicycle chain. 'Put this through the handles too, just to make sure, and don't unlock it till morning.'

'There are guards outside.'

'That's what I'm talking about. Don't ever open this door. I and Dr Malik have the only other keys.'

Then he left, and Katya was alone in the museum. She turned the lock and slid the chain through the handles, but as she fumbled with the key, the lights went out all at once, and she dropped it.

'Shit.'

Salim had warned her about the power cuts. She fished around on the floor. There was a reddish gloam about the place, a kind of auxiliary lighting that kicked in slowly and cast strange shadows. Once the door was secured, Katya ran back to her room, her footsteps echoing. She wedged a chair up against the door, feeling silly. She found that her mattress springs were broken in one corner, so she used the book Salim had bought her to prop it up, making sure the lion's sunken eyes weren't showing.

The Internet didn't work, but Katya had some browser tabs open on her laptop already. She clicked over to one that had been open all week, there in the background of everything she did, as she'd packed her bags, handed in the notice on her flat, said goodbye to her mum. The news story, dated ten years ago. The picture was of her dad, the one the Home Office had asked for, that had flashed on TV screens for weeks afterwards. He was wearing a flak jacket that said 'PRESS' and a helmet, smiling mysteriously at the camera. The text, which she knew by heart, was infinitely detached: 'British-Iraqi journalist missing in Nineveh Province ... No trace ... Presumed dead ... No ransom.'

Katya took one of her pills. She lay on her back and tried to stop her body from shaking. She listened to the city outside and thought of the dream she'd had in the car. She ran her fingers over her face and thought about her mum, and what she'd told Katya when she first brought up the offer to join the Iraqi dig. The way her hands shook as they sat in their kitchen with the empty third chair between them.

'Kat ... If you want to go there, that's your decision. But don't do it for him. God knows, he was hard enough to rely on when he was alive.'

Katya rolled on to her side and felt the museum dark press around her, full of hidden movement, the car horns outside, the breeze picking up and buffeting the windows. She thought about one of the other Katyas stepping off their plane on to her Greek island, visiting hillside monasteries and white pebble beaches at weekends, drinking ouzo and retsina. A sensation passed over her like the restless motion of leaves in the wind.

'You idiot,' she said, tucking her hands back into her sleeves and curling into a ball. 'You fucking, fucking idiot.'

Aurya

Aurya and Sharo sat on the old kiln and watched the ships on the river. The seven cold winds of the month of Shebat ruffled their clothes, buffed their hair. They watched the men with head-wraps and hammers and adzes slouch along the quarry road in groups, and Aurya wondered from which one they'd stolen the onion. She chewed a ball of grass to fool her stomach. Later, a peddler came by with baskets of salt fish, but he didn't stop at their house. Aurya thought of how they would taste, and her mouth watered.

'Aurya, do you think he has olives?'

Sharo loved olives.

'Even if he does, how will you pay for them?'

Sharo sniffed. Towards evening a grain ship forged upstream filled with huge clay urns, lined with soldiers and thirty oars on each side, going to feed the men in the hill forts who kept the creatures of the mountains at bay. It always surprised Aurya when she thought about it: the endless river, this great vein of the empire, its lifeblood, flowing right beside their poor house with its broken roof. That in only a day or so, this same water would flow past the walls of Nineveh. Aurya ran her fingers along the bumps in her necklace, trying to feel the memory of her mother's touch in the stone.

'Sharo. You remember the time before I was born, don't you? Before the lion ...'

'Yes.'

'And you remember her? Mother, I mean?'

'I remember everything, Aurya,' he said, his voice faraway. 'I remember every word she ever said. Every old story she told. Everything except the night she died.'

'What was she like?'

He closed his eyes.

'She looked a bit like you. With brown eyes and hair in curls.'

'Like mine,' Aurya said, and Sharo nodded.

'Yes, but not short like yours. It was so long that when you looked up, it filled your sight. She had freckles here, and here.' He touched points on Aurya's face, dappling his fingertips over her nose and chin, and she brushed him off.

'Stop it.'

'When I was ill, she dipped a cloth in honey for me to suck on. And she always bought olives when the peddlers came through.'

Aurya breathed in, savouring every word like drips from that honey-soaked cloth. The grain ship slipped around the river bend and out of sight.

'Aurya,' Sharo said. 'Do you think the lion will be okay? The one in the well?'

Aurya hugged her knees. The sun was going down, turning white through the haze. Smells of charcoal and burnt onions blowing from another house made her irritable. She spat out her wad of grass.

'Don't think about it, Sharo. Why don't you tell me one of mother's stories now?'

'One of the ones from before the flood? The one with the lions?'

'If that's what you want.'

So Sharo began.

'This is the tale of Gilgamesh the King,' he said.

This is the tale of Gilgamesh the King.

It began in a time before anyone can remember, in a city between the rivers. The King of that city was called Gilgamesh. He was strong and cruel, and took the city's women for himself.

He angered the gods. And the gods went to the river, and made a man from mud, and breathed life into him.

'We will name you Enkidu,' they told him. 'Go live with the deer and the lions.'

When the King heard about the man of the wilds, he was afraid, and sent a woman from the temple to seduce him. And it worked. The wild man fell in love with her.

'I must follow her,' he told the animals. They smelled the human on him, and ran away when he approached.

The wild man and the woman went to the city to be married. And there the story might have ended. But one day, the King saw the woman in the market, and he too fell in love. Soon after, a messenger arrived from the palace.

'It is the right of King Gilgamesh to take your wife to bed before your wedding,' he told the wild man. 'Give her up or die!'

Somewhere in the reed bank, they heard a high-pitched, sniggering laugh, followed by a chorus of shushing. Sharo broke off his story.

'Who's there?' Aurya called out, though she had some idea already. From the tangled brush came Nebo-Pishtim, son of Nilmaher the village headman, wearing his fine tasselled clothes. Whenever she saw him, she thought of the faces of voles. Behind him came two friends, older boys with rough red knuckles, ones she hadn't seen before. Nebo-Pishtim's narrow eyes flitted to where Aurya and Sharo sat on the kiln.

'Aren't you going to tell us the rest of the story?'

'Smash your head, Nebo,' Aurya said. 'Can't you go torture a mouse or something?'

He turned to the others.

'Her brother's simple. And she's always lying about how her mother was from Nineveh.'

Aurya felt her face flush.

'At least my mother doesn't sell herself outside the temple, you son of a carp!'

She didn't think that was true. She saw Nebo-Pishtim's mother at market sometimes, and she always wore the best coloured veils. But something about it touched Nebo-Pishtim, and his face went as dark as a crushed reed. He picked up a stone from the ground and hurled it in their direction. It was a bad throw, but Sharo squealed and ducked. The bigger boys hooted, delighted at the reaction, and fished around for more stones. Another one whooshed over Aurya's head.

'Let's go, Sharo, come on.' Sharo gripped her arm tightly, whimpering a little, but he didn't move. She tugged, but he wouldn't budge. 'Come on, Sharo!' She pushed him as a small stone struck her shoulder painfully and another slapped into the mud behind them. 'Be brave, Sharo.'

A stone bounced against the kiln just to Sharo's side. Aurya pushed him again, harder this time, but Sharo stayed frozen where he was as stones struck him on the back and shoulder. Aurya felt a puff of fire in her throat. She jumped off the kiln and ran at the boys, leapt at the closest one. He was bigger than her, with hair on his face, but the attack took him by surprise. He tripped over his own leg, and Aurya went with him, landed on top of him and struck him as many times as she could, in the eye, on the nose. Nebo-Pishtim and his other friend leapt back, laughing and whooping. Aurya stood up, shaking, feeling her hair come untethered from its bunch. She clenched her muddy fists.

'Who will fight the wild Elamite?' Nebo-Pishtim taunted, and pushed his other friend towards her. Aurya felt the weight of her blade fragment tucked in her wool.

'Run home, Sharo!' Aurya shouted. He was still crouching on the kiln, staring down at her with glazed eyes. When she looked back, she saw too late the egg-sized stone in Nebo-Pishtim's hand. She didn't have time to duck. He whipped it at her, and there was a burst of purple. The sky and mud swapped places; the taste of iron. She felt hands on her. The world rocked back into focus and she could see the two remaining boys leaning over her, the sky washed grey overhead.

'Nice trinket,' Nebo-Pishtim was saying, and Aurya saw her mother's necklace stretched on its thong above her, the image on its greenish stone just showing as it dangled there. Nebo-Pishtim pulled once on the thread, and it bit into the back of her neck. He pulled again, and it snapped. Aurya tried to reach for her blade to cut him, but her arms flopped around on either side like dying fish.

'Don't. It's my mother's …'

Nebo-Pishtim straightened, shaking his head.

'Your mother wasn't from Nineveh. She was probably just a wild Elamite like you. The sooner you accept that, the better.'

The boys turned and disappeared into the reeds, the two kicking and jibing their bleeding friend. Sharo was still there, still peering over the kiln, tears wetting his cheeks. Aurya struggled to her feet and back towards the house. The rain began to fall. It felt cool on the lump that rose on her head, throbbing with every heartbeat. The lack of her necklace was like a severed limb.

'Aurya, Aurya,' Sharo said, sniffing, climbing down from the kiln and following her. She didn't look at him. 'Aurya, are you all right?'

She spun around, blood running in two warm branches down the side of her cheek.

'You just sat there,' she said, each word an axe blow.

'Aurya …'

'Look at the size of you! And you just stood there while they split my head with a rock and took our mother's necklace. You didn't even try to fight.'

'I was scared. I can't fight them, Aurya. They'd hurt me …' He trailed off, sniffing, and began to cry again. 'Aurya, can I tell you the rest of the story now?'

Aurya lunged at her brother and struck him on the chest with both her palms. He hardly moved, but his eyes widened in shock and hurt.

'I'm done with your stories,' she said, and looked him right in his wide brown eyes. 'You can defend yourself from now on, and tell your stories to the animals.'

Then she turned and ran back to the house. The spring rain came down in sheets. A brown river already ran from their door when she got there, rain pouring through the broken roof, and their father nowhere to be seen. Aurya's stomach snarled, and she felt dizzy. Some days she would crack open one of the beer jars and scrape out the leftover grain husks, but now the thought made her sick.

She went into the room beside their father's, where she and Sharo slept when the season was too cold to sleep on the roof. She pulled her mat into the dry corner and curled up on it. Outside, the rain spoke its hissing language to the earth, and a slow quarry cart rolled by on the road. The ruin-mound foxes barked in the old village, and a ukuku-bird made its mournful sound. Night came, and she cried herself into a restless sleep as the lump in her head beat like a tiny heart.

Aurya dreamed about lions. Not the usual nightmares where they chased her through the brush and the old village ruins, or the dreams where she saw her mother dragged away by those jaws. She dreamed she was a lion. She was trapped at the bottom of the pit, starving and scared. Sleep came and went and came again. She felt the pit rising on either side, earthy and dark, the stink of the dead and the rot all around her. More than once, she kicked herself awake and found that she was scratching the mat with her nails. She lay back, chest heaving, and listened to the night rain come down like the judgement of Shamash outside.

Katya

In the morning, Katya lay on her mattress in her office room, feeling heavy as a sack of rubble. She'd always felt like this in the mornings: weak, hopeless, limp, as though the act of dreaming had drained her in some way. When she was young, her dad would breeze into her room before school and flood the room with sun and a screech of curtain rails.

Katya, get up, he'd say. *You have to get up.* For years now, she'd begun each morning by saying it to herself.

'Get up, Katya,' she breathed, and stretched up off the mattress, bones clicking. It was late already, and she'd forgotten to fill out the forms before falling asleep. She rushed through them with bleary eyes, printing her full name in block capitals: Katya Hammadi Macaulay, her dad's surname, her middle name, looking like it belonged to someone else. The risk assessment forms read like a carnival of terrors.

'"In case of kidnapping",' she read aloud, '"follow these four rules. One: Befriend your captors. Two: Be prepared for a long stay. Three: Don't show weakness. Four: Look for a chance to escape and take it if you can."'

Good advice in general. She paused only once, over the question, 'Have you ever suffered from seizures?' She ran her tongue over her teeth for a moment, and then ticked 'no'. Suffering was a strong word anyway. You couldn't suffer if all you felt was blankness. She went to her desk and took one of her pills.

After a little while, she heard people moving about outside her door, the sound of voices. A minute later, a knock sounded, and she jumped. She'd forgotten about the chair she'd wedged against it the night before, and she shot up to move it away, embarrassed. She opened the door to Salim standing outside, smartly dressed as before, smile lines around his eyes.

'Oh, you're awake. How did you sleep?'

'Great. Like a stone.'

The museum had come alive: women in black abayas were moving from place to place with buckets and brushes. In the staff kitchen, one of them had already boiled some eggs, which they ate with fluffy diamond-shaped flatbreads and apricot jam. The women talked with each other over their food, and Katya could tell they were pretending not to talk about her. In the main hall, she and Salim met the curator, the Assyriologist Dr Taha Malik. Katya had been set his books at university, and recognised him from his photo. He was a giant of a man, with a full beard, curling hair and round belly. He clapped his huge hands together when he laughed, which was often and with a frightening volume.

'So you're our guest, the plant expert,' he said. 'Welcome, welcome, welcome.'

'There's a story about Dr Malik,' Salim said. 'They say that during the embargos he carried a washing machine on his back from Iran, through the mountains. He's also an encyclopaedia when it comes to the history of Iraq.'

The older man waved him away.

'You are a flatterer of the worst kind, Salim!' the doctor boomed. 'And who needs an encyclopaedia these days? But young lady, the washing machine story is absolutely true. Follow, follow, I'll show you around.'

'He's also a great expert on Mosul's bridges,' Salim said under his breath once the doctor's back was turned. 'I wouldn't get him talking about them if I were you.'

'I heard that!' the doctor shouted back at them. 'Young woman, the city of Mosul has five of the finest bridges in the whole region. Let me take you out on my boat one day to see them from the river.'

'I'd like that.'

Salim and the doctor showed Katya around the museum. She felt overwhelmed by it all, an archaeological paradise: the statues of the kings of Hatra, and the Islamic-era ceramics with their intricate flower designs, the cylinder seals used to stamp impressions into clay. All of it secret, wrapped in plastic, revealed only for her. She didn't stop until she reached the room with the lion hunt carvings.

'Carved by the Assyrians from slabs of gypsum, six and a half centuries before Christ,' Dr Malik announced. 'Right here in Nineveh, when Athens and Rome were just villages.'

Katya followed the scene around the room: the hunting King in his chariot, the commoners gathering to watch on the wooded hill, the soldiers with their spears and dogs, the flying arrows, the lions scattered dead and dying in all directions.

'This is King Ashurbanipal,' Katya said, and pointed to the man in the chariot, his braided beard made up of conch-shell whirls, and his peaked crown.

'That's right,' Salim said. 'The last great king of Assyria. He built the world's first library, conquered Egypt and Persia. And when he died, that's when the Assyrian Empire began to collapse.'

'The plug pulled out of a bath!' the doctor boomed. 'These are the greatest achievements of a civilisation, and they were made right before it disappeared for ever.'

'Like agave plants,' Katya said.

'What?'

'That's how I've always thought of it. They grow for years and burst into flower only once. Right before they die.'

The doctor laughed approvingly. Salim nodded and put his tongue into the side of his cheek.

'Yes. I like that,' he said. Then he sagged. 'Of course, these are just replicas. The original carvings are in London. You must have seen them.'

'A million times,' Katya said. 'When I was a kid, I was obsessed. I made my mum take me every time we went to the city. She told me they came from the same place as my dad.'

That lion again, the same one from the book, leaping up to bite the wheel of the King's chariot as spears drove into its back. That sorrow: visible in the lion's eyes, the veins bulging in its legs, the muscular tension.

'The lions look so real, don't they?' she said. 'So full of pain.'

Salim eyed her.

'Come on. You'll have plenty of time to explore. Let's go see the site.'

Katya spent the drive putting on suncream, and felt nervous the whole way there, though she couldn't describe why. She kept thinking about the lions, pierced with the King's arrows. Across the river, a broken scrubland rose from the lines of houses, the jagged lines of walls and towers, crumbling mud brick and stone.

'There it is,' Salim said. 'Welcome to Nineveh.'

They left the car and climbed the earthen bank that was once the ancient city's ramparts. The sun was only a pale white through the clouds but it could still burn, and Katya felt the grease of suncream on her arms and neck. They climbed up through the scrub of tamarisk, dotted with the delicate purple ziziphora flowers pushing through the rubble. Salim looked strange in this wild place, in his shirt and brogues. He had a way of bounding over the stones as they went, looking like a boy going through rock pools, and the sun gave his hair a golden tint.

'You can see all twelve kilometres of the city wall from here,' he said, reverence in his voice. 'The capital of the world, in its time. That's the North Palace, up there, and that's where the ziggurat once stood ...'

'That must be the Shamash Gate then.' He nodded.

'That's right. You should see the lamassu up there. They're beautiful. That's where we've seen the most looting, so we've been concentrating our efforts over there. And there's the Halzi Gate. When they first excavated, they found dozens of skeletons there, left unburied in the streets. From the day the city was destroyed.'

'I read about it. Lying in the gatehouse where they fell, with arrowheads still in their ribcages.'

Salim nodded.

'Look at it: an empire that ruled for a thousand years. And then in a few short years, it was gone.'

'The end of the world,' Katya said.

'And no one at the time knew that it was coming.'

They stood there for a moment and watched the wind blow over the brown land, over the rubbish and tyre tracks, loose limestone and shattered concrete pipes, blue plastic bags. While Salim spoke about the dig project, Katya tried to imagine the city in its former glory, the buildings rising up from the dust, all the people and animals, the temples and markets.

'This way,' Salim said with a serious note in his voice. 'I'll take you to see your part of the site. It was hit by looters just the other day, so that's where you'll start. We'll secure the site, set up a proper dig and see what we can save.'

Katya's site was a low mound of bare earth at the corner of two busy modern roads, rising from the middle of a dense residential area and overlooking the river. Parts of the Nineveh ruins had been built over, the new concrete city washing over it like waves over a reef, so that now white rooftops clustered all around, and a water tower loomed overhead. The ground was littered with broken stones, shredded plastic cartons and cigarette packets.

'That's the tomb of Jonah,' Salim said, pointing up to an elegant minaret on a hill. 'The people here love that mosque, so we've never been allowed to dig too near. But since the looters have had a go, we've got our opening. It's hard to know what's down there, but this whole hill is the collapsed remains of a large building of some kind. Some think it's another palace, or a barracks or arsenal.'

A gnarled and ancient olive tree pushed through the crumbling wall that edged the slope. The tree's bulbous centre was dead, with shreds of rusting chain-link fence absorbed into its body and names carved on its bark, but enough life remained for some of the limbs to put out heads of silvery-green leaves.

'So it's your choice where to begin,' Salim said. 'The looters have dug holes all over this patch. You can start over the other side of the mound, or get started here.'

Katya climbed up and examined the olive tree, its leaves rustling like foil in the breeze.

'I'll start here.'

Salim laughed.

'You can take the archaeobotanist out of the lab …'

He left her soon after, and Katya spent the morning making a basic walking survey of her new site. She mapped the clumsy holes dug by the looters and got to know the bumps and runnels of the wind-blown land. Archaeology moves from the known to the unknown: she paced the site and marked on her map the mounds with the greatest promise, looking for signs of ancient architecture beneath. It was like trying to guess the shape of the sea floor by looking at the waves.

Before lunch, Katya met the rest of the dig team. She was the youngest there by a few years, only twenty-six and with the ink still wet on her PhD. The registrar was an Australian woman called Mia who wore a wide-brimmed hat and drove a rusting white jeep around the various sites, collecting new objects to be catalogued in blue crates. There were two Italian women, Giulia and Martina, and an older Iraqi couple from the south, Raad and Khawla. These two pairs kept to themselves, tending to murmur to each other in their own languages. They all sat at folding tables beneath a canopy with the site map stretched out in front of them, the contours in the land making it look like a map of the weather.

'So the situation looks like this,' Salim said, rolling up the sleeves of his shirt and rubbing his forehead. 'The looting is getting worse. The gangs are getting bolder and more organised. Some could even have links to groups fighting in Syria, so they're well-funded, well-equipped and often well-armed. We've got to the point where the police are afraid of them, and the army can barely put together a patrol. So our job is getting harder every day. But that also means it's more crucial than ever. When we see evidence of looting, we secure the site. We set up a proper dig and catalogue the finds before more damage gets done.'

'Or before we run out of funding,' said Mia, but no one laughed. Everyone looked tired, windburnt, their faces smooth and pink as if they'd been at sea. After the meeting, they ate a lunch of rice mixed with tinned tomatoes and chickpeas that had arrived in a big stainless-steel pot, brought by a local caterer on the back of a 4x4.

'So what other food do you get here?' Katya asked Mia, who just chuckled and shook her head. Salim caught her eye across the table.

'In a month without wages, don't count the days,' he said.

'What does that mean?'

He broke his poker face for a moment and gave a crooked smile.

'Just a saying around here.'

It rained at intervals, thundering on the tarpaulin. Rivulets of water poured down between their boots. As they ate, the others asked about Katya's previous digs. She told them about her PhD in Italy, how she'd dug in ancient latrines looking for pollen particles dispersed by the plant life of the Roman hills: lavenders, basil, capers and bay. Then she told them about the Bronze Age wreck she'd excavated as a Masters student, off the coast of Lebanon: the remains of pistachios, figs and coriander mouldering in the subaqueous bottoms of clay jars, the thorny burnet used as padding for the cargo that traced the ship to its far home port. They asked her questions about palynology, ancient leaf marks and charred grains, DNA analysis and the collection of sediment cores. As she spoke, she noticed Salim listening intently, though he kept his eyes on his bowl the whole time. She savoured the gently impressed expression on his face, and returned to the thought of it many times that afternoon as she walked the site and mapped it inch by meticulous inch.

———————

Katya managed to get online that night, using a pay-as-you-go SIM Salim had given her. She sat in her room and read the news, regretting it immediately. She learned that 300 people had been killed across Iraq that month. Journalists called it 'a rising tide of bloodshed', as though bloodshed was something that welled up from the earth and ebbed with the moon. She read about the bombs that ripped through busy markets and mosques, the kidnappings, the names of militias and terrorist groups she couldn't keep track of, all reported in the same dispassionate way as they had once reported on her dad. The streets outside seemed quiet, though: the rumble of a plane high overhead, a fox or an ailing dog nearby, the soft hooting of horns. She thought longingly about the llama herds she might have seen in the mountains of Peru, and the sound the Aegean makes when it laps a pebbled beach.

Then, on a whim, she googled Salim. There wasn't much about him online: a University of Mosul profile, and an older one from a university in New Orleans. She read them both. She learned that he was born in Iraq, but studied in the United States, and returned as a translator for the US Army, then as an archaeologist. She bit one of her nails, and then felt a flush of guilt, as though she'd been spying on him. She went into her settings, clicked 'clear history' and shut the laptop.

Instead, she sat and read the book Salim had given her, glancing more than once at the lion hunt carving on its front cover. She flicked to a page that had its corner turned.

'You will never take my wife,' cried Enkidu the wild man.

And so the King came to meet him in person, and the two prepared to fight. The two of them crashed through the streets like wild bulls. They battled until the city crumbled to broken brick and ash around them.

Finally, the King prevailed. He pinned the wild man to the ground. The men with axes rushed forwards to kill him, but the King only laughed.

'I've waited all my life to meet someone like you,' he roared. 'A man who could give me a fair fight. And here you are! A wild man from the forest!'

He got up and offered his hand, and they embraced in the ruins. Later, the people crept from the rubble to rebuild their homes.

It was more or less how she remembered it: austere and distant, its words infused with a strange kind of brass, a cold and alien light falling over it all. Katya lay down on the mattress and listened to the sounds of mosque loudspeakers crackling into song in the city outside. She thought of every room she'd ever lived in – her room at home in Coventry full of old art projects and books on archaeology, collections of pressed flowers and paintbrushes with the bristles stuck together, the photograph of her mum and dad when they were young – her university flat in Sheffield with crumb-covered carpets and piles of clothes, photographs peeling off their Blu-tack on the walls – the room she did most of her PhD in, with the poster of a painting by Hubert Robert and the black mould working its way through the ceiling and all the plants in their pots on every surface: ficuses, bromeliads, succulents, aloes – and the way the street lights at night would shine orange through the condensation on her window. She thought about who might be living in those rooms now, and whether any trace of her was left. Then all the lights went off, making her jump. Another power cut. Salim had given her a torch today. She clicked it on and wandered out into the dim halls in her socks, her beam cutting geometries between the statues in their plastic wrappings. She tried out the echo.

'Gilgamesh, King in Uruk!' she shouted.

Uruku-ruku-rukuruk …

Without warning, a sudden terror filled her. She was certain for a moment that all the veiled statues were not statues at all; that the lot of them were alive, breathing, blinking beneath their coverings, completely still. She ran back through the halls, and the whole way she felt something behind her. When she got to her room, she wedged the chair back up against the door, and listened to her breathing rise and fall.

'You're an adult,' she hissed to herself. 'Get a grip.'

She got into bed and tried to sleep, but that feeling stayed with her. She kept drifting off only to feel the sensation that someone was standing in the room with her, in the shadows of the corner, watching her. She kept opening her eyes to check that no one was there. To calm herself, she did what she always did when she had trouble sleeping: she ran through her reel of memories of her dad, each one worn with use and crackling with absence.

Walking through the forest in green light, with her dad naming the birds he heard, and the leaves of the trees: beech, oak, elder. The poetries of his adopted country.

Visiting the broken shell of Coventry cathedral, a war ruin, like a cobweb of stone broken by sky.

The way he'd said McDonald's with a G and she made fun of him for it, and then he'd say the longest Arabic word he could think of. 'When you can pronounce that,' he'd laugh, 'then you can make fun of your dad.'

Katya thought of the fantasies she'd entertained when she was a child: that her dad was still alive somewhere, that he'd knocked his head and lost his memory and started living out another life somewhere with another family, that he'd been kidnapped and left on a desert island or on top of an inaccessible mountain, that he'd become a Buddhist monk in Tibet, that he'd simply fallen out of love with her mum and never wanted to return to England. How anything had seemed better than what she was being asked to believe.

———

After a few more days of surveying, Katya began to excavate her site. It had been a year since her last dig, and this was the first time she'd been the only one in charge. While she conducted her walking survey and met the local workers who manned the shovels and picks, she tried to find that quiet place inside herself, separate from the chaos of the world. With every step around that patch of wind-blown waste, the other Katyas in Greece and Peru faded from her mind. As the days went by, she began to feel at home in her work. She loved the ache in her muscles that set in on the second morning and deepened with each day, the weight of the pick and the shovel in her hands. She was proud of the mud and spots of silt that never washed out from under her nails, and her blisters that hardened into yellow callouses. While they broke the topsoil, her team of local workers helped her and taught her some Arabic words. *Mafi mushkila*: no problem. *Shams*: sun. *Ghabar*: dust. They laughed at her efforts. Once around midday, she looked up from her work to see someone watching her from the shade of a faraway tree jutting out of the reed bank near the river. Katya shielded her eyes and could just make out the shape of a girl, a little iota of colour. When she next looked, the girl was gone.

Over her first week, Katya sunk the first trenches into the earth, pebbled with stones and pottery fragments. Whenever she wrote down notes, she remembered her mum always tutting about her handwriting, 'It's just like your dad's.' A series of squiggles, indecipherable to others.

As she dug down through the soil's surface horizons, Katya imagined herself climbing down into the past. Everything was down there, if you knew how to measure it. It took only a centimetre for her dad to drive out of the desert and fly home to her. A few more, and the Internet shrunk and grew silent. Then the aircraft thinned from the skies. Half a metre down, in the lowest topsoil, the mechanised armies of Europe burned their peninsula to the ground once and then twice, nearly drowning in their own blood. A metre down, in the reddish subsoil, the railways disappeared. European armies chugged up rivers in their steamships, then back again by sail, plantations shrinking behind them. People unproved mathematics and forgot the explanations of things, then the constellations of lights that map the night winked out, and the air grew colder and clearer. Silkworms were smuggled back to China in bamboo canes. The buffalo returned in hordes to the plains of America, and its old inhabitants came with them. Another half metre, with the subsoil darkening to chestnut, and the two sides of the world undiscovered each other. Smallpox returned to the old world by ship. Great cities shrunk, and the roads that joined them faded. Forests teemed and spread. Rome burned again and again, growing each time; armies of horsemen riding back into the steppes and returning cities to life in their path. In the clay and loam of the deep subsoil, people began to worship gods who were jealous of one another, who bickered and warred among themselves.

As she moved deeper, Katya uncovered steel brooches and shattered pieces of pottery, countless in number and painted in a different style at each layer. She found coins of different eras, corroded blue-green and delicate as dry leaves, weights and bone handles, a stone sickle with a chipped edge, layers of ancient rushes, bricks with inscriptions stamped into them, date stones, olive pips and animal bones. All of them secret, hidden as the inside of an apple. In the evenings, in the gloom of the museum basement storeroom, she took the objects from their crates and cleaned them, sketched them, photographed them.

Finally, after weeks of digging, she reached it: the roof layer, charred and packed where it had caved in, cluttered with wind-blown sediment: the layer at which, twenty-six centuries before, the city of Nineveh had burned. She straightened and stretched her back, wiping the sweat mixed with suncream from her fore-head. A smear of ancient ash came away on her gloves and her face.

'The capital of the world,' she said aloud, and regretted it immediately when the wind whipped dust into her mouth and she had to spit. She crouched down and brushed away the soot. There was another layer beneath it. It was strange: a soft white dust, fine like icing sugar. She made a note of its depth and consistency, and then moved on. In her lunch break, she sat on the crumbling wall and thought about the gulf of time between then and now: cavernous, large enough to swallow her own life a hundred times over. How long ago that felt, and also not that long at all.

She stood up and saw the distant shape of that girl again, watching her from the shadow of the tree. She waved to her, and the girl ducked down and out of sight.

At lunch, eating the same chickpeas and rice every day, Katya got to know the other members of the team. There was Giulia, who had spent ten years in Pompeii, mapping the buried streets and gardens, preserving the red-painted murals in the houses and political slogans still daubed on the walls. Then there was Martina, who had followed the ghost of the Emperor Hadrian around Europe for years before getting bored and switching to King Ashurbanipal ('I always fall for complicated men,' she said, shrugging). Raad and Khawla had met at the college of archaeology in Baghdad. Raad had hated Saddam with a fury, but Katya couldn't help but notice that he admired the man's fashion: he often wore cowboy hats and sunglasses to his dig. Khawla was fluent in ancient Akkadian and Babylonian, and could read and write in three kinds of cuneiform. She was freckled, fierce and to the point, with a lick of reddish hair poking out from beneath her abaya. Most of all, Katya spoke to Salim. He often seemed distracted, his mind on other things, but he was calm and gentle and made her feel at ease around him. He spoke about broken pieces of pot and brick as though they were intelligent, subtle creatures who understood stratigraphy and carbon dating, who found their way to their particular strata according to their knowledge. Some evenings Katya and Salim went out into the city to get falafel or chicken and rice, peeling strips from the fluffy, crackling flatbreads to eat with smoky baba ganoush.

'This is the only good thing to ever come out of all the years of sanctions,' Salim said as they sat in his favourite restaurant. He gestured to the clay charcoal ovens in the corner. 'Iraqis never forgot how to make real bread.'

Katya realised later that this was one of the first times Salim had ever spoken about the past. It happened more and more as they went out in the evenings and he seemed to relax around her. On another night, he spoke about his childhood, in a suburb of Baghdad, his large family and his time in the United States. She began to look forward to those evenings more than anything else, and would get an excited buzz in her stomach whenever he suggested them.

After another week of digging, Salim came to inspect Katya's progress on the site. It was raining heavily and drainage had never been a strength of hers: it required a broad overview of the site when she was strong on the particulars and details. Water cascaded down the hill in runnels, frothing and carrying litter, opalescent with oil. When Salim arrived, he cast a look over the trench, and the water leaking through the white sandbags lining its borders. Katya tried to brush the water from her eyes, but only smeared her cheeks with mud. A puff of steam billowed out from under Salim's hood.

'Everything okay?' she said. He shook his head.

'The looters hit the other site last night.'

'Oh. Was it bad?'

'Yeah, they tore up the whole place. It keeps happening, and our resources are so limited. The army's useless. We used to be able to keep up.'

'Did they get anything?'

'Some writing tablets, we think. They get a lot for those. Collectors overseas give them lists of things to steal, then they go out and dig for them.'

'That's terrible.'

'Yeah. A lot of poor people here, desperate for money. And criminals too. We have a guard over here at night, but he's just one man with a mobile phone. And the police often have other priorities. Anyway, if you see any damage just catalogue it, collect what fragments you can and move on.'

'What if there aren't any fragments?'

Salim puffed out a long fern of steam but didn't answer. He looked down at her trench, which was filling with water. He seemed to notice it for the first time.

'That looks bad.'

'Yeah, it's a long time since I had to do so much drainage.'

'Don't worry. My speciality. Let me help with that.'

He jumped down into the trench, and she followed. The mud sucked at their boots, and the rain on their hoods made conversation difficult. Salim had to tap her shoulder to get her attention whenever he needed her to deepen a certain culvert or outlet. As they worked together, she began to feel their personal space overlap, their breaths moving through each other in the cold air. She began reading significance into every movement he made through the trench, each look or touch felt through her raincoat. Later, when they got back to the museum and brushed the mud from their faces, they each laughed at the way the other looked. When Salim said he had to go, Katya felt a faint feeling of loss tug in her chest, and she knew that she was in trouble.

Aurya

The day after her fight, and the day after that, Aurya kept away from Sharo. She saw him sitting on the roof sometimes, murmuring to himself – but whether he was telling stories to himself or muttering to his drawings, she couldn't tell. She returned the matting she'd repaired to the potter's wife, who gave her some wheat cakes in return and shook her head at Aurya's poor clothes and thin frame.

'That Tappum,' she said. 'Shamash bring him another wife.'

In the evening, Aurya found Sharo's sketches in the mud. They were all lions now: running, rearing, jumping. She rubbed them out with her foot so their father wouldn't see. She didn't have to worry: as it got colder, fog came in over the hills in the morning, and the rain fell in bursts, gushed in rivers down the paths to the quarry, erasing Sharo's drawings and washing away the last dying crops in their field. The cut on Aurya's head scabbed and swelled; she wore a headcloth to hide it.

On the second morning, Aurya saw Nebo-Pishtim and his friends by the river. She'd gone looking for birds' eggs and the fish she sometimes managed to trap in crescents of rocks built in the shallows. She could hear the boys sniggering but couldn't summon the fight to go up to them. Out of the corner of her eye, she thought she saw something swinging from Nebo-Pishtim's hand, but she didn't give him the satisfaction of looking. She just tightened her grip on her fish spear and muttered bitter prayers:

To the god of lost things
To the god of mothers
To the god of lightning

She watched the boats sailing past with indistinct figures moving about on their decks, cloaks over their heads against the rain, the barges gliding lazily along the towpaths, the ships heading off to better places. She felt like the long-fingered river weeds, rooted in place but always reaching downstream. In one of her fish traps, she found a small green-backed carp flitting from side to side, trapped, thrashing at the rain-mottled water in panic.

'I'm sorry,' she told it. 'I'm stuck here too.'

She speared the fish and took it away into the rushes to eat raw, wiping her bloody hands and mouth on the leaves.

That night Aurya woke up to hear her father screaming. This happened more often in the months when the air cooled. She lay there and listened to him shouting in his sleep about how his friends were dying, how the chariots of the enemy were circling them. She heard him throw himself awake, and then lie sobbing softly in the darkness.

———

On the third day after the fight, their father came home with some tough bread, the kind made from unsifted flour. He gave it to Aurya and Sharo with eyes made flinty by shame. They knew what he wanted, and were happy to play along: they sat outside on the flat stone slab behind the house and made believe for a while that he was a good father as fathers went, who protected them and brought them enough food to eat. Somewhere in the distance a reed flute played, and their father told them riddles.

'The tower is high; it is high, but it gives no shade.'

Aurya crunched a piece of charcoal in her bread and spat it out.

'A sunbeam,' she said. Her father grunted.

'You've heard it before.'

'No, I haven't. It's easy. It's high, but it doesn't give shade.'

The rings under his eyes were dark as a bruised reed, and his lips were cracked.

'Too clever for a girl,' he croaked. 'Fine, try this one. Like a fish in a fish pond; like troops before the King.'

Aurya shrugged.

'A broken bow,' Sharo said.

'The boy's got it,' their father grunted, put out by their good guesses.

'That doesn't make any sense,' Aurya said.

'Maybe not to you,' their father said, and laughed. It was an ugly sound, like a plough going through mud, but as they sat there and joked, Aurya felt like they could have been some other family.

'King's men coming tomorrow,' their father said, stroking the surface of the stone. 'The carters from downriver say it's a whole royal flotilla: soldiers and slaves and all. You know what that means?' Neither Aurya nor Sharo spoke. 'It means the King himself could be with them. Imagine that: King Ashurbanipal passing down the river and stopping at our little village. And to buy stone from your father! Make sure you don't embarrass me, children. You know what I mean: dirty clothes, begging them for food. And fighting.'

Their father leant over and narrowed his eyes. Aurya realised too late that she'd forgotten her headcloth.

'I've noticed the two of you haven't been talking,' he said, through a mouthful of bread. 'Which means you've been causing trouble.'

He took her chin in his dry, hard hand and inspected the wound on her forehead like she was a damaged piece of stone, turning her head one way, then the other. He breathed loudly through his nose and swallowed.

'This isn't going to help your bride price.' Aurya shook her head free of his grip and spat another piece of grit from the bread, a stone this time. She recognised the warning signs by now: every time the demon scratched on the inside of his skull, his eyes gave a little flutter. They were doing that now.

'Not going to tell me what you've been up to? Well, you know what I say: punish first, find out later.' He brandished his bread at them both like a judge's baton. The air felt heavy with anger, the smell of old reed matting and the promise of rain. Then he seemed to remember that he was trying to be kind, and rubbed his forehead with the thick slab of his hand.

'Do you know there's a lion in the old village well?' he said after a while. 'A beast of the high hills. And what do the watchmen do about it? Someone ought to split that monster's skull.'

He jabbed out, invisible spear in hand. Sharo give a gasp, and Aurya's heart sank. Sure enough, their father rounded on him.

'What? Are you frightened of a half-starved lion?' He laughed, that sound again, like stones falling down the quarry wall. Aurya could hear that demon scratching in the sudden high pitch of his voice, its long nails on the inside of his skull. He jabbed a finger into Sharo's chest. 'Look at you, moaning like a dove in its hole, and nearly the size of me. Always drawing your pictures in the mud. Yes, I've seen those, though your sister tries to hide them. When the next war comes, the recruiters will have you, be sure of that. They'll march you out into the desert to fight the scavengers, or up into the hills, to Elam. Then you'll know fear, boy. The mountain men creeping through your tents at night with knives. I should just throw you down there with the lion and get it over with.' He turned on Aurya. 'What about you? Not defending him any more?'

She took her last mouthful of bread.

'I'm going to the river.'

'With your belly full of my bread!' Her father made to swipe at her. She jumped out of the way, feeling the whoosh of air from his hand. Aurya ran across the field, where the plant that people called 'the reed of tears' had begun to crack through the earth everywhere.

'Scurry all the way to the Bitter River if you want!' he shouted after her. She gave only one look back at the house, and saw her father already cuffing Sharo around the head.

'Stop blubbering!' he was shouting. 'Do you think a soldier cries?'

Aurya ducked into the thicket and set off to the river. But instead of heading to the bank, something made her veer off in the other direction. She crept towards the old village ruins, past the little reed shrines people hid out there. When she reached the pit, she covered her mouth with her shawl and sat on the edge. The lion at the bottom looked even more starved and wretched than it had before. Its eyes were closed, but mist was still rising from its jaws and curling in the air. The shaggy tufts of its mane caught the gold in the sunlight, and its black beard was matted. Its ribs showed now, its hide scabbed with fly bites and white maggots curling from the wound on its foot. She took in its greyish pelt, the fold of skin hanging down the length of its belly, and wondered: what led it here? Did a larger male chase it from its mother, send it slinking down from the hills? Or had hunters pursued it with dogs and fire until it forgot its way home? Aurya sat on the pit edge and tried to feel triumphant about its suffering. She looked at the lion's claws, and thought of them tearing at her mother's clothes, those jaws clenching on her mother's throat. But somehow the sight just filled her with pity.

'If it wasn't for your kind, I'd have a mother now,' she called down to the lion. The animal didn't move. Aurya picked up a pebble and hefted it in her hand. She threw it and hit the lion between the shoulder blades. She expected the beast to let out a great roar and gnash its teeth, but it just flinched and gave a little whine, its shoulders darting together and then slipping back down. It covered its head with one paw.

When she got back to the house after sunset, Aurya found that her father wasn't there, and Sharo was asleep on the sagging roof despite the cold. Her brother always slept turned away from the river and the farmers' houses running along its other bank: the two of them used to go from house to house on that side, trading gypsum charms for grain, and Sharo could remember in perfect detail the pattern of bricks in each house, the woodgrain on their beams, their interlacing of roofing reeds. When he slept, he always faced the quarry and the hills that he'd never climbed, which sat in his memory as a dark and peaceful land.

Aurya went up and lay down next to him, and saw fresh bruises on his arms and neck. She watched his sleeping back breathe against the evening stars, each one of which he had given its own name, each one's position he knew with his eyes closed.

'I'm sorry,' she said, but she didn't think he could hear her. After a while, the trembling overcame her, and she crept back downstairs and curled up alone.

The next thing Aurya remembered was someone gently shaking her awake. She grunted, and pain ran through her forehead like a pounded nail. A dark form loomed over her. She knew by the beer smell that it was her father. One of his hands was running a twine of her hair through his fingers.

'You have hair just like your mother,' he said, and it wasn't a whisper so much as an intake of breath, as if he'd never noticed before. She tried to move and found the weight of him was pinning her down to her mat.

'What are you doing?' she breathed. Then his heavy hand swung down and struck her across the face. She cried out. Her vision swam, her ears ringing.

'What happened to the necklace?' His weight crushed into her painfully.

'I don't –'

He hit her again, the other cheek this time, and the taste of an axe head filled her mouth.

'You never let me sell that necklace. Such a cheap thing, and you never let me. It always reminded me, seeing it …'

Her father's other hand went to her cheek. It was smooth and dry, like old stone, and she flinched away from it.

'Shh shh shh,' he said, spraying spittle. 'Sharo told me what happened. You know he hates it when I hit him. And he can't lie either. Can't lie. He told me some boy took it. Or maybe you gave it away. Is that what happened? You gave the necklace to a boy you liked? You're becoming a woman now …'

'Get off me,' she said, and heard how tiny her voice was beside his. Barely a breath.

'What's the matter? You know I'm going to stop drinking, Aurya? Just one last celebration, just one last – and then I'll stop. Like you're always telling me. You'll get a fine price. You're so like your mother, you know. So good.'

Aurya felt the hot blood in her cheeks. Her free hand was a darting fish, down into the folds of her cloth, and then the cold sliver of the blade was in her hand. She pressed it against her father's neck. He stopped mid-sentence, and his whole body went rigid. She had already gone too far, she knew. He would beat her terribly for this. But she kept her hand there.

'Don't speak about her,' she said, her voice cracking like a boy's. Her father's nostrils flared, but he loosened his grip. He gently shook his head, and his mouth split into a huge, sad grin.

'Aurya, little duck. Aurya, take that blade away.'

'No. Get off me.'

'Aurya.' The lump in his throat bobbed up and down beside her thumb and the little metal shard. His grip tightened on her wrist, daring her, his teeth clenched. 'Aurya, put the blade down.'

'No!'

'Aurya, put it down and I'll tell you a secret. A secret about her. About your mother.'

'What secret?' she said, with strength in her voice this time. 'There's no secret.'

'There is. It's about the lion that dragged her away.'

Aurya gritted her teeth.

'Tell me.'

He shook his head, the corners of his mouth damp with drool.

'There was no lion,' he murmured, his gaze wandering off through the walls.

'What do you mean?'

'She didn't get dragged away.'

'You're lying,' Aurya said. 'Where is she then, if there was no lion?'

Her father trembled suddenly, a motion that racked his whole body.

'She's in the house of dust. That's what she always called it.'

'The house of dust? Where is that?'

A cruel grin worked its way across his face.

'If you put the knife down, I'll tell you.'

'You're lying,' Aurya growled.

'Aurya, little duck,' he breathed, another waft from his stinking mouth. 'The house of dust. Take that blade away and I'll show you.'

The stubble of his beard sanded her knuckles.

'Get off me or I'll cut out your throat.' She gave the blade a press with her thumb so he hissed through his teeth, and a warm wetness bloomed and trickled down her hand. 'I'll cut it right out and string it up like a rabbit.'

To her surprise, he let go. The feeling flowed back to her right hand.

'Aurya, little coot,' he slurred, lifting slowly off her. 'You didn't think – your own father …'

'Get off me. All the way off!' He raised himself, her blade still pressed against his throat. The usual sag seeped back into his shoulders, his hollow cheeks. Her father put both hands up to the air, his pink palms facing her, smooth of fingerprints. Aurya lowered the blade, and said each word slowly like she was speaking to a child.

'Where is the house of dust?'

There was a moment of breath. The shadows around them felt charged with a strange energy.

'I'm sorry, Aurya.' And then he lunged like a snake. He knocked the air out of her, grabbed both her wrists. The blade slipped from her fingers, tinkled on the ground behind her. He pinned her to the floor, his lips pulled back from his teeth.

'Put a knife to your own father's throat, would you?' he snarled as she kicked and struggled. 'Just like your mother after all!'

He was a sack of stones on top of her. That gust of beer again from his mouth, rotting barley, and the stench of something dead, too, underneath it all. Those points of light in his eyes.

'The house of dust!' He shrieked with laughter as her legs kicked under him. 'I told you, she's there, in the house of dust! Let me show you where to find her.'

Aurya saw a shadow move fast over her father's shoulder. He saw it too late. He tried to turn, but there was a crack and splintering. Grit and sharp fragments and dust filled Aurya's eyes, her hair. Her father fell on top of her, crushing her ribs.

'Aurya!' she heard. It was Sharo. He held the broken half of an empty beer jar, and he was shaking. He stepped back in horror and let the heavy piece of clay thud to the ground. Aurya heaved her father from on top of her, and his arms flopped to the floor on either side. She ran to Sharo, held on to him: the two of them backed away into the corner of the room, waiting for their father to get up and turn his rage on them both. He didn't. He just lay there, and a gurgling came from deep in his chest.

'Aurya, I'm sorry,' Sharo said. 'Aurya, I heard voices. I heard Father shouting. I tried to be brave, like the wild man. Like you told me.'

Aurya put her back against the wall, slid down and hugged her knees. She was shaking as if a god had passed by. She couldn't take her eyes off their father, lying there with his face in shadow. Still he didn't move.

'Sharo, get the lamp,' she whispered. She lit some of the last linseed oil with her hands shaking; the room flushed with orange light and that warm smell. She saw their father lying in the centre of the room, his mouth and eyes open. His middle finger twitched as if plucking a stringed instrument. A dark pool was beginning to spread from the back of his head, and the smell of vomit seeped into the air.

'Will Father be angry?' Sharo said.

'No, Sharo ...'

There was still time to help him. Aurya could turn him on his side, thump him on his back, wash the vomit from his mouth. Instead, she watched as their father's twitching weakened, slowed, stopped completely. His gurgling too. It took a long time. Eventually his chest was still, and the bulging veins faded from his neck and forehead. Crickets outside whispered their secrets to the ghosts and gods.

'We killed him,' Aurya breathed finally. Sharo let out a little whimper. 'We killed him. Ishtar save us. Sharo, look at me. No one can find out. Do you understand? No one can ever find out. It was an accident – it was a ...'

Her hands shook as she crept towards their father, afraid that he might suddenly gasp awake, reach out his hands and grab her. Hoping, almost, that he would.

'Sharo. What day is it today?'

'The fourteenth of Shebat.'

She felt cold spreading through her bones. 'Sharo, tomorrow is the fifteenth. The King's men are coming in the morning, to pick up the stone. Look outside. It's already blue over the hills.'

Aurya knew what happened to murderers. She found out two summers ago, when a drifter came out of the desert and killed the potter's daughter, when the guards from town marched down the road with a magistrate on a horse. Death, of course, but before that a hundred lashes, with salt cast on the wounds. Perhaps to have their noses or ears cut off. She hadn't watched like the others, but she remembered the man's shrieks: they could be heard all around the riverbank, echoing off the quarry walls. And before that, the river trial in the dark water, their hands and feet tied and left to sink in the forests of river weed and fish and silt and gloom. Already she couldn't breathe.

'We have to hide him. We have to hide him now.'

'Hide him ...' Sharo said. 'But Aurya, he's so big. Where can we hide him?'

Aurya was shaking. She paced in circles, darting around as if getting ready for a fight, shaking the fear from her hands like water. The wound in her head was still thudding.

'Somewhere nobody will look. We have to find somewhere.'

'Aurya, I'm scared.'

'Sharo, think – please, for once. Where where where ...'

'He's so big,' is all Sharo said.

'He's so big,' Aurya echoed, wringing her hands together. 'Come on, Sharo – we need a hiding place. We can't just throw him in the – in the ...'

With the light of the oil lamp washing against the walls of that small room, their eyes met.

Katya

Katya's life in Mosul followed simple rhythms. Most of all, she looked forward to her drives with Salim to and from the dig site, when she would see the cracked blue tile-work of neighbourhood mosques pass by, the jewellery markets beneath their sun umbrellas and the antique wood-fronted cafés of Mosul, the men selling oranges on the roadside with weighted copper scales, wearing faded shirts and bright keffiyehs wrapped around their heads. When they talked on these drives, she would learn fragments of Salim's past, hidden like beads in soil. She built her map of him like a dig site: how he had studied in New Orleans and seen the mists come in over the bay, seen the city drowned by hurricane waters and people searching through the ruins.

'I went to New York too,' he told her. 'Before the towers fell. You should have seen them; I thought they'd stand there for a thousand years. They have our artefacts in their museums too. And in London. Iraqi artefacts, spread all around the world. I still dream about bringing them home one day.'

Iraq kept calling him back. There was the sadness in him that comes from dividing the heart between two places. But when he came back for good, he found that the country he'd once known was gone, reduced to rubble by what he called the Second American War. What relatives he had left had fled to the cold cities of Europe, to Hamburg and Glasgow, and forgotten him.

'If a camera could see the whole universe,' he said to her once, 'it would see more evil than good. Many times more. And every generation we see that with a higher resolution.'

Sometimes in the breaks between their shifts, when they stood on the edge of the site and looked out over the blasted remains of Nineveh, Katya felt that they were the last two inhabitants of a sun-scorched earth, watching the sands roll forgetful over the world.

Salim's vague promises about other accommodation never materialised, so Katya remained in the museum. She spent the evenings exploring it: the empty staffrooms and storage cupboards, the small library with books in Arabic and English on Iraqi art and history, the generators and boilers humming in their cages, the parking garage in the rear, windows furry with grime, where a broken-down van without tyres sat on cinder blocks. She found a fire exit up to the flat roof, which had a view out over the city, over the sprawling ranges of rooftops, its gardens of radio antennae and satellite dishes, over the river and the bridge nearby, the small park on the other side. In a back room, she found a Kalashnikov rifle left in an umbrella stand. She explored the recesses of the museum's basement storeroom too, where artefacts sat in the dark on steel shelves. The daily finds of their dig were laid out here in meticulous order on steel tables, and she spent hours peering through her microscope at the different shapes of pollen grains she found in samples: citrus and pistachio, ribwort plantain, sea grape and tabor oak.

The Internet came and went. When she could get online, Katya would look up the new details she'd encountered in Mosul that week: the positions of stars, the traditional clothes of Assyrians and Turkmen and Yazidis, the lemongrass smell that drifted from the doorways of mosques, proverbs and the names of politicians, Iraqi football teams and Egyptian folk singers. She practised the sounds of Arabic, which despite her father's influence wilted like implanted flowers on the hardy soil of her tongue. Online, she read the news about Iraq, but she didn't recognise the country in what she read. She read about the civil war just over the border in Syria, the country's rulers dropping barrels of dynamite on to its own cities from helicopters. She read about Homs and Aleppo – like Mosul, cities of limestone, being eaten down to their skeletons. She read about how the part of your brain involved in reading is the same one used to recognise faces. She read about how one hundred tons of cosmic dust descends from space each day and settles on the earth.

Katya knew the moment she woke up that she was going to have a seizure. They always started with that familiar feeling, as if something had come loose in the world.

'Possibly connected to grief. A psychological root,' the doctors had always told her mother as though Katya couldn't hear, as though she didn't know what the adult word meant. To her, they'd said, 'It's like you have a tiny thunderstorm in your head.' This felt like a baby's explanation even then, but as she got older she couldn't shake the image: the aura's gathering clouds, the rumbling as the storm let off its first sparks. The most unsettling part was the déjà vu, which always kicked in close to the moment of seizure. She also got a lot of false alarms. She thought about calling in sick, but she couldn't bear the thought of disappointing the others, of sitting alone in the museum all day while other people did her time-critical work. She would be careful.

'Get up, Katya,' she muttered. 'It's time to get up.'

She took a pill, pulled on her boots, her hat and abaya, and went out to meet Salim. When she got in the car, she saw a young man of about eighteen sitting in the back seat, his hair oiled all the way to one side, thin wrists in a crisp white shirt like Salim's.

'This is my nephew Athir,' Salim said. The young man touched his head and gave a meek 'hi'. 'Athir's the only family I've got left in Mosul. He works in an auto repair shop, but he wants to be an archaeologist one day. I said he could come to work with me today. This is Katya,' he said to the boy. 'An expert in archaeobotany, the remains of ancient plants.'

'And animals sometimes,' Katya said. She gave a polite smile, but she didn't need another person present while she tried to hold everything together.

'You okay?' Salim asked, brow furrowing. She nodded.

'Yeah. Did you know that a hundred tons of space dust lands on earth every day? I read that yesterday.'

'Feels like it's all landing here,' Salim said, and brushed the sand from his wing mirror. He talked to Athir in Arabic for most of the journey, which was a relief for Katya. She looked out the window at Mosul's markets setting up: potatoes, cabbages, lemons, giant radishes in piles, watermelons sold from the backs of trucks. All the time she felt that growing sensation of lightness. It was happening faster than usual, and she knew it had been a mistake to come to work. She couldn't go blank in front of Salim after lying on her health assessment form. Could she pretend to feel sick? She glanced over at Salim as he scolded Athir about something, and then at her own hands, which were tucked into her sleeves.

That car journey lasted for ever, and Katya hardly spoke the whole way. Something about it reminded her of the grief counselling she'd gone to as a teenager, the group circle, everyone taking it in turns to speak about the people who were no longer there: the wives and parents and children. One woman who'd lost both twins, who kept tissues in the sleeve of her cardigan to dab at her swollen eyes. Her mum came too: 'It'll do us both good.' Katya's mum spoke sometimes: about her dad's insistence on returning to Iraq after the war, the way he'd had scars on his arm, cigarette burns from his time in one of the dictator's prisons, and the way a piece of him seemed always to call him back. Katya had never been able to speak in those meetings. It felt like a slice of apple was wedged in her throat. She couldn't talk about it, couldn't cry in front of these people the way her mum did. She just sat and stared at the whiteboard on which the facilitator had written 'GREIF' in spidery capitals and waited for it all to be over. Katya remembered sobbing every day. She remembered stopping in the middle of a task – making a cup of tea, doing her homework – and just staring, without going on, like a wind-up toy that had run out of wind. She remembered the voice of her teacher in class, the drone of an engine in the background. And the worst part was how understanding everyone had been. How much space they gave her, as though she was a bomb that might go off. The girl who'd lost her father, who they'd all seen on the news. And then the seizures. The first time, she thought she was dying. It was a rushing, popping light in front of her eyes, her brain retreating back through the stages of its evolution: bird, lizard, fish.

There was a crunch of gravel and Katya realised that she was there. She'd made it to the site.

'Here we are,' Salim said. 'Take care out there today. Stay safe in the sun.'

'Thanks,' she said, and to Athir, 'Good luck. Don't let him push you around.'

The boy nodded and gave a wide smile that showed no teeth. Katya climbed up to her dig, flushing with relief. As she got closer, she noticed with confusion that the usual local workers were nowhere to be seen. No guard either. When she got there, she found out why. The earth was scoured and pocked like a battle-field. Shallow voids had opened in the ground, and a spaghetti of tyre tracks led off to the road. She knew immediately what had happened, and stood there for some time, looking out over the ravaged waste.

'Shit.'

Why today? She phoned Salim.

'My site's been looted again,' she said. 'They've wrecked the place.'

He muttered something curse-like in Arabic.

'It's all right. It's not your fault, Katya. Hold tight, I'll be there.'

She walked around and examined the damage, puffing out her cheeks.

'It's not your fault,' she repeated, but she didn't feel any better. She could still feel the aura creeping up on her, but no hint of déjà vu: a good sign. She surveyed the sets of footprints printed in the sand, a used-up phosphorus flare and an empty packet of ciga-rettes. The looters had broken open the top of one wall she'd spent days carefully excavating, and disturbed the layer of white dust. Hollow shapes in the side of the trench showed where objects had been taken. Katya tried to measure and survey these, build them into her map, but she noticed too late that the cemented nail she'd used to mark the dig's horizontal plane had also been moved, throwing everything she'd measured out of alignment. She slumped down on the edge of one hole and swore loudly until she felt better. As she did, she caught sight of something in one of the looter's holes. It was a dark shape, jutting like a root from the earth. She stared at it for a few moments before realising what it was. A human hand. Ancient.

'Shit,' she said again. She jumped down into the hole and brushed away the white dust, inspected the carious bone and mummified flesh yellowed with sulphurous deposits. She made to fetch her brushes and sketchpad, but something stopped her. The hand was closed, balled like a monkey's paw, and she could just make out a small object clenched inside. She fished out the small brush from her pocket and reached out to touch the hand. Then she felt something strange. Hadn't it all happened like this before? Hadn't she stood on that exact spot before, listening to the wind whining against the crest of the hill and the hollows of the olive tree? A sensation as if time was folding over itself like a ruffled fabric.

'Got something there?' Salim's voice called out from a distance. Katya jumped. She heard his footsteps crunching behind her, and his nephew hurrying along behind him.

'Some human remains,' she murmured, hearing her voice a million miles away. 'The looters uncovered them. And a week's worth of headache.'

Her hands felt buoyant. *Not now*, she silently begged. She watched helplessly as Salim and Athir came over to where she stood in the hole and looked around the scarred site. Salim kicked a piece of shale so it skimmed across the dust.

'Turns out the guard we had on the site last night wasn't the usual one. No one can track him down, used a fake name. No surprises there. I'm sorry you have to deal with this.'

'It's fine. Good material for when I write my tell-all.'

'Just catalogue the damage for now. Piece together the fragments, try and put a story together.' He turned to Athir. 'You'll have to deal with this one day. Get out while you still can.'

Katya tried to think through the fog descending on her.

60

'Do you see that white dusty deposit everywhere?' she said. 'What is that?'

'Yes, that is strange,' Salim said, but he didn't seem to be paying full attention. 'Take a sample and we'll get it tested. I'll get Giulia and Martina over here for the next few days, help you put this mess back together.'

'Thanks.'

Salim peered down into the hole beside her, where the hand still jutted from the wall.

'Oh, look at that. Poor bastard. Looks like he scared the looters off.'

'Yeah. Could be from the day Nineveh burned.'

Even as she said each word, she felt that she had said them already, that she was repeating all this, just as it had happened before.

'Could be. That's exciting, though. Let's get the human remains excavated and back to the museum. We can do tests there, find out more. Hey, are you sure you're okay?' Salim said, eyeing her.

'Yeah. Just tired. The stress.'

'Okay. Take care of yourself. This place can take its toll on people.'

'Thanks. I will.'

'And by the way, Dr Malik is threatening to take us out on his boat soon. To see the bridges. It's best to practise your interested expression now.'

Katya laughed, and he gave her only the slightest look.

'Come on,' he said to Athir. 'Let's show you what a proper soil profile looks like.'

The young man nodded at Katya. She noticed that he had the same crinkles to his eyes as Salim when he smiled. She sat slumped against the edge of the hole with the body beside her, and listened with relief to Salim and Athir walking away. The thrum of their engine started up, tyres crunching the grit. She looked down at the leathered fist extruding from the earth. The aura had faded a little, and her head felt clearer. Maybe it was a false alarm after all. Katya crouched down into the hole again and let the white dust filter between her fingers. She took a sample in a plastic tube.

Then she reached out and touched a finger of the mummified hand. It was dry as bark.

The seizure hit without warning. She had only enough time to brace herself against the rough trench wall. Her last thought before the black fell over her was of the hand in the hole, clenched over something she couldn't see.

The world came back gradually, like water seeping through karst. Katya found herself shivering cold in the looter's hole, with a dog nosing down at her from the pit edge. She didn't know how long she'd been out. It was usually only ten minutes or so, but now the sun was high overhead, pale white through the cloud, and the day's cold had sunk right through to her bones. She pulled herself out and got on with her work.

———

Over the following days, Katya joined up the looters' holes into an organised trench, and excavated the rest of the body. Around the remains, she used the long brush that let her sweep delicately through the dust, and took photos from all angles. She wasn't an expert in this kind of analysis, but she thought the body was male. It was huddled in a foetal position, with that one hand reaching out. His teeth were visible in the partially mummified skull, the hair still curling black and lifelike. As she examined the area around the body, Katya found traces of wood and charcoal, rushes and large plant fibres. On the skeleton, she found marks of trauma along the rib bones and a cleave in the skull, along with an iron chip as though from an axe or sword. She stood up and felt the echoes of that day in the air around her: the day Nineveh burned. She could almost smell the smoke, the shouts of men bursting in with weapons. As the day went on, the wind picked up and the body disintegrated. Katya covered her mouth, but at times she found herself swept up in a whirlwind of corpse dust. Pieces of human grit stuck to the sweat on her forehead, got in her teeth. She found this horrible at first, but you can't find something horrible for ever. She couldn't shake the feeling of excitement: the magic of finding someone who had been completely lost, the joy of uncovering them, bringing them back into the air.

As Katya sketched and photographed, she kept coming back to that hand, the one that seemed to be gripping on to something; the way it reached out as though to hand her something. The transportation of the body was painstaking but successful. Back in the museum that evening, her face still greasy with dust and suncream, Katya and Salim laid the human form out on the steel table.

'His teeth show signs of dental microwear,' she said, pointing with the end of a pen. 'A carbohydrate-rich diet. Lots of grains most likely, marks from the accidental chewing of stones in food. So probably quite a poor upbringing at least. Some signs of wear around the wrists and elbows, some kind of repetitive strain perhaps. And look: he had curly hair.'

'Like me,' Salim said, pulling one of his locks. Katya crouched down and pointed to the clenched and blackened hand.

'I've written up everything else. Some pollen and phytoliths under the microscope. But ... I think there's something in there. Clenched in his hand.'

'You've got it all photographed and recorded?'

'Yes, all done.'

'Let's try it then. See if we can get that hand open without too much damage.'

Katya leant in, heart beating. She took some tweezers and tested the give of the knotted fingers, gently teased them apart. She was right: she could just make out a small object clenched inside, caked in black mud. As the fingers pulled apart, the flesh the consistency of chipboard, the object fell out into her palm. It was a cylinder of greenish stone. Katya gave an intake of breath.

'It's a cylinder seal,' she said, brushing some of the dried mud from its surface. Salim whistled.

'That's a nice find.'

Katya had seen objects like this in museums. They were peculiar to Assyria and Babylon: a roller carved with an image designed to print into a wet piece of clay, used to seal a contract. She let the little weight roll around in her palm, feeling its cool through the latex glove.

'What's the story behind that? The way he was clutching this when he died ...'

Salim ran his tongue over the front of his teeth and looked down at the blackened body.

'I don't know. A prized possession maybe. We'll know more about him as results come in, and we excavate more of the room, get some context.'

'Not my usual kind of find,' Katya said. 'Plants are easier to read.'

'I prefer stones,' Salim said.

Later that night, they picked up falafel and flatbread by way of celebration. It was a quick and furtive act like all their visits to public places. Salim made a show of being relaxed, but his eyes would move from time to time to the ends of the street, keeping watch for signs of trouble. As the vendor doled the rich amber sauce over their falafel, they talked about the find.

'It's not the first human remains we've found,' Salim told her. 'But it's certainly the most interesting. You should be proud.'

He told her about other bodies he'd uncovered, excavating in Babylon and Uruk. Katya told him about a tomb she'd helped uncover two years before in Greece: the bodies of two young people, a man and a woman, both with garlands of olive leaves and blue cornflowers around their necks.

'What is it about the plants?' Salim said. 'When everyone else dreams of finding brass earrings and arrowheads and lost cities ...'

'I don't know. Maybe it's their secret languages. They way they talk to each other in ways we're only just beginning to discover: chemical secretions in the soil, pulses of electromagnetism. These silent conversations going on beneath the surface. And the secrets they hide. Did you know that the Colosseum in Rome used to be covered in plant life, before the Fascists stripped it bare? A wild and overgrown garden where people gathered hay and herbs. African plants grew there, some so rare they weren't found anywhere else in Europe. The Victorians thought they might have been brought there on the fur of lions brought to fight in the arena.'

'And what do you think?'

'It's a nice story. Sometimes that's more important than the truth.'

European football played on a fuzzy television in the corner. On top of the refrigerator, a bird flitted frantically in a cage, a dried piece of orange rind hanging inside. While they ate, Salim told her some Iraqi jokes.

'A prisoner asks if the prison library has a certain book. "No," the guard replies. "But we have the author."'

'Oh god.'

'The Vice President asks the President, "How will you say goodbye to the people?" The President looks confused and replies, "Why, are they going somewhere?"'

'That's the worst one yet,' Katya snorted.

'They're all like that. I have hundreds more.'

The whole time, whenever Katya felt lost in the moment, she would think about the body in the earth. The evening sun caught Salim's curls, and she would think about that hair curling out of the dust; he handed her the wrapped falafel, and she thought about the dry hand with its broken fingers clutching the seal, reaching out through the ages.

It got colder. The nights were freezing, and there were daily blackouts – sometimes only a few hours, sometimes most of the day. Katya heard gunfire in the city some nights, Kalashnikovs like chattering birds. Some evenings the whole dig team went to a local shisha café and played dominoes while Iraqi pop music played. That's when she started seeing her father in the city, too. It happened once or twice at first, on the drives. She'd see a man in a white shirt or a dishdasha, on a bicycle or selling petrol at a roundabout, and she'd think it was her dad. She felt it so strongly for a few seconds, and she'd crane her neck to see as they passed.

'What is it?' Salim would ask. A few seconds, that's all it would last. Then she'd see that it wasn't him, sometimes that the man looked nothing like him.

'Oh, nothing. I thought I saw something.'

But each time, the feeling stayed with her, the feeling that she was being haunted, or that she herself was a ghost, immaterial, blown like a cloud of dust through the streets. On the days this happened, she would return to the museum and go down into the basement storeroom where the newly found artefacts waited to be catalogued. She would find the little cylinder seal, its greenish stone unlike all the others. How it helped her exactly she couldn't say – but she would take it in her hand and roll it around in her palm, test its weight and let its solidity bring her back down to earth.

The first night this happened, three months after arriving in Iraq, Katya skyped her mum for the first time. She felt guilty about not doing it earlier. Their connection was patchy and full of long breaks, but the sight of their kitchen in Coventry, of her mother and the little lemon tree on the windowsill made Katya want to cry. She felt like she could see the ghosts of it all in the background: all the arguments they'd had, her mum's depression and her new boyfriends trying to tiptoe around the sullen teenager, the slammed doors. She put her chin on her knees and rocked on her heels.

'I'm doing fine over here,' her mum said, in a moment of clear reception. 'There's some flooding, all the politicians are out on the news wearing wellies. How is it out there?'

'Oh,' Katya said, not knowing where to start. 'It's great. I mean, I'm working hard. Finding lots of things. Look,' she said, moving the laptop around so her mum could see. 'I'm staying in the museum.'

'Oh. Is it safe?'

'I think so. I've uncovered a building out there.' Her mum's image had frozen, broken into pixels. 'There's this white dust all over the ground; we don't know what it is. Also I found a body. He could be twenty-six centuries old, left over from when the city was destroyed.'

'What are you – I can't –' her mother's voice stuttered at her down the line. 'I'm sorry I can't hear you.'

'It's okay, Mum, don't …'

Her cat Hugo jumped up on to the table and walked in front of the camera, curling his spine around her mum's arm. She thought of the sensation of his fur under her fingers. Her mum tutted as she lifted him down.

'Is it what you wanted, Kat?' her mum's voice buzzed. 'Is it how you imagined?'

'It's better,' Katya said. 'I don't know how to describe it. I feel closer to him – Dad – just being here. Like I'm still getting to know him, even after he's gone.'

'Oh, Kat. You sound so like him sometimes. He'd be proud of you, you know? If he could see you. Your father's daughter.'

'Thanks, Mum,' she said, but the image had frozen again, and she didn't know if she'd heard. They gave up a few minutes later, waving goodbye in the brief bursts of movement.

'Please look after yourself, Kat. Please stay safe.'

Later, when she slept, Katya dreamed of her dad standing in the city of Nineveh as it burned. She screamed to him, 'Get out of there!' But they were in different times, and he couldn't hear her. That white dust coated everything around her, fine as icing sugar on his skin, and the crescent scars of the cigarette burns on his arm. He was writing something in the dust for her, something for her to find, but she couldn't read what it said.

Aurya

Sharo held their father by the wrists, and Aurya looped his ankles up into her armpits. Together they carried his bulk between them, stumbling and scraping him across the unsown field behind their house, hushing each other. The moonlit world was grey-blue. Aurya tried not to look at her father's slack face, the jaw bouncing on its hinges with every step they took. The flesh of his ankles had turned cold. Sharo gave a whimper of fear.

'Keep going, Sharo. And keep quiet. We're nearly there.'

Aurya listened out for movements in the canebrake as they neared the bank. She could see the rushes and willow wands cut out against the blue night, the stars and bright half-moon. It was the kind of light that made her own hands seem unfamiliar, a stranger's hands.

'Aurya, please,' Sharo was saying. 'Aurya, I can't.'

'Sharo, hush! Someone will hear …'

When they got halfway to the cover of the reeds, a lamp flickered to life in a nearby house. Aurya dropped her father's legs and ducked down on the stony ground, lying flat. Sharo followed her, and their breath made little puffs in the night as they lay there and watched to see if anyone would appear in the doorway. It was the potter's wife: she had nightmares since her daughter had died. She would light a lamp to drive away the ghosts while she prayed. Aurya counted to as high as she knew the words for. There was the smell of river water and smoke, along with vomit and urine from their father. The dry reed of tears rustled in the field all around, and the dawn blush grew a rind in the east. Finally the lamp in the potter's house went out.

'Let's go, Sharo, come on!' Aurya said.

'Aurya, I can't,' he whispered, and she could see that he was shaking. 'I don't want to ...'

'Sharo, we have to. They'll kill us. They'll come for us and lash us and sink us in the river. Do you want that?'

Sharo was making soft noises of terror in the dark. But he obeyed her, picked up their father's wrists again, and together they heaved him into the forest of reeds, towards the ruin of the old village. Aurya had been here many times in her dreams. Their feet sank in puddles. Their wools caught on thorns, and the broken walls of old houses made jagged lines against the sky. More than once, she thought they'd taken a wrong turn, that they would be lost out there with their father's body and the ruined ghosts until morning.

Finally they reached the pit. Aurya and Sharo crept to the edge, peered down into the blackness. At first Aurya could see nothing. Whether it was her eyes that adjusted, or whether the moon came out from behind the clouds, she began to make out the shapes of everything below, the heaps of food waste and excrement and broken objects piled up against the pit edge. In the centre, she realised with a shudder that the massive black shape she was looking at was the trapped lion. It was completely still, looking up at her: a night dweller, awake now. It shook its great head, and she could just make out the hairs of its mane shifting like waterweed. Then it let out that baleful sound that made Aurya want to crawl inside herself.

'It's hungry,' Sharo said beside her. Aurya thought she might faint.

'Sharo,' she said, with a pale voice. 'Help me do it.'

Her brother crouched behind their father's bulk, rolling him by the shoulders and belly, while Aurya moved his legs one by one, so they didn't cross over and stop him. The moonlight caught their breaths as they worked. Aurya could hear the lion's noises in the pit below, pacing, sniffing the blood in the air. At the point where the ground sloped down into the pit, their father rolled on his own. At the edge, he teetered, came to rest on the very lip. He hung there, between here and the underworld, and then he tipped over and disappeared into the dark. There was a beat of silence, and then a crunch. Aurya burst into breathless, exhausted sobs. There was a growling breath from the lion, and then moments later a sound like tearing cloth. Aurya prayed:

To the god of wells
To the god of lions
To the god of murderers

Then she turned away and put her arms around Sharo. Warmth rose off him in the dark. When they got back to the house, they found the shattered clay shards everywhere, their father's blood congealing on the clay floor.

'Sharo,' Aurya said, hearing her voice hoarse from crying, 'help me clean this up.'

'Aurya, are they going to kill me?' Sharo asked, his eyes wide.

'Sharo, shut up and go find something to clean this up!'

Sharo just sat down on the floor amid the debris, clutching his head. Aurya fetched their father's second shirt, and mopped up the blood on the floor. She burned the shirt in the cold fire pit, warming her shaking hands on the precious heat. She buried the shards in the earth outside. When she came back inside, Sharo was curled up on his mat, his whole body shaking.

'Aurya,' Sharo said, his back to her. 'Aurya, I can't stop remembering it.'

She lay down next to him and held him for some time, stroking his hair.

'Try to think of something else, Sharo.'

'I can't.'

'Tell me the rest of the story then. The story with the lions.'

He took a breath, and she thought he would refuse.

'The wild man Enkidu and Gilgamesh the King embraced in the smoke and ruins,' he said.

The wild man Enkidu and Gilgamesh the King embraced in the smoke and ruins.

After that, their friendship filled the King with good. And soon they decided that they would go on a great adventure.

'We should fix what we've broken,' Gilgamesh told his new friend. 'We should build a new gate for the city. There is a forest in a land far away, a twilight forest of tall cedars, perfect for gate beams. But the trees belong to Enlil, King of the Gods. He made a demon called Humbaba to guard them.'

The wild man was afraid.

'I have heard stories of Humbaba. The animals whisper about him. He is the lurker in the gloom, he has a thousand legs.'

'It's an adventure!' the King cried. 'What, are you afraid?'

So they gathered fifty men and set out into the wilderness.

He didn't tell much of the story, but it seemed to last a long time. Whenever Aurya listened to Sharo tell their mother's stories, it was like listening to two voices at once: her brother's soft voice, rising and falling, and the second, silent voice that first told him the story all those years ago. If Aurya listened hard enough, she could hear the suggestion of that voice, its rumour just below the threshold of hearing. When Sharo slowed and came to a stop, she lay there for some time beside him.

'Sharo. What do you remember from the day our mother died?'

He shifted where he was lying.

'I don't remember anything, Aurya,' he murmured. 'You know that. It's a locked door.'

'You must remember something.'

'Nothing.'

Aurya lay beside him and her whole body gave over to shivering. She thought of the way her father had cackled as he grabbed her wrists, the smell of his breath. She thought of the way the lion had looked up at her from the pit, those points of moonlight in its eyes.

'Sharo, have you ever heard of the house of dust?'

Sharo didn't answer. He was already asleep.

When Aurya woke up, sun was coming in through the window. She remembered all at once where she was, and what had happened. She heard drums and people on the river.

'Sharo, wake up!'

Aurya reached for the necklace that Nebo-Pishtim had stolen from her, but it wasn't there. She crawled to her feet and went to the door that backed out on to their field, covered in low morning fog. On the river, she could just make out a shape: a long boat cutting swathes in the water, lance-men with coloured shields lining the prow. The sound of it was all dulled by the mist: the bell, the jangling chains, the oarsmen's grunts and the slosh of their oars, the steady beat of the pace-keeping drum. Then from the fog bank came another boat, and another, until there were more than Aurya knew the numbers for. Between them was a small but beautiful craft, lined with ornate shields, its whole deck covered in a plum-pink awning. As the craft got closer to the bank, Aurya saw a man in robes of peacock colours sitting on a high seat on board, with a servant holding a palm leaf over his head, and a boy in a strange crane-feather headdress holding the bell.

'By the gods Nabu and Marduk, and the lord of the lands of Ashur,' the peacock-robed man cried out as his boat drew up to the bank. 'Where are you, mason? Come out!'

The boat landed on the bank, crushing a coracle moored there by the charrer and his sons. The feather-headed boy struck the bell rapidly. Behind him, the other boats dropped their anchors with a chorus of watery crashes. Aurya took a deep breath and tugged on her brother's shirt, and stepped out of the door.

'Sharo, we have to go meet them. Can you lie, Sharo? If they ask you anything?'

'I don't know, Aurya. I don't think so.'

She squeezed his shoulder.

'Don't say anything, Sharo. You promise?'

He nodded, but she couldn't tell if he'd understood. Aurya thought she might throw up. She steadied herself on the slab of gypsum, felt the smooth cool of its surface, slightly sheened with dew, and gulped the morning air until the feeling lessened. Then they made their way down the bank to the boat.

The man in the peacock robes stood up from his seat and puffed out his chest when he saw the two children. The teams of slaves dropped their oars and jumped off the lower deck, with their shaved heads bowed, laying down split planks on the mud. Aurya became aware of her bare feet, muddy clothes and the wound on her head as the finely dressed lord looked her over.

'You two, you beggar children,' the man said. 'We're looking for Tappum the mason. He was supposed to meet us here. Do you know where we can find him?'

'We're not beggar children,' Aurya called out. 'Tappum is our father. But he never came home last night.'

'Never came home?'

'Sometimes he doesn't come back for days. He has a demon in his head.'

The man scratched his nose and took a long breath. Aurya knew she had to get rid of these people, before they discovered her father's body.

'A demon … Well, we're here to pick up a piece of stone. That one.' He gestured up the bank to where the gypsum slab was visible through the trees. 'But we can't do that until the man specified by the contract is present.'

'The contract?' Aurya said. 'Why, what does the contract say exactly?'

The man massaged his temples, and flicked his boy servant's shoulder with the back of his hand.

'What does it say? Get it out!'

The boy with the crane feathers had a wiry frame and dark, close-shaved hair. He rummaged around in the piles of crates and cargo, and eventually produced a baked clay tablet, small enough to fit in the palm of his hand.

'Tappum the mason, son of Iarbi-ilu, has sold one slab of gypsum, having sworn its quality to be pure. The buyer is Bel-Ibni, on behalf of the palace of King Ashurbanipal. Both hearts are content. By the name of the gods Shamash, Ashur and

Ishtar and the city of Nineveh, in days to come, neither brothers, sons, family on either side –'

'Skip to the part about the collection!' the peacock-robed man barked. The servant with the palm leaf intensified his wafting. The boy stuttered and pushed his headdress back on his head, ran his finger along the tablet. Aurya watched him with wonder as he turned the lump of clay into words, as strange as turning a river rock into a sunrise.

' … the payment is complete, and the collection of the item will be conducted on the fifteenth of the month of Shebat,' the boy read. 'The King's servants will collect the stone from the house of Tappum the mason, and thereafter –'

'So he doesn't have to be here?' Aurya piped. The peacock man settled his gaze on her. She felt the callipers of his eyes testing her.

'Doesn't have to be here … and why do you care? Are you little thieves posing in this man's house while he's away? Trying to steal from him?'

'We're not thieves!' Aurya said, feeling her cheeks flush red. 'And we're not beggars.'

The peacock man made a clucking sound with his tongue. He gave his boy servant another flick.

'All right. We'll take the stone.' He motioned to two bearded soldiers already on the bank. 'Go and search around the river, will you? In case the mason's fallen asleep somewhere in the reeds.'

A light shaking passed over Aurya, but she fought it. The men wandered off in the direction he pointed, towards the old village and the pit, parting the reeds with their spears. Aurya said quick prayers:

To the god of briars
To the god of mist
To the god of orphans

At the peacock man's word, the labourers with their shaved heads filed up to the house to where the stone lay. They worked without instruction, lashing their ropes to the sledge, lining up and spitting on their hands before they set their backs in, their muscles standing out like balled fists. The ropes creaked and after a few heaves, the whole heavy load slid over the mud and knotted roots of the field. Aurya looked over the fine boats rocking on the water, at the men's clothes. She imagined the beautiful place they must come from. How terrible it would be, she thought, to go back to that house, where their father's ghost must already have begun to roam.

'Come here, girl,' the peacock man commanded. 'Put your fingernail marks on the contract.'

Aurya came up to the crane-feather boy, who didn't meet her eyes, and pressed her nails into the cool clay. She wished she still had her mother's seal necklace so she could use that to bind the contract – then these city people would know that she wasn't just a hungry river girl.

'Where are you taking the stone?' she asked in a tiny voice. The boy glanced down at her.

'To Nineveh, of course.'

Nineveh: that name, full of every childhood dream, hit Aurya with the strength of a strong beer. She looked back at the slaves heaving the stone, the mud oozing beneath its runners, the slave driver shouting as he flicked at the men's heels with a reed, inching it closer to the boat with every heave. When it was on board, these people would leave for ever, and then Aurya and Sharo would be alone. And then a powerful notion swept over her, all at once and full of certainty, like the appearance of a brightly coloured bird in the trees.

'Our father did tell us one thing,' Aurya said to the peacock man, her voice shaking.

'What is it?'

She drew closer to Sharo, feeling the comfort in his presence.

'He said my brother and I had to go with the stone, to make sure it reaches the city.'

'There's no need for that,' the peacock man said. He slumped back down on his high seat on the deck.

'He insisted,' Aurya said, hearing the desperation in her own voice. 'He said not to make the deal otherwise.'

The peacock man sighed, and the scribe handed him the tablet. He took out his cylinder seal, larger and more ornate than her mother's had been, and rolled it into the clay with a flourish.

'You've already made the deal, river girl. And I'm not about to start taking legal advice from a hungry little –'

'Master Bel-Ibni!'

The peacock man looked up with pursed lips and saw the two soldiers he'd sent hurrying out of the reeds. Aurya saw by their white looks that they had found the pit.

'What is it? Speak, men.'

'The mason ...' the taller began, but then glanced at the two children. He bounded through the mud and up the gangplank to whisper into the peacock man's ear. Aurya held her breath. The peacock man's cheeks fell, and he removed his fine cloth cap. His eyes moved very slowly down to where Aurya and Sharo stood, but still he didn't quite look at them.

'Your father ... he had some kind of a demon inside him, you said?'

Aurya stuck out her jaw.

'Yes, my lord.'

The man scrunched his cap in his fist.

'It seems your father has met with an accident. It seems he has fallen into an abandoned well, where a lion was trapped. A terrible accident. A frightful thing.'

Aurya raised her hands to her mouth, covered her face. There could have been tears underneath, she thought. It would be easy to believe. The stone slab was still moving down the bank; she felt its progress trembling the ground through the soles of her feet, and with each passing moment, her chance to escape that place was disappearing.

'Please, my lord. We want to come with you, to the city,' Aurya said. 'We have family there. A cousin. We can stay with them.'

The peacock man shook his head.

'This isn't a children's tablet house. I'm sorry about your loss, but this is the royal flotilla of the King of Assyria. And it's an overnight journey to Nineveh.'

And just then, there was a blast from a horn. Everyone froze and turned to its source: the plum-pink awning on the boat still moored on the river. Its entrance split open like a flower and two soldiers in armour stepped out, with a servant blowing the horn trumpet. The peacock man turned in what looked like fright. Everyone, all the soldiers and sailors on the boats, threw themselves on to the deck. Even the slaves heaving the stone dropped their ropes and fell into the mud. The peacock man ducked down on one knee as fast as he could. Aurya watched, stunned. From the tent, a man stepped out. He was tall and thick-chested, with black kohl lining his eyes; his beard, streaked with lines of grey, was plaited and full of beads. His robe was a deep blue, embroidered with gold flower patterns. He wore a shimmering band around his head and another coiled band around his bicep, and another on his wrist with the pattern of a blossoming flower.

'What is going on here?' the man said, speaking slowly but effortlessly, loud enough for everyone to hear. He was a man who had never been rushed in his life, who always took as long as he wanted to speak. His accent was beautiful, redolent with gold and petals, more refined than the most educated teacher Aurya had ever met. There were rings on his fingers, and clusters of golden pendants hanging from his ears.

'Radiant lord, my King, my sun,' the peacock man said, his head down, his voice changed completely. 'It's nothing, a short delay. We are about to be on our way.'

The King cast his eyes around the riverbank, moving as if through honey.

'Who are those two dirty children?' he said. His eyes were half-lidded, lazy.

'Just the children of this mason, my lord. A brother and sister. They live here on the riverbank. It seems their father was killed by a lion. They're asking to come with us to the city.'

'A brother and sister,' the King said dreamily. He smiled, well-worn lines crinkling his eyes. 'And they want to go to the city? Bel-Ibni, do you think this could be the auspicious surprise you saw in the entrails yesterday?'

'No, my lord, I don't think –'

'Well, we can't take that risk, Bel-Ibni. Let them aboard. What are we waiting for? Get them some food as well. They look starved, like little walking skeletons.'

'Of course, my lord,' the peacock man said.

'And that lion. Has it been captured?'

'It's still at the bottom of the well, my lord.'

'Very good,' the King said. 'Have the slaves build a cage, and we'll bring it back with us to the capital. You see, Bel-Ibni? This is why I still love to come on these journeys. You never know what the gods are going to throw your way.'

The King returned to the shade of his tent, the soldiers following him, the awning closing over him. There was silence. For a few moments, no one moved from the ground. It was as if lightning had struck the boats with a boom and deafened them all. Then everyone slowly got to their feet, a couple of birds cawed overhead and the slaves with the ropes began hauling the stone again, cubit by cubit through the mud. The peacock man turned to Aurya, his face flushing pink.

'There's room in the back,' is all he said. 'Hurry and get your things together. And you lot down there, build a cage for that cursed lion!'

Aurya bowed. She took Sharo by the hem of his clothes, dragged him back up the bank and through the scrub before anyone could change their minds.

Katya

As Katya excavated the room where she found the body, spring
came to Mosul. The heat rose, softening the ground, and sprouts
of grass pushed through the grit and stones. Small fox-like creatures began to hang out in groups in the scrub of wild mustard
and yellow thistles beyond the dig site, letting out high-pitched
yowls as she worked.

Excavations progressed in a more thorough manner now
they'd discovered the body: delicate work with trowels and
brushes. Salim and the others helped at her site, and they focused
on cutting a clean soil profile and mapping the floor level. They
uncovered wooden beams and rush matting, clay lamps, water
basins and chisel-like tools, slowly building a picture of the room,
linking one object to another. While they worked, Katya thought
Salim made excuses sometimes to come and talk to her.

'Looks increasingly like some kind of industry going on here.
These tools and basins everywhere ...'

Katya nodded.

'That might fit with the repetitive strain we saw on the skeleton,
on the elbows and wrists. The fusions we saw on the vertebrae.
Always leaning over, working on something repeatedly.'

'Yeah, that's good thinking. Let's not get ahead of ourselves,
though. We'll have to get some proper analysis done.' He glanced
up and shielded his eyes against the sun. 'Oh, look. We've got a
spectator.'

Katya followed his gaze: the distant tree where the girl was standing once again, just watching them from afar.

'Oh, yeah, I've seen her out there a few times. Pass me the binoculars?'

The distant tree swam into view. The girl looked like a teenager, dressed in a floral dress, jeans and an abaya. She was leaning against the trunk and watching the dig, eating something from a bag.

'Moslawis are curious sometimes,' Salim said. 'But you should be careful. The looters put out spotters too, local kids they pay to keep an eye on us.'

Katya waved to the girl, who ducked behind a wall just as before, disappearing from view.

The afternoons were just as busy: Katya spent hours in the storeroom cataloguing new finds that came out of the dust room, taking photos and sketches, zipping them away in their self-seal polythene bags and building her map of the site. She spent time studying the body too, taking more samples to send off for lab analysis, scraping from beneath the fingernails to parse them for pollen grains and organic particles, scanning the skeleton for enthesopathic lesions. The whole time, she kept another object nearby: the little hollow cylinder seal. It sat on her desk in its clear sachet, with the printed scan they'd taken of the design that wrapped around its surface: a lion, a garden and a river. She glanced at it occasionally as though some new clue might have emerged on its patterned and greenish surface.

Dr Malik arrived at the museum with Salim on a Saturday morning. Katya heard the museum door opening and came downstairs with her toothbrush still in her mouth. The doctor spread out his arms when he saw her, nearly filling the whole doorway.

'It is time to see Mosul's bridges!' he announced. Behind him, Salim rolled his eyes.

'Wight ngow?' Katya said through the toothpaste foam.

'Right now!' the doctor boomed.

Dr Malik drove the three of them at great speed down some narrow alleys near the river, overtaking cars on narrow streets and honking furiously even when he was on the wrong side of the road. Katya saw Salim gripping the seat in front with white fingers as they were thrown from one side to the other and pedestrians leapt out of the way. The men drinking tea and playing backgammon on the roadside looked up as they shot past. Katya tried to fix her eyes on the road: she saw a cartoon of Mickey Mouse painted on the wall of a school ahead, and an old lime tree with one half of its branches dead and shrivelled, the other verdant with leaves. Salim breathed out a long breath when the doctor hit the brakes and jumped out.

'This is my palace,' Dr Malik announced. It was a large, stately building with a long veranda, overlooking the reed banks of the Tigris. 'Come, come, come,' the doctor said, and boomed, '*Ahlan wa Sahlan*!' in greeting to a man standing on a wall a few houses over. A concrete statue of Gilgamesh wrestling a lion formed the centrepiece of the doctor's neat mowed lawn. It looked as if it had been modelled after him. A small white boat was moored at the bottom of the garden, half hidden by the reeds. On the opposite bank, a group of unsupervised cows grazed.

'Get in, get in!' Dr Malik urged them. The boat didn't look large enough to comfortably hold all three of them, and when the doctor stepped in, the front end nearly lifted out of the water. Salim got in hesitantly, and then put out a hand to help Katya. When she took it, their eyes met for a moment, but he looked away instantly. The doctor gunned the motor and began to speak in a booming voice.

'Listen! For thousands of years, our two rivers have fed this land with life. They carry silt down from the hills and fertilise everything you see around you: the wheat, the palms, the oranges. Head just one kilometre in either direction, and what do you see? Desert. Dust. But here – this is where life begins.'

Salim lit a cigarette and caught Katya's eye with a look that said: there's much more of this to come. Katya let her fingers skirt the water as the boat pulled away from the bank and they made their way downstream, Salim's blue smoke ribboning them all.

The sun had been getting stronger every day, and it now baked her skin, dotted her with new freckles: her mother's skin.

'This is the first bridge!' the doctor said after some time. 'Made of iron!'

It was shady underneath. A runaway goat had made a nest under the arch on the opposite side. The air smelled of mud and rubbish, and the sound of traffic went on overhead. Salim tipped his head at her encouragingly, out of sight of the doctor.

'It's amazing,' Katya said. The doctor beamed.

'Amazing. Yes, that is the word!'

Salim nodded in approval, staying quiet as the doctor went on about the different arch designs and materials, the dates and designers of each of Mosul's bridges, checking with Salim when he didn't know English words.

'You know,' the doctor said as they picked up speed and the warm paper breeze smoothed Katya's cheeks, 'the problems in Iraq today are all the product of magnetism.'

He raised one finger and gestured to the approaching bridge ahead.

'The earth's magnetic field follows a certain number of lines all around the planet, stronger in some places, weaker in others. Like lines on the surface of an orange.'

Katya nodded, unsure of what to say. Salim was looking off to the side.

'And this country lies right on one of those lines,' Dr Malik went on. 'All the violence of the earth occurs along them, and the world's great rivers follow them too – look it up if you don't believe me! The rivers follow geography, and people follow the rivers, though they don't know why. Cultures flow down them, and dust, and stories too, and the dead when they go to heaven follow the rivers, flying over our heads. That's why bridges are such powerful things. Lodes of iron. Yes, Salim? Lodes?'

'Lodes. Sure.'

'In Iraq, it is the same,' the doctor went on. 'The Assyrians, the Sassanids, Genghis Khan, the Ottomans, Saddam, the Americans. All of them without knowledge obeying the laws of magnetism, which is the most hidden but most powerful force there is.'

'Maybe they should tear the bridges down,' Salim said, looking away to hide his smile. 'Might be an idea if they're causing all these problems for us, Doctor?'

'Salim, you might not believe it. You might joke about it. But you follow those forces too.'

Every time the boat rocked, Katya felt her thigh touch Salim's. Her lips were dry; she found herself watching his hand on the edge of the boat, noting its movements as it edged closer to hers, then further away. When they landed back at the mooring and all got out, did his hand flicker for a moment on her lower back? In the car on the way through the city, the doctor wound again through the narrow streets again at breakneck speed, and when he stopped outside the museum, Salim got out of the car with Katya.

'Thanks, Doctor, I can walk home from here,' Salim said, a little breathless. The doctor bellowed some farewell in Arabic as he shot away, making a yellow taxi screech to a halt at the junction.

'That's one way I don't intend to die,' Salim said, and caught her eye. 'I'll see you in the morning then.'

'Well, I thought ... do you want to come in?'

'Come in?'

'Yeah. There are some dominoes in the top room. We could play. If you're not busy.'

Salim looked unsure for a moment. Then he nodded and followed her upstairs. She still felt the rocking movement of the boat beneath her. They tried to sit on the museum floor while the statues of kings wrapped in plastic loomed over them, but the air conditioning was broken, and the only place they could find that was cool enough was the parking garage, where a breeze blew in under the sheet-metal gate. They sat on blankets near the old rusting van parked on its cinder blocks.

'Why do they keep this old thing around?' Katya said, and tossed a piece of gravel so it made a satisfying hollow sound against the van. Salim shrugged.

'No idea. It hasn't worked for years. Probably used to need a part they couldn't get during the embargo, and now it's too rusted to even screw the tyres on. Either that or it's an important part of the system of magnetic balance around here.'

Katya laughed. Salim didn't meet her eye, but he looked pleased. She had always thought dominoes was a child's game of luck, but the way Salim played it involved constant calculation and conniving. He won three games, but then Katya's luck changed and she won two in a row. Every time Salim placed a domino, he snapped it down triumphantly.

As they played, they talked more about the dig, the room with the tools and basins and the body they'd found with the cylinder seal clenched in its hand. Then Salim told her about the First Gulf War, which he'd seen as a boy. He told her how one day when a large bomb went off in his neighbourhood, he went out into his garden to see the ground covered with the bodies of little birds, killed by the shock wave. How his grandfather, a lover of birds since he was young, had stood on their porch and quivered with rage.

She told him memories of her dad, picking each one out like a polished marble from a bag: the crusty breads she'd eaten whenever he'd taken her to visit a friend's restaurant; the cryptic crosswords he'd done and how he'd chewed the end of his pen as he did them; the scars on his arm that she'd thought looked like the marks of an alien language; how he'd rubbed argan oil in his beard, a kind that came in a yellow bottle.

'Oh, I know that brand,' Salim said. He looked like he was about to say something, but his phone buzzed. He frowned at it, then answered and spoke a few brief exchanges in Arabic.

'I'm sorry,' he said. 'I have to go. My nephew Athir's got in some kind of trouble.'

'Nothing serious?'

'No. He's just not very good at paying the right people. It's a skill you need around here.'

Katya knew her disappointment was written on her face, and she tried to hide it.

'No problem. I hope he's okay.'

Salim got up with a sigh and gave her a bashful goodbye, leaving his dominoes on the floor in a little henge. Once he'd left, Katya let the air out of her lungs in one long breath and then checked what was left in his hand. He'd been letting her win.

Katya took the seal back to the dig site the next day, with the aim of examining it further in its context. That inscrutable little stone, rolling around on her palm. That day, her trowel seemed to sense things hidden in the earth, nudging through the loam and dust. She turned up a beautiful shard of glazed pottery, and a mother-of-pearl bead before lunch, fallen in a crack between two sections of the wall. The next day she brought the seal back again. In her breaks, she rested in the sparse shade beneath the ancient olive tree, watched white birds roosting in the houses that climbed the riverbank, men with flocks of sheep in the wetland stretches. She breathed the smells of the rubbish fires, of sewage and barbecued fish, pear blossom and orange buds, petrol, kebab shops, crushed grass. In high winds, there was the sound of skittering shale, and the masses of antennae on the rooftops trembled as though the city itself were a sensitive instrument, detecting vibrations in the air.

One evening, Katya returned to the museum to see a girl of about sixteen in jeans and a long-sleeved dress, sitting there on the kerb. The girl was crying, her head in her hands, taking little gasps of breath.

'Hello?' Katya said when she got close enough. 'Are you okay?'

The girl wore an abaya that covered her hair and shoulders, her face a white oval. Katya noticed the girl's hands, tucked into the sleeves of her dress, her shoulders hopping to her sobs. Katya put out her hand. 'Do you want to come into the museum?'

The girl looked up at her sharply, and drew her abaya to cover her face. But after a few moments, she met Katya's eye. She glanced around and then took her hand.

'Come inside,' Katya said. 'What's wrong?'

The girl didn't answer, but followed her into the museum. She looked around the dim entrance hall, at the huge bull guardians flanking the approach, and the statues veiled in their plastic coverings. When she pulled her hands out from her sleeves, Katya noticed a little red-and-white string around her left wrist, and a sooty stain on the palms of her hands.

'Want tea?' Katya asked in Arabic. The girl just shook her head, her face a mask of sorrow. 'Want telephone?'

'I can speak some English,' the girl said a little hesitantly. 'Your Arabic is very bad.'

'Yes, I suppose it is. What's your name?'

'Lola.'

'Lola. That doesn't sound like an Iraqi name.' The girl shook her head.

'No.'

'Where do you live?'

'In Ar-Rafidayn. Not far.'

'Are you a student? In school?'

The girl shook her head.

'No. Cooking.'

Lola had a young face, with freckles over the bridge of her nose like the marks on an egg. The girl pulled off her abaya with a brisk and frustrated motion that made hair fall over her tear-stained face.

'Well, I'm going to make some tea,' Katya said. 'I'll make two, and you can drink it if you want.'

Lola just watched her. She kept rubbing her hands on her clothes, trying to brush off the sooty black marks. Katya led the girl to the staff kitchen, boiled some water in a pan on the gas stove and found some yellow packets of Ceylon tea. She gave the girl a towel to wipe her hands: the girl sniffed, and brushed her palms, but the black wouldn't budge. It seemed to dirty everything it touched without ever lessening itself. Katya looked over the girl's floral dress, her jeans and abaya, and a stirring of recognition hit all at once.

'You're the girl who stands under the tree by the river,' she said. 'You watch us at the dig site.'

Lola gave a curl of embarrassment.

'I'm sorry. I like to look.'

'It's okay. You always hide when I wave to you.'

The girl nodded, and looked away with her face long and slick with tears.

'So what happened, Lola?' Katya asked eventually. 'Did someone hurt you? Do you want the police?'

'No. No police.'

'Okay. But if someone ...'

The girl closed her eyes and shook her head, tried again to brush the black marks from her palms, each time the motion more furious as if the marks were burning her.

'My brother,' she said. 'They killed my brother.'

Katya felt herself suddenly unequal to the situation.

'I'm sorry. Are you in danger?'

The girl threw the towel to the floor.

'Yes.'

Lola sniffed and rubbed her red eyes with the hem of her dress, tugged at the red-and-white cord around her wrist. The two of them leaned against the counters, letting silence stretch between them.

'The tea is terrible,' the girl said after a minute, her voice tiny. Katya let out a little breath of a laugh, but the girl kept that same flinty expression, staring down into the floor. By the time they'd finished their tea, Lola had stopped crying. She pulled her abaya over her head, tidied herself as best she could in the reflection of a copper-bottomed pan hanging on a nail, and then said, 'Now I go. Thank you.'

Katya followed her to the door and watched as she hurried away through the litter that blew down the street in spirals.

The next morning, when Salim came to pick her up, Katya mentioned her encounter with Lola.

'She said, "They killed my brother". What did she mean?'

Salim puffed out his cheeks.

'It could be anything. But I heard a shop got burned down yesterday. A firebomb. Near here.'

Katya thought of the dark marks on Lola's hands. The way she'd scrubbed at them. She shivered.

'Yes. She had soot. Here, on her hands.'

Salim nodded.

'They were Yazidis. Kurdish-speaking, from the north. I bet she had a little cord on her wrist, red-and-white string?'

'Yes, she did.'

'A terrible thing. A young man died, sleeping in the back room. Might have been selling alcohol secretly, or just didn't pay their protection money. The militias have their own logic, their own laws. And outside the city these days, the whole countryside is run by them.'

'That's horrible.'

Katya thought of the hardness in Lola's face, a pain like a piercing arrow.

'There are checkpoints of course, but these days anyone can buy a uniform and an ID card. There are gangs all over the city – and worse, too, though no one talks about it. That poor girl must have run as far as she could.'

'Was your nephew okay?' Katya said. 'That trouble you mentioned yesterday …'

'Yes, he's fine,' Salim said, shaking his head. 'I feel so responsible for him. When we were teenagers, his father and I used to repair cars together for money, always telling each other it was so we could both go to college. Then when the time came, I got the chance to study abroad. He said, "You go, Brother. We don't have enough for us both, and you were always the smart one." He stayed here through it all, and I went. Then he died, and I was all Athir had left.'

'I didn't know you lost your brother. I didn't know you had one.'

Salim nodded.

'Yes. What a world these young people will have to fix.'

After that, he didn't seem to want to talk. Something seemed to weigh heavily on his mind, and he seemed like a different man from the one she'd played dominoes with in the museum garage.

'Katya, keep an eye on the news,' he said as he left. 'There are dark rumours going around. And it's not good to be surprised out here. If it comes to it, we may have to get out of here at short notice.'

Katya thought about Lola as she worked on alone. She couldn't shake the image from her mind, of the girl with the blackened hands. She thought about her dad and what it meant to lose someone so young. She thought about the day her mum had got the call: her wail coming from the kitchen. She remembered going down to find out what was wrong and seeing the phone bouncing on its coiled cord, tapping lightly on the linoleum. Her mum curled on the floor with her head in her hands, and the cries coming out of her, deep, and unlike her voice. She remembered being taken to her aunt and uncle's house, whose ashen faces betrayed to her the seriousness of what was happening. The tuna sandwiches they gave her with too much butter, and her mother coming to pick her up in the evening, looking like she'd shrunk by half.

Once her work was done, Katya went back and sat with the body of the man from the dust room, lying now in its airtight sack, the broken array of its teeth still visible through the acetate. It was ready to be transferred to the lab. The men from the archae-ological department would come to pick up the body in the next few days, and it would be taken down to Baghdad. Katya felt sad to see him go. She sat and let her eyes wander over his leathered skin, and the contorted angles of his cheekbones, crushed by the weight of time and earth. She sat and thought about the colours and sensations that had once flickered on the inside of that skull, the loves and fears and uncertainty, the distances crossed by its dreams.

The next day, Katya went out to the dig. She was surprised when Salim joined her. He didn't speak much while he worked, but Katya liked his presence nonetheless, the calm and meticulous way he moved over the site with little flourishes of his hands, the sleeves of his shirt rolled up to reveal the sun-darkened skin of his forearms. They heard gunfire in the city, and he murmured the makes and calibre as he heard them.

'Kalashnikov,' he would say, the way her dad used to identify a bird by its call. 'Beretta. Glock.'

They improved the trench's drainage and uncovered a wider section of the white dust layer, found some more artisanal tools turned the aquamarine of corroded copper.

'More evidence of some kind of work going on here,' Katya said.

'Yes. I wonder what they made.'

Around midday, they took a break and sat on the wall in the shade of the olive tree, watching the wind cross the land and moan in its hollows. Salim seemed miserable, so Katya told him what she'd read about the plant life of Assyria, how the ancient kings had brought back trees and herbs from their conquests and planted them in their palaces. She told him about the lettuces that grew in ordered rows in the temple gardens of ancient Egypt. Then she let the sound of the wind settle in between them. Finally, Salim spoke.

'You can almost see them some days, can't you?'

Katya looked up at him, squinting in the glare and dust.

'Who?'

He gestured out at the site.

'All the people who used to live here. Walking through these disappeared streets.'

'Sometimes.'

Salim took several glugs from his water bottle and handed it to her. He coughed and looked sideways at her.

'I wanted to tell you, before I told the others,' he said.

Before I told the others. Katya collected that fragment to examine later.

'What is it?'

'Well … we're coming to the end of our funding for the dig. A couple of months at most. And I don't think we're going to get any more.'

'But … the body, the room with the dust …'

He shrugged.

'There's just no interest from on high. And with the security situation the way it is … We may have to take what we've got and write it up.'

'Wow.' Katya felt a sudden panic. 'I hadn't … you know …'

'Yeah.'

She bit her lip and felt a constriction in her throat.

'I'll really miss this place. And you. All of you, I mean.'

Salim nodded with his lips pursed, but he didn't get to reply. An army helicopter came flying over the ruins, staying low to avoid opportunist gunfire. He pointed up and screamed over the thwump-thwump of its rotors, 'That's their idea of patrolling for looters!'

They both shielded their eyes and mouths, helpless as the cloud of debris and dust swirled over them, ripping up their tarpaulin, and the branches of the olive tree swayed.

Aurya

It didn't take long to gather the contents of Aurya's and Sharo's lives. Their house already seemed abandoned, empty as a river shell. They found a dog nosing at one of the beer jars, but it dashed out at the sight of them. In their father's room, his empty sheepskin still wore his imprint. Aurya stood and stared at it for some time, and then picked up one of the beer jars, swung it hard against the wall with all her force so the shattering filled the empty house.

'Aurya,' Sharo said, watching as she picked up another jar. 'How will we find our cousin when we get to the city? Do you know their name?'

'We don't have a cousin in the city, Sharo,' she said, and hurled the jar into a cluster of others. Flies burst into the air, fizzing in panic. 'It's just something I said. So they'd take us with them.'

'But the city,' Sharo said. 'Aurya, what will we do once we get there?'

'Don't ask stupid questions,' she snapped, trying to still her breath. She kicked another jar, and it toppled and split. But she knew it wasn't a stupid question at all. 'We'll find something to do and someone to help us. People in that city must be kinder than out here.'

'But Aurya … the city will be so big. It's going to hurt my head. I won't be able to draw it all …'

'Do you know how much Father owes to that crook Nilmaher?' Aurya said, picking up the last jar. 'If we stay here, we'll lose this house, and we'll be up at the crossroads before the end of the month. We've got no choice, Sharo.'

'I trust you, Aurya.'

She threw the last jar against the wall, left a rose of beer dribbling down the bricks. Then she went to the door and looked down at the ships lining the bank, the men busy heaving the stone on board. Another group of slaves was building a lattice, lashing together stripped lengths of young willow: a cage for the lion in the pit.

'And there's something else. Father said something before he … something about our mother.'

Sharo's face didn't move. He watched Aurya closely.

'What did he say?'

'He said there was no lion. That she never got dragged away.'

Sharo's eyes wavered just slightly.

'Did he say anything else?'

'He said something about a place called the house of dust. He said that's where she is. Sharo … do you remember anything about that day? The day she died? Could our mother still be alive?'

She expected him to say something, but he just went on staring at her. His eyes were black and deep, the way they always went when memories were flickering behind them.

'Sharo, tell me if you know anything!'

'She's not alive, Aurya. She died that night.'

'How do you know that if you don't remember anything, Sharo? Was there a lion or not?'

Sharo put his hands on his head.

'Aurya, it hurts. I can't think about that day. It's a locked door. Every time I bang on it, it hurts.'

She put her hand out and touched his shoulder.

'Sharo … if there's any chance that she might be alive, we have to find her. Maybe someone in the city will know where the house of dust is. Your lion's going to the city too. You'd like to follow him, wouldn't you?' Sharo nodded, head still in his hands. 'We can't stay here, Sharo. It's an adventure. Like in the story. Right?'

After a few more moments, he lifted his head, dark eyes big and watery. Then he looked around the house at the patches of light and shade falling in the broken rooms.

'We'll look after each other, Aurya. Like in the story. We'll protect each other.'

Aurya nodded, and the two of them stepped outside, watching together as the slab of stone began the slow journey up the gang-plank and on to the boat, its ropes crackling and men shouting and heaving around it.

'But, Aurya,' Sharo murmured, 'you shouldn't lose yourself in hoping. Our mother is dead. I'm sure of it.'

Aurya was about to snap back at Sharo, but just then she saw a movement nearby, in the reeds that ringed their field. Up ahead, a small face peered from the undergrowth, looking even more like a river vole than ever. It was Nebo-Pishtim. His eyes narrowed at them as they approached, and flickered for a moment over the wound on Aurya's head. He wasn't with his friends, and he had a strange look that she'd never seen on his face. Her necklace still hung on a string around his neck, and she felt a flash of anger.

'You're in big trouble, Nebo,' Aurya shouted at him. The boy bared his teeth but didn't come any closer out of the reeds.

'What are you talking about?' he hissed.

'I told the watchmen you took my necklace.' She gave a cold smile and approached. 'See those men down there? They're from the capital.'

She watched Nebo-Pishtim's eyes wander over the flotilla of boats, the man with the peacock robes, the scribe with his tablets, the dozens of soldiers with their bright armour and pointed helmets, their beards and long spears.

'You're lying,' he said. 'The watchmen would never … not for a little …'

She smiled a little wider and counted a few heartbeats, let the fear do its work.

'You don't think so? Didn't I tell you my mother was from Nineveh?'

She watched his mouth open, his mind working furiously. Then she pointed down to the bank.

'And look what those slaves are building, Nebo.'

'What?' he spat. She allowed herself a pitying smile.

'It's a cage.'

When she looked back, he'd gone pale as cut tamarisk. She held out her hand, palm outstretched. Trembling a little, he took off her necklace and handed it back to her, careful not to touch her hand.

'I know what you did,' he said, his voice high and strangled. Aurya paused.

'What's that?'

'I saw you,' Nebo-Pishtim said. 'Last night, out near the pit.'

And Aurya realised what it was, that strange look in his eyes. He was afraid. She watched him, her whole body numb. She tried to keep her face calm.

'We weren't out by the pit. You imagined it.'

'I was throwing out our old matting,' he said. 'I hid when I saw you. "Sharo," you said. "Sharo, help me do it."'

Aurya grabbed Sharo's hand and turned to walk down to the boats.

'You're a liar,' she said, trying to control the pitch of her voice.

'I'm going to tell everyone,' Nebo-Pishtim shouted after her. She kept on walking without looking back, feeling the ground suddenly unstable beneath her feet, her whole body alive with fear. 'I'm going to tell everyone what you did!'

———

When Aurya and Sharo returned to the boat, the team of slaves had already heaved the slab of gypsum on board. The men's backs shone with sweat, their faces wrinkling with effort along well-worn lines, calling to each other in a strange language of brass and cool water.

'Put your things over there,' the peacock man said sharply. 'Abil-Ishtar, search them and put their things away!'

The boy with the feathered headdress nodded, and beckoned for Aurya and Sharo to follow. He made them turn out the folds of their wool cloaks, and when he saw Aurya's blade fragment, he put out his hand.

'I'm sorry. Not with the King here.'

Aurya gripped the piece of iron tightly, but then let the boy have it. The siblings sat down among the crates and earthen jars like pieces of cargo. Aurya made quick prayers:

To the god of cities
To the god of gamblers
To the god of hinges

The boy brought them two clay bowls of barley porridge flavoured with fried leek. It was the most delicious thing Aurya had ever tasted. She ate it without even using her hands, slurping up the porridge and licking the clay-tasting bowl clean. Beside her, Sharo did the same. The young servant boy looked a little afraid, as though he'd just fed two wild animals.

'Is your name Abil-Ishtar?' she said, wanting to prove she wasn't a wild Elamite.

'You can just call me Abil.'

'Abil,' she repeated.

'Yes.'

'Do you work for the King?' she asked, trying not to sound impressed.

'No. I work for master Bel-Ibni, and he works for the King.'

'He's a servant too?'

'Yes, a servant. And many other things besides. A doctor, a soothsayer, a reader of the oils.' Abil looked out towards the reed bank.

'I'm sorry about your father,' he said.

Aurya kept her gaze on the deck, felt the whole of it shifting low on the water as it took on the weight of the stone.

'He wasn't a very good father.'

Abil shrugged.

'Still. The lions are everywhere these days. There's been a plague of them, killing the cattle, taking women and men from the villages too. They come wandering down from the hills, follow-ing the river. Even as far as the gates of Nineveh. I heard of one nobleman whose head slave trapped one in his attic and had to keep feeding it until his master came back.'

The thought gave Aurya a crawling feeling on the surface of her skin.

'Why are there so many?'

The boy shrugged.

'Who knows what plans the gods have?'

'And why are they putting it in a cage? Why can't they just kill it?'

The boy motioned to the plum-pink awning at the centre of the flotilla.

'The King wants lions.'

'What does he want them for?' The boy didn't answer, just straightened the crane-feather crown on his head.

'Your brother's quiet, isn't he?' Sharo shifted beside her.

'He is sometimes. When he's not telling his stories. Our mother knew all the ancient stories, from the time before the flood. And Sharo remembers every one she told him. Word for word.'

'That's impressive.'

'My brother's like that. He can remember everything. Everything that's ever happened to him. He gets this memory-pain though, when too many new things happen at once. It hurts, and then he has to draw things to make the hurt go away.'

Abil watched Sharo with curiosity, tongue pressing into his cheek.

'He can remember everything?'

'Yes.' Aurya became suddenly aware of how much she'd given away. 'Please don't tell anyone.'

Soon the lion's cage was ready, and the men hefted it up on poles. All the while they'd been building it, Aurya had sat on deck and watched the people of the village gathering up on the reed bank. She could see their heads appearing through the undergrowth: she recognised the charrer's boys, the potter and his wife, all of them looking down with the nervous, curious eyes of deer. Could Nebo-Pishtim have told them already? None of them, at least, seemed brave enough to approach.

The best place to hide was in the crowd, she thought, and most of the men were now gathered around the empty cage. Aurya went to find Sharo, who was crouched on the bank beside the gangplank. He was drawing a lion in the mud with a reed, with several soldiers gathered around him, watching.

'Sharo!' she said, eyeing the men warily. 'Come on now, stop that. You want to see, don't you? When they rescue the lion?'

Sharo shook his head.

'No, Aurya.' But she took his hand and pulled him away. 'They're not going to hurt him, are they, Aurya?'

'I don't know. It's what it would deserve.'

Aurya and Sharo followed the men through the reeds. When the soldiers reached the old village and peered into its abandoned well, they tutted their tongues and curled their lips.

'Stand back, children,' one said in a foreign accent. 'Not a sight for you to see.'

Aurya and Sharo held each other in the vine-strewn ruin of one house, with tamarisks bursting out of its windows. They watched as the men made loops of rope, tested their strength, and then threw them down into the pit. From the bottom, the lion gave out a roar with every throw, and Aurya's stomach clenched like a fist at the sound. It was a difficult shot, but soon one soldier snapped the rope taut and dug his heels into the earth. The slaves rushed to hold him and stop him from being dragged in. Aurya reached for Sharo's hand as the rope jumped and leapt in the man's grasp. The creature in the pit gnashed and snarled, but before long, the men had the lion snared by a dozen ropes. They all stood on one side and pulled together. The animal's sounds changed.

'Aurya, they're hurting it,' Sharo said.

'Isn't this what you wanted, Sharo? It was going to starve down there.'

The slaves heaved to a count, and the ropes cut lines into the mud. When the lion came into view, Aurya didn't feel the fear she expected: she felt a burst of pity. It looked ridiculous. All four of its legs were pinioned in the ropes, which looped around its belly too. It looked as ungainly as a hoisted cat. Its tail was flicking furiously, and it whined in pain and terror as the men dragged it up the pit wall.

At the top, the soldiers prodded it with their spears, striking its rear with canes and driving it into the waiting cage. It had little choice: when it was in, they snapped the door closed and tied it shut. The lion was frantic, trying desperately to turn in the narrow cage, its tail whipping the bars, the ropes still wound around its limbs and body. When the men lifted the cage, the lion's claws flashed out and cut the hand of one soldier. He cried out the names of gods, and the men all kept their distance after that, but he laughed proudly as they headed back to the boats. One younger man lingered for a moment and glanced down into the pit where Aurya knew the remains of her father still lay. He reached into his belt and threw a crust of bread into the pit. He caught Aurya's eye.

'So he doesn't have to beg for crumbs in the city of the dead,' he said, and then hurried off after the others.

On the way back through the reeds, the lion whined like a dog. It lashed at the bars of its cage as the men stepped over rocks and willow clumps, rocking it from side to side. Aurya got as close as she dared, close enough to see the lion's eyes, huge yellow bulbs with a point of deep black in their centre. Those eyes rolled in their sockets, and the whole length of its hide shivered in fear. The rust of dried blood still painted its muzzle.

'Aurya, look at his paw,' Sharo said. Maggots curled in the pink wound. 'Aurya, do you think his foot will be all right?'

'It's for the gods to decide, Sharo.'

When they reached the boat, the people on board parted, and a tremor went through the crowd.

'What a beast,' someone said.

'Ashur, bind that cage tight.'

They heaved the lion up beside the slab of gypsum, near where Aurya and Sharo were to sit. The peacock man wafted away the smell: like an old fur coat, mixed with meat and dry hay.

'Get ready to leave!' someone shouted, and Aurya felt a thrill of fear. The boats dredged up their anchors, wearing beards of green weed. Wiry men put down poles into the mud with long, stretching motions, and the drums below deck began to beat like the heart of an enormous creature. This was the moment, then. The last moment that she could decide to stay. Aurya and Sharo sat together among the pots and bundles near the stones, watching the lion in its cage and feeling the shifting movements of the boat beneath them. Aurya had only ever been in the coracles the villagers used as ferries, which rocked and threatened to tip at any time. She thought it would be the same to ride a great ship, but this vessel moved slowly, steady as the earth. She looked around her at every joint and bolt holding the craft together, the ingenious interweaving of wood and the smell of bitumen rising off it all. Over the side, she watched her home, everything she'd ever known, begin to slip away. Their house's sagging roof slid away over the stern, and then receded, further and further. Then it all disappeared around the river bend, and she breathed out.

'What do you think it's going to be like, Sharo? Nineveh ...'

Sharo didn't answer. Aurya looked up and saw that he was busy watching the lion, not with fear or sadness, but with the hint of a smile as though the animal had told a joke that only he understood.

Towards evening, the jagged ruin of a riverbank fort came into view, half-sunken in the mud and reeds. The boats moored in a line along the shore, and the King's men gathered up thorn scrub to heap in a loose fence in the broken parts of the walls.

'No use if a lion wants to get inside,' one soldier said. 'I've seen a big male jump right on to the roof of a house.'

The King's guard built his tent against the crumbling rampart, and set a palisade of sharpened stakes around it, looped with more thorn scrub. Aurya couldn't help watching the King move around the camp. Something about the sight of him made her shiver. Men bowed like reeds around him, scared to touch him or even to get close. But there was something else in him too – a kind of fear that she saw he worked hard to conceal behind his eyes.

'Just think,' the King announced as he walked to his tent, 'this was once the border of our empire. And now Assyria rules half the world, from Egypt to the mountains, from Babylon to the Sealands!'

Some soldiers clapped or grunted. Soon fires squealed and popped around the clearing, and men laid their mats out on the brick mounds, the piles of shattered ancient pots, old green arrowheads. A bowl of porridge went around to each person, warmed this time, even a few dates that the soldiers had knocked down from the palms with stones. Afterwards, Aurya and Sharo sat on their haunches, soldiers and slaves all watching as the flames sent shadows dancing against the old walls. They didn't talk much. The King sat beside the peacock man, and they spoke about the hill forts they had inspected in the north, the tribes of wild horse people that lived outside the empire's bounds. Did they have the heads of horses or their feet, Aurya wondered? Which seemed more frightening? The King asked his servant the meaning of omens: the shape of a curl of oil he'd seen in his breakfast bowl, the movements of birds, the certain constellations covered by clouds that evening.

'They are good omens, my lord, my sun,' the peacock man kept saying. 'Our gods are winning the war in heaven just as we are winning our wars on earth. But there are some rites we should perform when we return to the city.'

The way he spoke scared Aurya somehow. There wasn't a shred of doubt in his voice. In the distance, behind the hills, the storm god Adad was rumbling and flashing. Aurya sat in the fire's warmth and tried to follow the conversation, but she couldn't keep her thoughts straight. Whenever she closed her eyes, she saw her father's body slumping into the darkness, heard his tearing flesh. The smell of his breath in the darkness. On the moored boat, through the reeds, the sleeping lion's shape cut a dark figure out of the stars.

Aurya realised with a flush of terror that she didn't know the way home. She had never seen a city before. She had never seen a town bigger than her own village, which on market days had been frightening and busy and full of noise. She laid her head on

Sharo's broad, soft shoulder. He was idly sketching a lion's paw into the mud with his finger.

'Can you tell me the rest of the story now?' she said, her voice small in the night.

'Where did I get to?' He knew, of course – he just wanted her to tell him.

'The King and the wild man,' Aurya said, and flicked a date stone into the embers, where it squealed. 'They set out on the adventure to the cedar forest, to fight the demon.'

'That's right,' Sharo said, and a thick tamarisk log in the fire popped.

> *The King and the wild man travelled the whole length of the land, across plains and marshes, through deserts and foothills where lions roamed, to fight the demon Humbaba and cut down his cedars.*
>
> *They reached the high forest gate, and Gilgamesh the King felt a terrible dread creeping through the trees.*
>
> *He said, 'Let's camp on this hillside for the night.'*
>
> *When they finally slept, the King was tormented by dreams, but Enkidu the wild man knew of these things and told him: 'These are good omens.'*
>
> *When the sun rose, the King strode through the forest with his axe, up to the tallest cedar. He raised his weapon and struck the tree.*
>
> *The tree sang in pain, snow fell from its leaves.*
>
> *The crows roosting in its branches took flight.*
>
> *And in the distance, the King and the wild man heard the sound of a thousand legs beginning to move.*

Sharo told the story quietly at first, under his breath. But before long Aurya saw that one of the soldiers close to them was listening. He nudged another soldier, and his friend turned and paid attention too, so Sharo spoke a little louder. She saw Abil prick up his ears as he wafted the peacock man with the fan. As snores rose, and men swatted at the insects that came whining from the marsh, Aurya realised that they were all listening. She looked over to the great tent where the King slept, and saw with a thrill of fear that he wasn't sleeping, but standing in its entrance and watching Sharo, his eyes shimmering and wet in the firelight.

———————

Aurya hardly slept that night. All around her there was a chorus of snores, the crunching footsteps of sentries patrolling the bank, the sleepless servants and slaves bustling through the shadows with pots of steaming water, jugs and folding tables. Aurya ran her fingers over the scab of her head wound and thought about what Nebo-Pishtim had said, his cold voice crying out after her. If he had told everyone in the village, how fast would news travel downriver? Aurya could feel the riverbank gods moving overhead, the gods of the ruins, and the voice of the wind, all hissing 'murderer'.

When she did sleep, Aurya dreamed that the lion had escaped from its cage. In the dream, it was stalking through the night, looking for her. She dreamed that the creature had the spirit of her father. It was hunting her, looking for revenge.

'Aurya,' it said in a breathy voice, not quite human. 'Aurya, I know you're out there. Where are you, murderer?'

She gasped awake, covered in sweat. Nearby, at the same moment, a man let out a high-pitched cry. Aurya's blood froze. She shot up and looked around, trying to make out the dark shape of the beast slipping through the shadows. None of the soldiers moved from their mats. Some scratched, rolled over. Then from the King's tent, there came another cry, and a deep, breathless voice.

'Bel-Ibni!' it said. In the darkness, she saw the silhouette of the peacock man emerge from his tent, and hurry to the King's enclosure. After some moments, the light of a small lamp lit up the tent. Aurya tried to get back to sleep, but it was impossible. She lay awake, looking at the crumbling walls lit by that lamp, and stroked the bumps and grooves of her necklace.

Unable to resist, she lifted herself up and crept through the sleeping bodies – the restless movements of fighting men in their sleep, the snores and twitches. On the wall above the King's tent, she saw the outline of a group of archers sitting and playing a game they'd scratched into the stone, but they didn't see her as she moved through the mass of sleeping bodies. Aurya stayed low and ducked close to the palisade. There were guards inside. The tent fabric wasn't one piece: it had gaps and folds that widened and closed in the shifting breeze. If she put her head through the palisade, Aurya could just about see inside. With a shiver, she caught a flash of the King's face. It was covered with blood. There was blood on his hands too, and his robe.

'Bel-Ibni,' the King said after a few moments, in that soft, deep voice. 'I had that dream again.'

'The lion dream, my lord?'

That was the peacock man.

'That fucking lion,' the King said, and used both bloody hands to comb back his hair, bristle the sweat from his beard. The peacock man passed the King a ladle of some liquid, which he drank from, and held a cloth to his nose.

'Not like that, my lord. You remember what I said? Don't apply the dressing on the side. Try to plug up the airflow, so the blood can clot.'

'That's what I'm …'

The cloth over the King's nostrils stained with a spreading rose. His weary eyes rolled back in their sockets.

'Shall I have a servant fetch some beer, my lord?'

'No, no, I'll be up all night. I just need sleep. But these dreams!'

'Why don't you tell me about it, my lord?' the peacock man said. 'I know I can never forget a nightmare until I tell it.'

Aurya watched the King, entranced: this man, who the gods lived and spoke through.

'It was just like before,' the King said, his voice swollen through his blocked nose. 'I'm sitting there in my library. I'm reading, and suddenly I know something's wrong. I hear water outside. Thumping and hissing. The sound of waves. And seabirds.'

'Seabirds,' the peacock man repeated. One of the guards stepped in front Aurya's view, and she started in fright. But the man's back was to her, and the King's voice went on. She couldn't tear herself away.

'I start to feel more afraid as the sounds get louder,' the King continued, 'and I get up and walk through the library to the entrance hall. It feels so real. I can feel the cool of the floor, and there's even that part by the door where the tile's coming away and no one's fixed it yet. I think to myself, "I must tell Bel-Ibni to have someone fix that tile!" And then I step out on to the terrace, and where I should see the city, where Nineveh should be, all I can see is an ocean. The waves, Bel-Ibni. They're taller than any building. They're taller than the mountains. There are people drowning down there, and ships and houses smashed to splinters, and the whole detritus of everything twisting and swirling.'

The guard stepped out of the way, and Aurya's view through the crack returned. In the dim light, the beads in the King's plaited beard made him look like some strange water creature with a multitude of eyes.

'And then what, my lord?'

'And then I hear a footstep down on the path to the palace.'

'Like a man's footstep, my lord?' the peacock man said, though he seemed to know the answer.

'Not like a man. It's a pad on the stone. And I look around, and I see a lion.'

'A lion.'

'A huge male. Ancient and ravenous, from the high hills. It's walking towards me, towards the library. Loping, tongue hanging. I want to scream and scream, but when I open my mouth, I find it full of dust. I try to claw out the dust, but more keeps coming, and the lion is coming up the steps, and I turn to run back into the library.'

The King lifted the cloth from his nose and sighed, massaging both his temples with one hand.

'That's when the water comes. The waves crash through the halls, and all the books and tablets are torn from the shelves and crushed together, and everything starts collapsing. Everything I've spent my life trying to build. And when the water hits me, that's when I wake up.'

The peacock man shook his head.

'Do the gods appear at any point? Maybe if they did …'

'No,' the King said, and waved a hand. 'No, it's just as I said. Just the library, and the ocean, and the lion. Ashur and Nabu and all the rest don't even poke their heads in the door. Bel-Ibni,' the King said, his eyes wide like the eyes of a child. 'I think the lion was my brother. I think it was the spirit of Shamash-shum-ukin, come to torment me. And the water. That was the great flood. The one in the stories.'

'What do you think it means, my lord?'

The King raised his eyes to the tent's ceiling. He let out a long breath so his lips fluttered.

'Bel-Ibni … do you know, when I became king, I thought we might do things differently. Not like our ancestors, I mean. Those bloodthirsty kings …'

'The old ways always come back in the end, my lord. They're always there, only buried beneath our feet.'

'Bel-Ibni, how many cities has it been now?'

'Difficult to count, my lord, without the records in front of me.'

'And when we bring the statues of their gods home with us … what happens to the gods?'

'We can't know for sure. But I suppose they stay behind, my lord. Gods without stones, wandering the ruin mounds.'

The King let out a long breath.

'Bel-Ibni … sometimes I fear we have awoken some terrible will against us.'

Aurya leaned closer, but just then a hand grabbed her shoulder from behind. She jumped, and let out a stifled squeak. Another hand shot up to cover her mouth.

'What was that?' the peacock man said. Aurya kicked out, and the person behind her spun her around. It was the boy Abil, his urgent eyes looking directly into hers. He dragged her away by one hand, leaping over the bodies scattered around, and just as the two guards burst from the King's tent, he pulled her to the ground on to an empty mat. She lay there beside him, her chest heaving, her heart beating, her whole skin alive with fear. One guard took a torch from the entrance, and its light washed over all the sleeping men. Through her lashes, Aurya saw drips of burning oil fall to the ground as the soldier lifted it high. Very slowly, Abil raised a finger to his lips.

The guards looked all around the outside of the King's tent, peered between the gaps in the palisade, and then walked a little into the reeds. Then one shouted up at the archers on the wall, scolded them for playing their game. After what seemed like a lifetime, they sidled back into the tent.

'Just a bird,' Aurya heard one mutter. 'Or a passing god paying his respects.'

On the ground beside her, Abil let out a long breath.

'They would kill you if they caught you,' he whispered, his eyes wide and urgent. 'You don't know enough to be afraid of them, river girl.'

When she thought it was safe, when the murmuring in the tent had subsided, and the light faded, she left Abil, crept back to her mat and lay there in the dark beside Sharo, listening to the chorus of snores. When she slept, Aurya dreamed of a dark room. Her father and Sharo sat opposite her, cross-legged, and water hushed nearby. They both held up round pieces of stone in their hands, so that their faces were perfectly covered. She couldn't see Sharo's expression, but she could tell that behind the stone, her father was smiling.

Katya

Katya and Salim stood outside and watched as the men from the archaeological department took the body away, sealed in its airtight container.

'Like saying goodbye to an old friend,' Katya said. Salim nodded.

'Look after him,' he called after the men. 'And be gentle. He's been resting a long time.'

In the car going to the dig, they sat in silence for much of the journey, watching the city slip by amid the morning traffic.

'Funny thought, isn't it?' Katya said as they crossed the river. 'That we never get to know how many times our bones will be buried.'

Out in the city, the greenery of spring had made way for summer heat, globe thistles and yellow chamomile sprouting in the verges. The morning sky was the impossible blue of Indian ink, the ground the colour of lion fur. Katya watched from the car window as they crossed the bridge, taking in the cattle cooling off in the shallows and grazing on the watercress that grew there, the birds roosting in the white houses that climbed the riverbank, the long queues for the petrol stations. Today was her six-month anniversary in Iraq. It had begun to feel familiar. Not like home exactly, but now her image of home was becoming blurred. She could hardly imagine the dig coming to an end, going back to the cold of her windy Atlantic island, leaving her work unfinished.

She imagined what it would be like for everyone she met to understand her when she spoke.

She climbed up to her site alone, and found that looters had struck again. The ground was pocked and cratered like the surface of the moon, an attack more audacious than anything they'd seen. The tracks of many bikes and spiralling footprints were pressed into the dust, the tamarisk bushes uprooted along the path of a large vehicle, and the whole place was given over to wind-blown litter. The guard was nowhere to be seen. Katya didn't feel the same devastation as before. Just a kind of weariness as she realised that she would probably spend her last days in Iraq trying to sort out this mess. Salim reacted differently. She called him, and he swore loudly down the line. Half an hour later, he arrived with Dr Malik, who came in a long, loose dishdasha, and they both helped her examine the damage, a dark cloud hanging over them all.

'Shit,' Salim said when he saw it. 'This is the worst yet.'

'What happened?' Katya asked. 'How did they get away with this?'

'The police say there was a mix-up with the scheduling of guards. Another one. Funny the looters knew all about it too.'

They made a map of the scarred site, marking little x's where damage had occurred. Salim's pencil jabbed angrily at his clipboard with each one. Dr Malik moved about the ruins with difficulty, the wind wrapping his dishdasha bandage-tight around his body. Dust and litter blew around him, and he gestured at the old tyres and water cartons, the plastic bags and shreds of barbed wire, the broken pipes and bricks.

'So much rubble,' he mourned.

'I know,' Salim said. 'We'll have to clear it before excavation can continue.'

'Clear it, clear it, yes,' the doctor said. 'And there's so much inside us too, Salim. Don't you feel it building up every day?'

When the doctor left, Katya and Salim continued working alone. They didn't talk much. Since he'd told her about the dig coming to an end, something in Salim seemed to prickle and withdraw behind a shell of professionalism. She watched him as he moved around the site in his usual crisp shirt and wide hat, trying to guess what he was thinking.

'There's still this white dust turning up everywhere we dig,' Katya said, trying to knock him out of his silence. 'Have you heard anything back from the lab about that?'

'No, nothing yet. I've chased them about it, and they say maybe next week.'

Salim didn't meet her eyes, and he crouched down in the trench. He ran some of the dust through his fingers. It had a silver sheen to it in the light.

'Sometimes you shouldn't hope too much for answers,' he said, and shook his head, then sniffed. 'I've found that out too many times. The stories down here aren't the kind that end neatly.'

'What's wrong?' she said. He took off his sunglasses, and she saw genuine sorrow in his face.

'This place. Sometimes it's all too much. Sometimes … I don't know. It breaks my heart. It feels like something's trying to claw its way out of the earth here. Does that sound crazy?'

'Yeah, a little,' Katya said. 'It sounds like something Dr Malik would say.'

Salim laughed coldly.

'Yeah, it does.'

They worked for the rest of the day to uncover what they could. Salim rolled up his sleeves. He swung the pick hard into the earth so his shoulder blades moved beneath his shirt, darkened by wings of sweat. They talked as they dug, or rather Katya talked: she told Salim about phytoliths, the microscopic silica skeletons of plant material that helped her map the seasonal work of a Neolithic village in Greece. She felt his mood improve as they catalogued the positions of lost objects, built their map of the damage. Later, in the car going back, he was quiet.

'What will you do after?' Katya asked him, as they drove across the river. 'Once the dig is over?'

She didn't mean it to sound as sad as it did. He shrugged.

'There's always something more. Always more work to do. I'll go back to Baghdad, look for more funding. What about you?'

'I don't know. Find another dig. Keep going until I've got enough to write a book, settle down and teach. You'll have to let me know if you're ever in London.'

He nodded and looked sideways at her briefly.

'I will.'

'We can go and see the lion hunt carvings together. The real ones.'

'I'd like that.'

When they parked outside the museum, Salim reached into his pocket.

'Oh, I nearly forgot,' he said, and took something out. It was a little bottle of argan oil, the kind with a yellow label that Katya remembered her dad keeping in their bathroom cupboard at home. She felt overwhelmed at the sight of it suddenly.

'Oh, my god. How did you find it?'

'It's everywhere here. Thought it might help bring back the past.'

'Thank you.'

Before she could stop herself, she leaned over and hugged him. They were both covered in sweat, grit and dust from digging, but she felt the muscles of his shoulders against her hand, and something moved low in her belly.

'I'm going to miss you,' she said. He nodded. Katya got out of the car and he pulled away, drove off into the evening. She sat down on the museum wall and unscrewed the bottle of oil. She took a breath, and memory came back to her in flashes of sensation: summer in their kitchen, lying on her dad's chest as a young child and watching the TV, him teaching her how to play football. The way he'd had nightmares sometimes and cried out in the night.

'I waited for you,' a voice said behind her, and Katya jumped. It was Lola, standing on the street outside the museum, keeping her distance from the guards and holding a blue plastic bag.

'Oh, Lola. It's good to see you.'

'Yes,' the girl said, with no inflection. 'You were digging. But now we can go to the park.'

Katya hesitated. She remembered her promise to Salim, never to go out on her own. But she'd spent months locked up in that museum, and this might be one of her last chances to see the city before going home. And anyway, she wasn't alone. She nodded.

'Let's go.'

They walked around the museum to the shade of the park and found a bench beneath a palm tree that was bending over a broken concrete fountain. A group of teenagers in jeans lounged on a rug beneath the tree, passing a shisha pipe. Lola opened her plastic bag and took out some grease-darkened newspaper wrappings.

'This is for you,' Lola said.

Inside were two stuffed aubergines, the smell of mint, spices and oil rising off them. Katya felt her mouth begin to water.

'Thanks,' Katya said. 'You made this?'

Lola nodded.

'This one is for me.'

Katya ate it messily, with her hand cupped beneath her chin to catch falling pieces, which made Lola giggle. It was delicious, full of smoke and rich tomato flavours.

'How is it?' the girl asked as they ate.

'It's good!'

'No, how is it?' She made a spade motion. 'Digging, digging.'

'Oh, the digging,' Katya said, rubbing the callouses on her palms. She thought of what Salim had said about the looters employing spotters and spies. But she felt she could trust Lola. 'Yeah, it's okay. But people keep coming in the night and stealing things from the ruins, destroying everything. Breaking things. I haven't seen you out by the tree for a while.' Lola shook her head.

'It is so busy.'

'Why do you stand out there?' Katya asked. 'Why are you so interested in the archaeologists?'

'I want to be one, one day. I want to be an archaeologist.' Lola moved slowly over the rough terrain of the word.

'You can be,' Katya said. 'Come and visit one day, and I'll show you around. You can see how we protect the site. How we dig.'

'When you find treasures,' Lola said through a mouthful, 'you take them back to your country?'

'We're not looking for treasure,' Katya said, swallowing. 'We're looking for pots, tools, the walls of people's homes, the food they ate, so we can find out the stories behind them. I look for plants mostly. Organic remains.' She picked out a seed from one of the aubergines, and held it out on her nail. 'I could find a little seed like this in a broken pot and that could be worth more than any treasure. We could trace its path back through ancient trade routes, decode its DNA, paint a picture of the world as it was all those years ago. Sometimes the rubbish dumps of ancient people are more interesting than their palaces. That's why the looting hurts us so much. People disturb the objects, take them out of their context. They break the story that's been waiting for thousands of years to be told.'

'But if you find something. A treasure,' Lola insisted, rubbing her fingers together to show value, 'you will take it.'

'No. In the past that happened,' Katya began. 'These days it would stay right here. So you can visit it in a museum.'

Lola didn't seem to hear. She was distracted by two older men wearing keffiyehs who walked past, talking and gesturing at the museum building nearby. She laughed and covered her mouth.

'They are talking about you,' she said. Katya looked after the men.

'What, why?'

'They say that the museum is … *maskoon*. It means someone is living there.'

'Oh. Word travels fast.'

Lola nodded.

'Yes. *Maskoon*. It also means "haunted".' She pulled a mock-scared face.

'Great.'

A warm breeze shifted, and the palm fronds overhead rustled in the silence that stretched out between them. Katya thought about telling Lola that she wouldn't be around much longer, that their dig was coming to an end. She couldn't find the words.

'Lola,' Katya said. 'I'm sorry about your brother.'

The girl turned her head away, and kicked her heels harder under the bench, crossing and uncrossing them.

'Yes,' she said quietly. 'I am sorry.'

'Do you have any other family?' Katya asked. 'Anyone to stay with?'

'No. My family …'

Lola made a hand sign that looked like birds flying away. What did that mean? It could be anything along a spectrum of tragedy.

'You don't have anyone?'

'The woman owning the kitchen. She lets me sleep above. But she is scared. Maybe leaving.'

'Scared? Of what?'

Lola shrugged, and met Katya's eye again.

'There are things in this city. Moving, out of sight. Monsters. Now it is not safe.'

'It's not safe? Lola, what do you mean?'

The girl looked away so Katya couldn't see her face.

'Even the gangsters are scared.'

'What is it, Lola?'

The girl refused to say anything more, just shaking her head when pressed. After another minute, she got up.

'Now I go.'

'Thank you for the food,' Katya said. 'It was delicious.'

Lola just nodded.

'If you dig up a treasure,' she said, 'you will give it to me?'

Katya laughed.

'You wouldn't want anything I thought was a treasure.'

Lola looked dissatisfied, but she ran off. Katya stayed there a few moments, watching the people come and go in the park, some families with children, birds pecking in the grass. She luxuriated in the feeling of being outside on her own. On the road, large trucks passed by, their horns as mournful as whale song. Then she got up and headed back to the museum.

After working to catalogue some new items she'd brought in that day, fragments of clay pots and old matting, she sat in front of the lion carvings with the little bottle of argan oil Salim had given her. She unscrewed the lid and breathed in its scent, and looked over the pain in the lions' snarls, the flying arrows finding their marks in their hides. It was only later, when she went back to her room and the dark of the museum at night descended on her, that Katya thought about what Lola had said: about the museum, and the city.

She fell into a fitful sleep. She awoke at one point with the sensation that there was another person somewhere in the museum. She didn't know what made her think that, but she felt it strongly. She lay awake and held her breath, listening for footsteps or any other sound outside the door, but there was only silence, just a bad dream blotting into the waking world.

Mia the dig registrar announced that she was leaving the team for a funded position in an Australian university. Everyone tried to swallow their jealousy, snapped at each other for a few days and polished their CVs. An atmosphere of doom passed over the whole team. Giulia and Martina went on leave, making knowing comments in cynical tones, and Raad and Khawla extended their time in Baghdad for a wedding. Soon it would be just Katya and Salim working on the site, wrapping up the last fragments of the dying project.

'Hey, do you want to hold on to my jeep?' Mia asked Katya on her last day. It was a wreck, an angular and dust-caked beast of a car with what looked like shotgun blasts of rust eating into the wheel arches.

'The jeep? I don't know ...'

'Can't you drive?'

'I don't have a licence.'

Having seizures from the age of sixteen will do that to you, she wanted to say. Her mother had taught her anyway, in car parks and side roads.

'Many people don't, around here. Just give the police a few dollars if you get caught.'

'Don't you want anything for it?'

'It cost nothing,' Mia shrugged, and handed her the keys. 'And she's been a good car – I'd rather she went to someone I know. Look after her, will you?'

And then she had a car. Driving gave Katya the kind of freedom she'd yearned for. As long as she was careful not to drive on the days she felt an aura, she could see the city without needing Salim: the winding alleys and long avenues of Mosul, the Friday crowds outside the mosques talking and buying sweet treats, the wooden doors and faded old domes and crumbling façades, the shopfronts and windows all broken in a different way, the cobblestones poured over with asphalt. In a shop with its shutter only half open, Katya saw an old tailor sitting at a sewing machine among mountains of coloured fabric. She saw a ruined mosque, with lime trees bursting their roots through its bricks and blue tiles. She drove with the back windows open, so the seats got coated in dust. That fine dust, settling over everything.

Dust seemed to rule her days. It covered her skin and hair, got in her teeth. She tasted it in the back of her throat. And in the days that followed, dust began to fill her and Salim's conversations too. They finally got their results back from the lab on the contents of the strange white powder that had coated the floor of the room with the body.

'It's gypsum,' Salim said, squinting at the readouts. 'Calcium sulphate. And some traces of other things. Ash, sand, organic compounds ...'

'Gypsum?' Katya said. 'So it's stone? What's stone dust doing all over that room?'

'Your guess is as good as mine. There are alabaster and gypsum deposits all around this region. They used to bring the high-quality stone from the hills of Kurdistan, to carve. And the ash will be from the burning of the city.'

'What does it mean?'

'I don't know. It might have been a workshop of some kind, a construction site working with stone. It might be evidence of what we've thought: that there's a palace underneath that hill, beneath the Nabi Yunus mosque. Hopefully we can come up with an explanation before we pack our things. Can you extend your trenches, uncover more of that room?'

'Sure, I think there's time. I can join them up, see what else we can find.'

'Sounds good. It would be nice to have a theory at least, to tie all the finds together. Something flashy.'

As Katya got back to work, the heat baked the dig site. Her skin went red along the tops of her arms, while her nose turned pink and peeled. The dust became unbearable. At lunch, she and Salim had to eat with their hands covering their bowls of rice, and work facing away from the wind. As the heat worsened, men began selling slabs of ice on the roadside, cracking them with metal bars and heaving them with hooked tongs into coolers in the backs of cars.

That night, she dreamed that she was out working in the ruins when that white dust began to fall from the sky all around her. It dusted the tops of everything, light as icing sugar, and then she realised that it wasn't dust, but pollen. Plants began to germinate out of the stones, seedless and alien, pale rootlets and sprouts curling all around her in a writhing time-lapse. They burst into flower: the opening umbrellas of lianas, bromeliads, amaryllis, blood lilies and cyclamen. Tropical flowers that didn't belong in this dry, desert place. And as they grew, the ruins beneath them crumbled.

———

It was a Tuesday. Katya had been working alone that day, with Salim off wrapping up the last details of the dig. The heat was intense, and she kept sweating off her suncream and having to reapply it every hour. The gypsum dust layer coated her hands and knees, got in her eyes. She excavated into the room's centre, where the remains of wooden beams, chocolatey in colour, stretched out into the earth. She wasn't expecting much as the trenches converged. But as midday passed and the sun began to slip back into the west, she uncovered a corner of stone. It was different from the baked bricks she'd been finding up until then: it was smooth and well-cut, stained by time to the colour of nicotine teeth. She kept going, sweeping the dust from it with her coarse brush. It looked like a paving slab. But as she went on unearthing its edge, she realised it was long. Perhaps a few metres in length. It lay flat on the earth, just in line with the white dust layer. Still she didn't think much of it – it was probably a large flagstone or lintel, she thought – not until she dug laterally and found that its surface became patterned. An intricate lacing of lines and whorls. She heard drums beating in her soul, trembling loose the dust and sand.

She continued brushing in a dream-like confusion. She was rushing and had to sweep away the earth that crumbled down from the trench wall above. The whole stone surface was carved. And as she dug, the patterns resolved themselves into shapes, the shapes into forms, until a whole image emerged, carved into the stone. At first, she thought she saw the gnarled branches of a tree. As she uncovered more and more, the branch became a claw.

She scrambled to fish her phone from her pocket and mashed the buttons until Salim answered.

'Hello?'

'You have to come here.' She heard her voice as if through cotton wool.

'Is everything okay?'

'I think I've found something.'

'What is it?'

'Just come and – come and see!'

When she hung up, Katya got back on her hands and knees, and dug with the tips of her fingers, clay and gypsum dust compacting under her nails. She realised her mouth was open and full of flecks of earth, and she spat without stopping. Then she took out the tiny paintbrush she used for only the most delicate work. When Salim arrived twenty minutes later, she was sitting on the trench edge, coated in sweat, her shoulders heaving.

'What is it?' he said. He'd been running.

She just looked at him and pointed down into the hole. He came up behind her and looked down.

'Oh, my god. Is that what I think it is?'

She nodded.

'It's a fucking lion.'

———

Katya and Salim worked with a kind of frantic thoroughness. They exposed the edge of carved stone as the hot winds came in from the west and battered them, snatched their hats and scarves, blowing litter. Piece by piece, the full image of a lion's head and outstretched claws came into view at the bottom of the pit. All the elements were there: the whirling mane, the wrinkles on the muzzle, the distinctive claws. When they got out of breath and had to stop to wipe the sweat from their faces, they would each stand back and stare.

'It looks like a copy of one of the lion hunt reliefs,' Salim breathed.

'No, look. It's not like any of the others.'

'It's holding something in its mouth ... what is that?'

'We'll have to excavate it all before it's clear,' Katya said. She photographed their find from multiple angles, with close-ups on the details. Salim clapped her on the back.

'Wow. I mean ... we've done it. This will make our careers.'

Katya's head was spinning.

'We have to tell everyone!' she said. 'The museum, the news, the police ...'

Salim bit lightly on his bottom lip and looked down into the trench. He shook his head slowly.

'No.'

'No?'

'Katya, we can't tell anyone.'

'What do you mean?'

'This is too big. We don't know who to trust. If we tell anyone about this – and I mean *anyone* – whispers will get around. Then looters will be out here the same night, cracking this lion into a hundred pieces. We need time. Time to contact everyone, get a government team down here, proper equipment, military protection ...'

Katya stared down into the hole, at the lion's deep, sad eyes, and whatever that was in its mouth.

'What can we do?'

Salim glanced around him.

'We have to cover it up.'

'Salim, we can't –'

'Katya,' he said, a hard edge to his voice. 'Do you want to save this lion or not?'

'I want to uncover it. I don't want to leave it behind …'

'We'll come back for it. I promise.'

She thought of her dad suddenly, the thought unwelcome, unasked for.

'You don't always get to decide if you come back.'

Salim paid no attention. He picked up the spade and shovelled earth back into the trench with care. Katya took a deep breath and scrunched her eyes closed. Despite everything she felt, he was right. She picked up her own spade and joined in, the lion disappearing again beneath the sand and loam. Afterwards, they smoothed the earth over, covered it in dust and wind-blown rubbish. They found a decaying tyre nearby, and worked together to drag it over the recently disturbed earth, marking the spot. They walked back to the car in a daze, and sat there for a few moments, both breathing out. Then Salim struck his hands on the wheel and let out a whoop, a triumphant Apache yell that made Katya jump and then burst out laughing.

'We did it,' she said. 'I can't believe what we just found.'

They stayed together for the rest of the afternoon. They went up to one of the museum's back rooms and sat with their faces close together, lit up in the strobing glow of an old monitor, poring over the photos they'd uploaded. They spoke hurriedly and under their breaths.

'It's unmistakable,' Salim said.

'Part of Ashurbanipal's collection,' Katya murmured, hardly able to believe her own words.

'I'd bet anything. It's the same artist, I know it.'

'But it wasn't put on the palace wall like the rest.'

'Or painted.'

'A missing piece …' Katya murmured again. 'What do you think it means?'

'It's hard to say with so little uncovered,' Salim said, zooming in and out with mouse clicks. 'It's the same depth as the ones in London, the same stone. But the composition's strange. All we have is a lion's head …'

'And its jaws, clamped down on something … a deer maybe, some kind of prey. A classic hunting scene.'

'This decorated piece here. Doesn't it look like the same design as the King's chariot? But it seems completely the wrong way around. Was this a practice run for the other carvings? A mistake? Maybe some kind of fatal crack in the stone that made it impossible to move ...'

'No. It stayed there on the workshop floor,' Katya murmured yet again. 'Those carvings were made around 640 BC, at best estimates. And the city was destroyed in 612 BC. And for all those twenty-eight years, this carving sat in the workshop.'

'Twenty-eight years,' Salim repeated. Their eyes met. 'Someone kept it there. They didn't destroy it. This mattered to someone.'

'Who? And why?'

Salim shrugged.

'I wish we could uncover it all right now. Maybe if we knew what the whole image looked like ...'

Katya peered closer.

'Do you think we hid it well enough?'

'God, I hope so. The looters are lazy. They won't dig so deep if they can help it. But if they see the disturbed earth ...'

Katya ran her fingers over the screen, felt the prickle of static on the glass. The lion's eyes were deep and recessed, full of a sadness that looked eerily human. She was going to say something to Salim, but she glanced up and saw that tears were glazing his cheeks.

'It's just so beautiful,' he said. 'Through all of this, through everything that's happened, this is going to make people proud of Iraq again. For one more moment, Mosul is going to be the centre of the world.'

She put a hand on his back and they stood there for some time, staring into the sunken eyes of the lion on the screen.

Katya could hardly sleep the whole night. The excitement kept washing over her in waves, and a restless fear that the looters might be out there right at that moment, moving the old tyre, attracted by the recently disturbed earth, crunching through the earth with their spades. More than once, she got up and crept through the halls, up to the roof, trying to spot the flicker of a phosphorous flare in the ruins. She didn't see anything, and what would she do if she did? She stood for some time and watched the city lights shimmer as the day's heat left the earth, and felt the tug of an unusual wind beginning to blow. She sat crouched with her back against the balustrade and rocked there for a few moments listening to the wind pick up over the city, full of heat and grit. She had a flash of a memory, without knowing why it came to her: coming downstairs once as a child and seeing her dad squatting just like that, his back up against the oven. He looked like he'd been crying, the constellation of little round scars visible on his hand. She knew he had trouble sleeping sometimes.

'Dad, what are you doing?' she'd asked. He'd glanced at her, a quick, frightened movement like a cat. Then he'd laughed.

'Oh. Nothing, dear. Come back to bed.' And then he'd taken her upstairs and she'd felt the rough carpet on her feet, and he'd put her into bed and tucked her in. 'Make sure, Kat,' he'd said, in just a whisper. 'Promise me. When you're older. Never hide when you should have run.'

Katya pressed her back against the wall and ran her fingers through her hair. What had he meant? She stayed there a little longer, then went downstairs. She took out the printed photos she'd taken of the new lion carving, took them to the room with the Assyrian lion hunt. She followed the scene around the room, trying to spot a gap in the story where another panel might go. There was the King in his chariot, the soldiers with their dogs and spears, the commoners flocking to watch. There were the lions, frozen for ever in their sorrow. There was a deathly silence in the halls. Then she went back to her room and lay down fully clothed. She dreamed of white towers hanging upside down in the air, their bells ringing.

She rocked awake at one point in the early morning and heard gunfire far-off in the city, a sound like bubble wrap popping. She drifted back to sleep, and when she woke up to her alarm, the gunfire was still going. That wasn't unusual. What was strange were the running feet and the trucks on the street outside the museum. Katya messaged Salim saying she was heading to the site, but didn't get any reply.

Outside, the guards weren't in their usual spot. Katya got into her car. There was the smell of burning petrol nearby, and the crackling of gunfire, more severe than usual. There was a column of black smoke in the distance. Still, nothing too unusual. But as she drove she noticed that something had changed. There were no queues at the petrol stations. The bus station where the crowds usually gathered for the bus to Erbil was almost empty, with only a few impatient drivers searching for passengers. An army truck drove past her on the other side of the road, with men hanging out the back, rifles out. It was driving just a little too fast.

Then her phone buzzed, in the tray beside the gearstick. She glanced down at it. Salim again.

'Stay in the museum,' it said. 'Not safe.'

Glancing up at the road and down at her phone while she drove, she tapped out: 'wts happening?'

Another army truck thundered past, flicking pieces of grit into her windscreen. Its tarp was only half-attached, flapping in the wind. Katya drummed her fingers on the wheel. Litter in the breeze. A child ran across the road. When the phone buzzed again, she snatched it up.

'An attack on the city. I don't know who.'

She became suddenly conscious of her breath. There were choruses of car horns, and she pressed down on the accelerator. She had to cross the bridge to turn around: the blue water stretched out on either side, and she could see more smoke, coming from the western districts. A strong river wind battered the car windows. In the near distance, a detonation like a heavy stone hitting the earth. And hadn't it all happened like this before? Hadn't she passed over this river already, with the smoke in the air, and the streets empty, the litter and dust in the air?

BOOK II

The Garden

Katya

When she woke up, Katya smelled smoke and petrol. Her pillow felt strange. It hurt her face. There was a hissing nearby: gunshots. She opened her eyes, but they kept blurring in and out of focus. Something was running down her cheek, and when she put her hand up to touch it, the tips of her fingers came away red. They were shaking. She wasn't lying on her pillow. Her head was resting against the steering wheel of her car. She lifted it on an aching neck, and saw the windscreen above her, smashed to a cobweb pattern.

There was a thump on the passenger-side glass. The shape of someone outside swam through the dusty glass. They were shouting something, but Katya's ears rang and she couldn't hear what they were saying. They were trying to get in. They came around to her side, and she panicked, tried to free herself from her seatbelt. The car door opened, and the face rearranged into the shape of Salim. He looked frantic, his hair wild.

'Shit!' he shouted. 'Katya, what happened?'

A seizure. How stupid could she be?

'I don't know. I must have skidded,' she said. She sounded drunk. Some gunshots popped nearby, and Salim looked up in fright. The pupils in his eyes were huge.

'I saw you from up on the site. You drove right into the wall. Are you okay?'

'Yeah, I think so.' She stretched her neck and it twinged painfully. One ankle was alight with pain.

'We have to get out of here,' Salim said.

'The car …'

'It's fucked. Front end looks like a crushed can.'

She slid herself out, and her legs buckled. Salim caught her, and she smelled the sweat and old smoke on his clothes. She looked back at the car, crushed up against the old city wall of Nineveh. Her senses returned, bringing with them a pounding headache.

'The bus station to Erbil,' she murmured. 'There were some drivers there when I drove past. I don't know how long ago.'

'Let's try it,' Salim said, and helped her take a few steps. Her right ankle twinged painfully every time she put weight on it. She felt a slight tremor in the muscles of Salim's shoulder as they went.

'It's fine,' she said. 'I can walk on my own.'

'Are you sure?'

'Yeah, it's fine.'

They stumbled together through the litter and debris between the road and the Nineveh ruins. Two army trucks sped past full of men, and Salim tried to wave them down, but they ignored him. They were heading east, away from the city. Salim screamed something at them.

'They're leaving,' he said. His face was pale. Further down the road, Katya covered her mouth as they saw an army Humvee burning, the air above it trembling. A man was hanging lifeless out of its driver's seat. She felt all her senses buzzing.

When they crossed the bridge back to the museum, there was an enormous boom, and a huge pillow of fire and black smoke rose over the western districts. Birds burst off in panicked flocks, heading east after the army trucks.

When they got to the bus station, they found it empty. The few drivers she'd seen earlier had left, and now desperate families were hurrying around, asking each other what was going on. A dog with an injured back leg was loping around in the rubbish and rubble beside the ticket kiosk. The wind whipped first one way and then the other, and little dust devils of litter were picked up on the road.

'Shit shit shit,' Salim was saying.

'We have to go back to the museum,' Katya said, trying to pop her ears with her jaw. 'We can lock the door – there's a gun there. In an umbrella stand.'

Salim frowned at her, and put his hand to her forehead.

'No, we have to get out of the city. If we get stuck in the museum …'

There was a chorus of gunfire close by, and they ducked. Katya felt sweat on her palms.

'Okay, okay,' Salim said. 'Let's go to the museum and try to get help from there.'

She took his hand and they set off back down the street. Salim saw that she was limping painfully, and he slung her arm over his shoulder before she could protest. They hobbled down the street together, and she could feel the sweat on the back of his neck, and the closeness of their cheeks. Soon the palms and the blank arched façade of the museum came into view. They ducked inside, bolted the door and secured it with the bicycle chain. Katya put her back against the wall, her chest heaving, her whole body numb. Salim put a cool hand against her forehead, testing her temperature, and she closed her eyes at the touch without meaning to.

'Do you feel okay?' he said. 'That's a nasty cut.'

She nodded and tried to look elsewhere.

'Mm, yeah, I feel a bit drunk.'

'You might have concussion. I'll need to stay with you, make sure you're okay. Let's find something cool to put on your head. Then we can go to the roof.'

Katya followed him through the museum, where the wrapped statues loured down at them. When they passed the lion carvings, Katya looked up at them and the dying cries of the lions became the thuds of bombs going off in the distance, the King's chariot wheels crackling like gunfire on the ground. Salim might have a point about that concussion. He took her to the kitchen and helped her wash the blood from her face and hair in the deep steel sink. She felt the water and his fingers in her hair, and hoped he wouldn't notice the way her arms burst out in goosebumps. He chipped off a block of ice from the cool box, and wrapped it in a towel.

'Here. Hold this against your head.'

'Thanks.'

They went to the roof. Mosul stretched out before them, looking like the set of a disaster film. Dozens of black plumes rose in a forest over the west, and helicopters flew low, fat dragonflies over the rooftops. Katya's head throbbed. She reached out and put her balled hand in Salim's palm, which closed a little around it. She thought of the man she'd seen hanging out of the door of his car, his arms limp over his head like a doll.

'I've never seen a dead person before,' she said, and then realised that of course that wasn't true. Not even close.

They stayed up there for a long time, watching chaos unfold in the city. Salim made many phone calls, his voice wavering between degrees of urgency. In the evening, the lights went out all over the city, district by district, until the whole of Mosul was dark and only the purple glow of the sun was visible. Katya's head was agony, her ears still ringing, her lip the size of a gooseberry. Salim had an unlit cigarette in his mouth, and kept striking a broken lighter, shaking it in rising frustration. Occasional flickers of tracer fire arced over the rooftops, unearthly as fireflies.

'Where are you staying tonight?' she said.

'There's an office next to yours. I'll go in there.'

'Okay.'

When night fell, with flashes continuing in the west and the rattle of Kalashnikovs, Katya said goodnight to Salim and melted into her mattress, fully clothed. She lay in a Z, feeling like a piece of architecture crumbling into the earth. She reached out into the space in front of her and imagined for a moment that Salim was lying there.

As promised, he slept on his coat in the room next door. She listened to his snores, warm and human in the dark. Exhausted as she was, sleep felt impossible. Her body jumped at every sound. She tried to calm herself by thinking about the meticulous processes of residue analysis, gas chromatography and mass spectrometry. When she finally drifted off, she dreamed of human skulls in alcohol jars.

In the morning, Salim got his hands on a SIM card that was Internet enabled. They took it in turn to use the dusty computer in one of the museum's back offices, and read about what was happening on different news sites around the world. Only vague terms were used. Insurgents. Attacks. Phrases like 'extremely serious', 'state of emergency' and 'maximum alert' appeared with frequency.

'My god,' Salim muttered. 'The roads must look like rivers ...'

When she got her turn, Katya found an email from her mother full of exclamation marks.

'I'm safe,' she wrote back. How much of a lie was acceptable? 'Please don't worry too much. The army's doing everything they can, and everyone's looking after me. You know how the news exaggerates. I love you. I'll be home soon.'

She couldn't help thinking about the promises her dad always gave when he left. She knew that's what her mother would think of too. For the rest of the day, she tried to lose herself in any work she could find, ignoring the injuries she'd received the day before. Her ankle still hurt when she walked, and her lip still throbbed. The cut on her head had scabbed and stopped bleeding, but she could tell she would have a scar, just showing beneath the line of her fringe. They checked how much food they had in the museum: enough for a week or two. To pass the time, Katya spent hours in the basement storehouse, checking the catalogue of objects kept down there, filling in new entries for the recently excavated finds in their crates, still smelling of mud and loam.

On the fourth day, Katya and Salim watched the battle from the roof. Her ankle felt better now. She could walk without pain. There was a low percussion of thuds in the distance, artillery fire, marking time. Puffs of billowing grey kept cropping up like mushrooms among the buildings. Katya wondered if there were people still living there.

'The generals are directing the fight from that hotel,' Salim told her, pointing over the forest on the other bank, the ranging reed banks and the funfair in the distance. 'The one by the river.'

Katya tried to shade herself from the sun that baked the roof, making the air hard to breathe. Dr Malik came around after lunch, and spent some time wringing his huge hands and talking with Salim on the rooftop. He was sweating, and his usual cheerful, booming voice had become a murmur.

'The idiots,' he said, as they watched the city being rocked by explosions, tremors they all felt in the earth. 'The army's killing people. Don't they care? And they're going to damage the bridges.'

A car alarm went off somewhere in the street below. When it stopped, a bird somewhere nearby picked up the same note. Towards evening, Salim took a call from the police chief, holed up in the hotel with the army command. Katya stretched her back against the parapet, and saw a woman in jeans and a flowered dress running down the museum approach. She could tell by the shape of her movements that it was Lola.

'Oh. Salim, I have to …' Katya started, but he was busy talking on the phone, and Dr Malik was too. Well, this was a crisis: she was as much in charge as anyone. She hurried downstairs as fast as her ankle would allow and opened the door. Lola's face appeared in the crack, tear-stained and pale.

'Please,' she said. 'They will kill me.'

Katya undid the bicycle lock and opened the door. Lola fell into her, shoulders racked with sobs. She was light as a bird.

'It's them,' is all she kept saying. 'It's the ones who killed my brother.'

Katya locked and chained the door behind her.

'It's okay. It's okay. You're safe now. I won't let anything happen to you.'

'The city is falling,' Lola said.

Katya put her arm around her and led her back through the museum.

'The whole city can't fall. The army's here.'

'No no no,' Lola kept saying, disconsolate. 'The city is falling. The army is leaving.'

Back on the roof, Salim was still talking on the phone. Katya looked for signs of trouble, any sign that what Lola said was true.

'Lola, see that hotel? That's where the generals are directing the battle. Salim's talking to them right now.'

Lola just sobbed and hid her face. Katya watched birds flying in front of the distant hotel windows, the sun reflected in its glass. Salim's voice rose and fell in concern. And then, all at once, every window in the hotel turned blank. Katya didn't understand what she was seeing. A ring of smoke mushroomed around the hotel, swallowed it, and Katya felt her breath catch. An expanding orb of shock washed over the treetops, the reeds, the antennae on the roofs like a sudden gale. When it reached them, Katya heard the boom, then a crack like splitting stone. Smoke and flames rose to engulf the building, pieces of debris spinning high into the air. Behind her, Salim stopped what he was saying into the phone.

'Hello?' he said. 'Hello?' He turned around, his eyes wandering to Katya. 'The line cut out.'

Then he saw Katya's face, and her finger pointing off into the distance to where the mountain of smoke over the river was turning black, flames and sparks leaping as if the earth had cracked and something was clawing its way out.

'The hotel,' she said. 'They blew up the hotel.'

Salim's face was white. Already the gunfire was getting closer.

Aurya

When Aurya woke up, it was the pale blue of early morning on
the riverbank. Dew had settled over everything, over her skin
and hair, in the webs that spiders had spun between the sleeping
soldiers. She could already smell the sun hitting the mud upwind,
but it was a sharper scent this far down the river. She blinked
awake and turned her head to where Sharo lay, but she saw with
a start that his mat was empty. She jumped up and looked around.
Everywhere she was surrounded by sleeping men, heads resting
on shields, the snores mixed with the morning birds, the crickets,
the river nearby. She saw the mud around Sharo's sleeping mat
was covered in drawings of lions. She scuffed them out with her
foot so no one would see. Where was he? She looked off into the
reeds that stretched out beyond the crumbling fort walls: nothing but birds taking flight in the morning, insects gathering in
clouds. She spotted movement in the brush far outside the walls,
but it was only a pair of deer nervous in the distance. Aurya
looked back to the boat, and that was where she saw him. Sharo
was standing up on deck with his back to her, beside the lion's
cage.

'Shamash,' she said and pulled her blanket around her, joints
aching in the cold. 'Smash his head.'

She picked her way through the sleeping bodies, past the silk
tent with the peacock man inside and the boy Abil sleeping across
the doorway like a dog.

'Sharo,' she hissed when she reached the gangplank, but he didn't turn around. She climbed up the groaning boards tracked with muddy footprints, steadying herself with her hands.

'Sharo!' she tried again. 'What are you doing?'

'Look, Aurya,' he said, and turned to her. 'He's going to lick my hand.'

Aurya saw that her brother's arm was inside the lion's cage, right up to his elbow. His fingers were stretched out. The animal, still wrapped in the ropes of its capture, was crouched. It was tense, its yellow eyes watching. Its tail flicked from side to side. The muscles in its hind legs twitched.

'Sharo! Take your arm out of there! I'm not joking!'

Sharo flinched a little at her voice and frowned.

'No, look, Aurya. It's friendly.'

She took a step closer, and the deck creaked. The lion let out a low, gurgling growl. Aurya took another step. The lion raised to its haunches and shook its mane. Then she ran forwards. She threw all her weight against Sharo so he stumbled back and let out a cry of surprise, his arm sliding free of the cage. At the same moment, the lion leapt. Aurya whimpered as it struck the cage side, snarling. Its jaws wrapped around the bars, full of teeth as long as her fingers, yellow as old bone. Its throat smelled like the cart of a meat seller who can't afford salt. The moment glazed, hard and polished as a stone, and then Aurya stumbled back, her heart in her throat. Her knees felt like reflections of knees in disturbed water. On the bank, men woke up everywhere at the lion's roar, reaching for their weapons. Guards burst from the King's tent, and shaved heads even emerged from below deck, accompanied by the rattling of chains.

'You made it angry,' Sharo said. 'It was going to lick my hand.'

'It … it wasn't, Sharo. It was going to bite your hand and tear your arm off. What did I tell you before? About hot soup?'

Sharo stuck out his jaw.

'He thought you were trying to hurt me.'

The silk tent on the bank bucked and bulged, and then spat out the peacock man with his robes disarranged.

'What's going on?' he shouted. His face blushed purple. 'What do you think you're doing up there? Sneaking around in the night like little thieves!'

'The lion is my friend,' Sharo shouted back to Aurya's surprise. 'His name is Enkidu. I don't care what any of you say.'

Aurya stared at him, felt all the strength in her legs disappear. She sat down with a thump on the edge of the boat. The crowd of armed men and labourers all stared for a moment. Then they shook their heads and exchanged murmurs.

'Grief does strange things to a person,' the peacock man said as he tramped up the gangplank, wiping his brow with his cap. 'But Shamash and Ashur, that boy is not normal.'

In its cage, the lion panted in huffs of steamy breath and circled, flicking its tail. Aurya listened to her own heartbeat still thudding like a fist on a door, and watched the men pack their things and undo the royal enclosure, their muddied hands moving without thought on the ropes and nails. One slave sang in his strange language as he worked.

Aurya watched the lion for some time, taking in the small scars that flecked its nose, its long curling tongue and whiskers that were shorter on one side. It looked back at her, and made a strange wheezy-whining sound as it did, followed by a huff of breath. She tried to see what Sharo saw in its eyes. She couldn't: only a kind of bored hunger in those yellow bulbs, emptiness in the dark slits at their centre. They made her think only of tearing cloth, of blood and hands grasping at its mane.

She sat there for some time, unsure if she would be able to walk, and watched Sharo as he trudged to the other side of the boat to sulk. She thought of the expression on his face as he'd kept his hand inside that cage, his chin jutting slightly forwards. It was only when half the camp was cleared and the fires of morning had begun to burn that Aurya noticed something beside the lion's cage. It was a pile of what looked like rice grains, in a brown patch on the deck's wood. She peered closer, unsure what she was seeing. Some of the rice grains were moving, and she realised all at once that they were maggots. She looked into the cage at the lion's foot, and saw that its wound had been cleaned. The fur around it was dark and matted. A pot of water sat nearby. She looked over at Sharo, who was hunched on the deck with his back to her, watching the birds gather in the morning sky.

––––––––––––

The King came out of his tent a little later, when the last of the camp was packed. He looked tired, but nothing like the frightened, bleeding man she'd glimpsed the night before.

'Fetch me beer, fetch me beer!' he boomed. 'The shapes in the oil are good this morning. Ashur is shining on this land and its King!'

Beneath the deck, slaves spat on their hands. Aurya now sat with Sharo among the cargo at the stern. She held on tight as each craft slid from the sandbar, and their waves rocked the fishing rafts and coracles of the early morning fishermen from villages nearby, the men swimming on inflated animal skins. She watched Sharo draw on the deck with his finger, making no mark but remembering the placement of each line, so that the picture emerged in his mind. She knew without looking that he would be drawing a lion.

Once the barges were back on the river and the peacock man had gone back to sleep, the boy Abil came and sat beside Aurya. He nodded to her, but didn't say anything, just sat there and looked out at the landscape passing by, the little villages and groves, all the reed-lined inlets.

'What did the King mean last night?' Aurya said. 'About his brother ... about the gods and their statues?'

Abil looked over his shoulder before answering. He fixed her with a hard look.

'Don't speak about those things here,' he said. 'You shouldn't have heard them.'

'I didn't mean to hear,' Aurya protested. 'I just ...'

'There was a great war,' Abil whispered. 'Between the King and his brother. Over who would rule the world. The King's brother is down there now, in the city of the dead. Or that's what the histories say.'

Aurya looked out over the ploughlands with their villages nestled in watercress and reeds.

'You know the histories?'

'Yes, of course. From the tablet house.'

'The tablet house ... What does it feel like, when you look at the marks on the tablets, and you turn them into words?'

'Reading? I don't know ... It's like hearing a voice in your head. Sometimes the voice of someone who's been dead for a long time.'

'Like speaking to a ghost,' Aurya said.

'Yes. When you say a word, it lives for a moment and then it's gone. But in the clay, it speaks for ever.'

Aurya nodded, not quite understanding. Abil looked at her, full of curiosity.

'We'll be in Nineveh by noon,' he said. 'How will you find your cousin when we get there?'

'Nineveh,' Aurya said, feeling the name run through her blood, full of every childhood dream. She looked at Abil, at his curly dark hair and innocent eyes, his young full face that had never known hunger. They were about the same age, she thought.

'We don't have a cousin in Nineveh. It was just something I made up.'

'Oh.' He bit his lower lip, his eyes wandering down to the deck. 'What are you going to do when you get there?'

'I'm going to find my mother. She was from the city once, and I think she might still be there.'

'Finding one person in the whole of Nineveh could take a lifetime. Maybe your brother ... if he really remembers everything, maybe he knows something that will help you find her.'

Aurya glanced at Sharo, still sulking nearby.

'That's the one thing he can't remember. The day she died. Or the day she left. I don't know which. But if the gods will it, anything can happen.'

'I hope you find her,' Abil said.

'Have you ever heard of a place called the house of dust?' Aurya asked. Abil licked his lips.

'There are lots of names of places like that in the city: the house of women, the house of singers, the house of weapons. But I've never heard of that place.'

Soon he had to take water to the slaves below deck. Aurya sat alone and watched the dusty land pass by, the palms wearing their brown beards of dead leaves. She imagined what it would be like to live in every town they passed, to know that wall broken by the roots of an olive tree; to grow up in the shade of that palm and see those hills in the distance every day. There were so many people in the world, she thought. So many lives. More than she'd ever imagined.

She looked over at Sharo still brooding among the cargo, and saw that he was holding his head in his hands and covering his eyes. She went and put a hand on his shoulder. He'd scratched the image of a lion into the deck with a shard of pot.

'Sharo, don't do that.' She looked around to see if anyone had seen.

'There's too much to see, Aurya,' he mumbled. 'You know how it hurts.'

'I know. I always thought I could walk the whole length of the world in a couple of weeks, from the Bitter River and back. But look at it all … It would take months. Maybe years.'

Sharo clutched one hand to his skull, but went on scratching his drawing into the deck. It was very lifelike, Aurya thought. She could see his fingertips turning white as he gripped the potsherd.

'The story,' she said, and reached down to gently take the piece of clay from him. 'You could tell me more of that story. Remember? Where were you?'

Sharo sniffed. But he nodded.

The demon Humbaba burst from the forest: the tearing claws of a lion, the fangs of a dragon, the tail of a serpent.

The King and the wild man fought, but neither could land a blow.

Around the clearing, the trees fell, and Humbaba screamed with rage and struck at them harder.

'Shamash, great sun god,' the King said, 'please help us.'

Shamash answered. He brought the winds to fight the monster: the north wind and the south wind, the cold wind and the biting wind, the rain wind and the hill wind.

The winds held the monster down. They tied up his limbs.

All around the clearing, the cedars crashed down. And then the monster opened its mouth and begged for mercy.

'Please, O King,' it gurgled. 'Take what you want from my forest. But let me live!'

'I don't think I like this story any more,' Aurya said. 'What kind of monster begs for mercy? Now I just feel sorry for it.'

Sharo put both his hands in his hair.

'I always feel sorry for everyone in the stories. I want to warn them what's coming.'

Aurya watched the birds circling over the boats, the high clouds.

'Sharo, do you remember anything that might help us? Anything about this house of dust?'

His eyes wavered a little.

'I don't know.'

'It must be in the great city,' Aurya went on. 'That's what Abil told me. Don't you think, Sharo? It sounds so grand. But if you could remember anything, Sharo. If anything came to you that might help us find it, you would tell me, wouldn't you?'

Sharo shook his head.

'Aurya. We'll never find it.'

'What? Sharo, what do you know?'

'There's no house of dust, Aurya,' he said, and clutched at his head.

Aurya reached out and put her hand in his hair.

'Sharo, please – if you know anything about what happened that day, you have to tell me.'

'I can't, Aurya.'

A shadow passed over them. Aurya turned to see the peacock man standing in the way of the sun.

'You two,' he said. 'The King would like to speak with you.'

'The King?'

'Yes.'

Aurya looked at Sharo, and they both stood up. The peacock man led them to the prow and waited with the boat as they drew

140

up alongside the royal barge, and men on either craft threw ropes to one another. Aurya couldn't find any clues in the man's face about what was going to happen. Then she realised with a cold certainty what it was: Nebo-Pishtim's news had travelled downriver, fast as the summer insects. Aurya looked back at Sharo. She knew if he was asked, he wouldn't be able to lie. Would he understand enough to keep quiet, at least?

'Sharo,' she hissed, 'don't say anything. Let me speak.'

He nodded, but his memory-pain was still hurting him, and she didn't know if he'd taken it in. When the boats got close enough, the men threw down planks, and the peacock man led them across. Aurya stepped up on to the beams, and looked down to see the two vessels' oars clattering beneath her in the frothing green water. Soldiers stood everywhere on the King's barge. Ahead, the plum-pink awning shifted in the breeze. Aurya had never even met the headman of her village, Nebo-Pishtim's father, who, when the villages gathered, wasn't important enough to sit near the head. Beyond that canopy, the King of the World waited to question her.

'Just a word of warning,' the peacock man said, before they stepped inside. 'The King hears the voices of the gods. If you lie to him, he'll know.'

Aurya barely had time to gulp for air before he swept them into the tent. It was gloomy, an underwater light, and the King was sitting slouched sideways on a wooden throne, drinking from a glittering cup. The incense inside made Aurya cough. She took a step forwards, and noticed that the throne's feet were carved to look like lion claws.

'Ah, the river children,' the King said. 'The brother and sister.'

His voice was deep but dreamlike. Aurya heard the commonness of her own speech when it came out.

'Your majesty ...' she managed, her voice crackling like dry garlic skins. She didn't know any of the proper benedictions. The King took a sip from his cup and leaned forwards. As he did, Aurya saw with a shock that the liquid inside was a deep red. She thought of the lion, and the blood painting its muzzle. She thought she was going to be sick.

'What a funny thing, to find you two there on the riverbank. With that lion. Such a tragedy you have suffered, the death of your father. Isn't that right?'

Aurya nodded, unable to say anything. If she lied, would the gods tell the King silently, whispering in his ear? Or would they bellow from the shadows, so all could hear?

'My father died of disease,' the King said. 'He went yellow one day and wasted away. But my grandfather was murdered. It was a terrible thing. Murdered by those he trusted most.'

He took another sip from his cup, and his eyes passed from Aurya to Sharo.

'You – you love each other, don't you? You, boy – you love your sister?'

She saw Sharo nod beside her, and step closer to her.

'And you, girl – you love your brother, don't you? You would do anything to protect him.'

'Yes,' Aurya managed. The King gave out a long sigh, and drummed his fingers against his cheekbone.

'I had a brother once,' he said, and then sat back heavily in his chair, massaged his brow. 'Until not so long ago. It's a beautiful thing, to have a sibling. You'll never be alone, you know, if you look after each other. And protect each other.'

Aurya felt the King's large eyes on her. For a moment, they looked tired. She felt behind her for Sharo's hand. The King seemed to dream off for a second, and then his eyes wheeled back to the two children.

'Your brother,' he said, 'I have heard he has some special abilities. Is that right?'

Aurya nodded. How did the King know? She had only told the servant boy Abil, and she felt a sting of betrayal.

'Yes, your greatness.'

'A prodigious memory, my servant tells me.'

'Yes, lord.'

'Well, let's see it then,' the King said, leaning forwards. 'How does it work?'

Aurya looked at Sharo. His face was pale. For a moment, she was at a loss about what to ask him.

'Sharo, how many days did it rain last month?' He looked at her with mute desperation. 'It's all right, Sharo. You can speak now.'

'Twenty-one days,' Sharo said, without a pause.

'Twenty-one …' the King said, and waved to one of his guards. 'Go check on that with Bel-Ibni. He's always writing these things down.'

'It will be correct, my lord,' said Aurya. 'My lord, tell me a date that you'll never forget. Sharo can tell you where the stars were on that day. And the weather.'

'Impossible!' the King said.

'Try it,' Aurya said.

'The … let me see … the eighteenth of Tibbakh, three years ago.'

'The bull and the lion rose in the east,' Sharo said. 'The goddess on two lions crested the horizon to the south, with the scorpion high overhead.'

The King looked at Sharo with a long, hard look, his eyes far away.

'That was the night my brother died,' he said. He kept very still. 'It's a great gift you have, boy.'

Sharo shuffled his feet.

'I don't want to remember any of it,' Sharo said. 'But I do. The bark of every tree I've ever seen. The lichen on the stones, or the burnt marks on a piece of bread. It all just sticks, like it's carved into my head.'

The King's eyes stayed fixed on Sharo, and he nodded absently, pressing one of his knuckles into his lower lip.

'Fascinating. Thank you, children.' The peacock man stepped inside and put an arm around Aurya and Sharo.

'That will be all for now, children. The King has much to do.'

Aurya felt the King's watery eyes on her as they left. She expected him to shout after them, to call them back. But he didn't. They stepped out into the sunshine and the breeze, and the world felt new again like it did after rain.

'Aurya, why did the King want to know those things?' Sharo said.

'I don't know, Sharo.'

They crossed back to their ship, although Aurya's legs threatened to give way as she passed over the water. She glanced at the boy Abil, who was sorting through a pile of tablets. A burst of anger lit her from inside, and she went to him.

'You told them,' she said, the heat of accusation in her voice. 'You told them about Sharo.'

The boy looked up, mouth slightly open.

'It will help you,' he said, under his breath. 'If the King thinks you're special. You'll see.'

Aurya felt her face flush.

'You didn't have any right. You don't know what we've ...'

'You have to be careful,' Abil said, and motioned at the peacock man's stooped back. 'Master Bel-Ibni is in a dark mood, and he hates these journeys. He hates the flies, and the rocking boat. Even the dust in the workshop at Nineveh irritates his throat.'

'Dust?' Aurya said. 'In the workshop?'

'Yes.'

'There's a lot of dust there?'

'Of course. You can't chisel through stone without making dust. It gets everywhere ...'

Aurya's heart thudded. She was going to ask more, but the clang of the iron bell cut her off. Someone shouted out something that she didn't understand at first.

'Nineveh ahead!'

Aurya stood up and craned her neck in the direction the man was pointing. On the horizon downriver, a band of gold stretched out from the riverbank. It looked like a piece of jewellery dropped on the grassy plain. The slave drum beat a little faster at the call, and the lion in its cage gave a sonorous yawn. The great city lay ahead. At first, Aurya thought that Nineveh's city wall must be twice or even three times the size of a man, but closer up, with a growing fear and excitement, she saw that it was taller than the trees. Boats of every kind crowded the water, and the river sweated oils and broken things.

'It doesn't smell like I imagined,' she said.

'It's the biggest city in the world. What did you imagine it would smell like?'

'I don't know.'

The smell only got worse as evil spirits wafted over the ship, and the buildings began to crowd in on every side, the river hollows bursting with reeds. Bird droppings streaked the walls and ramparts; a nest of storks in one broken tower.

'Why did they build the city with that mountain inside?' Aurya asked, pointing to the sharp point at the city's heart. Abil laughed.

'That's not a mountain, river girl. It's the ziggurat. That's where the god Nabu lives, up there in its highest chamber.'

'People built that?'

'Yes, long ago.'

Gardens growing on the ziggurat's side spilled plants down its sides, and a flight of birds were white specks against its slopes. Heavy bells sounded. All around them, boats and rafts of all kinds bumped prows, and were piled with reeds and urns, baskets of grain; pepper and dried fishes; nets bulging with crab and river fish. The peacock man woke up as they bumped into a smaller craft, rocking them slightly, and he summoned Abil to him with a snap of his fingers. The boy gave Aurya an apologetic look and hurried off to his master. Sharo had found a piece of charcoal and was frantically drawing lions all over the bulwark.

'Stop that, Sharo!' Aurya said, and rubbed out his drawings with her foot. Everyone seemed too busy to notice.

'Aurya, it hurts,' Sharo moaned.

'Take a deep breath. Look down into the water.'

Dried beans and fish skeletons floated on the surface, and pieces of broken pots hid among the mud and weeds. The smell was even worse than before. They moored in the shadow of a huge gatehouse, thumping against the quay with a noise like a drum, and Aurya stumbled as the deck jerked beneath her. The lion in its cage gave out a frightened roar, and gnawed at one of its bars, whining.

'Aurya, who built all this?' Sharo said. He looked pale as ash.

'Giants,' Aurya said, looking up at the wall. The gate was tall and made of reddish wood, bound with gleaming bands. It made her think of the cedar trees in Sharo's story, of monsters and dreams. Flies filled the dock air, with the smell of smoke and cured meat, stagnant water, urine and fish. More spear-men and slaves were there to meet them, and trumpeters with curved horns for instruments, men striking metal bowls.

'Nineveh,' the peacock man said to Aurya, although his pride didn't allow him to look at her directly. 'It's the King's wish that we help you to find your relatives. So where are they? In the south districts no doubt.'

Behind him, a group of slaves bumped one stone slab against a mooring stone, and he wheeled around to shout at them. Aurya's mind raced.

'Aurya,' Sharo said. 'I want to stay with him.'

'Stay with who?' Then she realised that he meant the lion. At that moment, it was struggling in its cage and flicking its tail as the slaves lifted the cage on its poles.

'Sharo, you can't go with that thing.'

'His name is Enkidu,' Sharo said, sticking out his bottom jaw. Aurya looked around at the men scraping fish with knives in the stoops of shacks, the cats and beggars eating the scales straight from the road. Behind her, Abil touched Aurya on the shoulder.

'River girl,' he whispered. 'If you want to go to the workshop, you should ask now.'

Behind them, the King's barge docked and tethered, and the awning came down. Inside, the King sat on a throne carried by six men.

'The incomparable city!' he boomed. 'What a delight it always is to come home.'

The calves of the men carrying him quivered as they stepped down the gangplank, and another slave scattered a bag of sand beneath their feet for grip. Aurya tugged on Sharo's clothes.

'Sharo, we have to follow them. We have to go to this workshop.'

'Yes, Aurya, we have to follow Enkidu, or else –'

'No, Sharo – I think this could be the house of dust, the place father talked about.'

Sharo looked at her again with his big glassy eyes. He seemed to be thinking hard. With a quiver, he nodded. Aurya made a few quick prayers:

To the god of lost children
To the god of cities
To the god of flies

The peacock man stopped admonishing the slaves and turned back to her.

'We want to go to the workshop with you,' she said. The man narrowed his eyes. Up on his high seat, to Aurya's surprise, the King gave a great hoot.

'Ordered around by a little river girl!' he wheezed. 'How you have fallen in life, Bel-Ibni!'

The peacock man let out a high-pitched laugh full of falsity.

'My lord, surely you don't want me to ...'

'Bring them along, Bel-Ibni. I have a plan for them!'

'Shamash and Ashur,' the peacock man hissed at Aurya. 'Follow along then, and don't cause any more trouble.'

Katya

Katya and Salim watched men arrive in two Toyota pickup trucks. They wore khakis and herringbone vests, balaclavas and bandanas over their mouths, carrying guns and shoulder-mounted artillery. From the back of one vehicle, a black flag flew.

'Stay down,' Salim hissed to Katya. He was holding the old Kalashnikov they'd found in the museum staffroom, looking as if he'd never held one before. Down the museum approach, one man, who had a white skull design on his balaclava, rattled on the museum door handle, then thumped with the butt of his rifle.

'They're thieves,' Dr Malik said from behind them. 'The hordes of Genghis Khan. They want to loot the museum.'

Katya glanced around at the doctor, at Lola. Everyone was looking at one another to see how scared they should be. Down on the street, the men were rooting around in the front seat of one truck, and brought out a pair of long-handled bolt cutters.

'Shit shit shit,' Salim said, his fingers white on the balustrade. Katya felt it then: the worst thing she could possibly feel in that moment. The aura. Another seizure. She raised her hands out in front of her; they felt light, like two balloons. And hadn't it all happened like this before, with the smoke wisping over the rooftop, the smell of sulphur, the helicopters and trucks, the running feet? Hadn't she even thought these same thoughts before? Below, the skull man bellowed something.

'He says to open the door,' Salim said, his lips going grey. 'He says the museum's contents are forbidden.'

'What are they going to do?' Katya said, hearing her own voice from far away.

'Steal it all.'

'And what will they do with us?'

Salim's fingers tightened on the black metal rifle. In the fairway below, the bolt cutters sheared together, and the heavy bicycle chain hit the stone. Katya looked from face to pale face, and a voice in her head spoke up, clear as if whispered right in her ear. *Don't hide, Katya.* She stood up.

'What are you doing?' Salim hissed again. 'Get down!'

'I'm going down to meet them,' she said, watching herself as if from a great height. Before anyone could say anything, she was running down into the cool stairwell, with Salim shouting her name behind her. It was cool and shaded in the museum halls, and strangely calm. The noise of battle outside was muffled as if through earth, and the statues cast long shadows across the floor. Somewhere below, there were the sounds of hurried footsteps and rough commands. Katya crept down on to the mezzanine overlooking the entrance hall. She tried to blink away the feeling in her head and peered over.

The fighters were inside: they were dashing off down the museum halls, into the Assyrian section, the Islamic section, the Hatra Gallery. A man with round glasses and a folded notebook in his hand seemed to be directing them. In the hall behind her, Katya heard footsteps. It was Salim, ducking low, rifle in hand. He put his back against the mezzanine wall beside her, breathing hard.

'What are you going to do?' he said.

'I don't know. Just walk down there. Distract them. Maybe Lola and the doctor can get away.'

'To where?'

She shook her head.

'Maybe they can hide. Get away at night.'

Salim took a long breath, and she could feel him shaking beside her.

'Let's do it then.' His pupils were the size of coins. 'We're fucked either way. Let's do it together.'

Katya shook. She reached out, and Salim took her hand. They stood up and walked down the stairs together. One man in the hallway, the one with the skull on his balaclava, saw them. He shouted and let off two shots into the roof. Katya had never heard a gun go off so close: it made her whole body jump, as if someone had hit a table with a hammer while her head lay against it. Beside her, Salim held the Kalashnikov over his head and called out something. Men rushed at them and snatched his weapon away, checked their pockets and their waistbands. Katya smelt aftershave and petrol from them, felt the anger in their hands. They found her pill bottle, and rattled it in front of her. She knew it would be useless to protest, and they took it. Salim kept trying to say something to them, but they ignored him.

'What are you saying?'

'I'm saying that the army will come back. That they can give themselves up now.'

'I don't think they'll like that.'

Salim shook his head and said it again. One man butted Salim hard in the stomach with his rifle, so he wheezed and doubled over. The skull man gestured at Katya. The eye holes of his balaclava were ragged, as though burned through the fabric by the smokeless coals of his eyes. He pulled back Salim's head by the hair.

'Amreeki? Amreeki?' he growled.

Salim shook his head, his voice coming out in little sighs.

'Britanii,' he murmured.

'British,' Katya said. 'UK.'

One of the armed men, the one with the glasses who had been directing the looting with his notebook, pointed it at her.

'Where exactly?' he said. Katya reeled. He had a London accent. She looked over the thin features of his young face, the dark rings under his eyes, a tufty beard and a close-shaved head.

'Coventry.'

The word put a sudden flash on her tongue: moss and purple beech trees, leaves plastered on wet roads and the bricks of terraced houses. He shook his head slowly.

'You're in the wrong place now.'

'I know,' she said. 'Thanks.'

The English man kept his eyes on her as more gunmen filled the museum. He checked his notes and shouted more orders to his men, who filed into the galleries and past Salim and Katya up the stairs. *Please don't find the others*, Katya prayed. She could hear the smashing of glass, and an alarm went off briefly before a crackle of loud shots silenced it. Salim was still doubled over.

'It's just you in here?' the English man with the glasses said.

'Yes. Just us two.'

'You've been practising idolatry,' he said, gesturing around at the museum, at the winged bull guardians in the hallway. 'Worshipping these old gods.'

'No –' But the men grabbed her and Salim before she could say anything more and dragged them both beneath one of the displays. She glanced up at the implacable face of an ancient king. Men carried things away: small cuneiform tablets, pieces of jewellery, the cylinder seals on display. Then Katya heard the shouting of many voices from the mezzanine, and the booming voice of Dr Malik.

'Take your hands off me,' he kept saying. Men with rifles herded the doctor and Lola down the stairs. Lola's face was set in flint, and she struggled and shrugged off the men's grips every time they took hold of her.

'They found them,' Katya said. Salim's fingers tightened into fists.

'It was a bad idea lying to us,' the English man said.

'Thieves and brigands!' Dr Malik was shouting as he was dragged to the bottom of the stairs. 'Bandits!'

As they came down the stairs, Lola swung out a fist that struck the cap off the head of one soldier. The man let go of her wrist, and she ran over to Katya and Salim, her eyes desperate. The skull man pointed at Lola and muttered something that made the girl's muscles tense. Beside her, Salim groaned.

'What did he say?' Katya whispered.

'He said this one is a devil-worshipper. They're going to shoot us all.'

Katya felt the world fall away around her. The men with guns clubbed the bellowing Dr Malik, and drove him towards the door. Another two soldiers grabbed Lola and ripped her from Katya's arms as the girl screamed. Watching this scene unfold, Katya felt fury and desperation explode in her chest. The universe contracted: at its exact geometrical centre was that room, and the statue of the king that stood, hands clasped, above her. The idea came to her in an unexpected flash. She set both hands against that statue. Some of the men turned to look at her. Then she heaved. The statue moved easily, teetered past the point of balance and fell. The moment lasted for ever. Nobody moved. Every eye in the room fixed on her – on the falling statue as it toppled through its arc and hit the floor. It smashed into white-powdered fragments. The head snapped off, and the body split open. The room exploded with noise. The man with the skull mask rushed at Katya and grabbed her by the throat, pinned her against the wall. His rough-skinned fingers closed on her neck.

'How dare you destroy our property?' the English man yelled from across the hall.

'Look,' she croaked, pointing at the smashed statue. 'It's just plaster. A reproduction. A fake. Half of the stuff you're stealing is just plaster.'

The skull man tightened his grip on her throat, and her eyes bulged. She pawed at his arms, trying to loosen his grip. He was too strong, his eyes burning beneath his mask. As the thunder of her heartbeat rose in her head, she heard words passed back and forth between him and the English man. Then the grip on her throat lessened. Air poured back into her lungs, welcome and cool. She pushed his arm away; to her surprise, he let go, and she fell to the ground, gasped for air, coughed and massaged her throat. Guns were pointed at her from every direction. Even Dr Malik stopped his bellowing, as three soldiers held his massive frame against one of the bull guardians.

'You'll tell us which ones are real,' the English man said blankly. 'Or you'll die along with the rest.'

Katya allowed the silence to stretch out, gathering her words like scattered beads.

'I'll trade,' she said.

'Trade?'

'Yes.' She gestured at Salim, Dr Malik and Lola. 'Their lives for the stones.'

The skull man looked at her with a sneer she could see even through his mask, and turned away. But the English man shrugged.

'Their lives for the stones,' he said, and fixed Katya with cold eyes. 'I have a list. We'll come back tomorrow morning, and you better show us something good.'

'Don't give these animals a thing!' Dr Malik boomed, his arms still pinioned by the three men with guns. 'You jackals, you thieves.'

The skull man glanced lazily at the doctor and muttered a word. On the floor, Salim gasped.

'You sicken me, you animals,' the doctor was shouting. 'Iraq will outlive you. On the day of judgement, the waters will wash the earth clean of you!'

Katya covered her eyes before the gunshots sounded, but each one still pounded through her, made her skin jump on her bones. Dr Malik's voice became hoarse and then stopped. Katya's ears went 'eeeeeeee', a reverberating tone like struck crystal, and as it faded, the sound merged with the screams of Lola and Salim beside her. She kept her eyes covered while they dragged the doctor away, taking all three men to do it. When she opened them, she saw a streak of red-brown on the floor. She slumped back against the wall. The English man with the glasses watched her.

'I'll be back tomorrow,' he said. Then he gestured to Salim, still hunched over and groaning beside the statue's shattered remains. 'And tell your friend: the army isn't coming back. They're fleeing south and leaving their uniforms by the road. We are the lions of Mosul. A spark has been lit in Iraq, and the fire will burn until it covers the whole earth.'

The English man turned and gestured to his men, who tied the hands of Salim and Lola. They came towards Katya too. And all of this – the dust in the air, the men with their weapons, the people sobbing – hadn't this all happened before?

When Katya came to, it was evening. She could hear the wind hitting the windows. She wasn't in the entrance hall any more. She tried to lift herself, and found her skin come alive with bruises. She lifted up on her elbows, and saw she was back in the office room in the upper floor, lying on the mattress with the red glow of the auxiliary lighting making an eerie dreamworld of everything. Salim sat on the mattress edge, still hunched over and deathly pale. Katya's throat burned when she tried to speak, and she remembered the man who had choked her. It felt as if she'd swallowed a ball of sandpaper.

'Salim,' she said, and he jumped when she spoke.

'Oh, thank God. You're all right.'

'Where's Lola?'

'The girl? She's fine, she's sleeping next door. Katya, what happened to you?' She shook her head and massaged her throat. 'You were completely out of it,' Salim went on. 'Like you fainted. But your eyes were open.'

She cradled her head for a moment, felt the weight of her skull, all its contours and fissures. And what did it matter now? What was he going to do, send her home?

'It's epilepsy. In my temporal lobe. It's happened since I was a kid. Since my dad disappeared.'

Salim turned to look at her. He had a sticky patch of congealed blood on his forehead, tidemarks of dust and sweat across his face.

'You should have told me. How often does this happen?'

'Hardly ever. Maybe once or twice a year. But since I got here, it's been happening more and more. It gets triggered by stress, lack of sleep, dehydration …'

'None of that here, then.'

'I have pills,' she said. 'Or at least I did. I take them every day. But I've had two seizures now in the last few days. That's never happened before.'

'When you crashed the car.' He looked at her, and she nodded. 'God. You could have died.'

'The temporal lobe controls memory, so I get this feeling of déjà vu every time it happens. Like I've been somewhere before, like time is folding over itself. Usually I have a lot of warning.'

He put a hand on her foot. She could feel its warmth through her socks, and his skin touched hers where she'd worn a hole in the heel.

'What happened?' she said. 'With those men.'

'They took our passports. They searched everything, tipped out all our bags, went through all the cupboards. They had me and Lola tied up, but they seemed nervous about what to do with you. Your head was rolling around on your shoulders, and these guys … they're superstitious. You scared them. But that English one seems a bit softer than the others. A bit younger at least. The others wanted to split us up, lock us in separate rooms. But he told them to leave us.'

'Why?'

'I don't know.'

'And they took everything?' Katya breathed. Salim shook his head.

'I managed to save these.'

He pulled out both of their antique mobile phones and handed over hers like a precious bounty. She turned on the screen.

'No signal.'

'Yeah. It must be down for the whole province. Maybe the whole country. No Internet either, though they took the computers anyway. They took the chargers too, so we'd better save the batteries. I can duct-tape them to the underside of the desk.'

Katya handed back her phone, and he took it. The screech of the duct tape unfurling made her jump.

'I'm so sorry about the doctor,' Katya said.

'I can't believe they'd do that.' Salim sniffed, and massaged his forehead. 'Those monsters. He was one of the best men I ever knew.'

'He was like something from a myth. Larger than life.'

Salim nodded. 'I know what his heaven will look like.'

'Full of bridges.' A sob moved between them like an electric current passing from one body to the other.

'So now we're going to help the monsters who killed him,' Salim said quietly. 'We're going to sell his life's work.'

'We don't have a choice ...' she began.

Salim shook his head.

'They'll take that stuff and sell it, you know. Thirty, forty thousand for just one of those little tablets. They'll smuggle them to Europe and use the money to buy more weapons. Each one will make them stronger.'

'This can't go on for ever. And the pieces they want ... the ones on their list. They'll all have been catalogued, recorded. It's the other pieces we have to protect, the ones that haven't been studied yet. Salim, if we help them find some things, maybe we can protect others. Maybe we can buy enough time ...'

He looked at her with pain in his eyes.

'Katya, you don't know who you're dealing with.'

'Who are they? What do they want?'

'If it's who I think, then we're in a lot of trouble. Real end-of-days types. They want to put a torch to the world.'

In the dim red of the auxiliary lighting, Katya looked through the door to the carvings of the hunted lions, the stretched claws, the muzzles pulled back over their teeth.

'What about the carving?' she said. 'The one out there.'

Salim shook his head.

'We have to keep it secret. If it fell into these guys' hands ...'

'I won't tell anyone.'

Salim sighed and looked away.

'This is the luck I've come to know,' he said. 'The greatest find of my life one day, imprisoned by madmen the next. Who's the girl? Lola, did you say?'

'Oh, you remember her? Her family's shop burned down. Her brother was killed.'

'Oh.' Salim let out a long breath. 'I remember. You nearly got us all killed, you know. Letting her in here. These guys despise Yazidis. They think they're heretics. Worshippers of the devil.'

'They would have killed her if she stayed outside.'

'Or worse. Do you trust her?'

'I don't know for sure, but so far I think so.'

Salim squeezed her foot in a way that made a tingle in her stomach. He got up in one laboured movement and turned to leave.

'Well, you're going to have to deliver on your promise to these guys tomorrow,' he said. 'You're our ambassador to lunacy now.'

She nodded and felt cold, wrapping her arms around her shoulders.

'Katya,' he said. 'Be very careful. Please. Don't be fooled into thinking you can reason with them. And don't try to be clever.'

She held his gaze for a moment and felt the urge to reach out her hand to him. She looked away though, and he turned to leave. She listened to the squeak of his shoes as he went, to the soft sound of sobbing echoing somewhere in the halls.

Sleep didn't come. Katya lay for a while, feeling her fear wash over her in waves. All at once, the thought of her mother hit her like a car. Memories from ten years before, of her mum crouched before the television in the days and weeks after they got the news, her face contoured in its coloured light.

'Please be careful,' she'd said to Katya at the airport. When Katya hugged her, she'd felt how little she weighed, hollow bones like a bird. She'd promised she would come home.

'That's what he always said too,' her mum replied. 'Katya … I don't want to lose you to that place. Please. Please be careful.'

Katya hit her skull with the heel of her hand, ran her nails over her scalp.

'Idiot,' she gasped, and sobbed. She tried to find the quiet place inside her, but it wasn't where she had left it. She sniffed, got up and followed her feet through the hall. Salim was lying in his room. A mat was left out for Lola too, but there was no sign of her. Katya went out on to the roof, and jumped seeing a figure standing there, leaning against the balustrade.

'Oh, god, Lola, you scared me.'

The girl pulled a mock-frightening look. She wasn't wearing her abaya, and she was smoking a thin cigarette.

'I am very scary,' she said.

'I didn't know you smoked.'

'No,' the girl said, and drew on her cigarette so the ember crackled. 'Not always. Coughing too much.'

Katya leant on the ledge with Lola and glanced over the side. Guards with weapons walked up and down outside, pickups mounted with large guns were parked on the street corners. She tried not to think of the images that still haunted her from her childhood, the ones she'd searched for in moments of darkness: stills from grainy videos, masked men with swords, pale men kneeling. She thought of the man who wore the skull mask, the shining coals of his eyes.

'Lola, what do you know about those men?'

The girl shook her head. She leant over the balustrade too, and let out a long breath of smoke.

'No one knows much. But they are the ones we are afraid of. They want to kill Yazidis. They want to kill Shia and Christians. I think they are the ones who killed my brother.'

'They called you a devil-worshipper ...'

Lola tugged on the red-and-white thread around her wrist.

'Yes, I am Yazidi. In our church, they teach that God created the world, and made the angel Melek Taus its king. He is the peacock angel. People think our Melek Taus is a devil. They see the black snakes on the doors of our shrines too. They are afraid of us.'

Lola made her fingers into the shape of a gun, closed one eye and pointed it at one of the strolling guards below. Cigarette smoke ribboned her hand. She made a popping sound with her mouth.

'Can you shoot?' Katya asked.

'Yes. My brother taught me. He always thought there was danger for Yazidis. He taught me to fight.'

Katya reached out and took her hand.

'I'm sorry you're caught up in all this, Lola.'

'Yes, I am sorry too,' the girl said, and coughed. She offered the cigarette to Katya. 'Thank you. For letting me in. I would be dead, out there.'

Katya took a drag that tasted of burnt coffee grounds and handed it back.

'We'll look after each other. I promise.'

Katya watched the movements of the armed men on the road below, and when Lola finished her cigarette, Katya followed her down into the museum. As Katya lay in her room and tried to sleep, she remembered the words from the risk assessment form she'd filled out months ago, that practical, numbered advice. She rifled through her drawers for some time until she found it, crumpled and buried in the files.

'In case of kidnapping, follow these four rules,' she read aloud, feeling the solace of her own voice, in the firm and rational advice. 'One: Befriend your captors.' She thought of the English man, his voice hard as he'd threatened to cut their throats. Something to work on there. 'Two: Be prepared for a long stay.' No choice there. 'Three: Don't show weakness.' She puffed air out of her cheeks and rubbed her eyes. 'Four: Look for a chance to escape, and take it if you can.'

She whispered the lines to herself over and over, an incantation against the night. When she finally lay down, she fell asleep fully clothed with her hands tucked into her sleeves. She felt a strange tow, as though the night around her were the water of a great river pulling her down its winding course.

Aurya

Aurya watched as the boats of the King's flotilla landed one by one at the dock. Out of each one, the slaves drew a slab of stone bound to a sledge, just like the one they'd come with, until there were around a dozen lined up on the quay. With a shout from their handler, the ropes strained and the slaves dragged the stones all together through the towering gatehouse, and through the streets of Nineveh in a long line. They churned troughs in the roads and dislodged cobbles. The King, carried on his high seat, followed behind. Aurya and Sharo were caught up in the groups of soldiers and servants, clattering, fanning, all sweating and shouting and beating drums and clanging bells. The air was hot, with the smell of mud and cheese and baking peat. Through the gatehouse, Aurya saw pigs and dogs on the street. People pressed against the sides of buildings to let the procession of stones pass by, and many fell to their knees when they saw the King. People on rooftops whistled and cheered, called out, 'Praise King Ashurbanipal!' Others wandered as close as they dared to the lion in its cage, which looked more frightened than ever, letting out pitiable whines, its eyes wide and yellow. Everywhere the bright clothes and headdresses, the women's veils, the shop awnings, flashed bright against the baked brick and whitewashed walls.

The whole way, all Aurya could think about was the house of dust. Could this really be it? And might someone there remember something about her mother? They rose up a slight hill, and the ropes tied to the sledges of stone creaked like tall trees in the wind. Men poured jugs of water over the ropes when they began to smoke. Aurya kept glancing up at the rooftops and their gardens, at the bright clothes laid out to dry. It didn't smell so foul further from the river.

'Nineveh,' she kept muttering to herself, still unable to believe it. She looked at Sharo, and saw he was clutching his head again.

'Close your eyes, Sharo,' she said, touching his arm. 'Hold on to my arm and close your eyes.'

As the rise flattened out, a strange kind of birdsong filled the air, a cheeping like the nest of fledglings Aurya had once found in the crook of a tamarisk tree. She didn't have time to dwell on it: as the King's men marched, thin children hurried from the alleys to beg from them. One girl came up to Aurya and spoke to her in a language she didn't understand, gesturing at her mouth, making a sign for food. They were roughly the same age. A soldier pulled the girl away and sent her off with a kick.

Before long, an enormous pillared building came into view, fronted with cracked blue tiles and poplar trees sprouting nearby. A poorer house sat in its shadow, like an old man leaning on a son's shoulder. When they got closer, Aurya saw that it wasn't birdsong she'd heard. The noise was coming from the crumbling house's courtyard, where half a dozen men with cloths wrapped around their heads worked beneath an awning of woven palm leaves. They were chipping at blocks of stone with tools and mallets, giving off that soft cheeping chorus. The dust from their work curled in the air. A skinny man hurried from the building and down the steps, tufts of beard growing at irregular angles from his chin and cheeks. His eyes were bloodshot, watery and red-rimmed.

'My King!' he shouted, and gave a hacking cough. 'My sun! All the gods of the world bless you! I am the dust beneath your feet. What an honour, a great honour as always, to have you bring the stone in person …'

The King on his high seat waved the honours away.

'How are the preparations for the garden scene coming?' the King said. 'No more problems I trust?'

'Excellent, my lord. The apprentices can take their first impressions tomorrow, if my lord will allow it.'

The King nodded.

'That's what the signs demand. Come to the palace early, before the heat rises.'

'Of course, my lord. You are the sun that warms us, the cedar that shades us. And I have reminded the apprentices how important it is to you, that the details are absolutely correct, that no ...'

'Very well!' the King boomed. 'Shamash and Ashur, I've been on the river for weeks! Mason, we have these two children here, from the hills. Their father was killed by this lion, and you are to look after them.'

'My lord,' the skinny master mason began, 'we really have no need for –'

'The King didn't ask what you needed, mason!' the peacock man snapped.

'Keep them here for a week or two,' the King said, waving his hand. 'If they're lazy or eat too much, send them to the streets.'

The master mason's sore eyes washed bitterly over Aurya and Sharo. He gave another cough, and his shoulders sagged a little.

'Yes, my lord. They can sweep for us. The dust here has a will of its own.'

The other masons gathered around the blocks of stone, smoothing hands over the surfaces, muttering in approval. Aurya looked over the crowd, her heart beating heavily in her chest, hoping to see a shock of curly hair just like her own among the apprentices. She didn't see anyone, though. She noticed how their eyes were all that same reddish colour, how they rubbed them with the backs of their sleeves.

'Come on, Bel-Ibni,' the King announced with a sigh, 'I believe we're meeting a Hittite delegation this afternoon.'

'That's right, my lord,' the peacock man said. The King's entourage turned to leave, and the slaves went to pick up the slumped lion. As they lifted the cage off the ground, it let out a warning growl and tried to lash out at them with its paw.

'Aurya,' Sharo said, and tugged urgently on her sleeve. 'Aurya, where are they taking him?'

'It's not our business, Sharo. It's the King's lion now.'

Aurya caught Sharo's intention too late. She tried to hold him back, but he was off, running at the King's men and shouting.

'Where are you taking him?' he yelled. 'Where are you taking Enkidu?'

The peacock man spun around, and soldiers lowered their spears, forcing Sharo to stop. Two grabbed him by the arms, and he struggled in their grip. Aurya shouted her brother's name, but he didn't listen. The servants carrying the King's chair performed a complicated manoeuvre, and the King was turned slowly around to face the commotion.

'What in Ashur's name ... What's wrong with the boy?'

Aurya ran to Sharo and put both her hands on his cheeks. He felt hot, stained with tears. He had stopped struggling while the soldiers held him.

'Sharo, you can't be friends with this lion. Humans and lions can't be friends.'

Sharo shook his head and shouted through clenched teeth. Up on his throne, the King scratched his chin.

'All this for a wild beast,' he said.

'My brother loves animals,' Aurya said, without taking her eyes away from Sharo's. 'He loves this lion especially. I don't know why.'

'Loves the lion that killed your father?' The King stroked the plaits in his beard. 'Well, this lion will be given a home in my palace for the next few months. Come visit him whenever you like, boy.'

'Come and visit him?' Sharo said. His eyes met Aurya's.

'Yes, Sharo,' Aurya said. 'You can go and see the lion when you want to.'

Sharo thought about it for a few moments. Then he seemed to relent. The guards' grip on him loosened.

'Can I visit every day if I want to?'

'I'll tell the lion keeper personally. Mason, bring these two along with you when you come to the palace tomorrow.'

'My lord ...' the master mason protested, as if being told to carry a heavy stone.

'You heard the King!' the peacock man barked, and the mason shrunk. The soldiers let Sharo go. The King was turned around again, and the whole entourage filed out.

'By the gods, I could eat a hundred of those little birds in brine, Bel-Ibni,' the King yawned as they went.

The boy servant Abil gave Aurya a wave as he followed the King and Bel-Ibni, and she waved back. When the noise of the King's passage had faded down the road, the master mason with the tufted beard handed them each a broom made of dried palm fronds.

'Get sweeping,' he said. 'All the seven winds are coming in this evening.'

For the rest of that afternoon, Aurya and Sharo swept the steps of the mason's workshop. They swept all around the yard. Swirls of dust rose every time the wind hit the hillside, and it seemed there was no end to it, that every time one area was swept, another was covered again. All the time she worked, Aurya kept muttering to herself, over and over, 'I'm here. I'm in Nineveh.'

In moments of rest, she squeezed her necklace so hard that the stone turned warm and left its image printed on her palm. But if this was the house of dust, where was her mother? She said prayers to the new, strange gods that must now be watching over her:

To the god of sweepers
To the god of great cities
To the gods of language

When the apprentices called to them, Aurya and Sharo carried buckets full of debris from the stones they were working. One was carving an important-looking man holding a baton out in front of him, Aurya saw; another a miniature model of the great ziggurat, with its seven layers and long staircase to the top; another a kind of beast that looked like a fat river pig with an enormous nose.

'That's a strange-looking pig,' Sharo said to the man as they swept at his feet.

'Quiet, Sharo!' Aurya said. The man sniffed. He had dark skin and kept his hair shaved close to his scalp.

'It's an animal from Egypt,' he said. 'Where I was born. They swim in the great Black River. And they're much bigger than pigs.'

'Egypt … How did you end up here?' Aurya said. The man blew both of his nostrils on the ground, one after the other, and looked around.

'My name's Harkhuf. I was visiting Memphis to buy tools when the Assyrian army captured it. They were going to kill me, but I told them I was a stone mason, and I could make good relief carvings. That was one of the professions they were told to bring back with them.'

'That's lucky,' Aurya said. The man shrugged and lined up his chisel and round-topped hammer.

'That's lucky, she says …' he muttered, and gave the chisel the lightest tap, only enough to kill a wasp. 'Many were not lucky.'

'What was your home like?' Aurya said.

'Beautiful. At the edge of the Roaring Sea.'

'I'd like to see that one day.'

'Perhaps you will. And if you think the ziggurats here are impressive, you should see what we have.'

'Have you ever seen a woman around here?' she asked. 'With curly hair like mine.'

The Egyptian shook his head.

'No. No one like that.'

He looked too young to have been there for very long, Aurya thought: his palms still had some of their patterns. She would try someone else.

———

The evening smelled of damp earth and basil. The apprentices sat in a circle to eat, coughs sounding periodically, men spitting the dust from their mouths. They all ate a rough meal porridge, and Aurya felt its strength flowing into her as she ate. Sharo didn't eat much. He drew with his finger in the dust: a lion pouncing, a lion sleeping, a lion in a cage.

'What's in that building?' Aurya asked one apprentice, pointing up at the dark pillars that loomed over the workshop, now in shadow.

The man cast an eye upwards.

'That's the palace of the King's father, and the house of weapons. No one goes inside any more. Not since the war in Babylon.'

'Why? What's in there?'

'Ghosts, probably.'

Aurya looked up at the building and felt her stomach turn. This man looked older, as if he'd been in the workshop for many years; his hands were worn completely smooth and pink, like her father's had been.

'Do you remember a woman here?' she asked him. 'She had curly hair, like mine, but more of it, so it hung out in bunches.'

The man shook his head.

'We don't have any women around here,' he said. 'Usually.'

Aurya felt the sting of that. When the meal was done, the apprentices slouched to their beds. They brought Aurya and Sharo into a low wooden building where a cow also lived. Everyone rolled out their mats and camel-hair blankets, lying in rows like dried fish. Nobody lit a lamp. Aurya and Sharo lay together near the curtained door. The breeze blew in periodically; the mat was hard, and their blankets thin. Aurya touched her necklace and wondered where in all that huge city her mother could be. She thought about what the King had said to the mason, about throwing them out into the street after two weeks, and she wondered what it would be like to beg for scraps with the other hungry children, in this city where everything seemed so huge, full of languages she didn't know and the strange ways of its people. She drew close to Sharo for warmth. Without her asking, he started whispering the story to her.

The monster Humbaba begged the King to spare him.

'I will be your servant,' the demon said. 'I will cut down my beautiful cedars with my own hands and give them to you. Please spare me.'

'Don't listen to him,' Enkidu told the King. 'He's a trickster. Kill the monster before he poisons your thoughts.'

King Gilgamesh hesitated. But he raised his axe and brought it down on Humbaba's neck, and the monster's head fell to the forest floor.

They set fire to the monster's house, and laid waste to the forest. They tied the cedar beams into a raft. And then they set sail for home.

Enlil, god of the mountains, came down and walked among the ashes and stumps of his forest. He wept with rage, and vowed his revenge on the King and the wild man.

'Be quiet,' an apprentice hissed in the dark. 'It's going to be a long day tomorrow. We don't have time for your stories.'

Sharo hushed. Aurya tried to sleep, but she couldn't. She still felt the boat's movement beneath her, the river's gentle pull. Once she could hear the long breaths of everyone around her, she lifted herself, wrapped her blanket around her like a cloak and wandered out into the night. The city was a restless creature; she could still hear it all around, a soft murmur like water. She remembered the King's dream she'd overheard the night before, and thought that the city did look like a sea at night: a carpet of shimmering lights.

Aurya wandered through the workshop gate to where the old palace sat empty and dark. She wound in and out of its pillars, and crept close to its entrance, with the bull-men guardians on either side. She edged a little closer, peered into the black corridor at its main gate and reached out to touch one of the stone bulls' hooves. As she did so, a low moan came from within, and a gust of warm wind blew over her face. She felt a presence there, moving inside the palace at night. Something dark and fierce, waiting for her to turn her back. And then a voice came from within, hoarse and dripping with malice.

'You're a murderer,' it said. 'Aurya the murderer. You killed your father and fed him to a lion.'

Aurya felt her legs go limp. She turned and ran with the wind wailing in the halls behind her, back to the sleeping quarter, and dived under her blanket.

In the morning, the smoke of fires came drifting over the hill. The apprentices ate in the shadow of their half-completed stones. Aurya glanced warily up at the old palace, less frightening in the blue light of morning. Storks nested on its roof and streaked its sides with their droppings.

'Eat faster,' the master mason barked, although his cough was troubling him, and he didn't seem to have eaten anything. 'Which of you wants to explain to the King why we're late? Hmm?'

The apprentices put on their travelling sandals and wrapped up their tools, wooden tablets covered in a thin layer of clay or wax, and styluses, thin sticks with sharpened ends. Aurya and Sharo followed them all down the hill, the apprentices chattering gossip and rumour, shooing away the beggar children without really noticing them.

As they walked through the city, Aurya's heart swelled at every new sight: the stalls overflowing with dusty vegetables and shining implements, feathered charms, ostriches and men carrying deer with tied feet, a child playing with a clay cart. Even the smells wafting from the river and the alleys, the flies that gathered in clouds, the streets turned to mud with churning feet, didn't dull her sense of being in a strange and wonderful place. Sharo gave little whimpers as each bustling street passed them by: another thousand memories to lock away inside his head.

They climbed the hill on the other side of the river, and a palace came into view – brighter and newer than the one beside the workshop, its coloured tiles gleaming in the sun.

'The palace without rival,' the apprentices muttered to one another. As they got closer, the smells of incense and petals filled the air, and the city's foul odours faded. More of those huge stone bull creatures flanked the palace's main entrance, with wings and human heads, brilliantly painted. They made Aurya think of the monster Humbaba. Inside, men in fine robes and sandals hurried past with arms full of tablets. Slaves with spotless head-wrappings lugged urns full of water and armfuls of fans from place to place. Lords and priests swept past with an air of dignity, and Aurya noticed that all of them, every last one, was moving so as not to make the slightest sound. Even the whisper of Aurya's breathing seemed to echo faintly in the high eaves.

Aurya felt Sharo move closer to her as the noise of the world's details once again swept in on him. She saw the pain building behind his eyes, but he kept quiet. Aurya tried not to stare at everything, but as they got further into the palace, she noticed all the apprentices staring too, craning their necks down shaded passages lined with painted friezes. Even the master's eyes darted from side to side as they went, a sheen of sweat on his forehead. He named the stones he saw in the statues and lintels and pillars, as if they were the names of gods.

'Gypsum. Basalt. White limestone ...'

At the top of some stairs, the King's servant Bel-Ibni was standing to greet them. He had changed his robes to bright red with shimmering gold stitching, but he still had the bearing of a peacock.

'Hurry along now,' he said. 'The King is waiting.'

They followed him through the halls, and Aurya swallowed a growing sense of dread. Along every wall, huge, strange creatures in human clothes were carved: a man with the head of a hawk, the head of a dog, carvings of cities burning, armies fleeing before chariot charges. A stringed instrument sounded somewhere down the halls, the sound getting louder as they walked. At the end of the corridor, they stepped out into a walled garden. Peacocks and an ostrich walked in the shade, around the lyre player. King Ashurbanipal was reclining on a lounge chair covered in cushions. Around him, men held up fans and trays of drinks, sweetcakes and oils. They looked like statues, all frozen as if turned to stone, their eyes staring straight ahead.

'Ah, my devoted carvers,' the King said as the apprentices arrived in the garden. He raised a shining cup in one of his hands. 'We've been practising our positions!'

The servants didn't move. Flies crowded over the exposed food and liquids they held, over their faces and eyes. Sweat ran down their faces.

'Look at this new chair and table I had carved just for the occasion,' the King announced. 'Some of the finest work ever seen, don't you think? Make sure to get all the details just right.'

The legs of the table and the chair were carved to look like the feet of lions, etched with intricate designs and shimmering pieces of mother-of-pearl.

'If the wood carvers can do it in wood, the masons can do in stone, my lord,' the master mason scoffed, though Aurya could see the sweat darkening his robe at the back of his neck. She felt Sharo touch her arm and squeeze it in silent plea.

'Keep hold of me, Sharo,' she said. 'Close your eyes and think of the lion.'

'Aurya, I need to draw. Can I draw on the ground?'

She looked at the beautifully cut lawn. She closed his hand around her wrist.

'No, Sharo. Not here.'

'This won't take long, your majesty,' the master mason said, and then turned to the apprentices. 'Come on, take your impressions. Make sure the details are perfect – you heard the King!'

They all hurried to unwrap their tablets and styluses, all looking as dazed as Aurya felt. She watched as they stood in the shade and etched their wax tablets. Each one sketched a different piece of the whole scene: the trees, the King, his chair and table, the servants with their trays and urns.

'Why are they drawing it, Aurya?' Sharo said. 'Can't they remember it?'

'No, Sharo. Try to imagine what it would be like, not to remember everything.'

His hand tightened around her wrist. The head servant Bel-Ibni walked around adjusting the servants' poses. He raised the arms holding trays, smoothed back locks of hair, straightened folds in robes. Some of those holding uncomfortable positions began to shake.

'Have they still not found it?' Bel-Ibni shouted to a servant at the entrance, who fell to the ground.

'No, my lord. It seems it's been stored away in the hall of treasures all these years. I will tell the boys to hurry.'

Aurya hung back with Sharo and watched as the sun passed overhead. The shadows in the garden shifted, and the preening birds followed them. After some time, a servant holding up a tray fainted, and there was a crash of falling cups and a pot of oil that made all the apprentices jump. Soldiers came and dragged him from the scene, and another servant hurried to take his place. Soon a group of servants arrived from down the corridor, carrying a lidded pot between them, ropes looped through its handles. Aurya saw that the boy Abil was among them, and felt a flutter that surprised her.

'Finally!' Bel-Ibni said. 'Was it on the other side of the Bitter River?'

'A million apologies, my lord,' Abil said, out of breath. 'It was beneath a pile of loot from Susa and Memphis.'

Bel-Ibni waved his hand. He pointed to a tree hanging over the line of frozen servants.

'Hang it up there.'

They carried the pot over to the tree, and opened its lid. While Abil held the pot, one dipped his hand inside and oil welled up around his wrist. The man pulled out his hand, and Aurya saw what was in the pot. It was a severed head. It looked like it had been in the jar for a long time: it was yellowish-pale, its eyes pure white like marble. An iron hoop had been run through its severed throat, so it came out of its mouth and back in through the wound. The oil dripped along the curves of its upside-down face, bubbled from the nostrils and formed a long pendular line from the crown of its dark hair.

'Teumman, the King of Elam!' Ashurbanipal laughed. 'How have you enjoyed your stay in that pot, my friend? Is it as good as your old palace?'

Aurya felt the blood drain from her cheeks. The image flashed into her head of the dark palace she'd seen last night, the silent carvings and the wind howling in the halls. The hoarse voice calling out to her: 'You're a murderer.' Her father's arms flopping as he slumped into the darkness, and the tearing sound of the lion devouring his flesh. She felt weak, and a ringing began in her ears. She watched the servants get ready to hang the head in the low branches, barely concealing their disgust. Abil turned his face away, but his robes got covered in oil, which dripped down his legs and made his feet slippery. They slung the iron hoop over a branch. The white eyes stared down at the frozen congregation of servants.

'Make sure to get that expression into the carving,' the King wheezed. Some of the mason's apprentices had turned pale. 'Make sure to get it exactly right! That's exactly the expression he died with.'

Aurya looked up at the head, at the frozen servants all around and at the apprentices furiously sketching the scene on their wax and clay tablets. She felt the turn in her stomach.

'It's just a head,' she told herself. 'You're tougher than this. You've skinned rabbits and gutted fish. Are you so scared by an old severed head now?'

There was no time to dash away. The surge of vomit rose up in her before she could do anything about it, and she only just managed to turn and vomit into one of the flowering bushes that lined that garden. She tried to stand, but the world went black at the edges. She thought she saw Sharo beside her, but the voices around her sounded like the echoes of another world lying beneath the surface of the one she knew. She felt hands lifting her, and then the dark rose around her like oil and swallowed her up.

Katya

Katya woke early in the morning, and for a few seconds she didn't remember where she was. Those were beautiful seconds. Then the terror stuffed into her mouth like cotton wool. There was the distant sound of artillery, further away now, grumbling like thunder. Other than that, there was silence. She rolled over painfully, and thought of home. She didn't want to, but she couldn't help it: she thought of the lemon tree on the windowsill, of her mother, of their cat Hugo. She thought of grand words like The United Kingdom, The United States, words meant to describe the old powers of the world that sailed far above her now, blind and impenetrable as the hulls of ocean liners.

Salim was awake. She found him in his room, hunched over the dim light of his phone. By the look of his eyes, he hadn't slept at all.

'Did you get a signal?' she said. He shook his head.

'Just for a second. Enough to receive some texts. The other members of the team are safe. They got out just in time. My nephew Athir's still here, but he's safe – he's sending me news when he can.'

His voice sounded thin and starched, a shirt washed too many times. Katya stood leaning against the door frame, watching him.

'What does he say?'

'That the army isn't coming back.'

'What does that mean?'

'That we're on our own.'

Down below, thumps sounded on the museum door. Katya jumped at the sound. She saw fear in Salim's eyes, and he fumbled to tape the phone back under the desk.

'Sounds like my date's here,' she said.

'Katya, I meant what I said yesterday. Be careful with these guys. And don't trust anything they say.'

Katya walked down to meet the man, and saw Lola crouched on the mezzanine.

'Be safe,' she said. Katya nodded, and felt the girl's eyes on her as she descended the stairs to the entrance hall. The English man with the beard and glasses was standing there in the doorway, casting a shadow into the museum. He looked tired but flushed, colour lining his cheeks. He stepped further inside when he saw her.

'Time to show me some treasure,' he called out. Katya's hands shook, so she held them behind her back. Don't show weakness: number three.

'We don't have any treasure,' she said. 'All we have is historical artefacts.'

He only laughed, and looked up at the smooth faces of the lamassu.

'Devils, more like.'

She noticed that he didn't have a gun with him this time, but the rubber handle of a knife jutted from a sheath at his belt. It looked big, the kind a hunter would carry.

'After you,' he said when they reached the stairs down into the basement. She could tell he was mocking her with this show of politeness, but she did as she was told. She felt his presence behind her in the dark as they headed down, the scuff of his boots on the steps. At the bottom, she felt the storeroom's cavernous space, the smell of damp and dust. She fumbled for the light switch, and then the strip bulbs flickered on, illuminating the lines of shelves that stretched off into the dark, strung with cobweb architectures.

'Most of the things down here are too ugly or broken to display upstairs,' Katya said. 'Mostly worthless, forgotten things.'

This wasn't true. Some of the best finds from their dig were down here, awaiting cataloguing. Many of the museum's most important artefacts were down here for safekeeping, too. But she knew she had to play down their importance if she was going to save anything. The English man peered around in distaste. In the gloom, he didn't feel quite so threatening. They were about the same height. Befriend your captors, Katya thought.

'What's your name?' she asked.

'You don't need to know that.'

'I'm Katya.'

He didn't react, just took a blister pack of pills from a pocket in his vest and swallowed two without water, then scuffed the floor with his boot.

'No small talk then,' Katya said. 'You said you had a list of things you wanted. Show me something on it and I'll find it for you.'

She could tell he didn't like being spoken to like this, being ordered around – and by a woman. A flash of anger flared in him, but he just ran his tongue over his teeth and handed over his notebook. There was a printed page inside, a professional catalogue. Katya was surprised at the detail of the entries. She could tell at a glance that they were written by experts, art dealers. All the museum's most valuable artefacts were there, and she realised with a tug what it would mean to hand these over. She looked up and saw the man standing by one of the shelves, an object in his hands.

'These,' the man said, and picked up a cylinder seal from the shelf. 'These are worth a lot. We'll take all of these right away.'

Katya coughed. The seal in his hand was the one she'd excavated, pried from the hand of the dead man in the workshop. It hadn't been catalogued or studied yet, since she'd taken it to the site so many times. She knew that if he took it, it would disappear for ever, and its secrets with it.

'Your dealer will laugh at you if you show him that,' she said, as if its worthlessness was obvious. She reached out and took it from him, and she saw that flash of anger again in his eyes. It surprised her that he let her take it. 'Look. This is a reproduction made before the collection was moved down to Baghdad. For safekeeping. It's a fake.'

The man breathed out through his nose and looked down the lines of shelves. Katya felt her heart thudding in her head.

'Is anything here real?' he muttered. Katya slipped the cylinder seal into her pocket while he wasn't looking, and let out a breath she didn't realise she'd been holding.

'Yes.' She ran her finger down the page of his notebook until she saw it: a clay tablet, a fragment of the Gilgamesh Epic. It was famous. It had been exhibited and written about in journals, featured in a documentary on the BBC. It would be worth a lot of money. And more importantly, it had already been documented, photographed and studied. The lump of clay felt cold when she picked it up. It startled her. The man reached out hungrily with both hands.

'It's a piece from an ancient story, about a king called Gilgamesh,' she said. 'It describes the great flood, a story that gets repeated in the Bible and the Quran. It's one of the most valuable things here. And it's on your list.'

He brought the baked tablet up to his nose and breathed in. She knew how it would smell: earthy, with a hint of burnt hair.

'It's from King Ashurbanipal's library,' Katya said. 'He was a king who gathered clay tablets from all over the world. The library burned along with the rest of the city in 612 BC, but the texts were written on clay. They baked in the fire, hardened, set to last for ever.'

He fixed her with a long look.

'Our dealer will look at this, and make sure it's the right one.' He closed his fist around it. 'You know, the others think I'm wasting my time here. With you.'

'The skull man,' she said. He nodded.

'And the rest. They want to just pack this stuff up and sell it, fakes and all. But I know it's worth a lot more to the right buyers. So the dealers give me lists of objects, and I deliver them. If you help me, I'll keep you safe. And your friends up there too. How does that sound?'

'Good,' Katya said, unable to look away from his eyes.

'Good. And you know what will happen if you ever lie to me, don't you?'

Katya nodded.

'Our lives for the stones.' He gave a slow nod, and her hand in her pocket ran over the bumps of the cylinder seal inside.

'That's right. I'll be back when we hear from the dealer about this.'

Once the man had left, Katya went to find the others. Lola wasn't there, but she found Salim sitting on the mat in his unlit room, inspecting a lurid purple bruise across his ribs. He breathed with a little grimace in the corner of his mouth.

'Katya. What happened?'

She didn't say anything. She sat beside him and wrapped her arms around his neck, felt the warmth in his skin. Slowly he moved his arms around her and they lay down together.

'Where's Lola?' she said.

'She went up to the roof. Those guys scare her. She doesn't want to be inside with them.'

Katya buried her face in his shoulder, which smelled of tobacco smoke and sweat, soap and cologne. She listened to Salim's heartbeat, and the clicking of obscure joints in his sternum as he breathed. She took out the cylinder seal, turned it so the lion design was visible.

'I saved this.'

'Is that the one we excavated? From the body?'

'Yeah. It hadn't been documented. It would have disappeared for ever if they took it.'

'What did you have to give them?'

'The Gilgamesh fragment.'

He took a sharp intake of breath.

'Not much of a trade.'

'They'll take it all if we do nothing. That's what he told me. This way we can at least save something. The smaller objects, the ones that haven't been recorded. Otherwise all our work has been for nothing.'

Salim rubbed his face with his palm.

'Talk to me about something else,' he said.

'Like what?'

'I don't know. Anything.'

She thought for a moment.

'Do you know I could be in Greece right now? Or Peru? I got job offers in both. And I took this one instead.'

'Why?'

She held him tighter, and pressed her head into his chest. She felt his grip on her tighten too.

'My dad was a journalist,' she said.

'I remember.'

Katya felt that blockage again in her throat, that hard cold feeling like a slice of apple lodged there. The more she tried to push through it, the tighter it felt.

'He kept coming back here, to Iraq. A bit like you. My mum hated it. He always said he wanted to report on normal people, the people trying to get on with their lives with all the violence going on around them.'

Something about Salim, about the way he held her there, made the tight feeling in her throat lessen, and the words came easier.

'When I was sixteen, he came out here to report on the war. And then he never came back. Some men with guns threw him into a car, and that's the last anyone ever saw of him. There was never a ransom, never a video. He just disappeared. It was like he turned to dust and blew away. The first we heard about it was a phone call. It was in the news for weeks. And then the news moved on, and everyone just forgot about him.'

She felt Salim's breath deepen.

'What was his name?'

'Idris Hammadi.'

'Oh, god. I remember that case. I'm sorry. I had no idea.'

Katya took in a deep breath. The hard, dry feeling tightened in her throat.

'I used to play a game. When I was lying in bed, in the dark. I'd try to remember his face. Try to picture it. I'd think of running my hand over his nose and cheeks. The dots of silver in his beard. It got harder every year. Now I don't know if I passed him on the street … if he just walked past me one day, would I even recognise him?'

'He would recognise you.'

In the dim light, Katya reached up and kissed Salim. Their lips were dry, their bodies were shaking. They kissed each other and Katya felt fear washing over both of them in waves. As they lay there, Katya imagined that they were two skeletons lying in a deep hole, one on their back and the other curled on its side. She imagined the hundred bones in their feet falling together and mingling like game pieces, the dust falling helical through their ribs.

The gunmen came back later that evening. The man with the skull on his balaclava was leading them. They didn't say anything. They just rounded up Katya, Salim and Lola, and tied their hands in front of them with plastic ties. Katya felt a new protectiveness from Salim, the way he positioned his body in front of hers as the men approached. It didn't help: the men took them upstairs and pushed them into a storage cupboard along with mops and buckets and the smell of cleaning fluid. Then the men closed the door and locked it, and the three of them were plunged into darkness.

Katya sat against the wall beside Salim, while Lola lay on her side in front of them. Katya tried to block out the pain from the ties around her wrists, and how much she needed the loo. She reached out her little finger as far as she could and touched the skin of Salim's wrist. She felt his touch back, and let it calm the growing terror in her body. Lola murmured something to herself, some kind of incantation or prayer, and they all listened to the thuds and the cracking of glass as the men went around the museum, kicking in doors and breaking windows. They jumped at each sudden bang.

'What's happening?' Katya whispered to Salim. 'Do you think it wasn't enough? That tablet I gave them ...'

'Who knows,' Salim muttered. 'Maybe it doesn't even matter.'

'What do you mean?'

She heard his laboured breaths in the dark.

'Maybe it's all over. If they can take Mosul and hold it, who knows what they can do? They could take Baghdad. Maybe the whole world is unravelling.'

They spent an eternity in the dark. They had to use one of the mop buckets as a toilet. There was no water or food. Katya felt weak. Her tongue felt like Scotch tape, sticking to the sides of her mouth. She kept wondering what was happening. Had the men found out about the seal she'd taken? Had something gone wrong with the fragment of tablet she'd given them? Had she made a mistake?

The three of them talked to pass the time that first day, at first about nothing in particular. Katya talked about ancient plant samples she'd found in the ceramics and pottery of southwest Mexico, where wild grasses gave clues about the domestication of grains. Salim talked about the favourite finds of his career: the gold band he'd found in a sealed tomb in Uruk, the stone dice from Babylon, the 4,000-year-old clay brick from Dur-Sharrukin that still showed the paw prints of a dog that ran over it when it was drying. Then, as they got more scared and the darkness pressed in further on them, they began to talk about their families. Lola switched to Arabic, which she spoke more fluently than English, and Salim translated. She had a beautiful lilting cadence when she talked about her brother, how he'd flown kites with her from the rooftops and taught her to shoot, the way the village they'd left had irrigation canals she'd played in as a child, and about her father who had driven a bright yellow tractor. She recounted the day they moved to Mosul and how she'd explored the ruins of Nineveh on her own, pretending to be an archaeologist. Then about losing her parents, being left with only her brother, who ran the family shop while she worked in a restaurant kitchen. Then the day years later that she came to find its blackened skeleton still breathing smoke, and she knew she was alone in the world.

Katya told them about her home, the tower blocks sprouting out of the bomb craters, the War Memorial Park, the shell of Coventry Cathedral. She talked about her mum's depression, the way she'd never been sure which version of her would walk through the door. She told them about her dad, the way he'd sat at his computer and written with the cat on his lap and the sunlight passing through the steam rising off his coffee. She talked about the day she found out he'd disappeared, how she'd had to go to her aunt and uncle's and had sat there eating tuna sandwiches though her mouth was dry, and her mum had come back to get her with her face puffed up and red with crying, unable to speak, shaking with what looked like rage; how Katya had thought this anger was directed at her, unable to understand what she'd done. She told them about the fights she'd got into at school, how she'd never been able to speak at the counselling sessions, and the men from the Foreign Office coming into her house and sitting there in her father's chair, the awkward way they'd perched and muttered the same phrases, 'So sorry for your loss,' 'Doing everything we can,' each one seeming to contradict the last. The way she'd gone to see the lion carvings in the museum, and her mum had told her they came from the same place as her dad, the same place he'd disappeared into, a place that must have been like a fog, a place where people can just disappear and never be found.

Salim talked about America, about his relations living in Europe and the nephews and nieces he'd never seen. He told them about his mother and father, how he wished he'd visited them more, how he sent money home to them but never had the chance to visit. He spoke about his regrets, how he had been a man living in two places, with two souls. He talked about when his brother had been killed, when they had taken his body to be washed and Salim had seen a pomegranate tree growing in the corpse washer's court-yard, watered by the blood that flowed from the washing table.

They could tell that night was coming: the soft glow of light that crept in under the door faded. Salim and Lola talked together in Arabic, and then he tried in Lola's native Kurdish. Katya listened to the way they became different persons in each language, as though multiple souls bubbled up inside them.

After the first night, they were too thirsty to talk. Lola sang weakly, lying at Katya's feet. Delirium fell in the dark. Laughter and strange dreams. Katya rolled over and tried to lie on her side, but it was agony in her wrists. It was then she became aware of a presence moving there in the room with her. Was it Salim? Was he sleepwalking, or stumbling around in a fever? She turned and saw a dark figure standing in the corner, the shape of a man.

'Salim?' she said.

'What?' Salim murmured, from right beside her. The figure in the corner just stood there, tall and terrible.

'Lola, is that you?'

But Lola was still lying next to her.

'Salim, there's someone standing in the corner.'

'There's no one there,' he said, and she felt his hands on her face. 'Katya, it's just us in here. There's no one there.'

She hid from the figure, but it remained for the whole night. Every time she dared to look, she could see it standing there in silence, and in the morning it was gone. On that second day, Katya's dad appeared to her. He stood in the corner where the figure had been. She couldn't see his face, but she knew it was him.

'Dad?' she said, almost too weak to speak. His voice came out of the shadows.

'You're not going to give up,' he said. 'Is that what I taught you? To give up?'

'I can't. Please. It's too hard. I can't.'

'You have to keep going, Kat. Time isn't done here.'

'Dad. Why did you leave? Why did you leave me?'

'Never hide, Katya. Run.'

She looked up and he was gone. On the third day, she knew that they had been forgotten. They were going to die in that room. Time folded over itself, pouring in laps like treacle. She wasn't afraid any more. She wanted death to hurry up and take her. Stop taking its time. When she heard noises down below in the museum, she thought she was dreaming. Then the door burst open.

'Fucking hell,' she heard. It was the English man. 'Look what you've done to them. You fucking idiots. It stinks.'

'Please,' Katya croaked, squinting in the light. 'Water.'

The English man clucked his tongue.

'Water!' he shouted at the other man, who hurried off. The skull man didn't seem to be there any more. The English man took a few steps into the room, wrinkling his nose.

'Look at this,' he said. 'What a fucking mess.'

She looked up at him, and for a moment felt a real burst of warmth towards him, so strong that she thought she might cry. He cut her zip ties and she tried to get up from the floor, but her legs wouldn't hold her. She massaged the torn skin where the ties had cut into her wrists. When the water came, she gulped it down, and it tasted as sweet as peach juice. It took all her strength to pass it to Lola and then Salim. They all crept out into the light like cave creatures, blinking and weeping from reddened eyes. The English man stood and watched them with the hint of a sneer, and the pupils of his eyes a wide, pure black like polished stones.

'The piece you gave us ...' he said. 'It was good. Good stuff. The boss is happy.'

Katya sobbed on her hands and knees. Behind her, Lola was crying too, and Salim was holding her.

'You need to give me more pieces like that,' the English man said. 'So long as the pieces keep coming, you can stay out here in the museum, and there won't be any need for my friend to come back. You understand?'

Katya nodded, and despite herself, she glanced back at the dark cupboard where she thought she would die.

'For how long?' she said. 'When will you let us go?'

'If the ocean were ink for the words of God, the ocean would dry up before the words.'

'What does that ...'

'Here's my list.' He dropped a folded printout on to the floor beside her. 'Two hundred items. Bring me these, and we won't have any more problems.'

'Two hundred,' Katya murmured. She lifted her head weakly. 'But if I work for you ... shouldn't I at least know your name?'

The English man shrugged as though it didn't matter, and this frightened Katya more than anything else. She looked up into the black wells of his eyes.

'I'm Abu Ammar,' he said. 'Abu Ammar al-Britani, lion of Mosul.'

With those words he left, and Katya slumped exhausted to the floor, listening to Lola's sobs behind her and Salim's voice as he whispered to her that it was going to be okay.

In the hour after being freed from the cupboard, all Katya, Salim and Lola could do was drink glass after glass of water until their stomachs hurt. Then they cooked and ate handfuls of rice mixed with tinned tomato, and it tasted so good Katya thought she might cry. They piled into the showers, letting the water rinse the filth from their skin and their clothes, running almost black down the drain. They emptied the mop bucket, gagging a little as they did, and when they felt enough strength return to their bodies, they looked around the museum at the damage the men had done. Anything that remained of value had been taken: all the artefacts in the cases that were light enough to carry, all the electronics too, even the stationery. They had gone through the bookcases in the library and torn out the pages on Iraqi art and history, left them littered thick like a forest floor. Katya watched Salim from the doorway as he sorted morosely through the leaves, the fragmented images on the ground showing the minaret of Samarra, the gold dome of Karbala and the patterned intricacies of Kufic script. Salim smoothed them with his palm and put them back into their places, one by one. He lifted a copy of an old Safavid Quran from where it lay open on the floor and brushed the dust from its cover. She watched the gentle curve of his neck as his head hung, and remembered kissing him the day before they were imprisoned in the cupboard. It already felt like another life. She came up behind him and put her arms around his waist.

'I thought we were going to die,' she said. His hands moved up and pressed into her forearms, palms warm and soft.

'Me too. It didn't seem that bad, from up close.'

'I started seeing things. I saw my dad. He spoke to me.'

'What did he say?'

'Not to give up.'

'It's easy for the dead to say.'

She held on to him and felt the warmth of him next to her.

'Did they find the phones?'

Salim shook his head.

'No, thank God. They took everything else.'

'That's some hope at least.'

'Yes. But it won't do us any good if the signal never comes back.'

'Or the charge runs out.'

He nodded.

'In the meantime, we should take an inventory of everything we have here, anything they missed. We need a plan if that skull man ever comes back.'

It was a way to keep busy more than anything, to regain a sense of purpose after their imprisonment. Lola helped them look, her face a sullen mask. At times like this, she reminded Katya of the teenager she might have been anywhere else in the world, in a different life. Katya checked the staff offices, but they had been thoroughly ransacked. The only thing she found was a length of string. She almost left it, then had a thought. The cylinder seal was still in the pocket of her hoodie, so she took it out, ran the string through its hollow and hung the seal around her neck like a necklace. A lucky charm.

'Nothing useful back here,' she said, her voice still hoarse. 'Try the kitchen.'

They didn't have much luck there, either. They found a bag of dried rice and about thirty tins of tomatoes, some yoghurt and apricot jam and soft cheese, along with frozen diamond-shaped flatbreads. Salim clucked his tongue.

'Enough food for … I don't know, a couple of months, if we ration it. It doesn't seem like those guys have any interest in bringing us more food.'

Katya's stomach growled in protest. When Lola pulled open one of the cutlery drawers, she shouted out.

'Here!'

Salim and Katya came over, and they both looked down at what she'd found. It was a kitchen knife, about three inches long with a cheap bright red handle, that had slipped under the lining paper. They all stared at it in silence for a moment.

'I don't – I don't know if I could …' Salim muttered. 'You know …'

'Me neither,' Katya said. She felt her throat constricting a little.

'But … we should take it and hide it somewhere,' he said. 'Just in case. For self-defence.'

Katya nodded. She thought of what the English man Abu Ammar had said to her, down in the gloom: 'You know what will happen if you ever lie to me …'

'Let's hide it down in the storeroom,' Katya said. Lola nodded. 'Yes, hide it there,' she agreed.

Katya and Lola went downstairs together and found a shelf in the corner where old clay tablets were piled up and wreathed in spiders' webs. They located a place behind the tablets to hide the knife, and Lola gripped its handle.

'I killed a sheep once,' she said. 'My father said I had to do it. He said girls have to be strong, because hard times were coming.'

Katya watched Lola's white knuckles on the handle.

'Was it hard?'

Lola nodded.

'Yes. I loved that sheep. His name was Amir. I was crying the whole time. But my brother helped me. He showed me how.'

'What's the secret?' Katya asked, and though she meant it to sound like a joke, she heard her own voice hushed.

'No secret. You have to be fast,' Lola said, and jabbed out with the knife to demonstrate, drawing it across an imaginary throat. Her voice was serious, her eyes hard. 'Once you decide to do something, you can't hesitate. You can't doubt. You have to do it with all your soul.'

In the morning, Katya and Salim continued searching through the artefacts in the storeroom for the 200 on Abu Ammar's list. Lola helped, darting down the lines of shelves to fetch what they asked for. It was silent down there, the thick concrete walls muffling all sound, other than the hum of the fluorescent strip bulbs that fizzed and blinked intermittently. Katya ran her fingers through her hair.

'The first thing we should do is work out what's not on his list,' she said.

'Yes. We can hide them somewhere, make sure they're safe.'

Most of the finds from their dig were uncatalogued, so they gathered them together first. Katya remembered each moment of discovery as she went through them: her shard of blue glazed pottery, her mother-of-pearl bead, the blue-green coins and bone handles, some white dust from the workshop floor, stone-carving tools brittle as dry leaves, inscribed bricks, date stones, charred sesame seeds, olive pips and animal bones.

'Not much to save,' Salim said, letting some of the date stones tick through his fingers.

'It's something.'

'And what do we give them in return?'

Katya showed him the printed list again, and his eyes ran down it with a haunted expression.

'Imagine the pigs picking this stuff out,' he said, his voice curdling. 'Americans, Russians, Europeans ... going through our museum's catalogue like a brochure. Turning my country's history into a garage sale.'

The power went out, so they worked holding battery torches. They were both still afraid of the dark, of the shadows beyond those two pools of light. As they sorted through the objects, they kept up a constant chatter to reassure each other that they were still there. Katya told Salim everything she'd learned from her meeting with Abu Ammar.

'There's always this rage hidden just below the surface,' she said. 'You can almost see him quivering with it. He's young, I don't know how young. He's always quoting these religious passages, and he takes these little pills sometimes.'

'Captagon,' Salim said.

'What?'

'It's an amphetamine they make themselves in Syria. Keeps them fighting for longer, makes them a little crazy. But I hear the withdrawal is pretty nasty. You should be careful around him if he's coming off the stuff. And when he's on it, it might be a good time to ask for things.'

Katya nodded, and thought of the black look in the man's eyes. Salim took a sharp breath. He was holding a small clay model of a cart, an ancient child's toy.

'I love this piece,' he said. 'I'd rather smash this than give it to them.'

Katya felt the tension in his hands. She thought he'd do it. But then he sagged and handed the little cart to her. He covered his eyes as he did, and she heard him sniff through tears.

'I'm sorry,' he said. 'I keep thinking about the museums I visited as a boy. The Baghdad Museum. How much I loved that place. And after the war, hearing that the Americans let it be destroyed as if it meant nothing. Wondering what kind of monsters would do a thing like that. And now I feel like I'm losing my soul with every piece we give away.'

Katya weighed the little cart in her hands and thought about the child who had first owned it, and what they had gone on to become.

'Go upstairs,' she said. 'I'll do the rest for today.'

'No, you don't have to …'

'No, I mean it. We're nearly done anyway. You're exhausted. Get some sleep.'

He nodded and wiped some angry tears from his eyes, then leaned forwards and kissed her forehead. He left her alone with the artefacts, and the reverberating sound of what he'd said. Was she losing her soul too? Giving it away, gift-wrapped and ready for sale? By the end of the day, the tips of Katya's fingers were dry with the dust of the artefacts, and her eyes felt strained from peering in the dim light.

They didn't see the skull man again. Abu Ammar took charge of the museum, and his was a looser regime: he let the three of them wander the halls, even unlocked the roof so they could go out into the sun and look out over the city. The museum seemed to unsettle him, all its silent statues and strange gods, so he rarely came inside. In the evenings, some of Abu Ammar's men would come into the museum and split the three of them up, lock them in separate rooms for the night, sometimes camp out in the halls until morning.

But then one night they didn't come. All three of them stayed in their separate rooms anyway, afraid of what would happen if they didn't. They listened to the sounds of distant war rumbling over the city, and wondered what was happening.

'Why didn't they come last night?' Katya asked in the morning.

'Better things to worry about maybe,' Salim said, with a breath of hope in his voice. 'Maybe this means the army's come back.'

But the men came that night, and locked them away as usual. In the following days, planes began to fly over the city and drop bombs. Their thuds and cracks rumbled through the earth, as though great worms were burrowing deep below ground. A few days later, the same thing happened: the men didn't come that night. From then on this would happen once every few days, and they were left alone to wander the museum halls at night.

The days and nights went on like that, and soon they were left on their own in the museum more often than not. It was as if the men had forgotten about them. Through the nights when they couldn't sleep, Lola would sit in the library, reading the torn pages of the English books. Katya and Salim would lie in the dark in the office room and talk into the early hours: about their child-hoods, doing impressions of the teachers they'd hated, reciting the plots of movies they both knew. When they slept together for the first time, it seemed like the most natural thing in the world, like coming home, and afterwards they lay together in the dark without exchanging a word.

One afternoon, Katya found Salim sitting on the roof, looking out over the city evening. The roads were emptied of traffic, and the woodpecker Kalashnikovs rattled in all directions. Since their imprisonment in the cupboard, none of them liked to be alone in the museum when the power was out. Katya stood with Salim while he smoked cigarette after cigarette with shaking hands, then crumpled his empty packet and threw it over the edge into the wind. She ran her fingers over his fist closed against the concrete, and his muscles softened slightly. His hand opened and he held hers, both of their palms clammy.

'I managed to get some phone signal today,' he said. 'Just a flash, for a few seconds. Some texts came through. I think if I queue them up, I might be able to send them too, to local numbers at least.'

'Any news about what's going on?' Katya said.

'They've banned pickles.'

'Pickles?'

'They think people might ferment them into alcohol. They're mad.'

The dark marks under his eyes were laced with burst arteries. Katya watched him, and then ran her hand along the line of his unshaven jaw.

'Salim,' she said, 'be honest with me. What's the worst that could happen to us?'

He shook his head and wouldn't meet her eyes.

'What I'm most scared of?'

'Yes.'

'That they'll split us up. I'm amazed they haven't already. That we'll disappear into Syria. They have a network of prisons there. Run by men freed from the regime's dungeons. Torturers, men with broken souls. The things I've heard, Katya …'

The thinness of his voice chilled her more than his words. She thought of the news articles about her dad. Disappeared without a trace.

'Salim …'

He hid his face.

'I don't want to be in one of their videos,' he said, his voice tiny. 'I don't want my mother to see me. And Athir. That's what I fear most.'

'And me? What should I fear?'

He looked right over into the distance this time, and didn't answer.

'We're going to be fine,' is all he said, some moments later. 'We're going to get out of here.'

'Salim … if they split us up, and you escape, promise you'll find me?'

He turned to her, and she saw his eyes glassy with tears. He ran his hand along her jaw, making her shiver.

'I'd never stop looking.'

Katya put her head on his shoulder, and he wrapped his arms around her. The two of them rocked there for a while, and then sat down together against the balustrade. Katya felt a strange freedom in the way the sun warmed her skin: the same sun that fell on her home across the sea, the same light. From somewhere, the maddening smell of apricots drifted to her, making her mouth water.

They stayed up there for hours, watching the muted comings and goings of the city. A peanut seller rolled past with his cart, and gave some to the armed men waiting outside the museum, without taking any money. Patrols stopped on the street to chat with the guards. A woman put up washing to dry on a nearby rooftop. Around midday, Katya looked over the balustrade and saw with a stir that Abu Ammar was standing on the fairway in the palm-tree shade. He was giving some kind of sermon to his men.

'"If you see the black banners coming from Khorasan, join their army,"' he was reciting in English, his voice cool and clear. '"The East and the West will gather against us. Soon they will fight us with one hand."'

Every so often while they sat there, Salim's phone would buzz and bring him some piece of news or rumour. Every time, he hunched over its screen, shielding it from the sun with his hand, and repeated it to Katya in that same dark tone.

'They're lashing people in the Bab al-Tub Square ... they're searching vehicles for hideaways ... they've killed the professors in the university, and moved heavy equipment into the campus ... they've set up checkpoints on the roads ...'

She wrote out a message to her mother on his phone and tried to send it. 'Mum, please don't worry about me,' it said. 'I'm safe, I love you.' She wasn't surprised to see the 'sending failed' message when it came. As the sun set, and the moon came out a perfect white, Katya looked up into the deep blue sky, where a tiny dot glinted like a star, circling higher than any bird: a drone, a distant eye watching and waiting. She waved at it and brushed the hair from her face as the wind picked up around her.

That night, she and Salim lay down together on her mattress, and Lola came to join them, the three of them curled up together. When she closed her eyes, Katya felt the illusion of her hands moving over objects, the way legs can still feel the motion of the sea after hours on land.

'We have to get out of here,' Salim murmured. 'We have to escape.'

'How?'

'We'd need a car. We wouldn't get far on foot. Some weapons. Some way of getting out of here unseen. A distraction.'

'But if we tried, and they caught us ...' Katya whispered. She could feel Salim shaking beside her.

'They've already caught us. Katya, never trust a word they tell you. You've made this deal, but you have no idea what you're doing. The moment we run out of pieces for them to sell, they're going to kill all three of us, or make us wish we were dead. Outside ... in the city ... Athir says they've been crucifying people.'

In the dark, she heard the papery sound of his lips moving together in silent prayer. She ran her fingers along the line of his bow-shaped lips. When she slept, she dreamed that she was responsible for hundreds of little statues, some the size of small children, others as small as mice, all with wide black eyes. Some were in good condition; others fell apart even as she tried to hold them together. She woke up and found someone choking her. A shadow above her, crushing its hand into her throat so she couldn't breathe. Then she woke up again, gasping and reaching to her throat in the dark. Salim was gone. There were sounds coming from the hall, the sound of shuffling footsteps. She got up and peered out of her door, into the lines of the exhibits. She saw a dark figure in the hall, a little hunched. Her skin went cold. It turned, and the shape in the dark resolved into the figure of Salim.

'Salim, what are you doing?'

'Nothing,' he said. 'I just had an idea.'

'Salim, what are you ...'

'It's nothing. Nothing. Go back to sleep.'

Aurya

Aurya woke up feeling as if she were suspended on ropes, swinging in the breeze, and her eyes swam. She found that she was being carried in a piece of cloth that smelled of ash and cinnamon. A figure was holding either end, and through the cloth they looked like men made of shadow. Panic crawled over her. They thought that she was dead. They were carrying her to her grave, to be buried.

'No!' she croaked and thrashed out in fear. 'I'm not dead! I'm still alive!'

One of the men burst out laughing. She craned her neck and saw that it was Abil. He was struggling a little with his end, while Sharo held the other.

'That's good to hear.'

'It's all right, Aurya,' Sharo's voice said, and Aurya twisted to see him better. 'You fainted. But we're going to see Enkidu now. We're going to see my lion!'

Dread still echoed around her body. She tested her legs and stood up, weak and cold, the world like a reflection in a pool that someone had disturbed. There was the taste of vomit still in her mouth.

'The King,' she said, feeling a rush of embarrassment. 'I threw up in front of the King.'

'He's seen worse, I think,' Abil said. 'Once an emissary from Judea came to see him during the war, and the King made him stand on one leg for the whole of their meeting. The man wet his robes.'

Aurya noticed that there were still specks of oil on Abil's cloak and legs. The image of that head, the oil dripping down its face, its white eyes and the way the King had cackled as it was strung up in the tree, kept flashing back into her mind.

'Who was that man?' she asked. 'That head?'

'That was the old King of Elam,' Abil said. 'He died years ago. That was the last time we marched up into the hills, and the last time the Elamites made war on us.'

'Our father fought in that war,' Aurya said. 'And against the Medes.'

'It was a hard war.'

They soon arrived at a squat building off the palace's outer courtyard. They were met there by a shirtless man with a shaved head and a thick mat of hair on his chest. He was chewing something breathily.

'These two are here to see the lions,' Abil said. 'Did the King send you a tablet about this?'

'Yes yes yes,' he muttered, and turned inside, gesturing for them to follow and chewing a little faster as he went.

'I have to go,' Abil said, catching Aurya's gaze with a nervous flash. 'But I'll see you soon, when Master Bel-Ibni comes to inspect the carvings.'

'Thanks,' Aurya said. 'See you soon I hope.'

She took Sharo by the hand, and they both followed the animal keeper inside. She noticed the patterned tattoos that wound up one of his arms, dots and lines intertwining along the wrist. The smells of hay and animal urine were heavy in the air, huffing noises from the stalls. Horses were stabled there, feet hobbled with ropes, and further on, donkeys and a pen of camels that groaned like old men. Sharo's eyes were wide with joy at the sight of the animals, and his memory-pain didn't seem to bother him.

They stepped outside into a rear area where a balustrade overlooked a sunken enclosure. When Aurya reached the parapet, ripples of horror washed over her. Below were maybe a dozen lions: huge males with thick, matted manes of black and gold;

lean females with sharp eyes; young lions with manes only half-grown. They were lounging on the pit's shady side, purring and grunting to each other in their own language. Aurya thought of all the dreams she'd ever had about lions chasing her through the reeds; all the dreams about her mother, and one of these beasts dragging her away. Sharo struck his palms together in excitement.

'Look Aurya – there he is!'

He pointed, and she followed his finger. There in the corner, slightly away from the other lions, was the young male that Aurya had first seen in the old village pit. It was curled in on itself, eyeing the other lions with suspicion but not fear. It licked the wound on its rear foot, fringed by a new growth of pink skin.

'He's doing well, Aurya,' Sharo said. 'His foot's healing.'

'Yes, Sharo. Looks like it is.' She glanced at her brother, bobbing on his toes on the parapet edge. 'What is it about them?' she asked. 'Why do you like the lions so much?'

Sharo looked at her and blinked.

'They're the last really wild things left.'

The shirtless animal keeper watched them without curiosity, scratching his belly. Aurya saw that on the parapet on the other side of the lion pit, a goat was waiting with its feet tied together, its eyes rolling back in its head in fear at the sounds and smells from the pit below. She thought it would be better if Sharo didn't see that part.

'Thank you for showing us,' she said to the animal keeper. 'I'm sure he'll come back to see them again soon.'

The animal keeper shrugged. Whatever he was chewing seemed to fill him with a kind of vacant calm.

'Any time he likes. Before the spring, of course.'

'What happens in the spring?'

He made the lazy motion of an arrow being pulled back in a bow, and then gestured towards the palace. Aurya's stomach dropped. She looked to see if Sharo had seen it, but he hadn't; he was leaning over the balustrade, bouncing a little on his feet, looking down at his lion.

'Be careful, Sharo,' she said. 'Don't fall in.'

Aurya and Sharo rejoined the masons at the palace entrance. Aurya took Sharo's arm and walked back through the city with the apprentices. Nineveh had turned sleepy in the heat of midday. Men sat in the shaded spots between buildings, playing games with knuckle bones on lacquered tables, groups crouched around the same beer jars, sucking from their reed straws and laughing in hoots. The whole place looked different now. Menace shifted beneath everything.

In one open square near the river, Aurya saw a crowd gathered in front of a platform where women and men bound with ropes and chains were standing, wearing only filthy cloths, their heads newly shaved. A fat man with a thin stick was calling out prices to the crowd, and they were shouting back at him.

'What are they doing?' Aurya asked Harkhuf the Egyptian.

'They're selling slaves,' he said with tired eyes. 'The King had a good war in Medea last season. Means the price has really dropped.'

'Those are Medes?' Aurya said. They didn't have hair like animals or mouths full of pointed teeth. They looked like normal people. A woman was dragged up on to the platform next, some clumps of hair still clinging to her shaved scalp, and the frenzy of the crowd increased. Aurya turned a corner in the street before she could see what happened. As they climbed the hill back to the masons' workshop, hungry children followed the procession of masons at a distance. The master clucked his tongue at them and pretended to pick up a stone from the street, which made them scatter, a trick people used on dogs.

As soon as they got back to the workshop, the apprentices began their work. The Egyptian handed Aurya his tablet, the shape of the King scratched into its wax surface. The men all copied out their lines on the stone with charcoal, and Aurya couldn't help staring as the King's face came into view: the shape of his jaw, the geometry of his almond eyes. She could see the artful flicks of the wrist the apprentice gave to each stroke.

After a few moments, an apprentice to her left, who was sketching the King's chair and table, faltered. He let out a whimper. He looked at his wax tablet again, and then back down at the stone.

'Master,' he said, and the mason grunted. 'Master, there's a problem.'

The master mason didn't look over.

'What is it?'

'Master, I made a mistake.'

'No,' the master growled, swinging around.

'I took the impression correctly,' the apprentice stammered. 'But when the girl ... when she fainted, I went to catch her, and I must have smudged the sketch I made.'

'What do you mean? Smudged where?'

'Here, my lord. The King's new chair and table. I can't see the design on this side.'

The master hurried over and peered at the tablet. The colour drained from his face. He seized the apprentice by the front of his wool cloak, then struck him hard on the cheek so he dropped his tablet and stylus. The crack of the blow made all the other apprentices flinch and stop their work.

'The chair! The table! You idiot, how could you come back here without them? You know how the King is about details. You saw how proud he was of that new table.'

'Master, I'm sorry. Please forgive me.'

Aurya watched with a cold guilt creeping over her, the man's cheek turning red. She knew this was it: that the mason would now throw them both into the streets.

'Can't you go back to the palace?' Aurya said, her voice tiny. 'Take another sketch?'

The master's hard gaze rounded on her. The apprentice's eyes turned watery and large, and he shook his head, silently pleading with her to be quiet.

'Go back to the palace, in the middle of the King's ablutions?' the master hissed. 'I might as well cut off my own hand. And tomorrow he's out in the Westlands, and then the day after that ... smash all their heads!' he screamed, and his face went bright

197

red. 'I should have known this would happen, taking in urchins off the street!'

Behind her, Sharo scuffed the earth with his heel.

'I can do it,' he said.

'You keep quiet, boy,' the master growled, jabbing one shaking finger at him. 'By all the gods, I will have you out of my workshop by tomorrow.'

'No, I can do it,' Sharo said. 'Look.'

He bent down and took the stylus dropped by the apprentice, then squatted down in the white dust covering the ground and began to sketch out the design of the table: the lion feet on each leg, the decorative finials, the ornate central piece. As the master watched, he let the apprentice go, and his jaw became looser in his skull.

'What is this? What are you doing, boy?'

'This is the table,' Sharo said. 'And this is the chair design.'

He sketched that too, the curlicues of decoration on the King's lounger, the hanging tassels. The master strode over, squatted down in front of Sharo.

'How is this possible? Are you making fun of me, boy?'

'Sharo remembers everything,' Aurya said, her voice soft as a reed pipe. The mason flashed her another look. The apprentices gathered around what Sharo had drawn in the dust.

'He's right,' one said. 'I remember that part with the tapering design along the lower edge.'

'And those lion feet are exactly how they looked,' another said. 'I'd bet next month's rations.'

The master rocked on his heels, breathed through his nose and looked hard at Sharo.

'If there's one detail out of place,' he said, 'if there's one little finial in the wrong order, the King will notice. Do you understand that, boy?'

'Yes.'

'It will ruin my career, my life.' He reached out and took Sharo by the hand, squeezing him so he winced with pain. 'And if it's wrong, I promise you one thing, boy. However the King punishes me, I will punish you ten times over. If I go one month on half rations, I will make sure you go ten months. If he takes one of my fingers, I will cut off all ten of yours. Do you understand me?'

Sharo pulled his hand away from the man's grasp.

'Sharo,' Aurya said, 'are you sure?'

Her brother fixed his eyes on the master, and she could see the same hatred and fear he'd had when looking at their father.

'I'm sure. I can see it in front of me right now.'

The master stood up, put both hands on his head so his arms looked like two handles of a jar. Little puffs of dust rained down from his hair.

'Fine. Draw it on the stone.'

Sharo got up from the dust and went over to where the slabs lay. The crowd of apprentices backed away from him. He took a piece of charcoal and knelt over the stone. Aurya held her breath. Then Sharo sketched the same details on to the stone: the seat beneath the King, the table, both with their delicate ornaments and lion feet. He lingered over those feet especially. He never once looked back at his sketch in the dust, but when he was finished, the master mason and his apprentices compared the two and found them to be identical. Even the master looked down at Sharo's sketch and nodded.

'Incredible,' one apprentice said.

'I've never seen anything like it.'

'Ashur is great ...'

That evening, the apprentices quizzed Sharo in a constant babble. They tried to catch him out at first, tried to overwhelm him with questions. They asked him what day of the week he'd first eaten a date, first seen a mountain, first heard Akkadian spoken, and then they'd ask the same question some time later, to check if his answers were the same. They asked him things they remembered: how the constellations had looked on days that were important to them: their weddings, their children's births, when they'd gone to the star-gazers to get the signs read. Each one nodded in grudging agreement when Sharo told them, his eyes closed as he reeled off the constellations: 'The furrow and the frond were in ascendance, the bull of heaven was high overhead ... the mad dog and the true shepherd of Anu were each in the east and west … the great twins and the standing gods crossed the mountains and hid towards dusk…'

By the end of the evening, they were getting him to tell them star positions for important days they didn't know, so they could take them to their astrologers and find out if their new chisels would bring good luck, if their wives would be faithful, if they'd get good commissions for their work. Aurya watched Sharo get more and more tired, holding his head as their requests went on, but he kept telling them what he knew, alone of all the people of the world. Finally they moved on to asking him how it felt.

'It makes me exhausted,' he said. 'I'll be talking to someone, and at the same time, I'm remembering something. The things they say make all these memories come back. If I follow the memories, one leads on to another. It's like a dark palace: so many winding corridors, the walls covered in images. I get lost quickly. I could spend the whole day chasing through those corridors. Sometimes I wonder if I went too far, would I ever come back?'

Aurya listened in silence. Sharo had never said any of that to her. Perhaps she'd never asked him. Perhaps deep down, she'd always felt something like what her father told them: that Sharo was simple, incredible maybe, but simple. For just an instant, she thought she understood what it must be like to be him: the burden he carried, and why he hated to see suffering. As she listened to Sharo speak, she looked over the apprentices' heads, to where the shadowy old palace sat empty and silent, cutting out a black outline against the stars.

———

In the morning, the master announced that Sharo would be taken on as his newest apprentice. Some grumbled that he was too young, that he was just a boy from the hills, and how would he pay the fees? They didn't grumble loudly. They all seemed to understand that the boy in front of them was something special, and it made them afraid.

'With a few years of good training,' the master said, 'I could make you the greatest artist in Nineveh.'

Aurya looked around the crowd and saw their eyes full of envy; shifting, dark expressions.

'I will learn,' Sharo said softly. 'But I won't leave Aurya. So if I learn, she learns.'

'Sharo,' Aurya said. 'You don't have to …'

'No. That's all. I'll stay here if she can stay.'

The master looked down at Aurya with a little twitch in his lip, and she felt as detested as a stray cat.

'If that's the price, then so be it,' the master mason said, and clapped his hands. 'It's settled then! Quick, grab some beer from the store and let's drink on it.'

The fifty days of summer heat were a long way off, but the morning sun still beat down on the two children as they sat in the workshop. The seven winds blew a haze of dust that occluded the city. An apprentice brought two rough pieces of stone, and placed one down before Aurya and then the other for Sharo. The master held a reed in his hand that he swung idly, making a swooshing noise.

'Stones like this one,' he said, 'grow like roots in the earth's depths. They have seen the underworld and its creatures. They saw the birth of the heavens; they saw Anu, Enlil and Enki draw lots over who would rule the earth, the waters, the sky. They watched as the gods knitted our bones. Sometime after the flood, this stone was cut from the hills north of here and used to build a bridge. You can tell by the soft colour on its underside. Then it became the lintel of a house – see this cut here? And when that house crumbled, it was placed in the bottom of a wall. When the wall collapsed, men brought it here to Nineveh. The works of men, crumbling and cleared away, made new and new again.'

The mason scored Sharo's stone with a sharp copper tool. He left a shallow cut.

'The stone will remember that mark until dogs screech and ostriches bark. Until Nineveh is just a pile of bricks in the dust. Until the flood returns, and the world is covered again with water.'

'Until this speech is finished,' Aurya whispered when his back was turned, but Sharo didn't react. His eyes were fixed on the master, and Aurya felt a flush of irritation. She looked down at her stone, which looked more lumpish and uglier than Sharo's. As the morning wore on, the master taught them the blessings to say before they began their work, how to ask the stone to remember, how to hold its form while they carved. Sharo repeated the blessings to his stone. Aurya leaned in close to hers.

'You're an ugly piece of rock and I hate you,' she said, so the master couldn't hear.

'You can tell a mason by the smoothness of his hands,' the master said. 'While the farmers and builders roughen their hands, the dust wears ours away.'

He held out his palms, and Aurya saw that they were just like her father's, completely without fingerprints, padded like the feet of cats. He gave them each a chisel and a rounded mallet, and demonstrated how to hold them. The tools felt heavy and dumb in Aurya's hands, their wooden handles polished as smooth as bone. She watched Sharo fumbling too, his tongue sticking out a little while he knocked chips from the stone. He looked the way he always did when he drew in the riverbank mud: concentrated, content. Sharo took to the work naturally. He understood what the mason told him on the level of instinct, like a young bird realising that it had wings. Aurya struggled with everything. Every day, she pinched her fingers between the mallet and the chisel, and her eyes smarted with the whitish dust that rose in clouds from their work. On the third day, she struck the chisel too hard, and her piece of stone split along an ugly line.

'Useless,' the master said as he threw the cracked piece over the wall. 'The stones always remember.'

By the end of the week, Aurya was close to tears. Her new stone was a mess of chips and misstrikes, but Sharo had managed to carve the basic shape of a flower, which the mason gazed at with greedy eyes.

'Well done, boy. Very promising.'

For the rest of the day, they went back to their chores. They sat at the long stone water-basins and sharpened the chisels and scutching tools with rough stones, wetting them as they had been shown. At night, as they lay in the barn with the other apprentices,

Aurya rolled close to Sharo, looking for his warmth in the dark. He was half asleep, but he put an arm around her, and she felt the soft papery texture of his hands. She kept thinking about her mother, about how she was no closer to finding her in this vast city.

'I can't do it, Sharo,' she said. 'The carving. I feel so useless.'

'You'll get it soon, Aurya. You've always been the clever one. I just remember things, that's all.'

'Sharo, I think we've made a mistake. I don't think this is the house of dust. We have to go out into the city and find out where it is.'

Sharo swallowed beside her.

'Aurya, I don't think you'll ever find it.'

A bitter salt feeling rose in her throat.

'Don't you want to find her, Sharo?'

'She's dead, Aurya.'

A sliver of anger stuck in her heart like a stone chip.

'If you know she's dead, tell me how she died, Sharo. I know you're hiding something. And I won't believe it until you tell me. So was there a lion? Or no lion?'

That little chip of stone dug in deeper. Sharo didn't want to find their mother. He liked it in the workshop. He didn't want to leave. Aurya sensed his breathing in the dark.

'Do you want me to tell more of the story?' Sharo said. Aurya nodded, trying to tease out the little flint wedged in her chest.

'Yes, tell it.'

'They killed Humbaba,' Enlil mourned. 'They cut down the cedars in my forest. Now I will bury them in their city's dust. Send the great bull of heaven and wipe them from the earth!'

The bull of heaven thundered down from the sky. When it roared, palaces burst into flames. People's houses shattered.

The King and the wild man took up their spears and went out to fight the bull of heaven. The bull dashed and gored, and the city burned. But the fight was long, and the bull grew tired from its wounds. Finally, the wild man leapt over its head and pierced it with his spear.

They feasted, victorious, but that night the wild man had a dream.

'For killing Humbaba,' the gods said in his dream, 'for killing the bull of heaven, one of these two must die.'

And the wild man woke in the morning, knowing that he had been chosen.

'The story's getting sad,' Aurya said, half asleep against her brother's warmth. She felt him nod above her, and then he swallowed.

'There's an important part coming up,' he said. 'It might answer your questions. But I don't know if you'll want to hear it. I can start telling you a different story if you want.'

There was something strange in his voice, but Aurya was drifting halfway between dreams and the real world. She didn't have the energy to question it.

'No,' she murmured. 'I want to hear how it ends.'

When she fell asleep, she dreamed that she was trying to carve her mother out of stone, but her hands were too clumsy. Every time she tried to chip out a detail from her memory, the stone broke away in an ugly splinter. Before long, the whole piece was ruined and it looked nothing like her mother at all.

Katya

The next day, Salim didn't come down into the basement. He consumed himself with dark muttering, making frantic notes on a scrap of paper pulled from a library book. Katya headed down into the dim-lit storeroom alone, and went on gathering the artefacts into crates. She apologised to each object as she went.

'I'm sorry, Sumerian grinding stone. I'm sorry, Assyrian student's tablet. I'm sorry, spun-glass bead. I'm sorry, figurine of Gilgamesh.'

The little clay statue looked up at her with its wide pearly eyes. She felt its weight, the cool, dry surface, the patina of dust. What was wrong with Salim? She looked for him later, but he had locked himself in one of the maintenance cupboards. She could hear him praying inside. She put the tips of her fingers on the door, and felt his despair emanating through the wood.

'Don't leave me alone,' she whispered to him through the door. 'Salim, please don't leave me alone here.'

Katya went to find Lola instead. They played dominoes sitting on swivel chairs in her room.

'Are you okay, Lola?'

The girl nodded.

'I hate dominoes.'

When they got bored with the game, they rolled out into the hall on the swivel chairs and raced through the exhibits to the trundle of the little wheels. Lola shrieked with laughter while

Katya chased her, and for a few minutes they both forgot where they were.

Later, Katya found Salim pacing up and down in the lion hunt room, muttering to himself. His face was unshaven and his eyes were bloodshot.

'Salim? Are you okay?' He looked at her and his eyes widened. He grabbed her by the sleeve and gave a wide grin.

'Katya,' he said. 'I think I've got it.'

'Got what?'

'I think I know how we can get out of here.'

'You do?'

He nodded and put a finger to his lips. He took her by the sleeve and led her down to the ground floor, into the gloomy staff area and through the utility rooms where the boilers and air-conditioning units sat silent without power. It was dark down here: little desert mice scuttled into their holes as Salim flashed his torch in their direction.

'Where are we going?'

'Shh, come on.'

Salim opened the door to the parking garage, careful not to make a sound. It was empty but for the hulk of the old van standing on blocks in a pool of rust-orange water. Katya remembered sitting there and playing dominoes with him only months before, ghosts from another life. Salim motioned at the corrugated-iron entrance door, and put his finger to his lips.

'There's a guard just on the other side of that,' he whispered. 'They've locked it with two padlocks on the outside. I saw that from the roof.'

He beckoned and crept across the concrete floor to the van. As she followed him, she saw that the bonnet had been wrenched open, and a tarpaulin on the ground had engine pieces laid out on top of it. Four tyres leaned against the wall. Katya felt a bottomless despair begin to rise through her body.

'I found the tyres in the maintenance room yesterday,' Salim said, his voice just a murmur. 'Someone was using them to prop up a desk. They're old, a bit rat-chewed, but they'll still work. I spent all of yesterday looking the whole thing over.'

'But … Salim, look at it …' Katya began, and he put an urgent finger to his lips, pointing to the steel door. Outside, the crunch of footsteps on gravel. Katya lowered her voice. 'Salim, look at it. It's a heap of junk. And even if we get it going, we'd still have to get out of the city.'

'It's not as broken-down as it looks. It needs a new fan belt, some petrol, new spark plugs. And we could make it, I think. I know the city roads. Half these guys are foreigners – Tunisians, Saudis, Egyptians – and most of the rest are country boys. I've known this city all my life. They'd never catch us. And I think I can get a good fake travel permit like they've been handing out to their drivers, in case we hit a checkpoint.'

'Salim …'

He put out his hand and touched hers.

'My nephew Athir. You remember him? He works in auto repair. I can get a message out to him, and he can get us the parts we need. Then we just find a way for him to smuggle them in here.'

'Smuggle them in? Salim, you've seen the guards. The locks on the door, the men patrolling in the streets. Athir's just a boy. How can he smuggle anything inside here?'

'We'll find a way. We have to find a way.'

Katya looked into his wide, wild eyes, and wondered if he had actually lost his mind. What was better? Madness or despair? That night she lay and rubbed her thumb over the cylinder seal where it hung at her neck. She thought about home, and wondered what her dad would say if he could see where she'd ended up.

'Oh, Katya,' she imagined him saying, as she felt the rough bumps and crevices of the seal. 'You've gone and done it now.'

When she slept, she dreamed that she was driving a large and powerful car down a hill, with Salim and Lola in the back seats. She dreamed that the brakes had failed, that the car wouldn't stop, and all three of them were hurtling to their deaths. And who was it sitting next to her in the passenger seat? She couldn't see their face.

The next time Abu Ammar came to the museum, it was a hot day, the air full of car horns and the occasional crackle of gunfire. He brought a kebab wrapped in greasy paper, with a flatbread and lettuce.

'It's for you,' he said, and placed it down on the table in front of Katya. The smell filled the basement storeroom, and she felt her traitorous mouth flood with saliva. She wanted to leap at it and stuff the food in her mouth, but she forced herself not to react.

'Thanks.' She didn't know what else to say. Befriend your captors. 'We have some of those artefacts for you.'

Abu Ammar nodded, and rifled through the crate of objects.

'Great, great.'

His hands lingered over a plaster cast of the goddess Ishtar. He had long fingers, which drummed on the goddess's waist. When he caught Katya watching him, he pulled his hand away.

'Is Abu Ammar your real name?' she asked quietly. 'Or did you make it up?'

A flash of anger.

'All names are made up. Your name is made up too.'

'That's true.'

'It's a kunya. They gave it to me when I came to fight.'

She looked around and tried to think of something else to say to him. She was desperate for some kind of news from outside, so she tried to probe.

'It sounds very dangerous out in the city at the moment.'

'What do you mean?'

'Nothing. Just, it must be nice to be down here, instead of having to fight out there.'

She realised immediately that this was the wrong thing to say. Abu Ammar took a step towards her.

'I've killed men before,' he said. 'Do you think I'm too young?'

'I didn't mean that.' She took a step back. His pupils were large and black again, the implacable eyes of a cat. She eyed the knife sheathed in his belt.

'"The plants of the earth grow, then turn to hay and blow away in the wind."' He ground his teeth for a moment, then relented a little and rubbed his eyes. 'They need me down here. I know the value of these things. I learned at university. From my life before. And we need money to keep up the fight.'

Katya thought about what Salim had said: was this man really as dangerous as he seemed? They were nearly halfway through Abu Ammar's list of objects. And what happened to them when they were finished? She needed to buy time.

'If you ask me,' Katya said, 'the real finds are still out there.'

'Out there?'

'Out in the ruins. Before you came here, we found valuable things every day, in the ruins of Nineveh. If you let us, we could try and find more. We know it better than anyone.'

She was overselling it, she thought, but Abu Ammar was listening.

'We can't let you out,' he said. 'We'd have to send guards with you, and we need the fighters. The imperialists are closing in again.'

She nodded, shrugged as if it didn't mean much to her.

'Sure, I get it. It's too risky.' She didn't glance up, but she felt that phrase working on him. Silence stretched between them, and Katya felt her mouth watering at the smell still rising off the kebab. She held the silence as long as she dared. 'What's that poetry you keep quoting?' she said finally. 'It's beautiful.'

Abu Ammar's nostrils flared.

'It's not poetry. It's the surah of the Cave.'

'Oh.'

'From the Quran. It's about two men who go to sleep in a cave on a hill.' He sniffed. 'And when they wake up, three hundred years have passed. All their families have died. They go back to their city, and no one recognises the coins they carry.'

'That's sad.'

He shrugged.

'Sometimes I wish that would happen to me. Just lie down and sleep for centuries.'

He laughed, his eyes challenging Katya to laugh with him. She didn't.

'Maybe things would be more peaceful then,' Katya tested. Abu Ammar shook his head.

'When the dajjal – when the Antichrist returns, only those who know that surah by heart will be saved. I read it every day. I know every line.'

Katya avoided his eyes. Outside, the crackle of gunfire sounded.

'Well, here are your pieces anyway,' she said, gesturing to the blue plastic crate. 'They've been sleeping for thousands of years, just like those men in the cave.'

He watched her, and she sensed a tension in the way he held himself. Did he feel he had to prove himself? Whatever it was, it faded quickly. He bent and heaved the crate up, puffing out his cheeks.

'Lift with your legs,' she told him. 'You don't want to hurt your back.'

His footsteps clicked on the stairs, and she stood there running her thumb over her cylinder seal necklace. When she was sure he was gone, Katya felt the silence close around her. Then she fell on the kebab and devoured a third of it, licking the grease from her fingers. It looked like a slice of fresh lemon had been included, but she noticed that someone, perhaps Abu Ammar, had eaten its flesh, leaving only the rind.

She took the rest of the kebab upstairs and gave it to Lola and Salim, who were playing dominoes in the lion hunt room. They both looked up in astonishment.

'He gave it to me,' she said. 'The English one.'

Salim took it suspiciously, smelled it, but then they both ate it hungrily. Lola dangled the shredded lettuce from her fingers and dropped it into her mouth.

'Why?'

Katya shrugged.

'It's like I told you. He's hard to predict. But some days he seems almost nice.'

Salim shook his head bitterly, and his lip curled.

'I'd bet you anything he was the one who had us put in that cupboard. That's how they work. They break you down, then act like they're the ones looking out for you, protecting you from the others. Good cop, bad cop. They learned it from the American torturers.'

Katya tasted the oils and spices lingering in her mouth and thought about what Abu Ammar had told her about the story of the cave. She thought of the smooth tone of his voice and his slender fingers moving like the legs of spiders across the dry clay objects.

Later in the day, Katya read to Lola and Salim. After the destruction of the library, she only had one book: that old copy of *Gilgamesh* that Salim had given her when she first arrived in Iraq. She had already read it many times: it was battered and dog-eared. Katya didn't know how much Lola understood, but she listened with her eyes staring off into the distance. Salim lay on his back with his head on Katya's knee, and she couldn't tell if he was asleep or awake.

The nights were broken by nightmares. Worse than anything were the ones where Katya dreamed that she was free, that she was home. More than once, she woke up sweating and chest heaving, and heard someone creeping through the halls, shoes squeaking slightly on the floor. The first few times, she thought this was part of her dream – but the third time, she blinked fully awake and went to her door. Salim was moving around in the dark again.

'Salim,' she hissed, not wanting to wake Lola in the office beside hers. 'What are you doing?'

'The van,' he said, half turning to her in the dark. 'I can't sleep. So I'm going to keep working on the van.'

She took a deep breath.

'But Salim, the parts. There's no way to get them in here.'

He turned back.

'I can't sleep. And I can't get it out of my head.'

'Okay,' she said. 'Don't get caught.'

'I'll try not to.'

'Salim. Please don't get caught.'

He shrunk away into the dark without saying anything more.

Abu Ammar returned at the end of the week, sooner than expected. He looked like he was dressed for war: a camo vest, a black sash wrapped around his head and a Kalashnikov slung over his shoulder. He wasn't wearing his glasses. He looked slightly ridiculous, but he stood proudly in the entrance hall waiting for her, eyeing the statues suspiciously, his pupils the same wide black as before.

'Have you just come from a battle?' Katya said, although his clothes were clean and new, and she knew this get-up had some other purpose.

'Every day is a battle,' he muttered. She took him down to the storeroom as usual, and they walked along the shelves, the barrel of his AK-47 clicking against its shoulder strap as they went. Abu Ammar was talkative and energetic, unusually curious about the objects she handed to him.

'What's this one?' he asked, picking up a cylinder seal like the one hung around her neck, but carved from ivory.

'It's for printing your mark on a contract.' She took it from him and rolled it over her hand. 'They wrote contracts in clay, back then. So you roll this over the surface, and the image comes out. Kind of like your signature.'

The seal left its print in white on her palm. He gave a little snort, making a show of mocking the primitive object, but it didn't seem totally sincere. She looked at him. Without his glasses, he looked a lot younger than she'd first imagined.

'How old are you, Abu Ammar?' She'd meant it to tease him, but she heard it come from her mouth with a softness that surprised her. He flushed at the question, and she thought he wouldn't answer.

'Twenty-three.' He adjusted the rifle strap around his shoulder so the weapon shifted behind him. Great. He was younger than her.

'How did you end up here?' He shrugged, about to say something, but then his face hardened.

'We all follow secret paths.'

She turned back to the shelves, biting a thumbnail. But he reconsidered, puffing up his chest.

'This is the only good place left now. We're building a new nation here, free from the colonisers who've drained the earth dry, and drained people's souls too, left them empty. Everywhere else is rotten, all the lands they've touched and spoiled. You can smell the rot on the streets.'

'Oh.'

Katya watched him and felt the skin on the inside of her mouth with her tongue, the painful ulcers growing there. She tried to work out how dangerous this young man was, just by the look of his face. But you can't tell anything from a face. She picked up a piece of cuneiform detailing an ancient cure for nosebleeds.

'Want to know what this one is?'

'No,' Abu Ammar said. 'It's stuff to sell to fat Americans, that's all. One dying empire amassing the remains of another.'

She nodded and handed him a blue plastic crate full of items, trying to force softness into her voice.

'Here you go then. Hope it gets you all the money you need.'

He pursed his lips in a kind of half smile and turned to go, using his knee to lift the crate, making everything inside clink and rattle.

'Oh,' he shot back at her. 'I told the boss what you said about digging out in the ruins.'

'You did?'

'Yeah. He said you can have a trial. You go out there and dig, and if you find anything worthwhile, you can keep it up. But if you try to escape, or do anything we don't like, we'll kill the lot of you. That apostate professor, the snake-worshipper you're hiding upstairs.'

Katya nodded, her mind racing.

'Okay. When is this trial?'

'Tomorrow,' he said coolly. 'We start at dawn.'

He disappeared up the stairs, and Katya stayed frozen there for a few seconds. Then the power went out with a clunk somewhere deep in the building, and she was swamped in darkness. She walked upstairs in a daze, and halfway up began to run, taking the stairs three at a time.

'Salim,' she said, shaking him awake. 'Salim, wake up!'

'What is it?'

'They're going to let us outside. They're going to take us out to the dig site tomorrow morning.'

He blinked.

'What are you talking about?' He rubbed sleep from his eyes.

'Salim, tell me the truth. Could that van really work? Can you fix it?'

'I don't know. I think so.'

She looked into his eyes, which held her gaze without wavering.

'Your nephew. Athir. Salim, this might be crazy. But maybe he doesn't have to get in here, with the parts.'

'What do you mean?'

'He could hide things for us. Out there, on the dig site. If he can bury the … the fan belt, all the other parts in the earth. And if we know where to find them …'

'Shit,' he said, his eyes awake now, darting back and forth. 'It could work. It's so risky. We'll have to smuggle the things back inside.'

'We can wrap them in the canvas with the tools. Those guys won't know the difference.'

Salim poked the inside of his mouth with his tongue so his cheek bulged out.

'It's too dangerous. They'll kill us if they find out …'

'Salim, these people are fucking crazy. You were right before about that. We have to get out of here.'

He nodded and bit his lip so it turned white.

'Okay, let's do it.' He glanced at his phone, his eyes far-off. 'I'll text Athir now. If the signal comes back in the night, he should get it before morning. But where can we tell him to bury the things?'

Katya thought for a moment.

'What about the olive tree on my site? He could bury it down there, between its roots.'

'Do we really want to bring them that close?' Salim said. 'To the lion carving?'

'It's the best landmark I can think of. Your site's too big – too sprawling. But that tree is pretty hard to miss. Right in the middle of the city, beneath the Nabi Yunus mosque. And while we're there we can check on the lion carving, see if anyone's dug it up.'

'Okay.' Salim took out his phone, tapped furiously on its buttons. 'Let's fucking do it.'

That night, Katya could barely sleep. She drifted off in bursts and dreamt that she was back home: a painful dream. She saw her mother, and their house, their cat, but she realised that she had no right to be there. She didn't have a passport, or any of the correct papers. Men would come soon and arrest her, send her back to the museum. The panic rose as she felt them drew nearer, as her mother begged her to hide. When they knocked on the door, she woke up.

Aurya

Before Aurya knew it, the month of Shebat came to an end in Nineveh. The swollen river receded from its high banks, leaving watercress stranded in garlands on the muddy banks. Adaar came to the city next with all its religious rites and the noisy crowds outside the shrines, and then the growing warmth of Nisan, and all the while she and Sharo laboured in the workshop, sweeping and clearing rubble, sharpening the metal tools in the wide stone basins, fetching implements and water and jugs of beer for the other apprentices. Each day, a little more of the garden scene carving took shape. Aurya watched in awe as the flat stone in the workshop courtyard transformed into the scene she'd witnessed in the palace: the trees, servants, birds and the King himself sitting in the centre and raising his cup, the head hanging upside down from the tree branch.

Throughout this time, Sharo visited his lion whenever he could, usually once or twice a week. He always came back with stories about how well the lion was doing, how strong its injured back paw had grown, how it had found a place in the mysterious ranking of the pride. It was one of these days, when Sharo was away from the workshop, that the servant Bel-Ibni came to inspect progress on the garden scene carvings. He brought Abil with him. When Aurya saw the boy, she realised how lonely she'd been.

Aurya was glad Sharo wasn't there. This was the first time the palace would inspect the carvings since his contribution, and if his memory of the chair and table were anything but perfect, she hoped he would stay as far away as possible. While the apprentices watched in fear, and the master mason chewed on the hem of his cap, Bel-Ibni strode up and down the rows of white stone, his robe a deep blue, and tied with mother-of-pearl beads. He peered closely at the intricate designs. The master mason was white even beneath his patina of dust. While everyone's attention was fixed on the King's servant, Aurya edged around the crowd until she stood beside Abil. He nodded to her.

'How are you, river girl?' he whispered.

'Oh, I'm …' she sagged. 'I hate it here. They're trying to teach us to carve stone. My brother's so good at it. I can't do it at all.'

Abil nodded.

'I could never be a craftsman. That's why I'm going to train in the tablet house.'

'The tablet house?'

'Yes, it's next to the library. It's where young scribes go to train. They learn to read and write in all the different languages. There are so many books there. When I'm older, I want to read every book in the world, like the King has.'

Aurya nodded, imagining all the stories there might be, locked up in those scribbling letters, all the different worlds and foreign lands.

'I'd love to learn to read,' she said.

'You could,' Abil said. 'If you don't like it here, you could come to the tablet house and learn to read and write with me.'

'With you?'

He went red.

'With everyone.'

She looked at Abil, at his pretty eyes and slender wrists. Even as she thought it, she knew it was impossible.

'I can't leave Sharo. He's so helpless on his own.'

Abil nodded.

'I understand. If I still had my family, I'd never leave them for the world.'

'What happened to them?'

'They were Babylonian. They were captured in the war. The Assyrians marched them into the desert, hundreds of them, and left them to die.'

'I'm sorry.'

'Me too.'

They were silent after that. Aurya thought of the desert sun, the heat and the crowing of circling birds. She noticed with a rush of fear that Bel-Ibni was peering down his thin nose at the table and chair in the garden arrangement, the part that Sharo had drawn from memory. He was running his tongue over the front of his teeth. The mason was practically dancing from foot to foot.

'Who did this part of the carving?' Bel-Ibni asked, his voice hard and clear.

'The apprentices Harkhuf and Kibri-Dagan. But the sketching was done by the little river boy, my lord.'

Bel-Ibni nodded slowly.

'It looks good,' he mused. 'A promising start. How long will it take?'

All the breath seemed to leave the master's body at once, like a skin being deflated.

'Several more weeks, my lord.'

'No more delays,' Bel-Ibni said, and then looked down at his chest. 'Curses of Shamash, I've lost a bead … did anyone see it?'

He left soon after, and Abil gave Aurya an apologetic look as he followed. Her heart gave a gentle tug to see him go.

'Think about what I said,' he told her as he left. 'About the tablet house.'

'I will.'

Aurya felt truly alone. Later in the day, a crier went around announcing details of a runaway slave. Lamentations sounded from a death down the street. The workshop dust filled her lungs, her hair, settled on her eyelashes.

She felt clumsier every day. She made ugly scars with slipped chisels and pinched her skin with the mallet. Bruises swelled like purple berries across her fingers. When she tried to brush the dust from her work surface, small slivers of knife-sharp stone would slice little cuts in her hand. Sharo moved on to carving vine leaves,

218

birds, bunches of grapes. The master mason would stand right behind him as he worked, peering over his shoulder.

'And you did this just from memory?' he would say of a piece Sharo had made, showing birds resting in the curls of a grapevine.

'Yes, of course,' Sharo would reply. He never seemed pleased or proud of what he was making, but Aurya hadn't seen his memory-pain trouble him for days now. All this time, Aurya felt that sliver of stone sink deeper into her heart. Sharo knew something about her mother that he wasn't telling her. He claimed she was dead, but wouldn't tell Aurya how she died. And he would never help her find the house of dust.

When everyone had left the workshop, and the evening light slanted down through the canopy, turning the dust in the air into columns of gold, Aurya went over to look at Sharo's carving. She ran her fingers over its surface. It was beautiful: well-proportioned and detailed, lovingly shaped and polished. But it had something else too, something she couldn't name. She looked at the birds caught in mid-preen, tipping their heads to one side and looking at the bunches of grapes with the little beads of their eyes. The stone felt alive. Aurya's fingers tingled a little to touch it. Jealousy boiled in her gut. With a kind of numb shock, Aurya realised that for the first time in her life, her brother didn't need her.

Aurya looked out over the city, at the white smoke rising from workshops and houses, the coloured awnings flapping everywhere, the palms and the rolling greenery cloaking the river, the floating bridge of boats thick with traffic, and wondered where in this huge city she would ever find her mother.

The first time Aurya ran away, she expected to get in trouble. She thought she might be punished or beaten for it, but any clue about her mother would be worth a hundred beatings. After the first meal, she had wrapped her cloak around her shoulders and taken a basket of rubble with her down to the gate of the workshop as though to empty it over the wall. She felt the eyes of the apprentices as she went. Then when she reached the gate, she dropped into its shade, pulled the cloak over her head like a shawl and left the basket behind. No one had spotted her. She kept on walking, down the hill and past the beggar children, not quite believing that she'd got away with it.

Down near the river, she found markets and workshops at the water's edge, weeds growing up through cracked jars. She didn't speak to anyone at first. She ran away from some drunks gathered in a doorway who shouted at her. But in one workshop, an old woman sitting in a pile of coloured fabrics saw her and offered her a date. She took it.

'I'm looking for my mother,' Aurya said.

'Poor child,' the woman said, in a strange accent. 'Where did you last see her?'

'I've never seen her. But I heard she's somewhere called the house of dust. Do you know where it is?'

The old woman closed her eyes and shook her head, turning her face away, and after this she wouldn't say another thing. Aurya spent the day near the quays on the river, watching the ships unloading, wondering which of them had sailed past her old home on the riverbank.

When she returned to the workshop in the evening, she expected a beating at least. But the master seemed not to have noticed she'd been gone. He'd been teaching Sharo to use the circle-drawing tools, half-moon implements that turned against the stone with minute precision. Her brother looked up for a moment when he saw Aurya come in, but the mason paid her no attention.

As the weeks went by, she went walking in the city more and more. She learned the names of the different districts, the different gates. She held her nose as she walked through the streets lined with mud and waste, where people stayed close to the house walls to avoid the foul water, and merchants charged tips to let women ride their buffalo across. She watched the brick kilns in the south belch smoke and the soot-covered men, the heaps of broken pottery higher than the roofs. She learned where to find the copper market, the fish market, the grain market. She smelled the evil spirits that lurked in the courtyard drains, covered with planks of wood. She saw people vomiting in the streets, and men in drinking houses taking women into the back rooms. She got chased by a gang once, and by a pack of dogs another time, both times climbing on to a rooftop to escape. She saw a dead body in an alleyway, swollen and flyblown, half-eaten by the dogs. She learned how to recognise the Babylonian dialect, the Phoenician dialect, how the tenants beneath the Ishtar Gate elongated their vowels when angry, or how the Judean women in the east would snort when they laughed and sat veiled in their shops, how the bakers in the Elamite quarter put cloves in their bread. She heard all the city's rumours, and the news of wars and rebellions and famines that trickled in from the empire's edges as though from another world. Nineveh: when she tried to think of it all, to hold everything she'd seen in her head, it made her feel a strange kind of fear.

Everywhere she went, she asked people for the house of dust. It had a strange effect. They closed their eyes or shook their heads. They mumbled a mysterious reply or just hurried on, casting words of protection over her as if she were a wandering shade who'd taken human form to trick them.

It was a day like this that Aurya saw the army leave for war. Sharo had gone to see his lion, and she wandered out into the city. She was loitering on a scaffold near the fruit market when a horseman came trotting down the street on a white horse, leather wrapped around the bottom of its hooves. He shouted, 'Clear the street! The army of Ashur approaches.'

The fruit seller beneath her packed up the persimmons he'd laid on the street as though a storm was coming. The first soldiers came marching into the market square with the blare of trumpets and thumping drums. Aurya sat and watched as the spear-men and the archers came past, the men with their woven shields and spears clattering together over their heads, their thick beards and pointed helmets catching the sun. Then the cavalry on their horses, and the brightly painted chariots with studded wheels. Another column of spear-men came past, and then a huge siege engine like a wooden building, rolling on giant iron-studded wheels. It went on and on: hundreds of men, then thousands. By the time the sun was high overhead, the men were still marching past. They had been marching for hours. Aurya became sure that the same men were passing her again and again, that they were turning off into some side street and doubling back around. She climbed a little higher on the scaffold, and looked out over the walls, to where the snaking column darkened the road far-off into the distance, an endless stream of soldiers so vast she couldn't see the end. After that, the whole thing seemed frightening: that there should be so many men, that they should all be marching out to destroy some place she'd never seen.

That night, she dreamed that she was marching in that endless column, and that people ahead of her were whispering about something terrible that lay ahead. No one knew what it was, but they knew it was terrifying. No one could turn around; the tide of men drew them all on. Aurya tried to escape the column, but the marching bodies pressed in around her on either side. Ahead, the sky was turning orange, flickering with flames and belching smoke. All together, the men began to sing.

———————

The last months of spring passed slowly in Nineveh. The fifty days of heat were on their way, and in the fields outside the walls, the fresh grass was growing. On the slopes where the sun fell, flowers grew like a foam, and the sky over the city was filling with birds. People slept in the afternoons, in the shade of awnings.

The King didn't leave with his army. He rarely did, preferring to let his generals deal with his wars while he toured the kingdom or spent time with his soothsayers. He visited the mason's workshop one day when Aurya was there. She was glad she'd stayed; the King brought with him his servant and Bel-Ibni, who was wearing brilliant robes in orange and magenta, and Abil came with them. Aurya thought that he'd grown taller since she'd last seen him. She had too: her limbs were starting to feel too long, which didn't help her clumsiness. Abil's eyes sparkled a little when he saw her, but he was busy attending to his master.

'All health to your majesty,' the master mason said, and fell to his knees. 'I am your dog and servant.'

The King was wearing plain white robes that day, so it was almost blinding to look at him in the sun. He swept from place to place, impatient to see his garden scene.

'These clothes, Bel-Ibni … How much longer did you say I have to wear them?' he bellowed at one point.

'Just the twentieth and twenty-first, my lord. Until the danger of an eclipse passes.'

'Shamash, they itch …'

The carvings were nearly finished, and Sharo had even been allowed to perform some small detail work on the edges, and on the table and royal seat. The King leant down and inspected the minute vines and flowers, the cups and whisks held by the attendants. He reached out and brushed the powdered stone from the carving of the table.

'This detail around the chair and the table is magnificent,' he said. 'Who did this?'

'My lord,' the master mason gushed, 'it was the boy you brought here from the riverbank, in your infinite wisdom. He has a gift for the art of stone.'

The King turned around and looked at Sharo, who was standing still and silent, his eyes fixed.

'I knew it,' the King said. 'Didn't I say so, Bel-Ibni?'

'Many times, my lord,' said the servant. The King rattled the gold-flowered band on his wrist.

'Well done, boy. And his sister? How is she doing?'

Aurya pretended to get on with some work, moving her hands busily but uselessly around the piece of stone she was working on.

'Not nearly as well, my lord. I really think that …'

'Brothers and sisters should always stick together,' the King sighed, and looked up into the sky. 'Sometimes I wonder if my own brother … if we had known each other better at that age. Maybe it could all have been avoided.'

'Who knows what the fates hold for different paths?' the master mason mumbled, and he mopped some sweat from his neck and behind his ears. He cast Aurya a look full of bitterness.

'Well, this looks very good, very good,' the King said.

'Can I come and see my lion today?' Sharo blurted out, and everyone muttered nervously at his almost interrupting his majesty.

'Of course, river boy. You should see him while you can. There's not much time left!'

'What do you mean?' Sharo asked.

'Well, it's nearly time for the hunt. Just a week now, isn't that right, Bel-Ibni?'

'That's right, my lord.'

'The hunt?' Sharo said, furrowing his brow. 'What are the lions hunting?'

There was a moment of silence, and then the King burst out in laughter, and slapped his hands together with a boom. Everyone else hurriedly joined in and tittered. Sharo just stood there, not understanding, and Aurya couldn't bear to look.

'You will give your apprentices the day off work,' the King said before preparing to leave. 'They will all want to see the hunt, I imagine!'

The master mason bowed.

'Of course, your majesty.'

Aurya got to speak to Abil briefly before the King's entourage left. She noticed the crescents of clay under his fingernails.

'Is it any better for you now?' he asked.

'No. I still hate it here,' Aurya said. 'I want to come to the tablet house. I want to learn how to read.'

'You can. Tell me any time you want, and I'll ask the teacher. He owes me a favour since I got him an audience with Bel-Ibni.'

Aurya looked at Sharo, who was standing there alone among the chattering apprentices, still wondering about what the King had said. She felt that little sliver of stone sink deeper into her heart.

'When they kill that lion, it's going to destroy him. I'll be the only person who can calm him down.'

'I hope you do come to the tablet house,' Abil said. He seemed a little braver than he'd been before.

'Me too. I sometimes go and sit in the fruit market, near the old palm. Will you come meet me there on market days? You can tell me some of the stories you're learning to read from.'

'I will. I promise.'

He got up to follow his master. A little whirlwind of dust was gathering and dancing in the afternoon air.

That night, Aurya dreamed of the heat and smell in the animal enclosure. She was walking past the stalls where the horses and camels were kept, but there were people inside in their place. Their eyes followed her as she walked past, terrified eyes peeking through the gaps in the wood. She could hear them whispering: 'Murderer … murderer … murderer.'

'I'm not,' she tried to say, but they just kept on whispering. With a growing sense of dread, she walked to the sunken lion enclosure. Fearful noises came from the bottom. The lions were down there, lying and sleeping in the dust. Sharo's lion was there, curled into the shape of a half moon, and curled up beside it was Sharo.

'Sharo!' Aurya cried out to him. 'What are you doing down there? They'll kill you.'

Sharo didn't look up. Was he already dead? The lion lying beside him lifted its huge head and fixed its enormous yellow eyes on her. Its jaws opened and its long pink tongue lolled out.

'He'll never help you find her,' it rasped. 'You're on your own now.'

Aurya shot awake with a gasp. She turned and saw Sharo lying with his back to her, curled in that same half-moon position. The birds outside were beginning to call.

Katya

The morning came with a strange silvery light that settled over everything. The world to Katya looked slick, sheened as though made of chrome. Salim still had no reply from Athir, and they kept repeating the same questions to each other. Had the text gone through? Would he be able to hide the parts on such short notice? Could he do it without getting caught? Salim checked his phone every minute as they ate chickpeas straight from the tin and talked over their plan. Neither of them had much of an appetite, but they knew they had to eat.

'There's no way of telling if it went through,' Salim said. 'And if we go out there, take all this risk, and nothing's there?'

Katya pressed her tongue gently against the sharp edge of the can, felt the tingle of the ragged metal's charge.

'There's no backing out now,' she said, unable to summon anything more reassuring. 'We'll find out soon enough.'

After breakfast, Katya and Salim stood in the museum entrance hall and waited for Abu Ammar and his men. Lola was hiding upstairs, which she normally did when the men came to the museum. Katya hadn't told her about their plan. As Katya had hugged her and told her they'd be back soon, she looked at the girl's stubborn face and had a sudden vision of what would happen if they were caught. She thought of Lola waiting up there all day for them to return, alone and scared in the museum.

'Lola … stay safe. Please. If the men come here, hide, or try to escape any way you can.'

The girl nodded grimly and wrapped Katya in a hug.

Down in the museum hall, nerves sung in Salim's voice.

'So … You remember what we have to do?'

'Yeah.' That same quaver in her own voice. 'When you think it's clear, you start digging near the tree, try to find the parts if they're there. Then I cause some kind of distraction.'

'Yes. Save it until I move over to the tree.'

'Yup. And then you wrap up the fan belt in the canvas with your digging tools.'

'If it's there.'

'If it's there. But what if …'

There was a sharp series of thuds on the museum door. Metal, the butt of a rifle. Katya met Salim's eye, and he squeezed her hand.

'Let's do this,' he said. The door opened, and Abu Ammar entered with two men wearing scarves, balaclavas and stolen military gear. Katya was glad at least that the skull man wasn't among them.

'What's this?' Abu Ammar sneered, and pointed at Salim. 'You didn't say anything about bringing him.'

'I need him,' Katya said.

'No way. He's staying here.'

Katya held him in her gaze. Don't show weakness.

'He knows the site better than anyone. I won't be able to find anything without him.'

Abu Ammar ground his teeth and gave a long breath through his nose. But he shrugged and gestured to the men. They roughly handled Katya and Salim, zipped their hands together with cable ties and marched them outside, where a car was waiting that smelled of cigarette smoke and mud. The men put sacks over their heads, and Katya breathed in the smell of whatever it once held, a rich perfumed smell like nutmeg that made her want to sneeze. It was sweltering in the car, and the zip tie cut into her wrists where they were still tender and scabbed from the nights in the cupboard. Through the weave of the fabric, she could see points of light, the shadowy backs of two men in the front seats. Abu Ammar was in the passenger seat, she thought. The third man sat in the back with her and Salim, but he didn't sit between them. Katya felt Salim's thigh against hers. She reached out her little finger and touched his hand, feeling the warmth of his skin. She felt him flinch in surprise, but then he touched hers back.

The journey felt longer than usual. Katya described the position of the site to the men, but had no idea if they were taking the right turns. Eventually the car stopped, and those same rough hands pulled them out.

'Here we are then,' Abu Ammar said. The bag came off, and Katya blinked in the harsh sun, blowing her hair from her mouth. Abu Ammar cut their ties with his hunting knife. The blade touched the skin of her wrist, and felt hot as if it had been lying in the sun. Her clothes were already sticking to her. She turned to Salim, and he wrinkled his nose as a bead of sweat ran down it.

'In July, water boils in the jug,' he said.

'Quiet!' Abu Ammar shouted at them from behind. He used the barrel of his gun to push Salim.

They all made their way up the hill, the silvery mosque of Nabi Yunus glowing in the sun. Soon they were standing on the dig site, which looked abandoned and neglected since they'd last been here. The tarpaulin shelter where they used to eat lunch had come away on one side and flapped in the wind. Looters had dug more holes across the site, and tracks wound over the dirt in all directions. But the old tyre they'd left on top of the buried lion carving was still in place. She glanced at Salim, and saw that he was looking there too.

'Get to work then!' Abu Ammar commanded. He turned his back to them and popped a couple of Captagon pills from a silvery blister pack, swallowed them without water. Katya and Salim picked their way around the looters' holes as they approached the main trench and laid out the tools on their tarpaulin. Abu Ammar sat and smoked with his rifle slung across his belly, and the two guards sat on the wall, eyes narrowed against the dust and glare. One flicked the safety on his gun off and on, off and on.

Katya began to noisily move her tools around, until she thought it was safe to whisper to Salim.

'What do you think?' she murmured. 'Did Athir bury the parts?'

Salim took a deep breath, and glanced enviously at Abu Ammar's cigarette. He shrugged.

'It's hard to tell. The earth's been disturbed so much.'

He didn't look in the direction of the olive tree, and neither did Katya. She listened to its leaves in the breeze, and her whole body shimmered with that sound. They began work just like any other day, a surreal normality. Katya wasn't wearing any suncream. The sun baked her, and she tried to cover her skin where she could, turned up her collar and rolled down her sleeves. They plotted out the squares using thread, and trowelled into the holes, marking depth as they went. The meticulousness of the work seemed ludicrous now.

'So this is what you do,' Abu Ammar sneered after half an hour or so of their digging. He seemed bored. 'You come to this country and rob all its treasures.'

Katya stood up straight, covered in dust and earth, and looked up at him from down in the trench.

'No,' she said. 'We dig to learn things. To find stories, to understand the past. They stay in museums in Iraq, where they're kept safe.'

'That's the excuse of all thieves,' he said. '"I'm just looking after it."'

Katya flushed.

'We protect them from people like you,' she said, and immediately regretted it. But Abu Ammar just scoffed and kicked a piece of shale in her direction. He turned back around to face the city with one finger in the air.

'"Shall I tell you who the worst people are?"' he recited to one of the men. '"The ones whose works in this life are totally astray, but who think they're doing good."'

Katya noticed that Abu Ammar didn't speak Arabic to the others, and they didn't seem to speak much English. She stretched her back, felt the beginnings of heat rash across her skin. Gunfire crackled in the air over the city.

Katya dug methodically, but with desperation tingling in her fingertips. The earth at that level was crusted with pieces of pottery, but she hoped she would find something at least a little impressive, a figurine or coin from a later era even. But significant finds were rare. She thought about taking off her cylinder seal necklace and pretending to find it in the earth, but she couldn't bear to part with it, her guilty treasure, the comfort she squeezed during the night.

Katya soon became aware of Salim edging towards the olive tree. Time was running out. She watched him from the corner of her eye, glancing his way as often as she dared. She could tell by the fact that he didn't use a pick, just went straight in with the trowel, that the earth had been recently disturbed. Something in his tight, self-conscious movements made him seem unnatural though. She could feel Abu Ammar's attention wandering over to him. She had to find something right away.

'Hey,' she called Abu Ammar, who swung around. 'Look what I found!'

He shot a look in her direction, and she reached for the first thing at hand.

'What is it?' He came over, army boots crunching.

'It's a pot.' She tried to fill her voice with excitement.

'A pot?'

'Yeah – well, a small piece of a pot. You hardly ever see this kind. See this beautiful black paintwork on the outer rim? A dotted motif. You can tell the clay's been brushed with a handful of grass after being moulded too. And see the way it's bevelled around the rim? Shows the kind of rapid advances in pottery wheel technology you get around this time, mostly due to collectivisation of the …'

'Well, how much is it worth?'

'Worth?' She blew away a piece of earth clinging to the side of the baked clay potsherd. 'You mean in terms of scientific …?'

'No, cash. C.A.S.H.'

'Oh. Well, it's not really worth anything. But it's a fascinating example of –'

Abu Ammar knelt down and took the fragment. He spun around and hurled it over the wall, through the branches of the olive tree. Salim flinched with an obviously guilty expression on his face as the piece flew over his head.

'It's a fascinating example of nothing,' Abu Ammar said.

'Whatever. Thought you'd be interested.'

'I'm not.' He scuffed his boot into the dust and put his hand on the black hilt of his knife. Katya watched as he walked back to his vigil on the wall. He swallowed another couple of pills with a grimace, and there was the thud of an explosion in the distance.

'"And how many a city did we destroy while it was doing wrong?"' he began to recite. '"How many fallen into ruin, and how many an abandoned well and how many a lofty palace?"'

Katya's heart pounded, but she gave the sharpest glance in Salim's direction. He was wrapping something in the canvas, along with his trowel. She caught his eye, and he gave just the hint of a nod.

———

In the car on the way back, the men had tied Katya's and Salim's hands again, but didn't bother with the bags. The third man sat between them this time. Katya felt her body aching after the day of digging, her head pounding from the hours of sun. Her clothes stuck to her, but a fire lit her from the inside.

'That was a fucking waste of time,' Abu Ammar said. He kicked something in the footwell that clunked. 'You didn't find anything.'

'It's not something you can rush ...' Katya began, but Abu Ammar shot her a look that made her jaw clench shut. As they drove through the city, Katya saw burnt-out cars in the road verges, police cars with smashed windows. Huge queues snaked outside every petrol station, people holding empty jerrycans limply by their sides, hard looks on most faces. Men with guns patrolled everywhere, standing up in the backs of pickup trucks, many wearing American-style camo but with their faces covered. On the bridge near the museum, she saw some men driving an armoured car. More than once, she saw that same black flag, decorated with white script, on which she recognised the name of God. When they got back to the museum, the men left them there, but one spat a gob of phlegm on the floor as he turned away. The door thudded shut, and Katya counted to ten, closing her eyes and listening to the shouts and receding footsteps on the museum approach. Then she turned to Salim.

'Did you get it?'

He let out a long breath, and shook all over, as if he'd been holding in his tremors for the whole journey back. He unbuckled his digging tools, spreading earth, dust and clods of dry clay all over the floor. He pulled out a long loop of black rubber, one side toothed like a gear wheel, and a large drinking bottle full of amber liquid, the kind she'd seen sold at roundabouts in the city.

'The new fan belt, and some petrol.' His eyes lit up. 'My god, it worked! You did well with that potsherd. Did you hear him? "It's a fascinating example of nothing!"'

He burst out laughing, and Katya joined in, unable to hold it in any longer. The corners of her eyes bloomed with tears of fear and relief.

'Can you get this on the van tonight?'

'I think so. We still need a few more parts, though. Another couple of bottles like this, to get us south. And the fake permit. I guess Athir couldn't get it in time. We'll have to do this again. Just once more.'

Katya rubbed her eyes, feeling the exhaustion weigh down on her.

'That means we're going to have to give them something bigger. You heard him just now. "A waste of time."'

'What can we give him, when looters are hitting the site every night? They're getting away with everything these idiots would find valuable.'

'What about the carving?' Salim fixed her with a look. Suddenly all the warmth drained from the air.

'The new lion carving?'

'Yes.'

Salim's face set.

'I'm not giving that to these bastards.'

He turned up the stairs and towelled the dirt off the back of his neck with a handkerchief.

'Salim ...'

'No way. That's the greatest achievement of both our careers, Katya. And it's my history. The history of my country. It doesn't belong to us to give away.'

'It's my history too.'

'Then act like it!' he shouted, and she shrunk from the unexpected sting in his voice. She followed him up the stairs, past carvings of the Assyrian battles in the marshes, the campaigns of Ashurbanipal in Babylon, his civil war with his brother.

'Salim,' she said, 'I've been down there in the storeroom with Abu Ammar. I know what he is. I know what kind of people these guys are.'

'Oh, don't worry. I know who they are.'

He pointed to the carvings on the wall: the marsh people cowering in the reeds and waiting for the spears of the soldiers who hunted them; the Assyrian soldiers dismantling the cities of Elam with hammers, patient and thorough as craftsmen; the gleeful soldiers stripping the skin off screaming men, impaling the flayed bodies on poles; a mountain of severed heads in the palm shade; the prisoners lining up to die as a watching king drank wine.

'That's who they are.'

———

Katya felt caged in the museum. Every day she woke up surrounded by silent, watchful things. Without her pills, she had expected her seizures to get more frequent, but that hadn't happened. Instead, she felt a kind of low-level aura all day, that feeling of having been somewhere before, walked all these same paths, thought even these very thoughts before. Planes were dropping more and more bombs in the city, rumbles and flashes in the night. The statues couldn't hear her when she talked to them, but she talked anyway.

'How are you today, King Ashurbanipal? Still dead? Good, good. Oh, me? I'm trapped in a museum by an army of maniacs.'

Some days when she wandered the museum, all these strange objects gathered from every era of history felt ridiculous. What did they say about anything? The worlds they'd known were gone. Katya herself felt like a statue, a useless exhibit warehoused in a museum that never opened.

Days passed, wrapped in cobwebs. The man with the skull mask returned and then started coming back more often. The three of them spent some dark nights in the cupboard, but the men left them water now. All three would sit with their hands tied, with Katya trying to lie back on Salim's lap. On the other nights, when Abu Ammar came, they had some degree of freedom. Salim sneaked out and worked on the van then, which kept him occupied and seemed to fend off his despair. He cleared away all signs of his work every morning, not knowing what the next day would bring. Katya wished she had something like that, some act of resistance that would take her mind off the fear that crashed down on her in paralysing surges. But all she had was those objects, passing through her hands and into the crate. The fear was constant. It was an icy waterfall from her chest to her stomach that left her hugging her knees on her mattress in the office, listening to the sounds of chaos and ordinary life vie for control of the city outside. She thought of home, of her mother going through it all again: the Foreign Office, the appeals, the journalists. How much loss could one person take in their life, before it broke them?

It was only when Katya was down in the museum's belly, in the storeroom counting objects, that she really thought about what it would be like to die. What kind of death it might be. One afternoon, down there in the dark, she went to the pile of clay tablets where they'd hidden the knife. She shooed away a large spider and reached for it, felt the slight weight of its cheap red plastic handle, the blade slightly bent at its tip. She lifted it to her throat, and held it there for a moment, that line of cold against her skin. It couldn't hurt to practise dying, she thought, just like you'd practise anything else. Her palms moistened a little, and she could feel her rising heartbeat through the handle and the solid architecture of her throat.

Somewhere above, there was a deep boom like a roll of thunder, deeper than the low rumble of airstrikes. The floor shook slightly. Katya took the knife away from her throat, the spell broken. She put it down with a long out-breath and ran upstairs to the roof. She found Salim and Lola there, both wide-eyed and barefoot, leaning over the balustrade.

'What is it?' she asked. And then Katya saw it. On the hill above her dig site, over the site of the mosque of Jonah's tomb, a huge cloud of dust and smoke rose. Where the mosque had once stood – its slender minaret, its arches and neat terraced gardens – was a plume of smoke. In the streets all around, people were beginning to flock in that direction. Wails were already rising up over the morning air.

'What are they thinking?' Salim muttered, in disbelief. The mosques around the city crackled into prayer at that moment. At the same time, another explosion went off, and Katya flinched. Another plume of grey smoke.

'Another mosque,' Lola said. In the streets, people were putting their hands in the air, on their heads, covering their mouths. Salim reached in his pockets for cigarettes, then remembered he'd run out and swore.

'Do you think the carving will be okay?' Katya whispered. 'The lion carving?'

Salim took a deep breath.

'We buried it well enough, thank God.'

He placed both his hands over his face, his breath whistling between the gaps in his fingers, watching the smoke settle over the shattered ruin of the Nabi Yunus mosque. Then he started to laugh.

'Salim, what is it?'

It started slowly at first, but his laughter grew until he bucked and howled with it, tears rolling down his cheeks. Lola stepped away from him. Salim bent over and pressed his back against the balustrade, trying to control the convulsions.

'Salim, what's so funny?'

'I ... I can't help it. Do you know how long I've spent trying to get permission to dig anywhere near that mosque? How many forms and meetings with holy men and bribes to officials, just to get anywhere near that sacred place with a trowel? And now the city gets taken over by fanatics … and they just blow the whole thing up!'

Katya watched as he collapsed in laughter, falling to the floor clutching his ribs. And she couldn't help it: she began to laugh too. They stood on the roof rocking together for some time, with a bright clear laughter of the kind she hadn't heard in weeks. Lola watched them both in bemusement. As the convulsions faded from their bodies, the three of them watched the lonely figures picking through ruins, the bright colours of European football jerseys among the salvagers and the dust falling in the air like snow.

They had been imprisoned in the museum for six weeks. As evening approached, they watched the sun turn purple and orange on the horizon, the pinprick of Venus appearing in the sky. The dust gave a strange quality to the sunset; the jagged shadows of the ruined mosque stretched out over the rooftops, and night fell quickly. The city was blacked out still, but not dark at all. Where does the light come from, Katya thought? It was a soft, mysterious glow.

As the light of the day faded, Katya talked about the plants that had flourished in the bomb sites of London after the war: the flowers of fireweed covering the ruins like a purple foam, coltsfoot and fleabane, ragwort and Yorkshire fog. Salim and Lola both listened glumly. She told them about the rare seeds that the bombs set free from Kew Gardens and the Natural History Museum, the Peruvian galinsoga and the fugitive mimosas brought from China that escaped their sealed hothouses and began to grow wild in the rubble. Later on, they became aware of people gathering in the park.

'What's happening down there?' Katya said. A man with a megaphone began to shout. It was a strange sight since the city had fallen: people never gathered in one place now, but hurried around the streets with abayas or keffiyehs pulled over their mouths as if there was a plague in the air. Now there was a real commotion, and shouting, jeering. The coloured lights from the shops around the square were casting strange carnivalesque shadows across the park. Pickup trucks were arriving too, and the men with guns were clustered in groups. The one with the megaphone jumped up on to a bench, the same bench she and Lola had sat on weeks before, Katya thought. He was calling out to the crowd.

'What's he saying?' Katya asked. Salim shook his head, let a long breath out.

'The windiest militant trash.'

Before long, a truck pulled up with a kind of metal cage in its back. Many fighters stood among the crowd, men in the uniform Salim called 'the Afghan style': herringbone and khaki jackets, camo trousers, checked headscarves and Kalashnikovs. They were the ones jeering. Most people in the crowd were watching silently. The megaphone man was announcing something over and over, striding up and down the long bench like an actor pacing the stage.

'What are they doing?' Katya asked. She turned to Salim and saw that he had turned pale. Lola's face was set. The men with guns pulled from the cage three prisoners with black hoods over their heads, their hands tied. When they moved from the tree cover, Katya noticed with a shock that one of the escorts was Abu Ammar. He had a stiff grimace on his face, the coloured lights dancing on his spectacles. In his free hand, his black knife was drawn. The man on the megaphone announced something as the prisoners got closer, his voice lilting and theatrical. Abu Ammar pulled the hoods off the captives, one by one, and all the faces beneath were as grey as candle wax, as if coated in dust. Their eyes were closed, and they were murmuring. Beside Katya, Salim took a breath.

'Come on,' he said. 'Don't watch this.'

'What is it?'

'They're going to kill them.'

'Why?'

'Whatever reason they can think of,' he gasped, and threw up his hands. 'For fighting back. For trying to leave the city. For having a jar of fucking pickles!'

He turned away and made for the stairs. Katya looked down at the scene. The audience had fallen completely silent, and a deathly hush hung over the park. Surely Abu Ammar, the man she'd stood next to in the storehouse dark, who'd brought her a kebab, a man three years younger than her, couldn't do what he seemed about to do.

'Katya,' Salim called back, with desperation in his voice. 'You won't forget it, if you see it. I mean it. You won't forget it for the rest of your life. That's what they want.'

Katya shuddered and took one last look at Abu Ammar, who raised his black knife to the air. The blade's heat came back to her, when it had brushed against her wrist the other day. Down in the park, the men with guns kicked the bound captives in the back of the knees so they were forced to kneel. Katya turned away and followed Salim, her stomach churning, and breathed steadily through her nose to avoid throwing up. Lola followed her, and just as they closed the fire exit door, she heard jeers from the fighters down in the street.

It was cool and dark in the museum. There was no power. The three of them sat in silence and shadow before the carving of King Ashurbanipal in his garden. Katya ignored the scars on the King's face, where the men who destroyed his palace and burned his city had tried to erase his image from the walls. She imagined she was there in that garden, beneath the leaf shade, the birds and vines overhead, the King raising his cup in a toast. When she noticed the severed head hanging from the tree on the left, carved faithfully and skilfully, she jumped up and ran away through the halls. No one followed her. She ran through the museum, not knowing where she was going, just wanting to run as far as she could. Finally she reached the room with the lion carvings.

She stared at the sorrowful lions scattered in the King's wake, at the lion jumping up and biting that wheel. She looked at the King, at his eyes cold and hard and slightly smiling as he drove his spear into the lion's back, at its eyes staring out at her through the millennia. Then she spoke aloud the passage from *Gilgamesh* that had been running over and over in her mind, the one that made her skin feel cold whenever she read it to Lola. She heard her own voice, high and scared, in the gloom.

"'I dreamt of the house whose people sit in darkness,'" she wavered. "'Dust is their food and clay is their meat. They are clothed like birds, with wings for covering. I entered the house of dust and I saw all the kings of the earth, their crowns put away for ever ...'"

Aurya

The hunt was all people were talking about in the city. Sharo seemed not to understand, or if he did, he didn't believe what he heard. He visited his lion more frequently now, going every other day. He always came back with more stories about it: how it had become friends with a female lion that it would playfight with, how he was worried it wasn't happy in its enclosure, how he could tell by its voice that it yearned to wander the hills the way it used to.

When the day came, it was hot and clear. Aurya tried to talk Sharo out of going.

'You should stay here,' she said, as they sat on the workshop wall and watched the city morning. 'This isn't something you should see.'

'I'm coming.' There was a stony determination in his eyes. 'They told me Enkidu is going out into the fields with the King and the other lions.'

'Sharo ...'

Aurya looked her brother in the eye, and thought that she could make him stay, if she had to. But that sharp sliver of stone stuck in her chest. Over the past few weeks, as all her attempts to find the house of dust had failed, as she began to lose hope that she would ever find her mother, the sliver had started to whisper to her. Sharo wasn't a child any more, the voice of that sliver said. He had forgotten their mother and left her to search this vast city alone. He refused to tell her what he knew. He had abandoned her. It would do him good to see the hunt, the sliver whispered. It would make him grow up. It was only as Aurya walked down the gravelly path from the workshop, and Sharo skipped along and spoke excitedly about the lion, that she realised that the voice whispering from that cold sliver was her father's.

They met Abil near the fish market. Watery blood formed miniature waterfalls down the sides of the drain there, the evil spirits of its stench lurking heavy in the air. Skinny desert cats mewled on the rooftops. That day, the crowds were heading in only one direction: to the Shamash Gate and the fields to the east. Men carried baskets stacked on the backs of donkeys, with pots and jars hanging from sticks slung over their shoulders.

'Come on,' Abil said. 'I know the best place to watch from.'

They passed beneath the shadow of the gate, and walked down the road away from the city. Soldiers supervised the excited crowds, flying pennants from their spears.

'Will he be all right?' Abil whispered to Aurya, motioning to Sharo. She nodded, the sliver sharp in her heart.

'It'll be for the best. He can't keep this up for ever.'

As they walked out into the country to the east, Aurya cast an eye over the city defences, thicker on the side facing the mountains than the river side: the moats and low banks, the towers and small forts bristling with men, staring off in the direction of the grey hills from which all danger approached. On the road, a line of carts moved. On each cart was a cage built of thick planks, and inside each cage one of the King's lions paced. Their grunts and roars and whines sounded above the noise of the crowd, and the onagers pulling the carts looked desperate with fear. The people lining the verges jeered at the caged beasts.

'Look, Aurya – it's Enkidu!' Sharo said, pointing to one cart. All the lions looked the same to her.

'That's not its name, Sharo. Animals don't have names. Come on.' She tugged at his wool. 'Don't get lost in the crowds.'

The three of them pushed through the clamour and climbed the mesquite scrub until they reached a low tree-clustered hill overlooking the plain. A stone monument of some kind stood at its top, around which people gathered for the best view. People beckoned as they clambered up the root-riddled soil, calling in all the city's languages. Children roamed in groups, running and fighting each other, and rough gangs of city people vied for the shaded spots under the trees. At the top, Aurya, Sharo and Abil lifted themselves up on to the stone monument, and sat in one of its alcoves containing a shrine. Aurya put her back against the carved stone and listened to her heart thud in her chest.

From up there, she could see out over the ploughlands and scrub, right to the blue desert hills in the distance, their talus dappled by the shadows of clouds. In the open space outside the city, a huge mass of people had gathered, thousands of them. It looked like half of Nineveh. They formed an enormous circle on the plain, its inner edge a line of soldiers, two and three men deep, their tall red shields forming a wall, their spears bristling inwards. Some held thick-necked black mastiffs on strained leashes. In this wide rounded arena, a chariot kicked up clouds that eddied in the wind, and Aurya recognised its rider: King Ashurbanipal, wearing his pointed crown, two spear-men riding with him.

'Aurya, what are they doing?' Sharo asked her.

'I'm sorry, Sharo,' she said. 'Please don't hate me.'

'Aurya, I don't understand.'

She looked at his face, at the fear and uncertainty washing over him, and felt her heart break.

'Sharo, I'm so sorry.'

He turned around and looked at the carving they were leaning against. He gave out a stifled shriek, and people all around them turned their heads. Aurya saw what was carved on the stone behind them. It was a lion hunt. It must have been 200 years old, cruder than the carvings made at the mason's workshop, but it was clear what it meant: the lion leaping up at the ancient King's chariot, the King's bow arched and tense, ready to deal death to the jumping animal. Sharo's face had gone completely white.

'Aurya, what is that?'

'Sharo …'

'Aurya, what are they going to do to Enkidu?'

'It's for the best, Sharo. You can't be friends with a lion for ever. It's a wild beast, a beast of the hills.'

'No, Aurya!' he screeched. She'd never heard him like this. 'No, you can't let them do it!'

'Sharo, you can't stop it. You can't change it.'

His eyes were wide and wild, rolling around in his head. He clutched out at her and Abil as they tried to hold him still.

'Sharo,' she shouted, 'calm down!'

'I won't let them do it!' he screamed, and he pushed her aside. And then he was off. He crashed down the hill, knocking people over, crying out and swinging his arms.

'Shamash,' she hissed.

'Quick,' Abil said. 'They'll kill him if he interrupts the hunt.'

They ran after Sharo as he broke through the people gathered on the slope. He knocked over picnics of olives and turnip paste, and angry hands grasped out or swung at them as they followed. Abil's wool coat got torn off and he left it in the hands of a shouting bearded man. The two managed to reach the bottom of the hill, but on the flat ground, Sharo ran even faster, stumbling and crying, towards the backs of the arena crowd gathered in its great circle. The lions in their cages were already being led through the crowd. People's hands reached up to mock them and touch the cages. The beasts lashed out at the bars, smelling the stench of the baying dogs, hearing the thunder of the chariot wheels on the earth.

When Sharo hit the crowd, he bowled people over, knocking them aside. Aurya and Abil had to follow in his wake, edging around the angry people. She felt their wool cloaks and the sweat on their skins, the smell of bodies, crushing her like an olive in a press. She gasped for breath and felt Abil's hand grab hers from behind.

'We can't lose him,' she shouted back to him, and felt him squeeze her hand through the crowd. 'I can't let them kill him!'

They burst out to the front and found Sharo kicking and wailing, gripped by two strong archers, who lifted him almost off the ground. One gave him a slap as if he were a sleepwalker, and the other threw a knee into his stomach. Sharo kicked and struggled but they held him tight.

'Sharo,' Aurya called out to him, and rushed to him. 'Sharo, please calm down.'

'Is he with you?' one of the archers asked.

'I'm sorry. Please! He's my brother.'

'Does he have a devil in him?'

'Sharo,' Aurya hissed and took his chin in her hands, tried to fix his roving eyes in her gaze. 'Sharo, look at me. This has to happen. Lions and humans can't live together.'

'Aurya, they can't … I can't …'

He struggled again, and one archer grabbed him by the hair.

'Please,' Aurya said, 'he doesn't know what he's doing.'

'The law is the law,' the archer said, and drew an oiled knife from his belt. 'Interrupting the hunt means death.'

Bodies crushed behind her, pressing her into Sharo, and Abil bumped against her too.

'Please,' Abil yelled at the archer. 'Wait a moment! I work for Bel-Ibni, the king's servant.'

The royal chariot thundered past, and though his back was to it, Sharo's whole body shuddered and he let out a moan.

'Wait until after the hunt,' the other archer said to his friend. He looked a bit younger, had fewer scars on his face. 'The blood will aggravate the dogs.'

Aurya looked at the two men and her brother still struggling between them.

'Sharo, please stop. Look at me. These men will kill you if you don't stop.'

In his chariot, the King had a cold look of victory. Knots of muscles wound through his forearm as he tested his bowstring, and he leaned into every turn with skill. The chariot driver lashed the horses. The hooves made the earth jump beneath Aurya's feet, and Sharo let out a scream of despair.

'Sharo,' Aurya said. 'Sharo, you have to listen to me. Your lion is already dead. It's the King's will. There's nothing we can do.'

Sharo was sobbing now, and Aurya kept talking to him as the archers held him. On the plain, the lions' cages had been laid out in a line, and Aurya saw that on top of each one, there was a smaller cage with a child hidden in it. A beat on a drum began like a fast heartbeat, and the blare of a horn sounded. In the arena, she recognised the servant Bel-Ibni as he stepped out from between the red shields.

'The king of the world, the light that shines on the dust, King Ashurbanipal,' he announced, throwing his hands to the air. In his chariot, the King raised his bow over his head. The crowd burst into cheers and stamped their feet so the earth trembled. 'Behind our walls, we rule the world,' Bel-Ibni went on, his nasal voice resounding over the dusty earth. 'Here we have conquered the demons of the wild and of the hills. We have conquered our enemies in the deserts and the mountains. And we have conquered the enemies inside ourselves too! Each of these beasts represents one of our victories. Praise Ashur! Praise Marduk!'

People whistled and chanted as Bel-Ibni edged behind the shields. The horns blared, and the child hidden in the compartment above one cage reached out a pair of wiry limbs and pulled up the lion's cage door. Moments passed, and then the lion stepped out. It was a huge male, its neck and shoulders thick with muscle, mouth hanging open, long tongue panting. It left the cage with slow steps, flinched at the rumbling of the wheels and the thunder of hooves on the earth. It raised its head and gave a roar that made people in the crowd step back. Aurya shuddered. It was the noise of her nightmares, an ancient fear, dredged up from the days before the flood.

Two, three more cages were opened, and the lions stepped out, two smaller males and a female. They flicked their tails, swung around in circles and shielded each other. The mastiffs behind the cages snapped at them, and the wild beasts jumped away into the arena centre, growling and circling each other's backs for protection. They were terrified but still fierce, and let out deep roars.

'Don't worry, Sharo,' Aurya said. 'It's not Enkidu.'

'I know,' he said, the lump in his throat bobbing furiously as the archers held him. The lions now darted out into the arena, and the King's chariot rounded on them, penning them in. The King raised his bow and drew an arrow. There was a moment of held breath, and then it flew, a whistle like steam escaping the lid of a cooking pot. The arrow missed, flew and hit a cage behind the lions: a bang like a hammer on the wood. The crowd let out a long sigh. The animals leapt back, circling and growling in fear, pawing the earth. Aurya's necklace was slick with the sweat from her palm.

The King frowned and barked an order to his driver, who adjusted something in the chariot. Sharo's lip was wobbling, his eyes scrunched closed. The King drew another arrow, and his chariot took a pass close to the group of lions. The soldiers on board jabbed out with spears. Another arrow zipped from the King's bow, wobbling in the air like a living thing, a darting sparrow. This time it struck one male lion in the flank: a thump like a dull drum. Aurya felt that strike. Her fists balled and her heart said: kill these monsters. That's for all the people you've dragged away. The animal let out the yowl of a scalded cat, and then a bellowing roar. An answering roar went up from the crowd. Another arrow flew, and another. Each one hit with that same sickening thump, yelps of pain from the lions, who limped with arrows stuck in their haunches and limbs. One lion coughed and gurgled, and blood spilled down its jaw. It pawed as if trying to burrow a hole like a rabbit, and the crowd hissed. Aurya couldn't look away.

Only one lion staggered on. It was the female, arrows jutting from its limbs and back. The King drew near it and motioned for the soldiers to give him his spear. He raised the weapon high overhead, with a flash of its iron tip. The crowd cheered all together, flecks of spittle in the air. The King jumped down before the injured lion, which tried to lift itself on its front legs. Its limp back legs pawed at the earth.

'Ashur,' the crowd was screaming. 'Ashur, Ashur, Ashurbanipal. He fights with lions. The lion of men!'

The King thrust the spear into the flesh above the animal's shoulder. The she-lion let out a long whine. The King dug his feet into the dust and pushed the shaft in deep. He was now only a foot away from the lion's snapping jaws, and then twisted the spear so it let out a yelp and dropped still. The dogs around the arena smelled blood; they bayed and strained on their leashes. The King tried to pull the spear from the lion, but it wouldn't budge. He gave up after a few tugs, and then got back into his chariot, rode around with his arms raised to cheers. Aurya let out a breath. Her heart thudded, and each beat said: kill these monsters, kill these monsters.

The remaining cages opened, and more lions came out to their deaths. There were six this time, and Aurya spotted what she thought was Sharo's lion, the last to emerge from its cage, smaller than all the others. She could see the bald spot of the scar on its back leg. It looked terrified, its eyes wide; the bodies of the other lions lying limp and arrow-stuck all around, blood browning the sand. It gave a mournful call. Held in the archers' grip, Sharo began again to kick and writhe.

'Turn me around!' he screamed.

'Sharo,' Aurya hushed him, 'please don't.'

'Turn me around!' he shrieked, lashing out with his feet, and to Aurya's surprise the men gave in and turned him to face the arena. Aurya saw the sweat standing out on the back of his neck, his quaking body, and she reached out to touch his shoulder. His skin was stony. He didn't react, just watched without flinching as the chariot made another thunderous pass, sending dust and grit into the crowd so people coughed and covered their faces.

Arrows flew. The King killed two females quickly with blows to their throat and chest. Then one of his spear-men lunged out and struck a young male, sending it curling on to its side. The bodies of lions were heaped around their cages. Tears ran down Sharo's cheeks, down his neck and collarbone. The lions fell until only Sharo's lion and the biggest male of all were left. This other lion was a true beast of the high hills. A scar marred its muzzle, its mane thick and black. It shielded Sharo's lion with its body as the King made one pass, then another. One arrow lanced into the ground beside them. The great lion let out a roar and dashed at the King's chariot, edging around it and darting in its path the way Aurya had seen market cats play with rats. The crowd were jumping up and down and screaming, raising their hands to the air.

'Finally a beast with some fight!' a fat man near Aurya screamed out. Sharo's lion watched the huge male dicing with the chariot and tried to get away. It edged behind the cages, but the dogs on the soldiers' leashes strained after it, gnashing their teeth, slobbering and baring their pink gums. The soldiers tensed their shield wall, spears bristling. Sharo's lion spun on the spot, hopeless and trapped in the arena. Meanwhile, the huge scarred male reared up at the chariot, exposing the full cavern of its mouth, its long yellow teeth. The King's men looked afraid. The King couldn't get a good shot, and he shouted an order to the chariot driver, who turned to gain greater distance.

The huge lion seemed to sense an opening. It had fought other lions in its time, Aurya thought. It knew the weakness in turning your back. As the King's chariot rounded, the lion dashed with incredible speed and pounced. The crowd breathed in all together, and fell silent. The moment lasted for ever: the lion in mid-air, leaping towards the exposed rear of the chariot, the expressions of the King and his guards frozen in shock, spears held out in flimsy defence. Sharo whispered something, but Aurya didn't hear.

The lion fell on the chariot wheel, and both the King's men desperately drove their spears into its back, their faces masks of terror. In an instant, the lion was dragged over the wheel, and some mistaken instinct made the soldiers hold on to their spears. The animal followed the turning wheel over the chariot and down to the ground below, and the men were thrown like pieces of rag into the air. The lion went under the wheel. The crackle of bones sounded in the arena's sudden hush. The crowd groaned in unison. The wheel bounced over the mess of the lion's body, and with an even louder crack, the chariot's axle gave way. The horses broke their halters, and the whole vehicle bucked upwards and turned over in the air. Screams began to erupt around the arena. The King tumbled overhead, tangled in his driver's reins, pulling him under. The chariot rolled on top of him and dragged him in the dust.

Sharo's lion saw its opening. As the crowd fell silent once again, it darted at the King. Its body was a bow of pure animal speed, dust rising at each beat of its paws. The trapped King saw the beast coming, and raised his hands to fend it off. The lion grabbed him in its jaws, clenched his waist and shook him like a doll. The King let out a shriek of pain and fear, and his hands grasped and pulled at the black mane as it mauled him. Then the uproar of the crowd began like a clap of thunder. All around the arena, the circle broke. Soldiers dashed forwards. There was a great screaming, a clamour of feet and voices.

'The King is fallen,' people bellowed. In the chaos, the archers holding Sharo loosened their grip. He broke free, himself suddenly a wild thing, and dashed to where everyone else was looking: to the twisted wreckage where King Ashurbanipal was trapped beneath his chariot, and the lion gripped him in its jaws.

Aurya ran after Sharo, to where a clearing formed around the King and the lion. The King was pale as ash, and bleeding from several wounds. The skin of one arm was grazed bloody where he'd skidded. He was moving though, and letting out groans and whimpers as Sharo's lion shook him in its jaws. Both his hands pawed at the animal's face, tried to gain some purchase on it, clutching at its mane. The lion didn't move. Its eyes swivelled between the people and dogs gathering around it, and its back legs tapped in fear against the ground. But it didn't let go of the King.

'Get back!' Ashurbanipal screeched, panic in his voice. 'Get back and shoot it!' The bowstrings all around creaked. But no one loosed an arrow. 'Shoot it!' the King shrieked again.

'Your highness?' an archer begged him. 'What if we miss?'

'It will tear you in its rage!'

No one moved. And then Sharo stepped out from the crowd.

'Enkidu,' he moaned, reaching out his hand. Soldiers turned their arrows to face him. Their bowstrings creaked, and they shouted at him to stand back. Sharo was going to die: Aurya knew it in that moment.

'You?' the King whined. 'The river boy?'

He let out a hiss as the lion's teeth clenched again around his waist. It tore at his tunic, with the sound of rending cloth, and ran its claws down his face, marring one of his eyes. The King's hands twisted like roots. Sharo kept walking, alone now in the circle of people. Aurya tried to cry out to him, but her voice was hoarse, and came out dry as whispering leaves. This was the end of it all, of all the years she'd looked after him. The lion saw Sharo. Its yellow eyes rolled up to meet him, and it let out a little yelp, muffled by the King's body. Its grip lessened a little, and then a low moan escaped its jaws. Sharo stepped closer and reached out to put his hand in the lion's mane.

'Shh,' he said. 'Let go of him. Let go, Enkidu. They'll let you live if you let go.'

Bowstrings ached all around. And slowly, with its eyes fixed on Sharo, the lion opened its jaws. The King let out a gasp of pain as its long teeth withdrew, stained with blood. His gilded tunic was soaked black, his skin and hair were covered with dust and ragged strips of flesh hung off him. Aurya held her breath as the lion let him go, and then raised its head to Sharo. It opened its mouth, its pink tongue curled and wet and red, the ribbed maw of its throat. And then the arrows flew, without a thought for the boy. The first one hit the lion between its ribs with a thump, and it let out a whine. Sharo screamed.

'No!'

Two, three more arrows struck the lion in the neck, the legs, and then the men with spears ran and drove their weapons into its side, stabbing again and again as Sharo screamed its name. It didn't try to fight back. It shuddered with each blow.

'Enkidu!' Sharo was screaming. 'Enkidu, I'm sorry.'

Men rushed from all sides and heaved the chariot from the King. He couldn't stand. His legs were limp and broken, and they had to bring a wooden bier to carry him. He was gasping in little breaths, wincing, and Bel-Ibni suddenly rushed to him, distraught and pale.

'My lord. I'm so sorry. I only just –'

'Bel-Ibni,' croaked the King. 'It's that dream. The dream with the lion.'

'My lord, what do you …?'

'I knew it meant something,' the King whimpered. Blood ran in rivers from his face and torn body, pooling in the wrinkles of his scrunched face, pattering in drops on the ground. 'I knew all along.'

Servants carried the King away, and the whole crowd stood stunned and silent as the boy, who had saved the King, dropped to his knees and wept. He dug his face into the dead lion's mane, his hands covered in its blood. People were afraid of him. They backed away and hurried away one by one, muttering darkly, performing the signs that warded off evil omens. As the crowd thinned, Aurya still stood with Abil and watched Sharo's back heaving with sobs. Around the arena edges, priests in their colourful clothes were chanting and using pine cones to pour oil over the dead lions, their blood brown in the dust.

'Sharo,' Aurya said. 'I'm sorry.'

'You knew,' he said. 'You knew this was going to happen.'

'Sharo, I didn't – I just wanted to …'

'Why didn't you stop them, Aurya? Why didn't you tell me?'

'Why do you care so much about that lion, Sharo?' Her voice was harder than she meant. 'You visited that thing whenever you could, but you never helped me try to find our mother. You never told me what you know. And you never helped me look for the house of dust.'

Sharo shook his head.

'There's no such place, Aurya. There's no house of dust.'

'Father said there was,' Aurya growled. 'He said our mother was there, in the house of dust.'

'He was lying to you. It's just a place in the old stories. A place mother told us about, that the ancients believed in. Father used to sit outside the house and listen while she told her stories. The house of dust is where people used to go when they die.'

'I don't believe you,' Aurya shouted. Then Sharo spoke through clenched teeth, his arms covered in the blood of his lion.

The wild man Enkidu knew that he had been chosen to die. He lay in his bed and felt death come closer.

'If only I had never come to this city,' the wild man moaned. 'If only I had stayed in the wilds, by the river.'

'But, my friend,' cried Gilgamesh, 'we have fought the bull of heaven together, and the demon Humbaba. Together we have lived a thousand lives.'

But the wild man dreamed of the place that beckoned him.

'It is a place where all the kings of men have gone,' he said, 'their crowns piled in a heap. They wear clothes made from

black feathers. Their food is mud, and their water is dust. Their
languages are forgotten, and they sit and wait in silence. This is
the house of dust, the place I now go.'

And the wild man held the King's hand, and by morning he
was dead.

Aurya reeled.

'But … Father said there was no lion. She was never dragged away.'

'He was telling the truth about that, Aurya. There was no lion.'

Her fingers tingled, and she balled her fists.

'What? What are you talking about, Sharo?'

He stood up and turned to her. People were flocking away in droves now, leaving the field strewn with the animals' bodies, the abandoned cages empty, the dogs and soldiers retreating back to the city. Corpse birds were circling high.

'There was no lion, Aurya,' Sharo said in a voice she'd never heard before. 'I could never tell you before. But I remember it all. The night mother died.'

'Sharo, what do you mean?'

He had a black look in his eyes.

'It was one of the fifty days of summer. The locusts had been and eaten everything away. And in our house, our mother was screaming, and you were being born.'

'Sharo,' Aurya tried to cry out, but she found she could only whisper, 'What are you saying?'

'And then you came. You were screaming and balling your hands. And there was blood everywhere. And the blood didn't stop. And our mother went pale.'

'Sharo, you're lying.'

'She died that night, Aurya.'

'You're lying.'

'You were the lion, Aurya. You dragged our mother away.'

'I don't believe you,' she said. Then she screamed, 'I don't believe you!'

Sharo just looked back at her, a look in his eyes as cold and flat as the eyes of an animal. Before Aurya knew it, she was running.

She heard Abil follow and call out her name, but she couldn't stop. She ran across the field, skidding in the dust, ankle turning in a hole, back to the wooded hill. She stumbled up through the roots and discarded things, the broken pots and old reeds, tears blurring her vision, gulping for breath between her sobs. At the top, she curled up between the roots of a tree and hid her face, sobbing into her arms. Abil caught up with her.

'Please don't cry,' he said.

'He was lying,' Aurya said. 'Everything he said was a lie.'

The boy looked down at her.

'I'm sorry.'

'I hate him!' she cried. Aurya gripped Abil by the wrist, feeling the warmth of his skin, looking up into his kind dark eyes.

'Abil,' she said, 'I want to go to the tablet house. I want to leave the masons and learn how to read. I never want to see Sharo again.'

Out on the plain, the dust rose in great clouds, twisting and swirling, obeying only the wind.

BOOK III

The River

Aurya

Aurya sat on the wall of her house and looked out over the courtyard, at the birds flitting in the pomegranate tree. The city's morning sounds rose all around them: market callers selling medicinal herbs and magic stones, knife sharpeners going from place to place, traffic in the nearby street. Aurya had a tablet on her lap, angled in what light fell through the leaves. It had taken most of the morning to read. Even after five years she was still slow and halting, and other things were on her mind. She watched the baker's children play out there in the courtyard, a boy and a girl. The tablet was the story of a city in the north that had disrespected its gods and been wiped out by a horde of dog-headed men from the hills.

'May depression descend upon your palace, built for joy!' she read. 'May the evils of the desert, the silent place, howl continuously!'

She thought her father used to sing about something similar, back on the riverbank, but she couldn't really remember if it was the same story. She ran her fingers over her mother's cylinder necklace and thought of all the days she'd spent in the heat of the classroom, the only girl among all the boys from rich scribal families, receiving the strikes with the reed wand whenever she misplaced a wedge in a letter. She rubbed the back of her hand at the memory. What had kept her going?

Behind her, Abil came and touched her on the shoulder. He kissed her on the back of the neck. His short beard tickled her skin and brushed against her hair, which she'd grown as long as she could. She now tied it with a cord, the way sellers tied bunches of coriander in the market, so it fought its way free whenever she left the house in her headscarf. She still wasn't used to the scarf: Aurya and Abil had been married for less than a year; a tiny orphan's wedding, paid for by the palace.

'How's your reading?' he said.

'It's sad. Everyone dies in the end.'

'It was so long ago,' he said, still kissing her nape as he spoke. 'All those people would be dead by now anyway.'

'That doesn't matter when you're reading it. Every time you read it, they come back to life all over again.'

She watched the baker's two children running in the courtyard, through the morning's sun and shade. Abil put his arms around her, so his hands rested on her stomach, and she froze. She pressed his hand gently, willing him to feel the unusual firmness there that had grown through the months of Tibbakh and Ilool. He didn't, never one for noticing what he wasn't shown. Aurya breathed a sigh as he left her and went back to his table to work on the half-finished clay tablet he was copying for the library. As summer came to an end, smells and tastes had changed in her mouth. She'd begun to hate the smell of cumin and the tang of turnip paste. She'd once loved the yeasty smells rising from the bakery in the courtyard, the charcoal and wet dough, but now they made her feel ill. She said her favourite prayer:

May the seven winds carry away my groans,
May the waters of the river flow cleanse me.

When the time came, they bathed quickly, rubbed themselves with olive oil and cheap perfumes, and both said some prayers to their house shrine. Then Aurya covered her hair and they left together for the library.

Barges unloaded at the docks at that time of day. The spice markets and charm sellers bustled, and already hooting laughter drifted from the drinking houses. Flocks of refugees held bowls by the Halzi Gate, their families close, their skins too small for their skeletons.

'There are so many these days,' Aurya said. 'There never used to be this many.'

'The gods are cruel some years,' Abil said, shaking his head.

'It's not the gods. It's the King,' Aurya said, keeping her voice quiet. 'It's these wars.'

'There've always been wars,' Abil said. 'You can't stop them, any more than you can stop the seasons or the stars. Poor wretches, though.'

They passed a large family crouched in the shade of an alleyway. Abil gave them a piece of bread, and they fell on it hungrily, splitting it between the smallest children.

'This feels different,' Aurya said.

'You shouldn't listen to everything you hear in the markets,' Abil said, and Aurya felt a rush of annoyance.

'I don't.'

'Anyway, it's just part of living in the city that rules the world. Of course everyone wants to come here. You might as well complain about the clay in the bricks or the stones in the walls.'

'That doesn't make any sense.'

'I mean the old kings built all of this with their wars.'

'They built the ukuku drinking house?'

'You know what I mean.'

As they went by the Shamash Gate, Aurya watched the refugees being herded together, and saw where a rough shanty town was beginning to form in the shadows of the walls. They passed the rest of their walk in silence, and Abil left her at the great library's gate. He didn't seem to realise that they had argued. It was at times like this that Aurya felt how much of her life was still unknown to her husband: she'd never told Abil about their father, about how he'd really died. Sometimes she thought he had married a different person from the one she was, and it made her afraid to think about what would happen if he ever found out. She still had those dreams sometimes.

Aurya headed to the records room to see what new tablets had been acquired. It was always cool in the library, full of the soft hubbub of reading voices. She scratched angrily at a bite on the back of her neck, and ran over her argument with Abil in her head. It was true that Nineveh wasn't the golden city that she'd imagined as a child – she'd learned to accept that, to appreciate the city in all its loud and dirty reality. But in the years since the lion hunt, another feeling had grown in her. A feeling that something was rotten in the city. Not just its mired streets and drains, the retch-inducing smells of the tanneries and slaughterhouses, or the black smoke that belched from the kilns. It was the way the city ground people down until whole streets were lined with beggars, while the rich hid in villas behind tall walls and hired guards. It was the markets of slaves she saw, that swelled with new chattel whenever the King's army came home, and the public executions of rival kings and rebellious lords; the hordes of prisoners tormented outside the gate, the men who had chains run through their cheeks, or nails put through their skulls, left raving mad in cages hung from the Nergal Gate, the men who the King kept in a kennel for days before the dogs got hungry enough to kill them.

The only place in the city that Aurya still loved, with the golden warm love she'd felt for the place as a child, was the library. It was a sanctuary, a place where the cruelty of the city outside couldn't penetrate, a place of peace and learning. As she walked through the painted halls, she tried to escape into the clay smell of the tablets, the oils and the wood burning in the braziers, the muttering of the record scribes with their numbers and weights, the poets humming as they wrote their songs for the King. Sometimes she walked past the tablet house, where the students were still reciting 'boo, baa, bee; noo, naa, nee,' learning to turn the signs into speech. If she didn't have work to do, she'd lean against the wall outside and listen as they recited the long lists of plants, animals, stars and stones by heart. She liked to watch them squash their balls of clay flat in their hands before beginning to write, breathe the aroma of that river mud fresh from the mountains with the spring floods.

That day, Aurya found a heap of new admissions to the library waiting for her in the library's courtyard, brought by the caravan driver Sin-Zababa. He was a thin man who dressed like a nomad and had a face that looked like it had been carved out by desert winds, eyes permanently squinting against sand and glare.

'Another lot of books for you,' he said in a dust-harshened voice, sitting down beneath the palm tree that grew in the courtyard. 'Gods know why anyone would want so many.'

'Send our thanks to whoever sent them,' Aurya said. 'Did they travel far?'

'A prince of Egypt this time,' Sin-Zababa said. 'He wants to gain favour with the King, and heard that his royal sire has been looking for some of these titles for years.'

Aurya looked through them.

'Tablets on astronomy, geography, a manual for making coloured glass … some papyrus. King Ashurbanipal will be pleased.'

'He better be,' the caravan driver murmured. 'The roads are dangerous these days, even travelling with the King's men.'

The King's love of books, at least, had survived his accident. In fact, it was the only thing he really took pleasure in. Whenever he heard about a rare tablet in a temple library or private collection, he would send a messenger to request a copy. Usually these new texts came in a steady trickle, but at other times Sin-Zababa would bring them in cartloads, their wedged cuts full of dust from the roads. Aurya liked to feel the new tablets' strange textures, their unusual clay or wax sometimes, others written in ink on wood, or reed paper. She would smell them, touch them and imagine the far-off lands they'd come from, and the learned people who used to own them.

'Safe journeys in the desert,' she said to Sin-Zababa, once the porters had emptied his cart of its contents. 'When's the next batch coming in?'

'Hard to say,' he said, and tapped his head. 'A lot of secrecy around this next one. Sounds like a big one, though. Good thing you like the work.'

He shouted to his onagers and flicked them with his switch, then winked and left along the road. Aurya spent the rest of the day adding the King's inscription to each new tablet and scroll, then filing them away in their proper place on the shelves. It took until after sunset. Shortly after she'd finished, she heard the voice of King Ashurbanipal booming through the halls.

'Your King has come to read the wisdom of the ancients!' he announced. Aurya's heart fell. The clap of the King's hands sounded in the corridor, and the slaves carried him towards the reading room. 'Careful!' Aurya could hear him shouting as they passed beneath the low-hanging lamps. 'Someone light another brazier, will you? It's cold in here. Do it with the sea wood.'

The King hadn't walked since the day of his accident at the lion hunt. He lay in his long chair while servants carried him from place to place, so that whenever Aurya saw him, she thought he looked like some slow grazing creature with twelve legs moving clumsily around the royal quarter. His voice had never weakened, though. While the King was in the library, Aurya stayed out of his way and avoided notice. The library was a sanctuary for her, and she felt his presence as a pollution, as though he tracked some of the world's cruelty in with him on the soles of his servants' feet, as though it followed behind him like a swarm of flies. She watched the King's servants take him through the halls to the reading room, and then went back to her work. She was tired – her sleep had been disturbed by dreams recently – and the warmth of the library and the smell of linseed oil weighed her down.

And then Aurya was walking in the streets of the city. It was dark and no one was there. The wall of a house beside her was built of a strange material. She stepped towards it and saw that it was made of human skulls. They were stacked one on top of another in place of bricks, grinning rows of teeth and cracked bone. She stepped back and saw that all the buildings around her were made of skulls. The whole city was the same: the palace and the ziggurat in the distance, even her own home. The handle of her door was made of finger bones that crumbled away in her hands. Then, in that city of the dead, she saw a shape moving towards her. She knew immediately what it would be. The lion stepped out of the shadows and spoke to her.

'You're a murderer,' it said.

'I'm not! I didn't have a choice.'

'You're a murderer in a city of murderers. And you'll die here along with your child.'

Aurya turned and ran. The library: she would be safe there. She knew it was the only place not built of death. But as she ran, the streets below her were made of the long bones of legs and arms, the curved bows of ribs. She began to slip on the uneven ground, and the streets of bones began to crumble away beneath her, and all the houses around her began to crumble too, the grinning skulls toppling and the hollow sound of bones clattering together in a thunderous rising sound, and she felt the tiny creature in her stomach turn to bones too. The bones closed around her waist, around her chest, crushing her with their sharp edges until she was reaching up and the bones were drowning her, their dust in her throat, and then she woke up with a cry, sweat covering her beneath her clothes.

'Are you all right?' someone asked. Aurya blinked and rubbed her head, and it took a few moments to remember where she was: in the library, in the room of records. It was one of the King's soldiers who had spoken. He stood in the doorway, running one hand through his thick beard. He had to lower his spear to step through the door.

'Yes, I'm sorry. I fell asleep … I had a strange dream.'

The man made a sign of protection. Aurya felt the parts of her body where the sharp points of the bones had pressed into her, looking for any damage.

'You work here, don't you?' the man said. Aurya hesitated, then nodded.

'Yes. I'm a junior scribe.'

'The King wants some tablets.' Aurya recoiled inwardly.

'The library porters should be able to …'

'They're all gone for the evening. You're the only one here.'

Was it that late already? Aurya's hands shook a little, but she got up and shook the sleep from her limbs. She thought what it would mean to meet the King, and wondered if he would know her when he saw her. She followed the soldier down the corridor. The man was right: she had lost track of time, and everyone else had gone home, the smell of their extinguished linseed smoke filling the dry halls. Only the King's reading room was lit, with the orangey-green flame of his favourite sea wood. As she walked towards it, Aurya thought of her dream and felt a dreadful trembling move through her body. She entered the room and saw the King sitting on his bier on matting perfumed with essence of basil, the fires' greenish flames giving the chamber an eerie glow. King Ashurbanipal swung to look at her with his big watery eyes.

'All health to the King,' Aurya said, and gave a bow. She became suddenly conscious of the roughness of her manners, the poor wool she was wearing. The King clutched at his blanket as if someone might try to rip it away, but there was no glimmer of recognition in his eyes.

'Who is it?'

'Just a library servant, my lord,' the soldier said. Aurya nodded, letting her curls fall in front of her face a little.

'What can I do to help you, my lord?'

The King raised his hand, covering the shining pink scars that still mapped his face like the lines of a river bed.

'Fetch me tablet three in the series "If the Liver is a Mirror Image of the Sky",' the King said. 'And Gilgamesh, for afterwards.'

Aurya nodded and headed off to the room of divination for the first text, and then the room of stories. There she ran her fingers along the tablets in their alcoves, some wrapped in reed paper, dry as the skin of onions. She found the ones she was looking for: the Gilgamesh sequence. They were too heavy to carry in one go. She took them two at a time, and the King smacked his lips and reached out his hands for each one. When she was done, Aurya went back to her work in the room of records, but she couldn't stop thinking about the sound of those dry lips.

As the evening went on, slaves and soldiers fetched things for his majesty, patrolling, checking the doorways and lighting different lamps. When she was done inscribing the new tablets and filing them away on the shelves, Aurya thought about going home, but something in her resisted. She still felt that flint of anger at the way Abil had spoken to her that morning, and that strange feeling of dread that had risen from her dream. Instead, she worked to put in order some records: accounts of barley shipments moving along the rivers on barges, and a desert train bringing cedar wood from the west down the faded hill paths. She thought of the boats she used to watch sailing past their house on the riverbank, of how she and Sharo would guess where they were headed. She wondered what had happened to their home in the five years since their leaving, whether someone else had taken it as their own, or whether it had become a cursed place like the old village, abandoned to crumble into the mud, with tamarisk growing through its windows. Some time later, past midnight, with the lamps running low on oil, she heard the King cry out.

'Bel-Ibni!' he shouted, with the voice of a scared child. 'Bel-Ibni!'

Aurya listened, but no footsteps moved to help the King, and no voices spoke up. He cried out again, unanswered, and Aurya's heart sank. She got up, swept through the halls to the reading room. The sight inside made her freeze. The King was covered in blood. The room was sweltering, and his slaves and bodyguards were gone. His eyes swivelled to look at her, and he wiped his face, further smearing it with the blood that was pouring from his nose.

'Bel-Ibni,' he said. 'I had that dream again.'

Aurya didn't know what to do. She went to the lamps, and took the rag that the lamplighter used to wipe oil from his hands.

'I'm not Bel-Ibni, my lord,' Aurya said, and offered the rag to the King. 'My lord, where are your servants? Would you like me to go and find them?'

He reached out and took the oil-scented cloth. His hands were shaking, and the gold band rattled together, too large for his wrist now. He wiped the blood from his face, some of it pooling in the claw scars on his neck and face so that they looked like fresh wounds. He clogged up his nostrils with the rag and tilted his head back.

'It was the lion dream,' the King said. Aurya's fear stirred. Sweat gathered on her body in the heat of the room, and she felt a faint suggestion of nausea. She tried to remember the words the servant had used to soothe the King all those years ago.

'Why don't you tell me about it, my lord? Sometimes it can help, to tell someone ...'

'It was just like it always is,' the King said. 'I'm sitting right here, reading. And then I hear the noise of the ocean. I go outside, and I see the whole city, all of Nineveh, covered by a dark sea.'

'Go on, my lord,' Aurya said, and fetched him some water from the urn, without taking her eyes off him.

'And then I hear the footsteps. And I turn and see a lion coming towards me,' the King said. He sounded as if he were close to tears. 'I know it's one of the lions that I've killed, Bel-Ibni. I think it might even be his ghost ... his ghost ...'

The heat in the room bore down on her. Aurya saw fear in the King's eyes.

'Whose ghost, my lord?'

The King let out a choke from the base of his throat.

'The ghost of Shamash-shum-ukin. The ghost of my brother.'

Aurya looked away, afraid that she was hearing something she shouldn't. She handed the ladle of water to the King, and he slurped from it.

'That's when these dreams started,' the King whispered, his eyes wide for a moment. 'After my brother died.'

Then he swung his head to look at her, and his gaze seemed clear.

'You ... You're the girl from the riverbank.'

Aurya shrunk under his recognition.

'Yes, my lord.'

'The girl with the brother.'

'Yes, my lord.'

'Your brother is a magnificent artist, you know.'

'So I hear, my lord.'

'He's only twenty-two years old now, and he's taken over the position of master mason. What a talent! A mind of pure recollection.'

Aurya shifted her weight from foot to foot. She thought she heard a chariot, somewhere in the distance. The heat in the room made the air close, made breathing difficult.

'I don't speak to him these days, my lord.'

The King took a long and laboured breath through his clogged nose and inspected the cloth for fresh blood.

'He is a magnificent artist. But he has been disobeying me. Such trouble I've been having with him.'

Aurya's hands tightened on the sleeve of her robe.

'Trouble, my lord? What kind of trouble?'

'I stopped speaking to my brother too,' the King said, in a far-off voice. He seemed to be slipping away again. 'I was never meant to be king – did you know that, girl?'

'No,' Aurya said. 'But my lord, what kind of trouble …'

'I was going to be a priest, like those old crows you can hear chanting up in the tower. It was our older brother who was meant to be king. He was the best of the three of us, you know. He would have made a great king. And while he learned to ride, and fight, and hunt, I learned to read. I'm the first King of Assyria to know how to read – did you know that?'

'No, my lord. But …'

'I've read every tablet there is. The cunning Sumerian ones, the dark Akkadian, the tablets written before the flood. I always thought if I could read the portents, on the earth, in the sky … maybe then I would feel like I was supposed to be the king. Our brother would have made a great king. He always stopped me and Shamash-shum-ukin from fighting. He was a great hunter too. He loved to hunt. He never fell from his chariot, never fell … and then when the sickness took him, it was just the two of us: me and Shamash-shum-ukin. Our father made him the King of Babylon, and I the King of Assyria. He told us to rule the world together.'

'What happened, my lord?'

The King lifted the rag from his nose and inspected it for fresh blood.

'Don't you know? You don't remember the war?'

'There were always wars, my lord.'

'Yes, but what a war it was. You didn't hear about it? Our siege of Babylon lasted for two years. Its people ate dogs and rats. And when my brother saw that he'd finally lost, when his last sortie failed, he set fire to his own palace. He sat there in the flames and smoke as it all crashed down around him and molten bronze poured down the steps in rivers. So stubborn, just like always. It was such a beautiful palace, you know. So many fine carvings. That's the other dream I have. The dream where I see him burning.'

A log in the fire popped and made Aurya jump. Footsteps sounded behind them, and two soldiers and a slave came back into the room. The King clutched at his blanket, and his face curled into a mask of rage.

'Where have you been?' he shouted. Aurya backed away into the shadows by the door, surprised by his sudden anger.

'We're sorry, my lord,' one whimpered.

'Be sure I will make you sorry,' the King snarled.

'A million pardons,' they mumbled, as they rushed to tend to him. 'The heat in here, my lord, it was making us faint.'

Aurya left the room, and the cool air of the corridor washed over her. She put one hand to her collarbone, damp with sweat, and felt her heart beating fast against the reassuring weight of her cylinder seal. As the servants helped to clean up the King's face and clothes, he snarled his threats at them, which echoed down the halls after Aurya as she tried to return to her work. She had dreamed of a lion on the same night as the King. And didn't the gods speak through the King?

On her way home, well past midnight, she saw a riot over a shipment of barley near the Shamash Gate. Ragged refugees from the Eastlands were fighting with soldiers, a mob of people yelling with contorted faces. The barking of war dogs and the screams of the dying echoed down the torchlit streets. She hurried home and found Abil already asleep on his mat. She lay down beside him, unable to sleep as the night insects fluttered against the shutters and the sky outside lit up with falling stars. She put her hand on her stomach, where that strange new life had taken hold. She lay there and thought of the dream she'd had in the library, and then she felt something: something that had been building in her for weeks and months, but that she hadn't realised was true until she whispered it into the night.

'Abil … Abil, I want to leave the city.'

He opened one eye and looked at her, breathed out through his nose. He put one hand on her cheek, and his fingers were clumsy with sleep.

'What? Aurya, why?'

'I had a dream. It made me so afraid. And I think something terrible is going to happen here.'

Abil closed his eyes again.

'Nineveh is the safest place in the world,' he murmured. 'You've seen the walls, haven't you? Nothing can touch us here. It's safer than the hills or the Sealands.'

'I know, but …'

'And you love the library, don't you? Whatever happens out there in the world, we'll always be safe there.'

Aurya bit her lip. He was right: she couldn't imagine leaving the library, her sanctuary. She pressed her mouth against the palm of Abil's hand, which was warm and still smelled of clay.

'I know. I do. But Abil … I can just feel it. Something terrible is coming this way.'

Katya

The air in the museum baked. With the frequent power cuts and no generator, the refrigerators in the staff kitchen had cut out. Flies swarmed around the remaining food, and soon the exhibit hall was full of them. At night, the sounds of their journeys from room to room stopped Katya from sleeping. She would wake up feeling their legs tickling her face, her lips. So she slept with her coat over her head, and dreamed of the execution in the park, the look in Abu Ammar's eyes as he'd approached the men with his knife. She dreaded seeing him again, knowing what he'd done.

In the morning, she woke up beside Salim, and they lay in each other's arms for some time. When he spoke, he kept his eyes closed, and his voice cracked.

'I wish I'd met you in some other place,' he said. 'Or some other time. I wish we'd met like a normal couple.'

'I don't know. I've had worse first dates.'

'Yes, me too.'

'Where would you take me?' she asked. 'Please no museums.'

'Maybe dancing. Do you like dancing?'

'Not really.'

'I could teach you. I know a good place in New York.'

She laughed, but a sob sneaked up on her. It was painful to think of that other couple, that other Katya and Salim, taking walks through a city at peace, drinking in bars, eating meals in low-lit restaurants. She gripped his shoulder and pressed her face into his chest, breathing raggedly.

'We have to get out of here,' she muttered. 'Salim, we have to get out of here. We have to tell them about the carving.'

Salim's jaw clenched.

'We can't.'

'Salim. They won't let us go out to dig if we can't show them something.'

'Katya …'

'And you still need more parts for the van?'

He combed a hand through his beard, which had grown thick, and let out a long breath.

'We need new spark plugs. And Athir's got the permit to travel. A good fake, he says; should get us past the checkpoints if we really can't avoid them.'

'That's all we need?'

'Yes. Just one more dig, and we'd have it.'

'Salim,' she said, and ran her finger along the line of his cheekbone, joining up three freckles in a triangle, feeling the fragile lines of his skull. 'I didn't tell you this before. But we've nearly run out of things on his list. This is the last box we've got to give them. And then what's going to happen to us? We could end up in the park, like those people. Or in Syria. Or worse.'

He swallowed.

'We'd be trading one of the greatest finds in history. To criminals. And it's all just for a shot at escaping that doesn't even have half a chance of success. I still don't even know if the van will start. We'd still have to overpower the guards on the door, unlock the garage. And then we'd be driving it through a city controlled by murderers. The whole thing is madness, and if it doesn't work, we'd have given that lion away for nothing.'

'I know.' He held her gaze.

'They'll destroy it, you know.'

'Yes.'

'One way or another. They'll break it up to sell in parts. Or when they find out it's too big to transport, they'll just smash it out of spite. They want to erase the past.'

'I know.'

'And we've not even begun to understand what it represents. That lion: the mystery of it, the story behind how it got there. It could transform what we know about that world, about our own history.'

Katya nodded, feeling her heart heavy as a stone.

'Yes. But would you die for that?'

Salim shrugged morosely.

'Dr Malik did.'

'Would you make Lola die for it?'

They got up and washed, finding comfort in all the old rituals. Salim held Katya's hair while she poured the water through it, and she felt his fingers on the back of her neck. Then they all sat and ate chickpeas for breakfast. Lola looked glum, sensing the tension between them. Katya could tell that the same conversation was playing over and over in both of their heads as they sat there in silence. When they were done, they drank the sweet earthy juice from the tins too.

One of the ways Katya passed the time was helping Lola with her English, and teaching her what she could about archaeology. Since most of the books in the museum library had been destroyed, they had only two sources of material for their conversations: Katya's copy of *Gilgamesh*, and the plaques and information signage of the museum. They walked around and Lola read out the descriptions of the missing objects taken by the men, or those wrapped up in their plastic coverings.

'Statue of the Kings of Hatra,' Lola would read, and Katya would look up at the empty pedestal and nod.

'Very good.'

They wandered together through the halls where the carvings of the Assyrian wars still hung, too large for the men to have moved. Then they entered the room of the lion hunts and stood there for some time looking at the dying lions, the arrows sticking from their backs, the depths of their eyes. Then Lola pointed to one of the signs.

'What does this say?' she asked.

'That's a letter written by King Ashurbanipal in his old age. Can you read it?'

Lola squinted.

'"I cannot do away with the strife in my country and the dissensions in my family,"' Lola read, her voice halting. '"Illness of mind and flesh bow me down; with cries of woe ..."'

'Sadness,' Katya said when Lola looked at her.

'"With cries of woe, I bring my days to an end. On the day of the city god, the day of the festival, I am wretched; death is seizing hold upon me, and bears me down ..."'

'Very good,' Katya whispered. They both gazed at the stricken lions together. Katya cast her eyes over the King's commanding stare as he stretched his bow, his eyes blank and without feeling.

'The people who are lived here,' Lola said eventually. 'Where did they go?'

'The people who *lived* here,' Katya corrected.

'Yes. Where did they go?'

'The Assyrians? They were destroyed. They started many wars. They were cruel. They thought they were invincible.'

'Invincible?'

'They thought they could never be beaten, that their empire would last for ever. But after King Ashurbanipal died, the whole empire began to collapse. It happened so fast. One day they were the greatest power in the world, making carvings like this, making art and music and war. Then, about thirty years after this stone was carved, all their enemies joined together. They defeated the Assyrians in battle and marched through their lands, burning their cities, emptying them and burying them in the sands. And finally they burned Nineveh too. Hundreds of years later, when the Greek writer Xenophon travelled through this area, he saw the great ruins in the desert and he was amazed by them. They were larger than anything he'd ever seen in Greece, but no one who lived there even remembered who had built them. These towering walls.'

Lola let out a long sigh, and looked up at the lions.

'Enough learning today,' she said. 'Can you read to me now?'

273

They went upstairs and sat on their mattresses; Katya got out her *Gilgamesh* book, battered and softened to the texture of felt with use. Salim sat in the doorway with his back against the frame, his hands making the motion of smoking cigarettes, though he didn't have any left. Katya watched them both, Salim and Lola, the quivers manifesting in different parts of their bodies: hands, eyelids, lips. She opened the book and read to them.

When the wild man Enkidu died, King Gilgamesh went mad with grief. He would not let the priests bury him, until worms fell from his nose. He wandered the wastes dressed in a lion skin.
* 'I want never to enter the house of dust,' he shrieked. 'I want to bring my friend back from that dark place. I will go to the dead land and find the secret to eternal life.'*
* He walked through a world that had lost all joy.*
* The trees were grey and like the hands of the dead.*
* The sky was grey and like a washed robe.*
* The earth was grey and like the ash of a fire.*
* The King approached the gateway to the dead land. He entered the mountain gate, and dark fell around him.*

Katya stopped reading when Salim began to snore, his head rocking low on his neck. Lola was asleep too, lying on her back. Katya leant over and kissed the girl on the forehead, careful not to wake her.

She knew it was a bad idea, but she went up to the roof anyway. The usual jets were circling overhead, the sound of them like a heavy ball of marble rolling on a stone floor, dropping their bombs with a flash and rumble in the city outskirts. It was strange, how some sights became normal, the more you saw them.

She went to the balustrade and looked over into the park. Even though she knew she would see it, she still wasn't ready for the brown stains on the path, the grass trodden by the crowds. On the spiked railings along the park boundary, three dark objects were speared in a row. As she peered at them, the shapes rearranged themselves in the gloom, until she saw what they were. The hair on the heads was matted with blood, mouths gaping. She stifled a sob, covered her mouth with her hand and hid behind the balustrade, pressing her back into the stone.

———————

When Abu Ammar came to collect the last box of artefacts, Katya tried to see if anything had changed in him. He was tired: his skin was grey and there were dark marks beneath his eyes, his hair unwashed. Katya couldn't believe it, to look at him. He still looked so young.

'How are you?' she said. He just waved his hand.

'My path is filled with hurdles and thorns.'

He walked close behind her as they took the stairs down to the storeroom, heavy footfalls. The power was out, and he used the light on his phone to send light branching through the shelves. He'd brought her another kebab, something that seemed to be part of their relationship now. She noticed again that the lemon's flesh had been eaten. She never acknowledged the food in any way, and never ate until he'd left. Abu Ammar flashed his torch over her face, making her blind for a moment.

'These are the last objects on your list,' she said. She picked up the crate of artefacts and handed them to him. 'What's going to happen to us now?'

'I've told you about asking questions.' His voice sounded more like a mumble today. 'Hurry up. I've got places to be. People counting on me.'

'Abu Ammar. What's going to happen to us?'

He turned away from her for a moment, and she heard the popping of those pills from the pack. He swallowed some with a grimace.

'"And your Lord is the Forgiving, full of mercy,"' he said. '"Rather, for them is an appointment from which they will find no escape."'

'What does that mean?' she said, hearing the fear in her own voice. 'Abu Ammar, stop speaking in riddles for a moment and tell me.'

'"I will not cease travelling until I reach the junction of the two seas ..."'

'I saw you in the park,' she said. He cut off his recital, and she saw his eyes flash towards her in the gloom. She regretted saying it instantly. Her throat closed as he looked at her, and – did she imagine it? – his eyes glanced at her neck.

'Did you?' Strange emotions passed over his face for an instant. Then it hardened. 'Good.'

'What did those people do?'

Abu Ammar tested the weight of the crate in his hands. She heard the wistfulness of the drug enter his voice.

'Does it matter?'

'I guess not.'

Katya looked at him, his features sharp in the light from his phone. She wondered where he'd gone to school, the first girl he'd fallen in love with, what his favourite flavour of crisps were. She knew the drug's effect wouldn't last long.

'Abu Ammar, I have something to tell you.'

He looked hard at her for a moment.

'What?'

'There's something buried out there, on the hill beneath the mosque you blew up the other day. Something very valuable.'

'Another piece of pot?' he snorted. 'You can keep it.'

'No. It's much more valuable than that. Priceless, even.'

'How priceless?'

'You know those lion carvings they have upstairs? The plaster copies?'

'Yeah. The real ones are in London.'

'Not all of them. We don't know why, but at least one panel was left out of the final display. It's in the ground at the base of the mosque. And if you want, we can show you where it is.'

Abu Ammar stared at her, and something in his lip quivered. Then he lunged forwards and grabbed her by the throat, knocking the air out of her. Katya stifled a cry.

'"Grave is the word that comes from their mouths,"' he snarled, '"they speak not except a lie!"'

The phone light in his other hand sent a frenzy of lines and shadows darting through the shelves, but his face was in darkness. Katya's back pressed painfully against one of the shelves.

'Please …' she managed.

'What else have you been hiding from me?' he hissed.

'Nothing! I promise.'

Katya felt the shelf teetering behind her, about to fall, the clattering of objects as they tipped over and rolled to the floor around them.

'Every day I'm trying to help you,' Abu Ammar hissed. 'Every day I tell the others you're worth keeping around. And you repay me with lies.'

Katya tried to speak, but he closed his hand tighter. She felt her head swim. The objects on the shelf behind her knocked together as he held her against it, and she realised with a rush that he was pressing her against the shelf where the clay tablets were stored. The shelf where they'd hidden the knife. Her free hand felt behind her, over the cobwebs and dust, the dry edges of the tablets. Her fingers stretched out, and brushed the plastic handle. Abu Ammar's torch lit up the veins in his throat and the blood vessels in his cheeks showing pink and orange through his skin, his lips pulled back from his teeth. His breath smelled like lemons. Katya took a deep breath and gripped the knife.

Then he let her go, all at once, and Katya sobbed in fear and gasped for air. She let the knife fall back down to the shelf. She'd been so close – and what would have happened then? Abu Ammar stepped back and rubbed his eyes, making the torchlight bounce. Then the power came on, and lights flickered on all around them. They both blinked. It seemed like a different world, and his face flushed with a surprising expression, something like embarrassment.

'I'm sorry,' he said, and rubbed his eyes as though just waking. 'When people lie to me … it sets me off, you know? It brings back all the people who've lied to me in the past.'

'It's okay,' she croaked, massaging her throat.

'You don't seem like the others,' Abu Ammar said. He reached out and with his index finger brushed Katya's hair out of her face and behind her ear. 'You could have a good life here you know.' He didn't meet her eye, but Katya stared at him. *Don't react*, she told herself. *Don't react in any way.*

'They're giving me a house round here,' he went on, and rubbed his nose. 'A big house, on Nineveh Street. Couple of servants. Luxury, you know? You could live there. If you want.'

Abu Ammar glanced down at the kebab, where he'd left it on the nearby desk. The smell of it was thick in the air.

'I …' she tried, but no more sound came out.

'Just think about it,' he said, still not meeting her eye. He picked up the crate of objects, and they rattled. 'I'll tell the boss about the thing you've found. If he thinks it's worth it, we can go out digging in the next couple of days. Stay ready.'

'Sure,' Katya breathed, the terror of a hunted animal coursing through every corner of her body.

'I hope you're not lying to me, though,' he said, his voice sing-song and strange. 'Oh, Katya, I really hope you're not.'

That was the first time he'd ever said her name. When he was gone, Katya put her hands on her face, and stretched the skin over her bones, pulling it away from her eyes. She stared down at the kebab sitting on the table.

'Shit,' she said out loud, and then the lights blinked out again with a fizz, plunging her into a darkness that seemed ancient somehow, the untouched darkness of a cave many miles below the earth.

'Fucking fucking shit.'

Aurya

It was morning. The baker's brick fires filled the courtyard with smoke, which made Aurya's eyes smart.

'And go where?' Abil shouted, throwing his hands in the air. 'Our lives are here. The library is here. And you want to leave it just for a dream you had!'

'It's not just the dream,' Aurya said. 'It's everything. It's like a stone in my shoe, like a piece of food in my teeth. Abil, let's get on the next boat and head downriver. Let's go to Babylon or Egypt – or to the Westlands.'

'You think they don't have slaves in Egypt?' he said. 'You think there aren't wars in the Westlands?'

'I don't know, Abil. I just can't shake this feeling.'

'What's changed with you? You used to love the city. You always used to talk about it. Ever since that day on the riverbank when you told me you'd always wanted to come here.'

What had changed? Aurya let her hand rest on her stomach.

'Abil ...' She nearly told him.

'I don't want to hear any more about this. Nothing is going wrong in the city. It's been a bad war, but I've lived here all my life. I know how it works. The empire will crush these enemies as it always has. The refugees will go back to their homes. Then things will go on as usual. And Aurya, our lives are here. You get to work in the library. You love the library, don't you?'

He took her by both hands and looked her in the eyes.

'Yes.'

'And I'm doing translations for the King. This text I'm translating was baked before the flood. We're touching great things every day we live here. The world is cruel, but we have to find the parts of it that aren't. The parts that make the rest of it worth it.'

'I know, but Abil ...'

He sighed and turned away, grabbed his work things and left the house on his own. Aurya was alone at the top of the steps, breathing in the smell of charcoal and aniseed from two houses down. She stood there for a few moments, feeling the blood pound in her head. Then she ran down the stairs, into the courtyard and threw up in the drain. A woman, airing her clothes on the ledge of a high window, looked down at her and nodded knowingly.

'Don't tell anyone!' Aurya called up to her, but the woman just kept nodding and went back indoors. Aurya washed her mouth out and went to work in the library, chewing some fennel seeds on the walk. She tried not to think about the argument with Abil. She felt the usual feeling of peace descend over her the moment she stepped into the shaded halls: a place of quiet, a place separate from the bloody business of the city outside.

She spent most of the day ordering and tidying tablets, fetching texts for the soothsayers and medicine men. It seemed a group of doctors were competing to cure the King's nosebleeds: they were always coming in and asking for the same medical texts on bloodletting and poultices. Every time Aurya picked up a tablet, she thought about Abil, and her face flushed with anger and helplessness. But he was right: there would be slaves in Egypt too. There would be wars, too. And in the library, at least she could escape all of that. At least here she was at peace.

Later, more tablets arrived in a cart, swelling the library's collection by several hundred.

'Where did the King find all these?' she asked the carter Sin-Zababa, but he only shrugged. He had lost what weight he had, and looked tired.

'Out west. That's what the tablet says.'

It took all day to go through them, placing the King's official tag on each new book. It was mindless work, and while Aurya did it, she ran through her conversation with Abil again and again. She raised the tablets to her face, breathed in the air of the far-off lands. When she did, she thought she smelt a hint of smoke on these new tablets. But her sense of smell had changed recently as much as her taste. She put a hand on her stomach and prayed:

May Nabu enlighten me like a mask of gold,
May the dream I dream be good; may the dream I dream come true.

Towards evening, when most of the other workers had gone home and she thought she was alone in the library, she went quietly to the medical room, and searched through the shelves until she found what she was looking for. She took the tablet out and brushed away the dust.

"'If a woman is pregnant and the top of her forehead is yellow, the child is a boy,'" she muttered to herself, following the lines of text with her finger. "'If the top of her forehead is white and shines, the child is a girl.'"

A poet had left a bronze lamp on the table, and she tried to look at the reflection of her forehead wrapped around the dull metal. The colour of the lamp made it impossible to tell, though. Aurya placed a hand on her stomach. It was frightening: the feeling that her body wasn't her own, but something that happened to her, unstoppable as a flooding river. She went back to the tablet.

'If she has an appetite for foods preserved in vinegar, her child will be a boy. If she has an appetite for sweets, a girl.'

Aurya tried to feel what her appetite was, but before she could decide, a voice behind her said her name, making her jump.

'It's Aurya, isn't it?'

She nearly dropped the tablet on the floor. She swung around to see a familiar face. It was the King's servant and soothsayer Bel-Ibni, dressed in a typically fine robe of blue and gold threads. He was running his fingers along the edges of the tablets lined on the shelves, rustling the paper wrappings.

'Yes, that's right.' She put the tablet back in its place, making sure the servant couldn't see what it was about. Aurya hadn't spoken with this man since her time at the workshop. She often saw him moving about with the same officious air, conducting the King's will here and there in the city, but it had been years since he'd last found reason to talk to her.

'I heard you spoke with the King the other day,' he said blankly. Aurya didn't know if this was a question or not, and the smooth lines of the man's forehead gave no clue. 'What did you speak about?'

'About ...' Aurya's mind raced. 'About his dreams. And my brother.'

The servant gave her a hard look. He smoothed his moustache with fingers that had grown new gold rings since she'd last seen them. He watched her as if trying to read her.

'Well, the King would like to talk to you.'

'Right now?'

'Yes. He's waiting in the palace.' Aurya's insides moved.

'What does his majesty want?'

'I believe it's about your brother. The stone carver.'

'I don't speak to my brother any more. We haven't spoken for five years.'

'Even so. The King wants to speak to you. Please come with me.'

Aurya hesitated, but Bel-Ibni didn't give her another chance to protest. He turned off down the corridor. She shook her head and gathered up her things, put on her cloak. She followed him through the library halls, out on to the path leading to the palace, feeling suddenly afraid. The night was cold. In the ziggurat's high chamber, the priests were performing some great rite that had taken days, and smoke rose from its altar, lit from beneath by fires. Their chanting drifted down to her, and the night insects flitted and fluttered.

'Does my forehead look a certain colour to you?' she asked Bel-Ibni, as they passed the guardhouse, and he looked at her as if she were mad.

'What?'

'Oh, nothing.'

They passed through the palace gate. No servants rushed through its shaded halls now, no courtiers whispered in the cloisters. The painted carvings along each wall still clamoured in a riot of bright colour: the reds and greens and yellows of crushed seashells, and of rare kinds of trees and flowers and beetles. In the patches of occasional lamplight, she saw the garden scene Sharo had helped to carve in the workshop five years before, now finished and fixed in place along the walls: the King lounging and raising his cup, the servants standing in attendance, with the trees and vines all around. The head hanging in the tree nearby. With the colours added to the carving, it looked magnificent. Aurya thought she recognised Sharo's work here and there: that living quality in the curling vines and the courtiers' soft faces. Near to the throne room, they passed a long corridor, and Bel-Ibni stepped inside it for a moment.

'Look,' he said, gesturing. Small oil lamps were burning at intervals on the floor. There were no carvings in there: all the walls here were blank, just cavities of baked brick. 'Here's where the King's next series of carvings is going to be placed,' Bel-Ibni told her. She looked around the room, at the long lines of waiting spaces.

'What are the carvings of?'

'They will show the King in his chariot, hunting lions the way he used to, when he was young.'

'Oh.'

The servant led her on to a pair of doors. He put his hand on the brass fittings, then paused for a moment before opening.

'You have probably already seen that these days the King ... is not the way he used to be. It is best not to anger him.'

With that warning, he pushed on the door; a waft of warm air, smelling of hay and wood smoke, breathed from inside. Aurya stepped into the room, and Bel-Ibni stayed outside, pulling the door closed behind her. She saw that it was a high vaulted space, full of statues. They were large and small, made of stones of all shades, some of metals that glinted in the dim light; some horned, some with the beaks of birds or the faces of monkeys; some with wide, frightened eyes of white ivory. The statues stood all around the room like a strange kind of audience. In front of them, the King sat in a long chair, with the greenish glow of burning sea wood lapping over him. His crumpled legs were covered, and he was reading from a tablet.

'Come in, come in,' the King croaked, and raised a hand to cover his scars. Aurya tried to remember the proper honorific.

'My King, my lord, my sun. I am the dust upon which you step. Seven times and again seven times, I …'

'It's the river girl, isn't it?' the King murmured, cutting her off. Aurya coughed.

'Yes. Bel-Ibni, your servant. He told me you wanted to speak to me.' The King put down the tablet. Aurya's gaze wandered around the wide eyes of the statues looming out of the dark, the frightful expressions on their faces. 'My lord, what is this place?'

'This? This is the house of broken idols. This is where we keep all the gods we take from our enemies. The gods we take from their shattered temples, their burnt-out palaces. We bring them back here to live out their lives, so they might serve us as they served their former masters. This one with the horns, we took from the people of the seacoast. This bird monster is from Egypt.'

'They look sad.'

'Perhaps they are. They've travelled a long way from the lands they used to rule.' He coughed. 'Just like you, little girl. You've come a long way, since that day on the riverbank.'

'Yes, my lord. I have.'

'Bel-Ibni tells me you're indispensable in the library. One of our best workers. That you've been helping to order the new tablets as they come in. We should have a large load coming in soon. You'll see.'

'Yes, your majesty. Thank you. I've always loved those stories. It's an honour to work with them.'

'Yes, the stories,' the King said. 'I've always loved them too. This one especially. Have you read this one? The story of King Gilgamesh?'

'No, my lord.'

'But it's the most famous story of all,' the King said dreamily, his brow furrowing. 'The first half I always love: the journey to defeat the demon Humbaba, the fight against the bull of heaven. And the second half, after the death of the wild man Enkidu …

when the great king goes off in search of the secret to eternal life. How can you have missed it?'

'My brother ... he used to tell me the story. It was a way of calming him down. But he never got to finish it.'

'Your brother ...' the King slurred.

'Yes, my lord. I don't think I want to know how the story ends.' The King nodded.

'I don't want to think about my brother either. It's why I haven't set foot in Babylon, since we reclaimed it. Or my father's palace, across the river, where the two of us grew up, running together through those halls. I always loved Babylon, you know. The glorious blue tiles of its gates, the shaded groves, the water-birds. Of course now,' he waved at his blanketed legs, 'I can't travel anywhere. I sit here and direct the happenings of the world, seeing only through the signs the gods choose to send me.'

He fluttered one hand at her, as if to say that she was one of these signs. Aurya shifted her weight from one foot to the other.

'And while I sit here,' he went on, 'our empire flourishes. Our armies trample the lands of our enemies, scatter the bones of their ancestors, bring their gods back to Nineveh. And my artists – my artists are creating the finest works the world has ever seen.'

He coughed and cleared his throat.

'And that's why you want to speak to me,' Aurya said, tingling with fear.

'Your brother ...' The King's eyes wandered off as if he could see through the walls, out into the city. 'Your brother is refusing to perform his work. I have explained to him what I want him to carve, and he has refused.'

'Can't one of the other carvers do it for you?' The King just laughed, cold and clear as a clapping hand. He spat some phlegm into the brazier with a hiss, and the light flickered across the faces of the surrounding statues.

'There are no other carvers,' he said. 'What used to take a whole team of men now takes only one. All the others were reassigned, sent off to the far corners of the empire, to Dur-Sharrukin and Nimrud, to work on dull fortifications, to carve stone stelae on old hilltops. None of them can create work of the same beauty. The same detail.'

'My lord, Sharo obeys strange gods. I haven't spoken to him for years. What can I do to change his mind?'

She already knew what the answer would be.

'Go and speak to him. Convince him to carve what I have ordered him to carve, and nothing else. Or I will lay down the sentence reserved for those who disobey their King. You know what that is, don't you, girl?'

'Yes,' Aurya tried to say, but it came out as a hollow pipe. The King ran his fingers over the ancient marks in his tablet, and Aurya caught the glance of one statue with wide, frightened eyes.

'And while you're there, get him to tell you the rest of this story,' the King said. 'Maybe you can explain to me what it means in the end. We need the young … the young minds. For the future.'

The door creaked open and let in a bar of light from the hall. Around the room, the wide eyes of the captive gods lit up. Bel-Ibni beckoned.

'I will take you to see your brother now,' he said. Aurya's stomach plunged.

'Now?'

The servant nodded.

'We should let his majesty get some rest.'

Aurya stepped out into the cool grey hall, with one last glance back at the idols imprisoned in the gloom of that room. Tiny bats were beginning to gather in the rafters. The servant closed the door on the King softly, careful not to make a sound.

'It's late,' Aurya said. 'Can't we go in the morning?'

'You know,' the servant said, 'It was only last month that our armies finally conquered Elam. His majesty told me for weeks how much he would like to be its king, how he wanted to wander its vineyards, to learn its language and read its books.' He ran one of his ringed hands over his cheek. 'Only days later, he gave the order to burn the whole land, to tear its cities down to stones, to scatter the bones of its kings and leave it to the gods of the ruins. Our men are still at work there as we speak.'

Aurya's hand came up to her mouth.

'What happened to the people there?' Aurya whispered, but the servant ignored her.

'I tell you this to show you how quickly the King's moods change these days. That your brother is alive today shows how much respect he commands in the palace. How much the King loves his work.'

'But tomorrow ...'

Bel-Ibni pursed his lips.

'Tomorrow his majesty might feel less inclined to mercy.'

'If that's what you think, then let's go. But my brother must be asleep by now.'

The servant shook his head slowly.

'Your brother has changed a lot since you last saw him,' he said, and ran a hand through his hair. 'I'm told he hardly ever sleeps.'

They walked through the city with a band of soldiers, who shoved with their spear butts at the crowds that still gathered around the drinking places. People reeled in the lamplight of beer houses, rocked on wooden benches and sang, sobbed and snorted, fought in the mud, talked over each other, jabbing at the air with their fingers. They passed a band of refugees begging on the river-bank, desperate faces lit by torches. They soon reached the crown of the hill where the empty palace stood, the palace of the King's father. A mass of memories passed over Aurya, after-images over-lapping and erasing one another. She remembered the fearsome presence she'd once felt moving in the old halls. Already the dust was whipping up into the air in a great spiral, and she could hear a solitary chisel striking stone. Aurya prayed:

May Makhir, the god of dreams, settle upon my head,
Let me enter Beth-Saggil, the palace of the gods.

As they rounded the crest of the hill, the mason's workshop came into view. Aurya saw drawings etched into the mud. They came one at a time at first: the scratched figure of a bird or a person, or a man with a donkey. As she got closer, the drawings sprawled everywhere in the clay earth, and where they reached the walls of nearby houses, they became charcoal etchings, climbing on every surface: drawings of a busy marketplace full of performing animals and bubbling crowds, the priests in the ziggurat performing their rituals, the herdsmen taking their animals through the water gate to drink – and lions, everywhere lions. Aurya's skin tingled at the sight. As the mason's workshop came into view, the chisel grew louder, and Aurya saw a solitary figure in a pool of torchlight at the centre of its courtyard, wrapped in a shawl and hunched over a huge piece of stone.

Katya

Katya found Salim sitting with Lola in front of the lion hunt carvings. It was a position all three of them had begun to take habitually throughout the day, a base they always came back to after wandering the museum or going out on to the roof. Salim was staring up at the lions with empty eyes, and when she got closer, she saw that he was holding some printed pages, photographs of their excavation of the body from the dust room. She sat beside him and put an arm around him, laid her head on his shoulder. She looked at the photo, remembering the day she'd found it – how long ago that seemed. The body was as she remembered it: foetal and shrunken, its one hand extended, fist balled around the seal now hanging from her neck. She ran her fingers along Salim's shoulder, along his neck and collarbone, and tried to work up the courage to tell him what she'd done. That Abu Ammar knew about the lion carving out there in the earth.

'Did you ever notice the direction this man was reaching?' Salim said, his voice far-off. He tapped the directional markers in the top of the grainy printed image, beside the metre rulers they'd laid out beside the corpse. 'Lola pointed it out.'

'South?' Katya said.

'Southeast, more like. Or south-southeast.'

'What about it?'

He shrugged.

'It's just funny. It's the exact direction of the Tigris. The river.'

'It is?'

'Yes. Like he was reaching downstream.'

Katya ran her tongue over her teeth. She took a deep breath.

'Salim,' she said. 'I told them.'

Both Salim and Lola turned to look at her.

'Told them what?' he croaked, but it was clear he knew.

'Salim … I'm sorry.'

She thought he might shout or curse her, but he didn't. He just nodded and stared straight ahead, his chest rising in one deep breath. And then he placed his head against her shoulder. Katya felt the weight and warmth of it, and looked up at the carvings on the walls. Even the King in his chariot, frozen in those moments for millennia, looked tired these days. Would he ever get to put down that spear?

'We're doing it then,' Salim said. He ran his hands through his hair, which was growing long and matted. 'Twenty-six centuries of history, just for another chance at life. I can't even imagine what Dr Malik would say.'

'I know what he'd say,' Katya murmured, and swallowed. She knew what her father would say too. 'But if we don't get out of here, they're going to kill us. And the one that keeps coming back, Abu Ammar …'

'What?' Salim said, eyeing her momentarily. Katya felt, strangely, a burst of shame. She just shook her head.

'We've run out of artefacts, Salim. It's the end. Unless we can get that van working.'

He nodded, and reached out a hand to touch her cheek.

'We've come too far to stop now. And honestly … what does all this even matter any more? These stones …'

'Don't say that.'

'Look at them,' he said bitterly. 'Dead stones and broken things, gathering dust. What use are they to anyone?'

'They're here so we can remember,' Lola said softly.

'No,' Salim said. 'They're here so we can forget.' He pressed the tips of his fingers into Katya's cheek, and breathed out slowly. 'I always wondered how Nineveh could have fallen,' he said. 'The whole city destroyed, all at once. Just like that. But now … I think

I know how it felt. I didn't see any of this coming. I'm sorry. It was my job to keep us safe.'

She kissed him on his forehead, his eyes, his lips.

'We're going to get out of here. Just one more dig, and we've got the parts. Just one more dig, Salim. Then we're free.'

Katya put her arm around both of them, and they all sat there and held each other until the rumble of bombs in the city outside disturbed their peace.

They got the text that evening. Athir had hidden the parts just as before, buried beneath the olive tree. The new spark plugs, some more petrol and a faked permit to travel. Salim's hands shook when he read the text.

'Now we just wait for that English bastard to come. When do you think it'll be?'

'He didn't say. Just something vague, like "the next few days". And what if the looters … or someone else … what if they go digging on the site and find our things? What if it's all gone by the time we get there?'

Salim shrugged and put his head in his hands. He looked exhausted, his face all angles and hollows. But he reached out and drew her close to him. She felt the shaking of his body, but his warmth passed between them.

Katya spent the nights with Salim in constant fear. They knew that every passing day increased the chance the hidden parts would be dug up and stolen, or blown away in a storm, or carried away by a stray dog. Lola developed a cough. She looked pale and thin, a photo negative of a person.

On the third day, they heard a knock on the museum door. The three of them were eating the last flatbreads they had left. Katya and Salim jumped to their feet in panic. Lola watched the two of them with wide eyes, chewing slowly.

'Shit,' Katya said.

'Fuck,' said Salim. 'Stay calm. Stay calm.'

'Just like before. We go to dig. You go to dig by the olive tree. And then I distract them when you find it.'

'If I find it.'

'If you find it.'

They both hugged Lola before heading to the entrance hall. 'Please come back,' she said. 'Katya, please come back.'

They went down to meet Abu Ammar. He was there in the hall, flanked by two gunmen with covered faces. He nodded grimly at Katya and Salim as they came down to meet him, offering their hands to be zip-tied. Katya felt a strange new energy from Abu Ammar since their conversation in the storeroom. He avoided looking at her. He treated her briskly and made one of the gunmen tie her hands while he did Salim's.

The men didn't bother putting bags over their heads this time. It was sweltering outside, oven air, and the air-conditioned car was a relief. As they drove off, Abu Ammar turned around and fixed Katya with a long look. She couldn't work out its meaning. She glanced around at Salim, who was staring out of his window purposefully, the muscles in his jaw clenching and unclenching as the empty city passed before his eyes. Katya ran through their plan in her head: the olive tree, the dig, the distraction. They went by the blackened cavities of many bombed-out buildings. Abu Ammar was browsing the Internet on his phone, flicking through news articles. Katya saw flashes of military hardware, satellite photos of landscapes and cities, men in black standing over other men kneeling in orange jumpsuits.

'"And his fruits were encompassed by ruin,"' Ammar muttered. '"He turned his hands in dismay over what he had spent on it, while the fruit collapsed on its trellises."'

They parked the car on the road below the site, and Abu Ammar pulled them out into the bleached sunlight. They walked across the bare ruined ground for some distance, stumbling in the dust and broken brick, until the shattered mosque on the hill came into view. They arrived at the site, and Katya knew immediately that the looters had been there. The ground was littered with more cigarette packets and flares, fresh tyre tracks winding along heavily used tracks up to the site. New holes had been cut in the earth, their trenches torn apart, and there were holes beneath the olive tree too. She glanced over at Salim, and by the shade of grey he'd turned, she knew he was having the same thoughts. But still, mercifully, the lion carving remained covered: the broken tyre they'd used to mark the spot hadn't been moved.

'Over there,' Katya told Abu Ammar. 'That disturbed patch of earth, beneath the tyre. That's where we found the piece. And we think there could be another fragment over there, by the tree.'

He gave a snort.

'Get digging then.'

The earth should have been easy to dig, having been disturbed before, but Katya was weak. Hunger had thinned her out, and her joints felt too bony. It confused her senses too, made the scent of the earth, of loam and clay, smell delicious. When she straightened up, she glanced over and saw Salim digging beneath the olive tree. His face was pale. He shot her a desolate look. The parts weren't there.

A series of booms sounded in the distance, and the howling of a jet. Abu Ammar and his men ducked behind the olive tree wall, muttering to themselves.

'"Your enemies will summon one another to attack you as if inviting others to share their meal,"' Abu Ammar muttered. He stood up and raised one finger to the sky, while his gunmen remained under cover and watched him with weary eyes. More planes streaked, the thumps of bombs going off in the city. It went on all day. From the hillside, Katya could see the new ruins they made in the distant skyline, buildings folded in on themselves like cardboard boxes. She thought what a relief it would be to have one of those bombs snuff her out right now, for it all to end in an instant.

After some time, Salim slouched over to her. She knew what he would say just by the desolate look on his face, the sad, shallow holes he'd dug in a ring around the tree.

'It's not here,' he muttered, his eyes fixed on the earth. 'There's nothing there.'

'Keep trying,' she said. 'It's not like we've got anywhere to be.'

'They might get suspicious.'

'They might. But it's our last chance.'

It took hours for Katya to reach the layer with the stone. Its smooth surface emerged slowly. Here was the King's chariot, with its gilding and intricate details, the harnesses and finials. Salim was right: the chariot was the wrong way around. It was upturned. She uncovered its wheel, and found it broken, the spokes shattered. Beneath the chariot, King Ashurbanipal lay trapped, his legs crushed, his spear and bow fallen from his hands, his crown toppling from his head. And a lion, one of the animals that the King was slaughtering in the other panels, had the man himself in its jaws. As she uncovered more and more, Katya forgot where she was. The piece went on further into the trench wall, and she uncovered it gingerly, with shaking hands.

'Hey!' she called to Abu Ammar. 'There's something new here.'

He was smoking, and looked over with irritation. Salim glanced up at her too, watching her keenly. Abu Ammar sidled over to her, and Katya pointed down at the emerging image in the stone. He just stood there and flicked his cigarette down into the trench.

'What is it?'

'It's the missing piece of the frieze.'

'Just dig it up,' Abu Ammar sighed, and wheeled back around. 'You didn't say it was this big. It's too big. We'll need to get a crane up here to lift it out.'

He shook his head and dialled someone on the phone, talked for a little while. Katya climbed from her trench and went to Salim.

'Come and see it,' she said.

'What?'

'Come and see what we would have discovered, in another life.'

His face fell, but he nodded. Katya led him over to her trench.

'Look. There are two new panels.'

'That's ... incredible,' he breathed. 'My god. What does it mean? Is that the King? Crushed beneath his chariot? There's no mention, in the texts ... and what does the other panel show?'

'I'll keep digging. You keep looking by the tree. Maybe we got the place wrong. Maybe ...'

'It's no use.' His eyes stayed down in the pit with the lion. 'I looked everywhere. It's all been for nothing.'

She reached out and touched his shoulder.

'We're stuck here anyway. Don't give up.'

'Hey!' Abu Ammar shouted. Katya turned and saw a real flash of rage in his gaze. She withdrew her hand from Salim's shoulder.

It took about half an hour to clear the second panel. The carving showed a lion lying like so many others, arrows jutting from its hind legs and back, its tongue lolling from its mouth. Kneeling over it was the figure of a boy, his face a mask of pain and sorrow. Katya paused over the image for some time, and felt her fingers reaching instinctively for the cylinder seal hanging from her neck. The boy's expression, that desperate loss and hopelessness, was the same look that had crossed Salim's face. It was the same thing she felt. Suddenly there wasn't enough breathable air in the world. They were going to die there: she felt it so acutely in that moment, the pure, terrible reality, that she couldn't bear it. Katya heaved herself from the pit, scraping her knee. Tears popped in her eyes, and she ran to the ancient olive tree, its leaves shimmering silver in the breeze.

'Hey!' Abu Ammar barked. 'What are you doing?'

Katya stopped and turned to look at him. She breathed in, brushed away her tears, ashamed of them.

'I need to pee!' she yelled. It was true, and the directness of this seemed to silence Abu Ammar. He wrinkled his nose and waved his hand. Katya jumped down over the wall and behind the olive tree. No one tried to stop her or follow her. They had guns after all, and where would she run?

Out of view, she pulled down her trousers and crouched in the shadow of the tree, among its roots that ran deep down into the ancient mound. She felt the relief on her bladder. As her eyes followed the stream through the dust and mesquite scrub, she thought of what Dr Malik had said once, about the rivers of the earth and its magnetic field, about all of human history flowing down through its geography. Then her eyes landed on something. It was a blue plastic bag like dozens all around her, like the rest of the litter in the wind. Only it wasn't in the wind. It was weighed down by something inside. She shook herself and pulled up her trousers, took a few steps down to the bag. There was earth caking the outside, too. Fresh earth, still dark like the edges of the looters' holes. She crouched down and reached out. Inside the bag was a bottle full of amber liquid, a square of paper covered in Arabic and spark plugs.

'Oh shit,' she muttered, and quickly looked over her shoulder to see if any of the men had seen her. They were beyond the wall, and the olive tree hid her from view. The looters must have found the bag in the night, one of countless plastic bags that littered the hill, then thrown it over the wall like rubbish. She took the bag and climbed back up the hill, heart pounding, and nestled it just behind the olive tree. Then she composed herself and stepped out into view. Abu Ammar was looking out over the city, hands on his hips, his pistol in its holster and his knife in a sheath at his hip. Katya walked casually over to where Salim was sitting with his head in his hands, and touched him on the shoulder. His head jerked upwards.

'Behind the tree,' she mouthed to him, and tipped her head in its direction. His brow furrowed, not understanding. And then his eyes widened. Katya jumped down into the trench and resumed digging. She took a long breath.

'Quick!' she shouted to Abu Ammar. 'Come see this!'

'What is it?' he growled. 'I told you, I don't care. Just dig it up.'

'No. I mean it. You have to see this.' He came over with irritation playing all over his face. 'You see,' Katya went on, 'we've always wondered what happened to the Assyrian King Ashurbanipal. In the last years of his reign, it's like he disappeared completely. No one even knows how he died. People have theorised about illness, madness, remorse over his brother's death. But this carving might be a clue.'

Katya could see in the corner of her eye that Salim was edging to the tree.

'So?' Abu Ammar said.

'So perhaps we have an answer now. Perhaps this is what happened to him. It's one of the great mysteries of Assyriology – the disappearance of Ashurbanipal.'

'What's it worth?'

'It's the most important discovery for generations. It's priceless.'

The tip of Abu Ammar's tongue ran along the edge of his lower lip. Salim was at the tree now, bent behind it. Katya willed herself not to look at him directly, but Abu Ammar still sensed something in the direction of her attention. He turned to where Salim was crouching. Katya shot out her hand and touched Abu Ammar's wrist. She brushed her thumb against his skin. His eyes lanced back to meet hers. He tried to pull away as if scalded, but she held him, felt the narrow bones in his wrist, the hairs on his skin that seemed to prickle at her touch. He seemed all at once very frightened, and Katya felt a tingle of terror deep in her own heart. She fixed his look. Then he yanked his hand away, his lips curling and pale.

'What are you doing? Don't touch me.'

'Sorry. I'm sorry.'

Behind Abu Ammar, Salim was wrapping something in the tarpaulin, hands shaking, but his eyes were on Katya. He gave the slightest nod, his face the colour of ash.

The two of them worked in silence for the rest of the day, unable to catch each other's eyes for fear of giving something away. When a new group of armed men came with a crane and its scared-looking driver chugging up the slope, everyone gathered around the trench and watched. The chains pulled taut and the stone slid from the earth, grinding the trench sides as it came, and for the first time they saw the whole thing in one go, both panels. The dust slid from it in sheets. It was all there: the boy, the lion, the King crushed beneath his chariot. Katya felt exhausted tears cool her itchy eyes. She realised in that moment what she'd done, and how history would remember her.

'We discovered something that would have changed the world,' Salim murmured beside her, as if reading her mind. 'And we sold it for a chance at our miserable lives.'

On the way back to the museum, the men didn't bother tying Katya's and Salim's hands. They let them sit beside each other in the back seat, as the car eased their way through traffic. Ahead of them, two pickup trucks drove with the huge slabs of stone weighing down their rears. Abu Ammar seemed deathly silent. As they drove down Nineveh Street, its evening markets came to life, hung with coloured lights. The sun dimmed in purple and orange, and the mosques crackled to life with the muezzin call to prayer. Katya reached out and touched Salim's hand with her little finger. She glanced from the corner of her eye, and saw that his lips were moving in silent prayer.

Aurya

The years had changed Sharo more than Aurya could have imag
ined. She stood in the entrance to the mason's workshop and
watched him, lit by reed torches. He turned and saw her, and she
felt a fish bone in her throat. His skin was covered in white dust,
and his eyes were red as a waterbird's. They were the sore eyes of
a stone worker, the skin around them puffy and dark. A kind of
sadness had worked its way into his face, which was now thin and
stubbled with wispy hair.

'Sharo?' His face remained fixed, but he pulled his shawl up
over his dusty hair and put down his chisel and hammer on the
piece of stone.

'Hello, Aurya,' he said flatly.

'Sharo …' She stepped into the workshop's shadows. 'It's been
a long time.'

A breeze picked up the reed matting overhead, and a curtain of
dust peeled off into the air, carrying the acid smell of stone.

'It was two thousand days on nineteenth of Tishrin.' He used
a thick hand to brush the dust from the stone he was working
on. Aurya recognised his hands: the hands of her father, strong
and sanded smooth. Sharo had been carving the King in his chariot on to the stone, the emerging form of a lion jumping up to
bite the wheel. It was still lumpen and ill-defined, but it was
unmistakable.

'Oh Sharo.' She came over to him and wrapped her arms around his shoulders, pressed her cheek into his neck. 'I'm so sorry. I'm sorry for everything.'

His skin felt cool and hard, but slowly his hands reached up to wrap around her. Tears made tidemarks in the white dust coating his skin.

'I've missed you, Aurya.'

'I missed you too, Sharo.'

She ran her hands through the tight curls of his hair, and little puffs of dust rose from him.

'But I know why you're here.'

She looked into his eyes, the dark irises couched in those river beds of red. Sharo gestured back to the entrance, where Bel-Ibni was standing with one hand clasped in the other.

'Yes. They sent me.'

Sharo nodded and turned back to the stone.

'They want me to carve something that didn't happen.'

'Yes.'

'It's no use, Aurya. I can only carve the things I've seen. Nothing else makes sense.'

She sat down on a bench beside the piece of stone Sharo was working on, and he drew the shawl further around his face, and went on working. She listened to the click of his hammer and chisel, and then reached out and touched his hand, brushed the dust from the little hairs on its back. She ran her fingers over his, and felt the dry, hard skin, knew his fingerprints would now be worn away completely. He paused and looked up at her.

'Sharo, you're risking your life. The King … he could kill you if you don't do as he says. He'll do terrible things to you.' She dropped her voice. 'He's going mad.'

Sharo shrugged, but his face was a mask of misery.

'Sharo, why are you doing this? For that lion? After all these years?'

He put down his tools again and fixed her with a look for a long time. Then he stood up.

'Let me show you what I'm working on.'

He led her around the corner to the wide courtyard behind the workshop, and she gave a little intake of breath. In a semicircle, a dozen flat slabs of stone were gathered, each etched with intricate carvings. The work was spectacular. Every detail was perfect. Here was the king in his chariot; here were the lines of soldiers, with their dogs baying on their leashes; here was the wooded hill with its monument on top, a carving within a carving; here were the people beckoning to each other as they gathered to watch; here were the lions in their cages, with the children on top releasing them; here were the arrows darting through the air to their targets; here were the lions dying; here were the priests pouring oil on the slain beasts. Everything was there, exactly as it had happened.

'They keep telling me to make the lions more fearsome,' Sharo said. 'They say they should look like fierce beasts, so the King can look brave as he kills them. But that's not how it happened. Not at all. They told me this lion's tail was too long, even though that was exactly its length. The King even wants me to carve him wrestling a lion, pinning it by its throat with one hand.'

Aurya thought of the King peering out from under his blanket and laughed despite herself. In the flickering light, the lions seemed to come alive: their sad faces scrunched in pain, the blood gushing from their mouths, their straining limbs still clinging on to life.

'And that part over there ...' He waved towards the workshop building. 'They say that part shouldn't exist at all.'

Over in the shadowy corner, in the direction Sharo was pointing, were the final pieces: two panels, carved in the same immaculate detail as all the others: King Ashurbanipal trapped under his chariot, a lion gripping him in its jaws, with Sharo standing there. The next scene showed Sharo kneeling beside his lion's limp body and weeping. Aurya covered her mouth.

'Oh, Sharo ...' A void opened inside her, and she held her brother, realising only then how much she had needed him.

'Sharo. What you said, that day. The day of the hunt. About our mother. Was it true?'

Sharo turned to look at her with haunted eyes.

'I'm sorry, Aurya.' She held him tighter. 'I should have told you earlier. Father always told me we had to lie to you, about our mother. About the lion dragging her away. And after he died … I didn't know what to do. You kept talking about the house of dust, and I didn't know how to tell you. You've always been better at those things than me.'

'I'm sorry too, Sharo. For everything.'

He nodded. Aurya noticed something in the corner of the crumbling old wall.

'You planted an olive tree,' she said. 'You always loved olives.'

'Yes. Olive trees can grow for a hundred years, sometimes many hundreds. No one really knows how long. And the man down the road said he'd pickle them for me. You should hear it when the wind picks up, Aurya. It blows right through the branches. It almost sounds like it's saying our mother's name.'

'What was her name?' Aurya said. And wasn't it strange that she'd never known?

'Ashana. Ashana Nur-ili, daughter of Adad-Kudurri-Usur.'

Aurya bit her lip.

'Sharo, will you tell me the rest of her story sometime?'

Sharo nodded.

'I can tell it now if you'd like. Our mother always cried at these parts.'

Aurya sat down beside him as he carved, the tapping of his chisel punctuating the story as he spoke in the same soft, even tone she remembered from so long ago.

King Gilgamesh clambered on his hands and knees through the dark tunnel. Darkness lay all around.

He could not see the hand in front of his face.

He could not see the path ahead.

He could not see the ground beneath.

After days of travelling through this dark place, he reached the end of the tunnel, and the river of the dead. Gilgamesh found the ferryman Urshanabi and told him of his quest to find the secret of life.

'I will take you across the river,' he told the King. 'But you must cut down one hundred and twenty trees to use as barge-poles, for each tree will wither and die the moment it touches those waters.'

Gilgamesh did as the ferryman commanded, though it took many days. Then they made their offerings and set out across the river of death to meet with the immortals.

'But be warned,' Urshanabi told the King, 'you will never find what you seek.'

Sharo paused there and stopped his tapping on the stone.

'I'm not going to tell you the rest,' he said.

'Why not?'

'So you have to come back.' She felt a bubble of tears. She put her arm around his shoulder.

'I'll come back, Sharo. But your carvings … they're going to kill you if you don't stop this. The King is going mad.'

'Then that's what they'll do.' He turned back to his work. 'I can't forget any of it, Aurya. And what I remember goes into the stone.'

He brushed away the dust from his work. Aurya felt a great sinking in her heart, a weariness in her limbs. The night air was cold, and she knew Abil would be worried about her. Aurya breathed out and turned to leave. Sharo picked up his chisel again and made a couple of gentle strikes.

'Aurya,' he said, and she turned back to him. He sniffed. 'You should leave this place. This city. It poisons everything it touches.'

'I know. I'm trying.'

Sharo smiled.

'You grew your hair. You look just like her, you know.'

Aurya nodded and felt a smile break through her tears.

'Thanks, Sharo. It's good to see you again.'

She walked from the workshop, leaving Sharo behind with his stone. Bel-Ibni was waiting in the shadow of the gate, and looked questioningly as she approached.

'Well? Will he stop this nonsense and carve what the King wants?'

'I think so,' Aurya lied.

Aurya saw the muscles in the servant's jaw clench and unclench. And then, for the first time, she saw a fluttering of real fear in his eyes.

'That boy is going to get us all killed.'

When she got home, Aurya lay on her mat with Abil and listened to the movements of the city night outside, the yowls of cats and drunks, the huff of oxen and the slushing footsteps of patrolling soldiers in the muddy streets. She felt the muscles in her stomach, the strange creature growing just beneath the surface.

'Abil, I want to talk to you.'

'You don't still want to leave, do you, Aurya? I told you: our lives are here, in the city. And these dreams you've been having, these feelings ... they're just your imagination. Everything is just as it's always been.'

She held on to him, unable to let him go, while the night moved around them. She wanted to tell him, but telling him would make it real. And what was it inside her? Was it a child, or a lion? She lay in the darkness, feeling the warmth of her husband's body, and the city's invisible spirits moving in their enormous numbers in the sky overhead.

'Abil?' He didn't answer. She listened to his breathing and knew that he was asleep. 'I'm going to have a child.' The words went unheard, disappearing into the night as if never said. 'I'm so scared.'

The new trove of tablets that the King had promised arrived in the following days. There were hundreds of them, arriving in carts and barges, stacked in wicker baskets and flax bags stuffed with straw. The caravan driver Sin-Zababa came with them, but he seemed in a strange mood to Aurya. He had got even thinner, and pale as ash. He didn't want to talk about the tablets at all.

'Long journey,' he kept saying. 'Too long, a very hard road.'

He waited out by the library gate as the tablets came in, and set up an awning under which he would spend the night, chewing some kind of mountain grass he kept in a pouch.

Aurya had to stay late to catalogue the new finds as they came in. She marked each tablet with the King's inscription before stacking them on the waiting shelves: stories and poems, histories and king lists, manuals and lists of laws, word lists for the dead languages, hymns to the gods, psalms and songs. All this time, her thoughts wandered over Sharo and his story, over Abil and the dark shroud she felt creeping over the city.

Sometime after sunset, Aurya made some excuse and headed to the room of records. The place was huge. It sprawled across many shelves, stuffed with tablets stacked in piles and tied with string. It took her a long time to find what she was looking for: the manifests of vessels. She counted back the years. The tablet she found was scratched and old, but the writing was clear enough. She ran her finger down the list of names. And then she found it.

'Ashana Nur-ili, daughter of Adad-Kudurri-Usur.' There she was. Her mother's name, stamped in the clay. 'Departed by boat headed north with Tappum the mason, son of Iarbi-ilu.'

That was all it said. Aurya sat down on a seat nearby and stared at this one line in the clay as goosebumps broke all over her arms. She felt the grooves in her necklace as she read it over and over, imagined the day it must have been written, the young woman setting out by boat with her new husband. Then, when the shaking in her body had passed, Aurya put the tablet back on its shelf, and went back to work.

Once everyone else had gone home, Aurya brought a pitcher of beer to Sin-Zababa, who took it with a far-off look in his eyes.

'Thank you, Miss. It's been a long journey.'

'They only get longer,' she said, and the driver nodded.

'Back on the road tomorrow. Back on the road tomorrow.'

With the library empty, Aurya could take as much time as she liked to read each text as they passed through her hands. She stopped to read one strange tablet that imagined an argument between a palm tree and a willow, over which was the superior tree. Then she read about the goddess Ishtar's descent into the underworld, how she passed through every gate into that dark place, and at each one removed an item of clothing until she stood naked before the land of the dead. When Aurya reached the story's end, she saw something that made her stop: a dark spot on the baked clay, like a blot of ink. She scratched at it, and her fingernail came away with a rust-coloured rind of red. She examined it, drew it close to her face and breathed in. There it was: under the tablet's earthy clay smell, and the slight hint of smoke from the tablet's firing and the dust, there was the copper tang of blood. Aurya picked up another slab of clay and peered at that too. There was another one: a dark spot, larger this time, and a deeper red. She searched through the piles of new tablets, peering closely at each one. After checking a few more, she found another spot, and then another, until finally she picked up an ancient king list, and found a long dark thread of dried blood staining the clay, pooled in the letters' deep cuts. Aurya said a prayer under her breath:

Give me unto Marduk the merciful.
May my mother Ishtar forgive me.

'In the name of Ashur and Nabu, Ashurbanipal the King of Legions enters his library!' came the King's booming voice, making Aurya jump. The usual clamour accompanied him: the clang of bells and banging of drums, the grunts of the slaves beneath the bier, the fluttering of pennants and ostrich feathers. Servants and slaves hurried along ahead of him, flicking fly whips, and his soldiers lowered their spears so as not to knock the hanging lamps in the ceiling.

The King and his entourage passed her doorway in a bustle and clamour of instruments and voices, and she straightened up. Abil was there too, walking behind the royal bier, carrying something in a red cloth. He caught Aurya's eye for a moment, his face pale. She took the bloodstained tablet with her and went to the corridor as the commotion made its way through the library. The greenish flames of sea wood were already flickering, and the King stopped in the reading room. Aurya wandered out through the chaos of servants and soldiers trailing through the halls, back to the library gate where Sin-Zababa was crouched beneath his canopy. The beer had combined with the grass the driver chewed to make his eyes sleepy and dull, but he raised his head to see Aurya standing there.

'Sin-Zababa, where do these tablets come from?' she said. He looked up at her with sad eyes.

'From a place just like this,' he said. 'An old stone library, in the palaces of Elam.'

'From Elam?'

'Yes.'

'I heard the King had Elam destroyed.'

'Yes.'

'And what happened to the people like me? The people who kept the books?'

Sin-Zababa took a long draught of his beer, and spat out the grains.

'When I arrived they were already dead. Some of them still holding the books they loved in their arms. Their throats cut, ear to ear. And the soldiers laughing.' He put his head in his hands. 'Shamash will judge me for what I saw.'

Aurya looked down at the thread of blood on the tablet, and felt her fingers pressing white into the clay. A pure anger filled her from within, blistering as the sun. Murderers, all of them. Murderers the King and murderers his soldiers – and they had made a murderer of her too. They made her file away their murderous loot with the blood on it barely dried. The image flashed through her head of a body tumbling into the darkness, a pair of eyes looking up at her, pricked with points of moonlight. The voice in her dream came back to her as blood rushed to her face, and the world seemed to rock around her. A murderer in a city of murderers.

Just at that point, the King's procession exploded out of the library in all its riotous noise. Abil was with them, still carrying his wrapped package. Aurya pulled herself together and hurried after the clamorous crowd, trying to draw close to him. Soldiers and servants bumped her, cymbals crashed in her ears and the ostrich and peacock feathers brushed her face, but she managed to reach him through the chaos.

'What's going on?' she hissed. Abil didn't dare look straight at her, only let his eyes flicker in her direction. She could tell he was afraid.

'It's this tablet. The one I've been translating.'

'What about it?'

'It's a ritual. The King is going to the top of the ziggurat to perform it.'

'What kind of ritual?'

'Ancient. Full of power.'

Aurya could hear a tremor in his voice. She looked up at the King, whose arms were raised, his head tilted back, his lips murmuring. When they stepped out into the night, Aurya saw that the ziggurat's highest chamber was lit with a flickering flame, and the night wind moved around her restless and full of shadows.

Katya

The pickup trucks carrying the lion hunt stones parked outside the museum. As they drew to a stop, one engine burst from the weight of the stone, and smoke began belching from its bonnet. The black acrid fumes made Katya cough as Abu Ammar walked her and Salim back to the museum. Inside, she caught a glimpse of Lola up on the mezzanine. The girl ducked down at the sight of the gunmen pouring into the museum. Timid workmen moved the two lion hunt pieces on forklifts and wooden shipping pallets, laying them out on the entrance hall floor. Katya walked around the huge stone slabs with Salim; both were awestruck, talking excitedly despite themselves.

'Look at the workmanship on the lion's mane,' Salim muttered. 'It's even better than the ones in London.'

'And we were right: no traces of colour anywhere. It was never painted, never put up in the palace.' Katya touched his sleeve. 'The story behind this; can't you just imagine it? The scenes the King didn't want anyone to see, but the artist who made them anyway …'

Abu Ammar was standing there watching them, the air darkening around him.

'What the fuck are we going to do with this?' he said. Katya and Salim hushed and both looked at him. Katya realised too late that she'd touched Salim's arm again.

'I said, what the fuck are we going to do with this?' Abu Ammar shouted.

'It's priceless,' Katya said. 'One of the greatest …'

He puffed out his cheeks, and his eyes were blazing.

'I've had enough of this.' He pointed a shaking finger at Katya. 'I won't be made a fool of by you. I'm calling the boss.'

'No, Abu Ammar,' Katya began, but he held up his hand and turned away from her as he dialled a number into his phone and spoke brief, cold words into it. Then he hung up and threw a burning gaze over them both.

'Tie their hands, you idiots!' he shouted at the guards standing behind them. The men came up and made them kneel, pressing a foot into the backs of their knees and zipping their hands together.

'Are we going to die?' Katya muttered to Salim.

'I think so.'

It didn't seem like a joke. They knelt there and waited for interminable minutes, until a car approached outside, and more armed men, their faces covered, entered the museum. Some were wearing blue jeans, while some were dressed in the usual Afghan style. Katya shrunk back as she recognised the skull man with his distinctive balaclava. Then another man all in black entered. He was short, but his head was tipped back, and his eyes roved coolly over everyone present.

'Who is this?' he said in halting English, his voice high-pitched and clear.

'Hostages,' Abu Ammar muttered. 'Prisoners, from the day we took the museum. She's a foreign scientist and this man too. But they helped us find …'

'Are there others?'

'One other,' Abu Ammar said. 'Hiding upstairs. A Yazidi girl.'

'Get rid of them,' the man said, his voice chilling. 'Kill him tomorrow for the camera. This woman. What is she? American?'

'British,' Abu Ammar said.

The man in black nodded.

'I will marry her.'

Katya felt her blood freeze. She cast a glance at Abu Ammar, whose lips were twitching. Beside her, Salim's face was lowered, his hair covering his eyes, but his lips were pulled back from his teeth.

'Of course,' Abu Ammar said eventually, his voice thin. The man in black's eyes passed for the briefest of moments over the lion hunt carving, still dark with earth in places.

'What is this?'

'Boss ...' Abu Ammar began.

'Destroy it,' the man in black said. 'Destroy everything in here. Feed it all to the camera.'

Then he turned to leave, his masked soldiers with him. The skull man was the last to go, casting a long and deliberate look around the room. Katya turned her head to Salim and saw that he was sobbing in silent exhaustion. Her whole body felt numb. For several moments, Abu Ammar just stood there in the entrance hall, refusing to look at anyone. Then he turned to the remaining soldiers and screamed, 'What are you waiting for? Get hammers. A drill. And a camera.'

'Abu Ammar,' Katya said, and she heard the pain in her own voice. 'Abu Ammar, you don't have to do this ...'

'Quiet,' he hissed, not looking at her. 'Just be quiet.'

The soldiers returned a few minutes later with sledgehammers and a pneumatic drill. One got out a mobile phone and started filming, and another had a handheld camera. Katya watched and felt her whole body racked with nausea.

The men strode around the museum, going from exhibit to exhibit. Where pieces were covered with protective wrappings, they tore them off as if revealing something indecent, and used their hands to tip them to the floor. They fetched stepladders and climbed to reach artefacts high up on the walls, hitting them so they fell to the ground in a shower of shards and dust. The plaster replicas smashed instantly, but the stone statues fell with deep thuds, cracking the floor tiles where they landed. The men put their feet on the backs of the statues and gathered in groups to swing their hammers over their heads, knocking chunks from the stone. Katya flinched with each blow. She felt tears running down her cheeks. In the air, dust hung in low clouds, catching the light, moving in swirls and eddies wherever the men passed through them.

'"I dreamed of the house whose people sit in darkness,"' Katya murmured. '"Dust is their food and clay is their meat. They see no light, they sit in darkness ..."'

The men's laughter and the hammer blows rang over and over in her head, and for each blow that rained down on the ancient figures, she saw Salim's body there instead, its fragile bones breaking, his warm skin splitting beneath whatever torments these men had in store for it. When their work was done, they came back into the entrance hall, kicking broken pieces, their boots covered in white dust. They gathered around the lion hunt carvings.

'Please,' Katya begged them from her knees. 'Please, anything but that. You don't know what you're doing.'

Abu Ammar came back into the hall and joined the other men. Without taking his gaze away from Katya, he reached out and took a sledgehammer so its steel head slid along the floor with a dull note. He raised the hammer over his head and with his teeth bared, he brought it down right on the centre of the carvings, sending a crack lancing up the stone. After the first strike, all the men around him raised their hammers too, and the blows came down again and again on the stones, until the two panels split into smithereens that crumbled like brown sugar beneath the blows. Katya just watched, unable to do or say anything. Beside her, Salim pressed his nose to the museum floor.

'Dear God,' he was wailing softly into the dust. 'Dear God, forgive us for what we have done.'

For some time after, the men kicked through the rubble, smashing any piece larger than a football. Abu Ammar looked exhausted, his shoulders sagging. He looked as if he could barely lift the hammer any more.

'You two,' he said to the two guards standing behind Katya and Salim, 'stay with the prisoners and watch over them for the night. We'll take the man out at dawn tomorrow, when the light's good. I've got something in mind.'

Salim was shaking. His skin had turned a shade of grey beneath its coating of dust. Katya watched as Abu Ammar pointed at her.

'Don't hurt the woman. You heard what the boss said. There's a snake-worshipper upstairs if you want her.'

They nodded. Katya felt a ball of rage ignite inside her.

'Don't touch Lola!' she shouted. 'Please. She's just a girl.'

The men hauled Katya and Salim up off the floor from behind, both kicking and struggling with their hands still tied, and Katya kept begging them, pleading with them. They didn't reply or give her any sign, just took them to the room upstairs where they found Katya's belongings and the stale smell of habitation. The men sat them both down on the mattress and left in silence, the office-room key clicking in the lock. Katya began to cry. Salim didn't speak to her. She tried not to listen as she heard Lola beginning to shout, the men laughing, dragging her downstairs. Katya heard Lola's cries of rage and fear and then the door to the storeroom opening and closing deep in the building. Barren minutes passed. Out of nowhere, Salim spoke.

'This is what the lion hunt carvings mean.' His voice was hoarse and full of effort. 'The artists, whoever they were. This is what they were trying to tell us. The cruelty of this world. They're telling us, "We see it too. You're not alone."'

Katya only wept. Time fell over them in folds, glutinous, turning one way then the other. She saw her *Gilgamesh* book lying open on the floor, and read it out loud, as loud as she could, to drown out the sound of her own crying, and Salim weeping beside her, and the cries of Lola, distant in the belly of the building.

Gilgamesh and the ferryman sailed across the river of death. On the far shore, they met the ancient one Utnapishtim. His eyes were milk. His beard was moonlight.

'I know what you seek,' he said. 'But you will never gain the secret of eternal life. See, you are exhausted. Your head is hanging. You want to live for ever, but you can hardly stay awake for one day!'

'Test me!' Gilgamesh cried. 'I will stay awake for six days and seven nights.'

Gilgamesh sat beside the river of death. But his journey had been hard, and grief had weakened him. Soon he nodded and lay down and then he was asleep.

On the seventh day, Gilgamesh awoke and saw seven loaves of bread laid out in front of him, one for each day. Each one was harder, covered in more mould than the last. And he knew that he had failed.

A muffled gunshot sounded somewhere in the building. A pause. Then two more. Katya lost her voice. She felt the whole of herself crumble from within, and burst into sobs of rage.

'My god, my god,' the words coughing out of her. She thought of the freckles on Lola's nose, the way her front teeth were turned slightly towards one another.

'She was just a girl. Such a sweet girl.'

Beside her Salim was sobbing too, his head hanging. The silence felt like a death all of its own. Katya heard the door to the storeroom opening, and footsteps coming up the central museum stairs, and she felt her whole body shrink with hatred. The key turned in the office door, and Salim whimpered. The door swung open, and Lola was standing there, her hands and clothes covered in blood. She clutched that little red-handled kitchen knife in one bloodstained hand.

'Ya Allah,' Salim breathed.

'Lola,' Katya whispered, unable to believe what she was seeing. 'What happened?'

The girl's eyes were wide and frightened. Her pupils were deep, inky wells, barely any iris visible.

'They put down their guns,' she said, her voice barely more than a whisper. 'When one came close, I did not hesitate. I was very fast. I stabbed him. I took his gun, and now they are both dead.'

'Are you sure?' Katya said. 'Lola, are you sure they're dead?'

'They are dead,' the girl said again, dropping the word like a stone, spots of blood dripping in glutinous threads on the floor. Focus swam back to the girl's eyes, and she staggered over to where Katya and Salim sat.

'Lola, cut our ties.' She did, though she was shaking the whole time. Once Katya's arms were free, she wrapped them around Lola. She smelt the blood on her, the smell of fear; the girl's bones felt weightless, and her skin was cold. The knife dropped to the floor with a wet clatter. Over Lola's shoulder, Katya met Salim's eyes.

'Salim. They'll be back any moment. They'll kill us when they find out. Can you get the van going?'

'I have no idea.' He looked down at his own quivering hands in front of him, as if trying to test whether he was in a dream. Then a shudder passed through the whole length of this body, and he shot to his feet with a crazed expression on his face. 'My God, I have no idea!'

Down in the museum's shattered debris, they found the wrapped tools with the parts hidden inside, just where the men had left them. Salim put them under his arm and ran to the garage in wide, bounding steps, pieces of stone and plaster skittering in his wake. Katya took Lola to the bathroom and washed her up as best she could. The water ran pink in the metal basin. She held Lola and whispered to her that it was going to be okay, that they would get out and that she would be safe soon. The girl was shivering and distant, but she held on to Katya's arm with a tight grip, as if the world was rocking beneath her.

'I did it just the way my brother showed me,' she said. 'I decided to do it, and then I did it with all my soul.'

———

It was past midnight when Salim finally came to them, his hands covered in oil, patches of grease on his face, his hair disarranged.

'I think I've done it. I think it should work now. But there's only one way to know.'

They all went down into the parking garage: Salim, Lola, Katya. They stood around in a circle as Salim got into the driver's seat and closed his eyes, muttered a prayer. Then he reached out and turned the key in the ignition. The engine spluttered and coughed. It choked, and then with the most beautiful sound Katya had ever heard, it thrummed into life, a throaty and wild roar. Katya and Lola jumped and cheered as loudly as they dared.

'We're going to get out of here,' Salim said, barely believing what he was saying, his hands flexing on the steering wheel. 'My god, we're going to get out of here.'

'It's really happening,' Katya said, and ran up to hug Salim where he sat in the driver's seat. 'You did it.'

He breathed out.

'There's just one more thing we have to do,' he said, and looked at Katya. His hands were shaking.

'What is it?'

'The door to the garage. It's locked from the outside, with two padlocks.' He lifted up a pair of bolt cutters from the toolbox on the passenger's seat. 'I need to go out with these and cut them both.'

Katya looked at him, his dark eyes and unruly beard.

'Salim, I'll go.'

'No, Katya, don't be crazy.'

She held his gaze and reached out to take the bolt cutters.

'Salim, it has to be me. I can't drive. You saw what happened before. We can't risk a seizure, a crash. You sit in the driver's seat with Lola and get ready to leave.'

'Katya, no …'

'Salim, *I* have to do this. Give me the bolt cutters.'

His face was full of pain, but he knew she was right. He didn't resist when she reached out and took the tool. She felt its weight in her hands, heavier than she expected.

'I'll be a few minutes,' she said. 'Just through the door, around the building to the back. I'll tap on the door when I've removed the locks.'

'Katya, be careful. There could be guards … and take your phone.'

She nodded and took a deep breath. Then he reached out and put a hand on her cheek, leant over and kissed her. She closed her eyes and felt his lips dry on hers, and for a moment her fear wasn't of pain or death, but of that lost future. Then, unable to bear it for a second longer, she spun away and set off through the museum. She turned back just once, to see Salim watching her, and Lola too, in her bloodstained clothes.

When she turned the corner into the ransacked museum, Katya was trembling. She was alone now. She thought for a moment of going down into the storeroom, fishing around in the dark on the blood-covered floor for the dead men's guns. But the thought terrified her. And she knew that if she fired a gun, the whole city would come down on them. She reached the main door and found that the guards had chained it shut with the bike lock. She listened against the wood. There was nothing outside, not even the sound of traffic. Just the distant booms of ordnance falling somewhere on people's houses, a sound as normal now as the howling of dogs. She lifted the bolt cutters and set them against the old bike chain binding the door, then pressed the long handles closed. It was easy: the chain melted like hard toffee in its jaws. She caught it before it hit the ground, but one link came loose and tinkled on the floor.

Katya held her breath and listened for any sound from outside, but there was nothing. She edged the door open and crept out into the warm dark, the stars brilliant over the blacked-out city. There were two men with guns at the end of the street, but their backs were turned, and they shifted their weight from one foot to the other. Katya opened the door as quietly as she could, and crept on hands and knees out into the night. She darted into the grass verges around the museum entrance, and around the side of the building. The men didn't turn, didn't seem to notice anything. The palm trees overhead made a sound in the breeze like falling rain. Over the rooftops she heard the roar of jets, the flashes of bombs going off in other districts, the smell of gasoline and fireworks, a rising chorus of barking dogs.

Katya ran the whole length of the museum in the shadow of its garden. She ducked down at one point when a bird took flight near her, and then there was the sound of running feet that set her whole skin alive. She dropped to the ground and waited, let the echoes pass, then crept on to where the parking garage door stood, leading to the road. There were no guards here either.

Katya looked around, and moved as silently as she could to the wide garage door. She found the first padlock, and set the bolt cutters' jaws against it. It broke easily enough, and the door's vibrating surface let out a deep metallic rumble. She darted a look around again, into the unlit streets and the dark windows facing them. There was no one there. She ducked down, crept the length of the door to the next padlock and set the bolt cutters against it. This one was stronger, better made. The cutters slipped on the hardened steel, grazing it. Her hands were sweating, and the tool slid around in her palms. She wiped her hands on her trousers and tried again, clutched the cutters in both hands and wedged the padlock into place with her boot. Then she applied the pressure as gradually as she could, her forearms shuddering. The padlock snapped with a clink, and she fell forwards against the garage door, letting out a resounding bang.

Katya caught her breath and dropped the bolt cutters, swung around to see if anyone had spotted her. A dark figure was standing there in the night. Katya stifled a cry, lifted up her hand to touch her necklace. The figure stepped closer and staggered a little.

'Katya?' It was Abu Ammar.

Aurya

Aurya followed the King's procession out into the open air, where insects were whirling. Clouds covered the stars.

'Come, all of you,' the King howled. 'Follow me to the top, and we'll see the ritual done together!'

Hearing the King's voice, a dog started barking nearby, then another, until a chorus of barks and howls filled the night. Aurya felt cold in the air. She tried to turn around and go back to the library, but a soldier put out his spear and shook his head, herding her back into the entourage.

'You heard the King,' he said. Aurya went to Abil and walked beside him. As they approached the ziggurat, servants came out of the palace, carrying statues. They were the gods she'd seen that night at the palace, the lost gods from the house of broken idols. Some were small enough to hold in their hands, but others were carried by two men, or six. Some were drawn on sledges by ropes. There were statues of copper and bronze, statues of iron, clay and stone, statues carved from gypsum and sandstone. There were statues of long, slender figures and of round, fat ones, statues of men and of women, statues with crowns and ones with the heads of baboons and birds and dogs and lions. They all gathered around the King, a silent procession of stone.

'Abil, what are they doing with those gods?' Aurya whispered.

'I don't know,' he said. 'They're the broken idols. Gods that rule over the ruined places.'

Aurya remembered the spots of blood she'd found on the King's new tablets, and the story Sin-Zababa had told her. The dark rind was still under her nail. She touched Abil's arm, warm and soft in the dark.

'Abil,' she said. 'Do you know where the library tablets come from?'

'What do you mean?'

'The tablets. The ones the King's always adding to the library. Do you know where he gets them?'

Abil looked uncomfortable.

'Oh … he buys them, usually. Sometimes people give them as tribute.'

'And what about in the wars?' Her voice was barely a whisper. 'Did you know he gets them in the wars too?'

'It stands to reason. Sometimes he must, just like he takes gold and precious woods.'

'And what about the librarians? The people who keep the books. Did you know he slaughtered all the librarians of Elam?'

Abil didn't answer, but his eyes flickered. She felt her insides move. What would it take to convince him? They stumbled along with the King and his entourage, surrounded by the bobbing stone heads of the statues, and their wide, astonished eyes. At the palace, a group of musicians joined them. One carried a lyre decorated with a bull's head, gilded and studded with blue lapis, while others carried a horn and a drum. Up ahead, the ziggurat's enormous bulk cut out a severe form against the sky, the flame in its highest chamber flickering like a lantern, the priests' chants drifting down to them. The slaves carrying the King mounted the first steep steps, slightly worn in the middle. The King raised his hands and shouted as they began to climb.

'Abil, I have something to tell you,' Aurya said, hearing her voice shake. 'Things I've never told you before. Never told anyone.'

The eyes of the gods all around washed still and impassive over her, eyes of ivory and lapis and mother-of-pearl. Abil eyed her too.

'I have seen the houses on the riverside burn,' King Ashurbanipal shouted. 'I have watched the flames in the water. I have seen the lions come down from the hills, ravenous.'

Aurya stayed close to Abil. He stared at a tall bird-headed statue strapped to a sledge, lying on its side as men hauled it up the ziggurat's stairs to the beat of a drum. The tablet he carried seemed to weigh suddenly on his hands, but he went on climbing. The city below shimmered, and the servants raised the smaller idols above their heads as they climbed, the broken eyes eerie in the night, an unreal procession of haunted faces.

'Abil, when you first met me, and our father was killed by the lion … it wasn't the lion that killed him.'

'What are you talking about?'

As if responding to the King's shrill cries, the chanting of the priests in the high tower deepened.

'My father tried to hurt me, and Sharo hit him with a jar. He wanted to protect me. But the blow killed our father, and we threw him in the lion's pit to hide our crime.'

Abil stared at her, his eyes wide and showing all of their whites. The statues around him stared too.

'Aurya, I can't believe it.'

'It's true. And I have to tell you this because I know the gods will punish me one day. They've warned me before. And if I ever do evil again, they'll punish me and everyone I love.'

The King's bier made slow progress up the stairs, and the slaves beneath it strained on knotted muscles. As Aurya spoke, men on the steps above fixed ropes to the chair and helped haul it up as though the King were a piece of heavy stone. All the time, Ashurbanipal's wailing went on.

'The bricks of Nineveh will blacken,' he moaned. 'The graves will spill and the creatures of the deep earth will claw their way up. To ash and crumbs, we will burn the cities of our enemies, and scatter the bones of their kings; all their people in chains, all our broken idols and all our gods in ruin.'

Aurya's legs grew heavier with each stair as they climbed. Cicadas hissed in the gardens that lined the ziggurat's terraces, the leaves susurrating in the winds moving over its walls. She looked up ahead at the orange glow in the top tower, listened to the chanting drawing the King up to its high chamber, and his cries, which were getting higher as he went. Terror overcame her. She didn't know what waited at the top of the ziggurat, but that gradually approaching flame, those soft and haunting voices, filled her with dread. She thought of the blood staining the tablets in the library, and then she thought of Sharo's carving: the lion leaping up to seize the chariot's wheel.

'Abil, that's why I can't be in this city one more day.'

Several of the slaves carrying the King stumbled and cried out for help, and the soldiers on either side hurried to shore up the bier from underneath, so he looked like a spider with dozens of legs clambering up the side of the tower. The lot of them shouted to each other, backs heaving on the steps, ropes creaking like trees in a storm. Some of the men carrying the statues put them down, a silent and watchful crowd. Even the musicians stopped their playing to strain beneath the King's weight. He went on chanting, oblivious. Aurya found herself alone with Abil, high on the stairs of that great tower, surrounded by the ruined gods.

'Abil,' she said, 'we have to leave as soon as we can.'

'Aurya, I'm glad you told me.' She could hear the uncertainty in his voice, his eyes on the scene of madness unfolding halfway up the ziggurat. He walked up several more steps and lifted the tablet he was holding. 'It makes sense of things for me. The look you get in your eyes sometimes, all far-off and scared. And the whole business with your brother and that lion. But it's in the past. You can't throw our lives here away, just for ...'

'Abil,' she said, and put her hand on one of his arms that held the tablet. 'I'm going to have a child.'

His foot caught on the stair. Expressions moved across his face like the shadows of clouds.

'I thought I could make a life in the library,' Aurya said. 'I thought I could escape there, among the stories. I thought I could do no harm. But this city ... No one who stays here is clean. Nowhere is safe from it. And when the gods come for their vengeance, it will fall on everyone who stayed, on everyone who knew what was happening and went on as if it was normal. If

322

you want to stay, then you're going to do it without me and our child.'

'Aurya,' he croaked, and then he turned and looked up at the ziggurat's high chamber. His eyes wandered over the King, and the slaves and soldiers propping him up, heaving him up the great tower, step by step, their arms raised and quivering. And then he looked down at the tablet in his hands. He placed it down and turned to face Aurya.

'Let's go,' he said. A cage full of birds burst open in Aurya's chest. She leaned in and kissed him. She took his hand, and they ran together down the stairs, the city a shimmering liquid beneath them.

'Aurya, where will we go?'

'Anywhere. Let's follow the river. South. To Egypt. They have great libraries there too.'

'Egypt. I always wanted to go there, when I was young.'

'We can start a new life there. Away from all this.'

They both looked up at the tower, the King's now-distant cries as he was carried to the top. She felt Abil's hand tremble.

'What about your brother?' he said.

'Sharo ...'

'Would he come with us?'

'I don't know.'

As they reached the bottom, Abil squeezed her hand.

'I'm sorry,' he said. 'I should have listened.' Then he laughed, his eye wide with disbelief. 'We're going to have a child.'

'Yes.'

Aurya held herself close to him and listened to his heart thudding beneath his ribs, the sound of the King's chanting still washing down from above as the night thickened around them.

In the morning, the city didn't seem to be any different from the day before. A breath of smoke rose from the ziggurat in the distance, the only sign that anything had taken place there the night before. Did Aurya imagine a slightly different quality to the light? A strange, shimmering silver that fell over everything, quite separate from the hanging morning mists.

Aurya and Abil spent the morning writing their letters on hand-sized lumps of clay, in their most careful script and formal language. They were not slaves, but they were not quite free either – Aurya had never asked for the details of this arrangement, but Abil assured her that requests were often granted. It took two days to get their reply. It came in the form of two fat lumps of clay sitting like a pair of toads on their doorstep. Aurya found them in the morning. She picked them up and read first one, then the other, then checked their backs for more. She tipped the clay in the sunlight to make sure she hadn't made a mistake. And then she ran indoors to find Abil.

'The King in his great wisdom and with the advice of the gods has decided to refuse your request,' she read to him.

'That's it?'

'That's it. And they say we're to be summoned to the palace tomorrow to explain ourselves.'

'We must be able to plead against it,' Abil said, as they paced the room together. It looked bare, now. They had already sold their furniture: the lacquered table by the window, and the cutting stone on the shelf.

'I don't believe it,' Aurya said. 'Why won't they let us leave?'

'I suppose we'll find out tomorrow,' Abil said, his face ghostly pale. 'They'll probably send us to some ration-keeper who wants to tax us double for leaving.'

They read over the tablets again, trying to gain some clue. They held each other well into the night and whispered their fears in the dark and their plans if they ever reached the land of Egypt.

'We'll build a house near the great salt sea,' Abil said, running his hand through Aurya's long hair.

'We'll learn to fish,' Aurya said. 'We'll find a place for Sharo, where he can carve his stones in peace.'

When the next day dawned, it was with a clear, cold sun bursting through the leaves of the pomegranate tree. Aurya and Abil walked to the palace together, in the city morning. At the palace gate, Aurya and Abil were received by the servant Bel-Ibni. He had accumulated more beads in his hair, more bangles and rings, so he now jangled a little when he walked. He had clearly been waiting for them.

'Ah, our two young scribes,' he began, one eyebrow slightly raised. 'Follow me. The King wants to see you.'

'The King?' Abil stammered. 'What does the King want with us?'

The servant only turned and motioned for them to follow. Although it was a bright and hot morning, the palace was cool and dim. Aurya could see Abil shaking a little. They followed the King's servant through the quiet palace halls, taking in the carvings. Aurya noticed the most violent ones this time: the Assyrian soldiers in their boats hunting down the marsh people as they crouched terrified in the reeds, the siege engines shattering the walls of Judean cities and the soldiers cutting off heads and displaying them on spikes. A creeping cold gathered in her body as she saw these things, and her desire to leave Nineveh rose up in her even stronger than before. Aurya prayed:

May my mother Ishtar forgive me, for I knew not what I did.
The fruit forbidden by Ishtar, I ate without knowing.

Bel-Ibni led them to the throne-room door.

'Whatever happens, I'm here,' Abil whispered, and drew closer to Aurya. She felt for his hand and squeezed it.

'So am I.'

Bel-Ibni reached out and pushed open the door. Inside, the King was sitting on his bier, not on the throne but beside it. He looked tired, as if the ritual he'd performed had cost some essential part of him. Aurya and Abil entered and dropped to their knees.

'My lord, my sun, the great king of all the heavens and the lands of the earth, we are your servants ...' Abil began, but the King waved all the blessings away with a hand, and gave a wet cough.

'Yes, yes. Enough of that. Enough, enough. Why did you come here?'

Aurya and Abil looked at each other.

'My lord, because you summoned us. You sent tablets ...'

'No,' the King cried out, and hacked out another cough before continuing. 'Why did you come here? You, the river girl. Why did you come to Nineveh?'

Aurya thought for a moment.

'I came because I'd always dreamed of seeing this city. And because I thought my mother might be here. I wanted to find my mother.'

'And did you find her?' the King asked, his voice high and wheezy.

'No,' Aurya said. 'I found out the truth instead. I found out that she died to give me life.'

The King nodded, but he looked far-off, through the walls.

'I never wanted to be myself,' he said, and rapped his fingers on his bier. 'I never wanted to be myself.'

Aurya and Abil stayed kneeling there on the ground, not knowing where to look. The King didn't seem embarrassed.

'My lord,' Aurya said, eyeing him carefully. 'I am going to have a child within the year. I've always dreamed of going to Egypt, to see the Black River and the Green Sea, to see the animals they have there.'

The King ran some fingers through his beard and tugged hard at one of its braids.

'You dreamed of Nineveh, and now you dream of Egypt. What do you think you'll find there?'

She hesitated.

'Peace, maybe.'

The King took a long breath in through his nose.

'I once dreamed of the same thing.'

'Please, my lord …' Aurya began. The King put out a hand.

'I will let you go,' he said. 'I will let you go anywhere in the world. But I have a condition.'

'Anything,' Aurya said, and beside her Abil bowed his head down to the floor.

'Anything,' he echoed.

'Your brother,' the King said, 'your brother must carve what I ask of him. He must obey me. If he promises me this, on pain of death, then I will let you leave Nineveh.'

Aurya felt numb. She remembered the determination in Sharo's voice the last time they'd spoken. She bowed her head and tried to hide the desperation.

'I will try. My lord, I will speak to him one more time.'

The King nodded and looked down at her with his smile of cold command, his wistful and faraway eyes.

'The river is always flowing, river girl,' he said. 'Even while everything else dies. It will always draw you onwards.'

Aurya thought about this as she backed from the room with Abil. She kept thinking about it as Bel-Ibni escorted them back through the palace's painted halls, out into the sun and the city's noise rolling around them. She remembered the way she'd once felt on the riverbank, like she was one of the river weeds, rooted in place but always reaching downstream.

Katya

Abu Ammar was drunk. Katya saw it immediately when he staggered closer. His pupils were wide too, the size of buttons. He had his handgun drawn, hanging slack by his side.

'Katya,' he said, 'I didn't want any of this to happen.'

She looked to where the heavy bolt cutters were lying on the ground, and thought about dashing to them. If she was fast enough, she could swing them and knock the gun from his hand. But Abu Ammar drew close to her, the weapon shaking in his grip. In the dark, he looked even younger than he was, a boy. It would take just a twitch of his finger.

'Abu Ammar,' she said, hoping she was speaking loud enough for Salim to hear her through the garage door behind her. 'Abu Ammar, you don't have to do this. You don't have to hurt anyone.'

He sniffed, and then gave a bitter laugh.

'That's all I ever do. I used to be good, you know. Good in school.'

'You can still go back. Abu Ammar, I can take you away from here …'

He lifted the gun to point it directly at her, and she raised her hands instinctively at the black full stop of the barrel.

'You can't take me anywhere. The boss wants you. And the boss … the boss is so cruel when people disobey him. He learned things, in the American prison.'

Katya gambled, and took a step closer. His face was gleaming with tears.

'Abu Ammar, put the gun down. Please, do it for me. I thought you weren't meant to drink?'

He burst out laughing, and snatched her by the wrist. His grip was iron.

'Those regulations don't apply to me. Come with me. I want to show you something.'

'No, Abu Ammar … please …'

'Come, I have to show you something.'

'No, it's late. What do you have to show me?'

'The end of the world,' he said, and pressed the barrel of his gun into her neck, an O of cool metal. He dragged her down a side street where his car was waiting and pushed her into the passenger seat. She took one last look back at the garage door, which screeched open one inch, then two, on its rusted mechanism. As it opened slowly, she just caught sight of the frightened faces of Salim and Lola looking out at her from underneath. Abu Ammar jumped into the driver's seat, gunned the engine and pulled away at great speed. Katya shook with terror as the dark city peeled away on either side. Could she grab the steering wheel, crash the car?

'Abu Ammar,' she tried, 'you can't do this. The boss … you heard what he said.'

'We're nothing to him,' Abu Ammar sobbed, and Katya noticed that one of the lenses of his glasses had a crack running down it. 'They're going to start burning people, you know. Like your friend back there. They want me to do it tomorrow.'

Katya felt in her pocket, and turned on her phone, its precious battery nearly gone. It buzzed to life in her hand, and she glanced down, trying to hide its green glow inside her pocket. There was some signal. She looked at Abu Ammar and tried to tap out a message by memory and the feel of the buttons.

'I don't understand …' she said loudly, to cover the noise of her typing. He was rolling his head around on his shoulders as he swerved from one side of the road to the other, as they crossed the bridge and headed off in the direction of the old city.

'The real war is coming,' Abu Ammar said. He slammed on the brake, and the car skidded to a stop. 'A war that will wipe the earth clean. And we're just the beginning.'

He took the keys from the ignition, got out of the car leaving the headlights on, and she heard his footsteps trudging around the vehicle, coming to her door. She pulled out her phone and checked the message she'd written.

'Salim,' it said, 'they got me. go without. love'

She pressed send just as Abu Ammar thrust the door open and grabbed her by the arm, causing her to drop the phone into the foot well. He dragged her out into the hot night and the full intricacy of the stars.

'The dajjal is coming soon,' Abu Ammar said, his voice high and deranged in the dark beyond the headlights. 'The son of Satan will walk the earth.'

They were in the ruins of Nineveh. The huge ancient walls loomed around them in the dark, the ravaged statues up at the gate, the palace's shattered remains. Abu Ammar pressed the gun into her ribs and held her by the arm, pushing her up the slope of the ancient wall. Katya kept her eyes on the ground to avoid stumbling in the dark. They carried on in silence, but when they topped the slope, with the ruins stretching out behind them and the patches of city light shimmering in the hot air before them, Abu Ammar began to sing very softly. It was almost a whisper. He turned his back to Katya and faced the city. She thought about rushing at him, trying to hit him with a rock or piece of brick, but she could only stand and watch. Far in the distance, there was the howling of jets, and then plumes of brilliant orange burst along the city skyline. They sent sparks into the air, and lit up the ruined place for a moment, the booms following soon after.

'This is how the world ends,' Abu Ammar slurred to her, and stumbled a little on the unsteady ground, the broken bricks underfoot. 'We can both die up here, if you want. Would you like that?'

'Abu Ammar,' Katya whispered, but she had no idea what to say.

'Do you know, I have this dream sometimes?' Abu Ammar said, and scratched his head with the barrel of his gun.

'A dream?'

Abu Ammar's knife was in his belt, Katya saw. Its handle jutted out just below his elbow as he stood there. Her eyes wandered over it, illuminated for a moment in the bomb light. She could grab it, she thought. The image of Lola flashed into her head, her clothes covered in blood, the way her whole body shook. The palms of Katya's hands began to sweat. How hard would it be? How drunk was he?

'Tell me about your dream,' she said.

'I wake up in a city,' Abu Ammar slurred again. 'I don't know where it is, but it feels like Mosul. Like Mosul might have been a thousand years ago, many thousands. And I hear the sound of water ...'

'Of water?' She took another step closer.

'Yes. But not a sound like rivers make. It's a sound like the sea. And I wander outside, and I see that the city is sunk. Sunk beneath the ocean. The waves are enormous. I feel so afraid. I want to scream. And then I run back inside, into these dark halls, like a maze. And I hear footsteps on the ground.'

'Footsteps?' She edged closer.

'And I turn around,' he said, 'and do you know what I see?'

He turned slightly towards her in the dark, and Katya knew that this was the last moment she might ever get. For an instant, without knowing why, she thought of what a precarious thing a chariot is. How unstable. How fragile.

'Do you know what I see?' Abu Ammar said again, a snarl entering his voice. Katya lunged forwards. She gripped the rubber handle of his knife, pulled it from its sheath with a slick noise. Abu Ammar stumbled back and made a noise of surprise, turned halfway to face her. With a shout, Katya drove the knife as hard as she could into his side. There was no resistance at all. He could have been made of butter. He let out a little whimper, hoarse and half-strangled.

'What do you see?' she breathed, and pulled the knife out, then drove it down into the top of his shoulder, beside his neck, right down to the hilt. His whole body gave a jerk and a shudder, and he reeled around slowly to face her, putting his hands on her shoulders as if he was going to kiss her. His breath still smelled of lemons. The knife stuck out of him, and Katya felt its handle slippery in her hand. She let it go. She stepped back, filled with horror, and Abu Ammar's hands dropped to his sides. He gave a little croak, and she saw too late that his right hand still had the gun in it. He raised it and pointed it at her.

'I see a lion,' he said. Katya never heard the bang. There was a blinding flash that lit up Abu Ammar's frightened face for a moment, imprinting the image in purple on to her retinas: the knife still sticking out of his shoulder, his horrified expression and wild eyes, the sheen of sweat on his skin. At the same moment, a searing pain burst in Katya's left thigh, as if an enormous beetle had crawled up inside her trousers and sunk its pincers into her skin.

Abu Ammar slumped to the ground, but didn't make a sound. All Katya could hear was a single pure white note, singing 'eeeeeeeee' in her ears. She tried to take a step, but her left leg crumpled beneath her, and she fell. Nearby, Abu Ammar's body was motionless, but she couldn't see anything in the dark. She lay there breathing in the clay and grass, the tang of blood all around her, the sickly smell of summer flowers and the gunshot's firework smell in the night air.

'Get up, Katya,' she whispered to herself, but her body didn't move. 'Get up. It's time to get up.'

Every muscle felt weak. Her skin was buzzing. She heard her father's voice in her throat.

'For fuck's sake, Katya, get up.'

She lifted herself to her elbows and rolled up to sit. She reached around for something to help her walk, and found a piece of old planking, hauled herself to one foot with its help. Sweat broke out all over her body. Her left leg was limp and useless, waves of heat pulsing from the wound. The bullet must have grazed the bone. Her makeshift crutch dug painfully into her armpit as she limped back over unsteady ground, stumbling on debris and litter, panting and sweating in desperation, leaving the body of Abu Ammar lying there in the ruins.

'I can still make it back,' she moaned to herself, her voice torn with pain. 'Maybe they haven't left. I can still make it back.'

She stumbled down the slope to Abu Ammar's car. He hadn't locked it or turned off the headlights, but there was no key in the ignition. It must be back on his body. She would have to go back into the ruins to get it, and she cursed herself for not searching him. She opened the door, fished around in the muddy foot well for her phone. She found it, turned it on, and it gave the dim glow of low-battery mode.

'1 new message'

She opened it. It was Salim.

'Katya. They came to the museum. The skull man. We had to leave. My heart is breaking. Do not go back there. Please survive. I will never stop looking for you.'

The phone's light died in her hands. She mashed the buttons, but nothing happened, and she screamed at it, hurled it back into the car. She knelt there for what seemed like for ever, the pain in her leg now red hot and thumping with her pulse. Her trousers were soaked with warmth; it felt like she'd pissed herself. She cried in exhaustion until she had nothing left.

'Get up, Katya,' she moaned to herself again. 'Get the fuck up.'

She staggered to her feet with the help of the crutch, and saw all the way along the road ahead, illuminated in the car's headlights, a group of men with guns hanging low in their hands, walking slowly towards her and pointing.

'Fuck.'

She pulled herself painfully to her feet and limped off with her crutch in the opposite direction, her heart pounding. The glare of the car's headlights would hide her for now, but she was slow and the strength was fading from her body.

'Fuck fuck fuck,' she gasped. She didn't know where she was going. She was going to die. The khaki of her injured leg was stained black, and the blood was turning cold in the night air, droplets ticking on the road. She struggled through the streets, crutch thumping noisily on the road, in and out of pools of light. Gnats swarmed in her vision. She looked back along the street, and saw the men reach the abandoned car, casting long shadows, looking around inside the vehicle with a torch. She had to get out of sight. She reached a complex of cinder-block buildings and barbed-wired yards, and ducked into an alley, sitting for a moment on a heap of cement sacks. She tried to catch her breath. Sweat coated her whole body.

She worked up the courage to glance back around the corner, and she saw the men – still over a hundred metres back, but beginning to walk in her direction. How did they know where she was? She crouched breathless with terror, watching them. They were pointing at the ground as they walked, their torchlight licking the road, and she realised that they were following the trail of her blood. With a moan of fear, she recognised the man with the skull balaclava leading them. She had to move. And she had to stop the trail she was leaving. She limped through the alley until it opened out on to the road leading to the bridge, each step an explosion of pain in her leg. She pulled off her left shoe, blood pooling in it, and then she threw it as far as she could. It spun through the air, leaving a long skein of blood along the dusty road. A false trail. Then she tore her trouser leg using the bullet hole for purchase and tied the remaining fabric into a tourniquet. She set off in the other direction, cupping her free hand beneath her leg to catch the blood still welling up from the wound in her thigh. And it worked, just about.

She made it to the bridge before the blood started dripping on the ground again, overflowing in her cupped hand. The street lights on the bridge were out; it was dark, and the shadows hid her. The great expanse of the river opened up beneath her. She glanced over her shoulder and saw the men back at the alley mouth. They turned left after the false trail, then stopped. They were confused, pointing at the ground where the blood stopped and shouting at each other. Would they find the shoe? How long would that buy her? The breeze blowing across the river washed cool on her sweat-covered body.

Katya limped on as silently as she could, cleaving close to the bridge's barrier and trying to stay low. Her good leg was starting to tire, but somehow she made it over, her left leg boiling, and she turned with a shudder of dread to see the men back on her trail, just beginning to cross the bridge. She hobbled through the maze of alleys until she turned a corner she recognised, a street of old iron railings and concrete pillars, the multi-coloured bulbs strung along the eaves of some riverside restaurant still lit by generator fuel. There was the smell of frying fish and petrol smoke. She couldn't remember why she knew this street, but she followed the landmarks she recognised: the cartoon of Mickey Mouse drawn on the school wall, the old lime tree with one half dead and the other heavy with leaves and fruit. She turned a corner, and another, and then she saw Dr Malik's old house, the grand riverside manor with its garden sloping down into the reeds. Lights were on inside, the steady chugging of a generator nearby, and loud laughter coming from within.

She crept into the garden. It was overgrown with weeds now, but the statue of Gilgamesh strangling the lion still loomed in shadow. She could make out the shape of gunmen inside, dressed as they always were, drinking and singing. They'd taken over the house. She stumbled as quietly as she could through the long grass to the statue, feeling her whole body tingling and numb, no longer able to hold herself on her crutch. She ran her hand over the hero's concrete legs and felt the pocks where the men in the house had been using it for target practice. She listened to her heart booming in her chest and tried to breathe.

As she sat there and hugged the statue's feet, someone opened a door, and a wash of light spilled out into the garden. Loud voices drifted on the air. Katya whimpered and dragged herself out of sight behind the statue, leaving her crutch behind. The fighter slung his gun over his shoulder, unzipped and pissed with one hand into the weeds and long grass. Just then, there was the sound of running feet and the men who had been chasing her arrived. The pissing man stopped, threw out a question to them. The man with the skull balaclava shouted something back. Inside the house, the music stopped and men came outside one by one, their laughter stopping.

Katya was barely twenty metres from them. She dropped low again, and dragged herself as silently as she could through the long grass and weeds, trying not to disturb them as she crawled down to the river. It was her only hope, she thought: to hide in the reeds on the riverbank, to lie there and let sleep wash over her, and hope that the men wouldn't find her. As she got closer to the river, the mud beneath her became damp, smelled more like water and sewage and oil. She brushed through the thistles and chickweed, and her fingers sunk in the earth as she pulled herself along, silt beneath her nails. Torch beams lanced through the garden. She heard footsteps approaching steadily behind her, and glanced over her shoulder to see the men walking through the long grass and weeds in her direction, forming a line, their guns and torches out.

Katya dragged herself into the riverbank reeds. She slithered over the mud and into the shallow water, which washed over her wound like a pack of ice. She sighed at the cool touch, a sheen of oil glimmering in rainbow colours on its surface, and that was when a torch beam washed over something sitting there in the shallows. A large white shape. Katya looked at it for a few moments, not understanding what she was seeing. Its own reflection was wobbling in the water that she'd disturbed. It was Dr Malik's boat.

Katya crawled towards it, the water lapping all around her, feeling her hands moving out in front of her like two balloons floating away from her. She reached for the edge of the boat, which gave a little thud as she slapped her hand down on it. It was real. She heaved herself inside, her muscles straining and quivering with the effort, and the little craft rocked beneath her weight. Then with the last of her strength, she reached up and untied the mooring rope, took the heavy boathook from beneath its tarpaulin and stabbed it into the mud. She looked back up at Dr Malik's house, lit up like an ancient palace at night. She watched the men combing its garden, their torchlights slashing through the dark, their shouts of confusion and anger. And then she pushed away from the bank. The boat bobbed out on to the water, light cut out in little crescents all along its black surface. Just as she pulled away from the shelter of the reeds, a torch beam in the garden flashed over her, a sudden sunburst that made her blink and cover her eyes. Shouts of anger rose up in a chorus. She fell back into the boat, and pulled the tarpaulin over her, smelling the dried mud on it, and the blood still seeping from her leg. The river rocked beneath her as it drew her into the central flow of its current, and the stars overhead moved steadily north. There was the rattle of a gun, and she didn't even jump, just lay on her back and listened to the fizz of bullets hitting the water around her, a few loud thuds against the boat, one ricocheting off the hull and spraying little pieces of wood dust on her face. She blinked and watched her hands float out in front of her as the river carried her southwards. She reached up to her neck, and touched the cylinder seal hanging there as one of Mosul's bridges passed overhead, a lode of iron, a blackness cut from the billion stars. She imagined for a moment that she could see the dust from space falling from the sky and settling over everything. And hadn't it all happened like this before?

Aurya

Aurya went alone to the mason's workshop, to give Sharo the King's demands. She rode on a donkey she hired from a porter near the docks, and brought crusts of old emmer bread with her, expecting to see the beggar children that always used to gather on that hilltop. A great fear rose in her heart as the donkey rocked beneath her along those old streets, all her memories overlapping, all the times she'd climbed up that hill after exploring the city, looking for her mother. The houses there were crumbling, brick walls repaired with mud, but pots still hung in the eaves and matted reeds laid out to dry. In daylight now, Aurya saw the palace of the King's father that had scared her so much as a child, with its cracked blue tiles and yawning dark halls. It seemed dead, as if its ghosts had been banished. The beggar children were nowhere to be seen, so she fed her bread to the birds instead.

When she arrived at the workshop and tied her donkey, she found Sharo already at work, his skin covered in the white dust. He was wrapped in a number of woollen cloaks though it wasn't cold, and hunched over a wide piece of stone lying flat on the ground. All around the workshop, children were working, playing or dashing about. They swept dust, sharpened tools, washed stone and took measurements. There were cats too, and dogs missing patches of fur. Aurya stood there in the gate and watched the chaotic scene for a little while before Sharo noticed her.

'Aurya,' he said, without feeling. She gestured at the children running everywhere.

'Who are these?'

One cat curved its spine around her shin and purred. Sharo turned and put his mallet and chisel in one hand, brushed his unruly hair from his eyes with the other, and took a glug from a blue-glazed pot beside his work station.

'You remember the hungry children who used to beg on the hillside? I recruited them as my helpers.'

'Do you need so many helpers?'

'No, probably not. They don't help that much, actually.'

One of the younger children ran up to him, and he tousled the dust from their hair with the shadow of a smile. Aurya stepped carefully through the commotion and put a hand on Sharo's shoulder.

'Sharo. I'm going to have a child.'

He put down his tools, and raised his hand to touch hers. Then all at once something cracked in his face, and he jumped up to wrap his arms around her.

'That's so beautiful, Aurya.'

She laughed, and fought him off, the way they would when they were children. Close up, she saw the red in his eyes. Tears made tidemarks on his face, cutting rivers through the dust.

'Sharo, I want to leave the city. And you should come with me. We're going to go south. Maybe as far as Egypt. You remember what that man told us, about the giant water pigs?'

He shook his head.

'You're going to be a good mother, Aurya. A great mother. But I can't leave.'

'Sharo …' She felt tears in her own eyes. 'I think something terrible is going to happen here. The wars are getting worse every year, and the King is losing his mind. It's like the whole fabric of everything is breaking apart.'

Sharo sat back down at his stone, and ran his hand over the surface, making whorling patterns in the dust.

'I know, Aurya. I feel it too.'

'So come with me, Sharo. You don't have to stay. Once you've finished your carving …'

He didn't answer at first, just went on brushing the dust from the stone. Where her father's hands had been dull slabs, Sharo's were like small birds flitting between branches, alighting on whatever they touched, weightless and effortlessly precise.

'Let me show you,' he said. He clapped those hands, and all the children hurried to him, flocking around the stone, grabbing hold of ropes and pulling all together. Sharo helped them to pull, and the stone in its frame lurched up from the ground. The older boys joined him in heaving against its pulleys. The beams and ropes cackled together, and the stone lifted slowly from the earth. Aurya stood back to take it in. The dust fell off the stone in sheets. Finally, it stood completely upright, and she could see the finished piece: the lion jumping up to seize the chariot. The deep, mournful recesses of its eyes. For a moment, she couldn't speak.

'It's beautiful, Sharo.'

He nodded slowly.

'Thank you.'

She took in a long breath.

'But Sharo ... there's something I need from you.'

'What is it, Aurya?'

'It's the King. We're trying to leave the city, but he won't let us. Not unless you carve what he wants you to carve. Sharo, if you don't, he'll never let us go. And whatever happens to this city will happen to us all.'

Sharo looked at the children hurrying around, playing games in the dust.

'Aurya, I told you ...' She put out her hand to touch his arm.

'Please, Sharo, I need to leave this city. I can't have a child here. I can't have this evil in its life.' She looked up at the carving, at the cold look on the King's face as he drove his spear into the lion's back. 'That evil.'

Sharo's eyes moved to follow hers. He took a deep breath and looked around the workshop, put his hands through his hair.

'I have to carve the whole scene,' Sharo said, staring into the lion's deep-set eyes. 'I can't leave anything out. But if the King wants ... if he wants, he can take only the pieces he likes. Let an apprentice change them later if he likes. I'll keep the rest here. The ones he wants to forget. This will be the house of dust after all, just like you said. A place where things go to be forgotten.'

Aurya laughed, and looked round at the powdered stone that coated the floor, coated the feet of the children and all of Sharo's face and clothes.

'The house of dust,' she said. Around the workshop, the children's voices started up again, and they continued with their work or their games, chasing the cats. She nodded. 'I'll ask the palace. I'll ask them if that's enough for them.'

'I'm sorry, Aurya. It's the best I can do.'

'Sharo,' she said, 'how does the story end? I want to know.'

Sharo licked his bottom lip.

'It's not really about the ending, Aurya. No story is ever about its ending.'

'I still want to know.'

Gilgamesh had failed to stay awake, and he wept.

'I do not want to pass into the house of dust,' Gilgamesh sobbed. 'I do not want to follow my friend into that dark place.'

The ancient one took pity on him. He told the King of a plant that grows on the ocean floor, which looked like the fruit of a dog-thorn.

'Whenever you eat of this plant, you will return to the vigour of your youth,' he told him.

Gilgamesh left the land of the dead. He sailed out to the ocean and tied stones to his feet, and sunk through the gloom. He found the plant and plucked it, then swam to the surface.

Many days Gilgamesh travelled down the river with the plant, back to the city of Uruk. He thought about all he had lost, just to gain the secret of life.

And then one night, sleeping on the riverbank, a serpent slithered through the reeds. It saw the plant hidden in Gilgamesh's bag, and swallowed it whole. When Gilgamesh awoke, he saw the flower was gone, and fell about in despair.

'I have lost the secret of eternal life,' he screamed. 'This whole journey has been for nothing! I have not found what I set out for.'

341

He followed the river flow, back to the city of Uruk. And on the riverbank, the people rejoiced that their King had returned. And when Gilgamesh stepped from the river, he stood in Uruk and looked out at the fine city walls, that would last until the end of time. He looked out at the palaces he had built, and the works he had created, and then he set his whole story down in stone.

Silence. The children had gathered around, putting their chins on their knees. Sharo coughed once.

'That's it?' Aurya asked.

'That's it.' She looked at him for a long time.

'Five years to tell a story, and it ends with no one getting what they want?'

Sharo shrugged, and brushed dust from his stone.

'They got something else, though.'

Aurya wrapped her arms around his neck and squeezed him.

'Sharo, I'm sorry about your lion. All those years ago. It was a good lion.'

He nodded.

'Thanks, Aurya. I'm sorry for telling you … you know. That day.'

She shook her head.

'It hurt for a long time. But I needed to know.'

They held each other there for a few moments longer, and then Aurya reached up to her chest, where her mother's seal sat.

'Here. Sharo, I want you to have this.'

'No, Aurya, I can't …'

'Take it, Sharo. I want you to have it. And if you're ever afraid, or feel like you need strength, just squeeze it in your hand as hard as you can, and think of me.'

He took the seal from her and held it in his fist, balled tightly around the little stone cylinder.

'I will, Aurya. When I finish my work here, I'll come to visit you, and your child. And then I'll give this back to you.'

Aurya nodded slowly.

'You promise?'

'I promise.'

'Will your work ever be finished?'

He didn't answer. Aurya felt a blockage in her throat, but she turned away.

'Goodbye, Sharo. You can always find me, you know. If you follow the river.'

He nodded.

'I'll remember that. Goodbye, Aurya.'

She gave one last look back as she left, and saw her brother still sitting there, holding the seal in his hand. She saw his fist close over it and squeeze.

On her way back down the hill, rocked by the donkey that carried her, Aurya looked out over the rooftops and courtyards of Nineveh, over the whitewashed temples and the brightly coloured awnings of the markets; the stork nests bristling from the walls streaked with white droppings and the smoking beehives of the kilns; the mountains of shattered pottery growing with weeds and the children playing with rag balls on the clay streets; the stone alley steps worn in the centre; the old melancholy wood fronts of the houses and the plants that grew in the cracks of the walls; the drinking houses and the mansions and the bastions of high stone from which the iron tips of soldiers' spears glinted; the gaggles of astrologers in the gardens with their charts and the thin men with hammers and axes and adzes, slouching along the mud roads to their work; the tailors sitting in mountains of coloured fabric and the crumbling old houses gone wild with flowers and daubed with painted signs; the barges pulled by oxen along overgrown towpaths and the rickety wooden bridges polished smooth by feet; the belching drains and the clatter and clang of a thousand industries; the cemeteries crumbling beneath groves of cypresses and palms and the men leading their cattle out to water through the painted gates; the palace tiles flashing in the sun; the library and the great ziggurat with its overflowing gardens rolling like tangled hair down its slopes – and all of it looked as if there could be nothing else in that place, as if it would stand there until the end of time. Immovable as a range of mountains.

She would think about that ride many times in later years. She would think of it many years later, in Egypt, when news of King Ashurbanipal's death came to her. She thought of it many times as the feuds over his crown consumed the kingdom, and the enemies of Nineveh massed in the hills. She would think of it when the droughts came, and the hordes of the Medes and Elamites overwhelmed Assyria's borders and marched down into the lowlands. She thought of it again when she heard of the final decisive battles fought in the river plains, and the fleeing of the bastard king. Then again when it was said that Nineveh was besieged, and she saw Judeans and Medes and scavenger tribes all celebrating together at the news, thanking their various gods. Every day she would wait at her gate, watching the road for Sharo, and that journey on the old porter's donkey would come back to her. Later, when she heard the news that Nineveh had been burned, she sat down with her back against the wall for a long time and felt a bottomless feeling that was beyond tears. When she heard that the city had not just been burned, but reduced completely to ash and dust, that its lands had been tilled with salt and all its people put to the sword, she thought of it again. She thought of it every day as she waited by her gate, watching the narrow road from the north. And every time she thought of that ride, she could almost feel the rock of the donkey beneath her.

———

Aurya watched the river birds flying overhead as the drums below deck began to sound, and the ship pulled away from the quay of Nineveh. She wrapped her wool shawl around her head and put her hand on Abil's arm. The boat rocked on the water as it came untethered and men drew its weed-covered ropes back on board, dropping them in wet loops on the deck. She sat among the urns of alum and sesame and breathed in the air of new beginnings.

It hadn't taken long to sell everything too heavy to carry. Aurya and Abil had never owned much. Perhaps it was the inclination of orphans, to always be ready for the next upheaval, the next great migration. As Aurya looked up at the city walls, she thought of

Sharo, and what he might be thinking right now. She felt at her chest, and for a moment experienced a shock to find the cylinder seal missing, for the first time in years. But it would come back to her, she knew. Sharo had promised. And if not in this life, then in the next.

The boat edged away from the quay, and men shouted their goodbyes to the people on the bank. Aurya said her own farewell to the city of her mother. She said goodbye to Sharo, to the library and to the dream she'd always had of living in that place. She laid her hand on her stomach and thought of her mother, and the journey she had made away from that same city, years before, perhaps with Sharo already growing in her belly. She tried to imagine the feelings that must have passed over that young woman: whether fear, or excitement; whether her husband had seemed good to her then; whether he had sat beside her as Abil sat beside her now, with his hand on her shoulder. Aurya prayed:

My tears I drink like the waters of the sea.
Let the river carry me away.
May the waters of the river flow cleanse me.

She put her hand in that water and felt its cool run between her fingers, felt its flow pulling her endlessly onward. The wind tugged at her hair too, and all of it, the wind, the current, the soft light that fell over the tops of the city walls, seemed to be drawing her south in a ceaseless downstream tow.

Katya

Katya swam in and out of consciousness. Her tongue stuck like Velcro to the roof of her mouth. She was starving. Had it been a day or two days? A week? It was early morning, she thought, still cool, and birds were soaring in pairs in the pinkish sky. There were flies, too, wandering over her lips, her eyelids. She couldn't summon the energy to swat them away. She managed to lift her head a little, and look out at the river around her, bounded with reeds. The boat rocked with her movements. Its floor was sticky with dark congealed blood.

Where was she? As she lay there, she listened to the crickets nearby, the soft slosh of water, and ran her thumb over the cylinder seal that still hung around her neck.

'I told you that you wouldn't find me,' her dad said from behind her. She jumped at the suddenness of his voice. She craned her neck to see him sitting on the edge of the boat just out of sight. She couldn't make out his face, but there was something wrapped around his neck. A snake, red-and-white bands on its scales.

'I wasn't trying to find you,' she said. 'I was trying to forgive you. I was so angry you left me.'

Did she say it or think it? She tried to sit up, but her foot slid in the blood and her arms were numb. Her thigh felt boiling hot, and she could feel her heartbeat in it.

'It always hurt me so much to leave,' her dad said. 'And it was you I thought of, in the end. You appeared to me, you know. In those final moments, out in the desert. It was as if you were right there in front of me. And you said, "Don't worry, Dad. It's going to be okay."'

'It wasn't, though.'

He laughed.

'No, I suppose it wasn't. I'm sorry, Kat. Perhaps you'll understand one day.'

'I think I understand already.'

'Maybe you do. But you told me something else too. You said you knew I wasn't gone. Not really. That no one ever goes. They only change into something else.'

'Into what?'

But there was only silence behind her. When she turned again, he wasn't there. High overhead, a white plane – not a military jet, but a passenger plane – glinted in the blue, a white crest of sky surf expanding behind it. It was the first one she'd seen in months. How far had the river taken her?

Katya closed her eyes and dreamed a little. She dreamed that the boat would come to a stop somewhere in the reeds, that it would crunch on to the bank. She would hear voices, the feet of children nearby. Then a young face would poke over the edge of the boat. It would be a girl maybe, a young girl with a thread of hair falling loose, head cocked to the side. Katya would lie there, and their eyes would meet for a moment.

Katya would croak out a plea for help. The girl would turn and call to her parents. More footsteps would come. Strong hands would reach down and pick her up, kind hands and gentle voices. They would call an ambulance, douse her wound with sharp-smelling iodine, staining her jeans yellow, bind it tightly with a patterned scarf. They would offer her tea. She would be too weak to eat. The women of the family would gather round her and pray for her while the ambulance came, a confusing scatter of details passing over her as she drifted in and out of consciousness: the flower pattern on the sofa cushions, the icon on the wall of a man with a green turban and kind eyes, the way one woman had a wine-coloured birthmark on her cheek. When the paramedics came, they would lift her into the white lights of the vehicle and take her away. In the hospital, the nurses would be warm to her, the doctors would know how to heal her, how to put her back together. She would lie in clean, cool sheets, listening to the reassuring beep of instruments as the painkilling drugs took hold. She would pass in and out of sleep, and dream of home. They would tell the reporters to leave her alone. They would send news to her mother that she was okay, that she was healing quickly. They would hold up a telephone for her to speak into, and she would burst into tears and murmur down the line, 'I'm okay, Mum. I'm okay. I'm coming home.'

She would ask about Salim. She would insist that someone send news about him, that he was travelling in an old white van with a young girl, that they should be careful not to shoot him at a checkpoint or turn him away. The doctors would be kind, but they would say that they had heard no news. Then one day when she was nearly healed, she would hear a knock on her hospital room door, and Salim would walk in. He would look exhausted, tears in his eyes. He would rush to her and wrap his arms around her, knocking the breath out of her. She would hold him there and grip her fingers in his curls, feel the warmth of his skin against her cheek.

'I'm so sorry,' he'd say, over and over again. 'I'm so sorry we left you.'

She would shake her head.

'You had to,' she would say. 'But I'm alive. We're all alive.'

'It's a miracle,' he would say. 'It's a miracle you got away.'

In the hospital's acid light, they would hold each other there for an age, both their cheeks wet with tears. Later, Lola would arrive. They would tell Katya about their miraculous escape, the hair-raising near-misses they'd had at checkpoints, the locals who tipped them off to waiting patrols on the road ahead, the terror they felt the whole way, the bullets that thudded into the van when they had to speed away from one checkpoint, missing them both by inches. Lola would tell her how they'd found her family in Baghdad, how she'd started to go to school again and would become an archaeologist like she always dreamed. Later, when the doctors told them it was time to leave, Salim would grip Katya's hand.

'I told them everything we did,' he would say. 'The police, the army. They know what we had to give up to those madmen.'

'And?'

'They know we had to do it. And I showed them the whole list of things we gave them. But I want to get it all back, Katya. All the pieces we lost. I want to trace where they smuggled them through Syria, into Europe. The US. I want to find the black-market sellers, the underground auctions where they sell this stuff. And I want you to come with me. Help me get it all back, Katya. Let's get those responsible. Let's make them pay.'

Katya would feel herself fill with exhaustion, and then she would think of her dad. She would think of the look on his face every time he'd left her, tired but full of flint. The way she'd always tried to understand that look. And from somewhere deep within her, she would feel a fire ignite. She would grip Salim by the arm, though she was still weak.

'Let's do it,' she would say. 'Let's get those bastards. Let's get it all back.'

They would kiss again, and she would breathe in the tobacco smell on his clothes, the soap on his neck, barely daring to believe that it was real, that they had both survived. Salim would promise to visit her again the next day, and he would. When she left the hospital, limping on crutches but full of energy, he would be there waiting for her. Her mother would be there too, standing beside him in a headscarf, there to surprise her. They would already be friends.

'Your father's daughter,' her mother would say, mock-scolding, and then burst into tears, running up to her and hugging her. 'I'm never letting you out of my sight again.'

Life would go on, winding like the river.

In the boat, Katya managed to lift up one of her hands, and brush a fly from her face. When she did, she found tears soaking her cheeks. She thought of Gilgamesh, sailing home along the river. She thought of the flower he found, the gift of life, lost for ever because once again he couldn't fend off the embrace of sleep. Her own eyelids were getting heavy.

Nearby, she heard traffic, the deep honks of lorry horns. She saw reeds around her, nodding as the boat disturbed them in the water. White birds overhead. Then with a bump and silty scrape, the boat lurched against something. The bank. She lay there for what seemed like hours, delirious with thirst. Time stretched out, and she felt the way she did when it was time to get up for work and she wanted to stay in bed: wouldn't it be so much easier to just lie there? Another five minutes. A beautiful cool was rising through her body, and her eyes began to close.

'Get up, Katya,' she murmured to herself. 'It's time to get up.'

Nearby, she heard small feet, and a child's voice called out something. The sound came closer. Then a head poked over the edge of the boat. It was a little girl, a thread of hair hanging loose over her face, head cocked to the side. Katya lay there and looked up at her, and their eyes met for a moment.

Acknowledgements

I would like to thank the following people, without whom the writing of this book would have been impossible. The British Institute for the Study of Iraq (BISI) helped me with research leads, and facilitated my first journey to Iraq. Thanks to Richard Dumbrill of BISI and the British Museum for inviting me to attend the Babylon Festival of Arts and Culture, as well as sharing his expertise on ancient Babylonian poetry and music. Thanks to Geoff Hahn for his expertise and professionalism in guiding me around Iraq on my second visit. Many thanks to Raad Al Qassimi, an unparalleled guide, as well as Saif Alshalah, Ali Hammodi and Athir Al-Adhari, and all the others who worked to keep me safe during my trips, and to share the beauty and spirit of their country.

A great deal of gratitude is owed to archaeologist Flint Dibble, who agreed to read the manuscript and act as a consultant on matters of archaeology. Thanks also to Rebecca Sharrock, who read the novel and helped guide the character of Sharo with her own experiences of Highly Superior Autobiographical Memory (HSAM). Thanks are owed to the Consortium for Arts and Humanities in South England (CHASE), who funded my studies during the writing of this novel. Thanks also to the stone masons at Gildencraft Stone Mason's Guild in Norwich, and Master Stephen in particular for teaching me some of the basics of stone carving. Also many thanks to Mary Thomson, Sarah Morriss and Myles Schaller for their expertise on the mysteries of spectrometry.

Many thanks to Rasha Al Aqeedi for her Moslawi's knowledge of Mosul's geography and culture, and her invaluable input into the novel. Respect and gratitude belong to Omar Mohammed, for his bravery in running the Mosul Eye blog for years, risking his life to bring news of the so-called Islamic State to the outside world, and many thanks also for agreeing to read this novel and advise me on it, as well as inviting me to visit Mosul. I would also like to thank Micah Galen and Daniel Rye (via Puk Damsgård) for their bravery in sharing their stories of surviving ISIS captivity in Iraq and Syria.

Thanks are also owed to the multiple translators and rewriters of the Gilgamesh Epic, whose work fed into my own: Taha Baqir, Benjamin Foster, Andrew George, Maureen Kovacs, Herbert Mason, Stephen Mitchell, Nancy Sandars and Robert Silverberg. All quotations from the Quran are taken with respect from the Saheeh International translation. Special thanks are owed to my teachers, especially Rebecca Stott for her infallible advice and inspirational conversation; to Petra Rau for her direct and honest advice; and to Giles Foden for his insight. I would like to thank all the readers who offered their considered comments and suggestions on the manuscript: David Greaves, Jacob Rollinson, Rebecca Sharrock, Margaret McLaughlin and David Cooper. I would like to thank my agent Eve White, without whom I would be lost, as well as my wonderful editors at Bloomsbury, Alexa von Hirschberg and Marigold Atkey, for their tireless work to make this novel as good as it could be. Thanks to Annie Kelly for her love, support and belief. The book is finally dedicated to all those who risk their lives to uncover the truth of the past and the present, and to the people of Iraq, who have fought so hard and suffered so much.

Note on the Author

Paul Cooper was born in south London and grew up in Cardiff, Wales. He was educated at the University of Warwick and UEA, and after graduating he left for Sri Lanka to work as an English teacher. He has worked as an archivist, editor and journalist, and currently teaches Literature and Creative Writing at the UEA and University of Warwick. His writing has appeared in the *New York Times*, *The Atlantic*, *National Geographic* and *Discover Magazine*. His debut, *River of Ink*, was published by Bloomsbury in 2016 to great critical acclaim.

paulmmcooper.com
@PaulMMCooper

Note on the Type

The text of this book is set in Linotype Stempel Garamond, a version of Garamond adapted and first used by the Stempel foundry in 1924. It is one of several versions of Garamond based on the designs of Claude Garamond. It is thought that Garamond based his font on Bembo, cut in 1495 by Francesco Griffo in collaboration with the Italian printer Aldus Manutius. Garamond types were first used in books printed in Paris around 1532. Many of the present-day versions of this type are based on the *Typi Academiae* of Jean Jannon cut in Sedan in 1615.

Claude Garamond was born in Paris in 1480. He learned how to cut type from his father and by the age of fifteen he was able to fashion steel punches the size of a pica with great precision. At the age of sixty he was commissioned by King Francis I to design a Greek alphabet, and for this he was given the honourable title of royal type founder. He died in 1561.

ALSO AVAILABLE BY PAUL COOPER

RIVER OF INK

'An extraordinary debut … *River of Ink* is what historical fiction should be: immersive, illuminating and captivating'
THE TIMES

From his humble village beginnings, Asanka has risen to the prestigious position of court poet in the great island kingdom of Lanka, delighting in a life of ease. But when the ruthless Kalinga Magha violently usurps the throne, Asanka's world is changed beyond imagination. To his horror, the king tasks him with the translation of an epic poem designed to civilise his subjects and snuff out the fires of rebellion…

Asanka has always believed that poetry makes nothing happen, but as lines on the page become cries in the street he learns that true power lies not at the point of a sword, but in the tip of a pen.

'Potent, beautiful and wholly absorbing … A wonderful, memorable debut' **Madeline Miller**

'Cooper endows his work with persuasive historical accuracy and detail, but the "juice" of his own work is the intensely poetic quality of his prose' *INDEPENDENT*

'Masterly … A powerful and timely fable about freedom, resistance and the secret might of the weak' *FINANCIAL TIMES*

BLOOMSBURY